One Crooked Thing

Timothy Roderick

First published 2020 Timothy Roderick
www.timothyroderickbooks.com

ISBN: 9798651175987

The characters and events portrayed in this book are fictitious. Any similarity to real persons, living or dead, is coincidental and not intended by the author.

Editor: Laura Perry
Printed in the USA

One

Los Angeles 1947
Several Days After It Happened

She traveled great distances to a church she'd never seen. She knelt, as she had hundreds of times before. But this time, she meant it. A square wooden panel large enough for some small offering to pass through slid to the side. An ornamental grid separated her from the priest; one more barrier between her and salvation. A haze from the burning frankincense and dim lighting cloaked her like her nun's habit and veil, offering some anonymity.

The Reverend Mother Margite's life was one of routine concealment, not for any precepts involving humility, but as an extra layer of protection from the things that go unseen. *It. Them.* Her nun's garb supplied one more buffer, providing a ruse, a costume meant to confuse.

At one point within the span of her long years, she'd believed in the power of robes, rosaries, and the cross. In her youth, with these as her anchor, she had attempted benefic works within the church's cloistered walls. But in the end, the trappings of religious faith had become little more than talismans, serving as a shield. They were only objects she'd used for her own ends. And they had worked, somewhat. They'd kept foul things underfoot—for a while at least. But such devices had never affected her soul, if ever she had possessed one.

Eventually, it would find her, she feared. They would find her. All seventy-two, yet just the one. They operated like the Holy Trinity, although they arose from a much darker source. She cast her gaze down so the priest might not look into her eyes and recognize the hideous monster lurking in such close quarters.

"Bless me, Father, for I have sinned…" The Reverend Mother hesitated then drew in a steadying breath. The phrase she'd just spoken, she realized, might be the only reliable truth she'd utter. Not because she'd developed a knack for lying, and not because she was afraid to state the facts. She realized there was only so much known by any one person. So a confession was, at best, half-truth.

"Yes, go on," he said.

Some perspiration puddled on her upper lip, and her hands trembled beyond control. That was unexpected. As far as she was aware, there wasn't the slightest contrition in her heart. Not now. Too much time had passed, and the road traveled, too crooked. She thought it ridiculous to quiver and drip this way. If she didn't know any better, she might conclude that she had some lingering regrets. There were none, and that alone might have been the source of her anxiety. Didn't this little interview end with an Act of Contrition? She wondered if she had the strength left to muster some up.

What was right or wrong? What was brought upon her without her knowledge or consent? And what were her options now that she'd committed certain acts and signed detestable bargains in the cinders and the soil of numerous graves? The Reverend Mother could see a network of truths proliferating before her. That provided no comfort.

She doubted whether God would intervene. How might he forgive, let alone reverse all that she'd done, all that she'd been up to this moment? The priests claimed they would wash it all clean in the blood of Christ with a thorough enough confession. There was always someone's blood involved, wasn't there?

"It has been two hundred and fifty-seven years since my last confession. And that one didn't end so well," she said.

The priest chortled. "What was that, sister?" He had a wispy-gray voice, and he probably wondered if his hearing aids faltered. "For a minute I thought you said…"

She saw no sense in making things up now. Nor in justifying any of it. Confessions were at their core transactional. This sin costs those several prayers, and all would be right as roses. Wasn't that right? Then why did her heart thump so? She had to get on with the business at hand, or what she'd set in motion those centuries ago might continue—perhaps forever—or as long as she feared encountering the inevitable. Everything came with its price, and she understood that. But there was worth in haggling over the final bill.

She cut him off, or she'd never get her words out. "I don't know where the beginning was. Nor which of my actions originated in sin or human error. Not because there was no beginning nor sin to what I'd done. But what has passed through my life existed long before me, mixing time and again between humans and those who are not. And none of it will ever stop, not for all eternity, unless someone, like Christ, like me, accepts what is fated."

"All of us are sinners, Sister. Can you be a bit more specific?"

"I suppose I should begin when the doctor summoned me. Faust, that is."

"Faust… what? Sister, either you need a doctor or a reminder that the confessional is no place for levity…" The priest coughed, but she continued, untouched by his judgements.

"I was once a good girl, from a good family. But after he infected me with conjuration, everything changed. I became like the shepherd's lost lamb and wandered as if in a fog where truth and tricks of the mind are as one. Though, to make my confession complete, I admit taking a role in how things played out. I could have turned back, but I thirsted after its promises. Its sweet enticements kindled desire, lust. And there was blood, yes, an ocean of it."

Los Angeles, 1947
Two Months Before It Happened

One red drop lingered and defied gravity. It clung to the mineral-streaked basin. Ren supposed it had no rush. Where was it to go, except down? It's all headed that way anyway, he thought. The water rushed and gurgled from the faucet, filling the cramped bathroom with a soft gray steam. Ren wasn't unnerved by blood. He'd seen plenty of it in his line of work and across his lifetime. Plenty more where that came from. Everyone's got quarts of it—just encased in skin, so no use in fussing when only a little spilled, he thought.

He leaned over the sink to verify what he saw. Events were sometimes less certain for Ren since he'd gotten back. That was two years ago, right after the war ended. It was a long time to be drifting between concrete experience and imaginary remnants of what happened during his turn away from home and country. As a result, he spent a lot of time double-checking. But he decided he had a good handle on things—he knew his mind, and they hadn't broken it while he was away. They tried, but he escaped. Besides, if he involuntarily recalled bad things that happened long ago, it wasn't the same thing as having some terminal disease. He felt fine. He could use a little more sleep, but he was fine. Ren just had spells, that's all—and he learned how to tough them out, like everyone else.

As he leaned over, his back ached, and there was a pressure in his chest as if he'd been swimming underwater at a great depth and was just able to come up for a breath. He noticed a second ruby drip with a long tarry-red streak that was much less reluctant to slip down to the drain.

With two fingers spread like the letter V, he smeared the speck and the streak. They felt thick and viscous as warmed maple syrup to his touch. He washed off what remained on his fingertips and regarded the blood markings in the sink. They were almost a design—a half-one at any rate. Even though he knew the thought was odd, he felt compelled to finish what he'd started. He smeared the blood more, creating fresh lines, waves, and curly cues that connected and crossed one another in a strange circular arrangement. To Ren, the formation looked like both a voluptuous woman's chalk outline and a lot of upside-down crosses. It was nonsense. He splashed the sink until a slight trace of red tinting bubbled and drowned around the drainpipe.

He wondered how long the faucet had been gushing like this. Or how he'd gotten there in front of it. That kind of confusion was never a welcome sign, yet it was happening with greater regularity.

It was early morning and still dark outside. And he remembered that the Sargent had called him with some urgency. He mentioned a hotel. The details and whatever else had followed were a blur. Ren's customary out-of-bed routine involved some foot-scuffing atop the creaky old floors, morning cheek-kisses in the dark, and scratching his backside while urinating. So that same sequence likely happened today. He relied on it being so. Otherwise, Gloria might catch on that Ren had gaps in his day, nearly every day.

It troubled him to lose chunks of time, but worse was the result. He might snap out of it and find he was sitting in some coffee shop with a strange meal in front of him, or he'd be walking in a distant neighborhood nowhere near where he'd blanked out. He'd even awakened at the Tijuana border once.

From time to time during these missing ticks of the clock—sometimes minutes, sometimes hours—he'd find himself in a strange, surreal landscape; always the same one. And when he'd return, he'd recall a handful of snapshot-mind-images, fragments, like jigsaw puzzle pieces. There were mud-cracked plains, a perpetually dim twilight sky. He sensed, off in the blurry periphery, that shadowy old presences lingered, watched, and waited for an opportunity. Hungry ghosts he called them.

Wherever this was, it certainly wasn't downtown Los Angeles. He concluded that he was only having nightmares. Lots of guys coming back from the war had them. But he knew a man couldn't admit to them; the doctors would label him a fruitcake. Then he'd wind up like the rest of them—castoffs rambling alleys and haunting the doorways of busted-up downtown shops and empty park benches.

Ren wasn't like that. He knew what was real and what wasn't. He realized he couldn't be in one place and then another with a turn of his head, or a cough, or stepping up a staircase. Especially not a strange place like that, with its undulating horizons and its structures and inhabitants formed from the formidable, nearly choking atmosphere.

Yet, when he stood within that darkened landscape, it was hard to dismiss. Everything seemed as tangible as a hotdog and a couple of cold ones at Wrigley Field. So he kept his experiences close to the vest.

The *dark-between* was what he named this unnerving realm—or whatever it was.

He knew the solution to his unexpected journeys, but he didn't like it. All the confusion and time gaps might disappear if he'd only use those little white pills. Then again, it didn't help that he drank too much. Doc Kelly had told him that opium was common for calming the worried mind and exorcising unwanted demons.

That was the miracle drug, the panacea for his fellow troops if they reported any sign of a trembling hand or a few lousy dreams. With a swipe of a doctor's pen, it could all go away. But Ren also saw how some of his buddies who took the pills wound up sleeping on sidewalks and drinking leftover swill from trashcans.

Doc Kelly said it was war nerves that did them in, not the medicine. But Ren knew that shit was poison, "war nerves" or not. And none of it was so bad that he couldn't still be a father to his Molly, a loving husband, or a good cop. Besides, whiskey was bracing, and it steadied his nerves just enough, thank you very much.

Aside from the opium, Doc Kelly had made other suggestions that Ren found useful, like living without too much excitement. That's how he and Gloria wound up in a small house that clung to the steep slopes of the remote Hollywood Hills. There was nothing wilder out there than coyotes and raccoons. Maybe a stray skunk now and then. And the doctor was right. Quiet and seclusion was as good as any medicine, maybe even better.

Gloria was a city girl, accustomed to the pace of city living. She had come out west with a vaudeville troupe. When that had crumbled, she'd wound up dancing for dimes under the name of Miss Nighty Whispers in a Chinatown burlesque hall. That's where he'd found her and saved her from that life. At least, he thought he'd saved her.

One evening, not that long ago, Ren had come home to find her sitting on the edge of the bed. She had her old programs and the feather fan she'd used in her act spread out across the blankets, and she sobbed into her hands. She never saw him as he loomed behind, and Ren knew better than to step in. He knew what that was about, but he never knew how to make it up to her. He tried to be the husband she wanted, but he knew he fell short of her expectations.

Steam from the sink clouded up the medicine cabinet mirror. However, the condensation was light enough that he might inspect his cheeks for skin nicks. He assumed he was shaving. Why else would he grip an open straight razor? Trouble was, he had no shaving soap on his face. He touched his skin, and it was thick with stubble. There were likewise no tiny, thin puddles of red on his face.

He double-checked, and then he spotted a shadow looming in the mirror. Beyond the sink steam, where his face ought to be, there was a cloudy outline, like the blurry things he'd encounter on the sidelines in the dark-between. Sunken black areas suggested where the eyes might be, and where there should have been a nose and mouth, there was a long misshapen blur. He wasn't sure it was a face at all. Not a human one, at any rate.

He squinted and leaned forward to get a better look. The face turned to its profile, as though it was watching whatever headed down the hall behind him. Ren slipped backward at the sight, but then he steadied himself and wiped the glass. Whatever was there had vanished.

Then the sounds he'd been hearing echoed in the distance started up again, but this time they were close by. They were clicks, as though they were emanating from some phantom machine. Just yesterday, he'd heard them down the hall with all the surrounding doors shut, leaving only a black space for the sounds to echo—however hollow and dull. He'd heard them again in the kitchen the night before that. When he'd gone to investigate, the clicks had seemed to move and surround him. And one time he listened with halted breath to the clicks coming from his closed closet while he laid by Gloria, who was fast asleep.

Where in the jackrabbit hell was that coming from? The shower?

He glanced toward the far end of the bathroom where he noticed the shower curtain move. There was no breeze, but someone might have been trying to hide there. It was a possibility, given recent circumstances. Blood rushed and senses sharpened as Ren clenched his fingers around the razor and took a bare step toward the curtain. The closer he stepped, the more he could make out a shadow, dark and hulking, moving behind the curtain. He poised the razor, ready to strike.

"Oh my goodness, Ren, that was an early call. What was it? Three in the morning? What's going on at this hour?" Gloria asked. She leaned in the doorway.

He caught his breath and turned. He glanced back, and the curtain had gone lifeless. There was a pain at his temples. He swallowed it down and reminded himself that Doc Kelly warned him that lots of things might startle him—even play tricks on his mind.

"Gloria. Ah jeez. I was hoping you would sleep through it. Is Molly still knocked out?" he asked.

There was a shelf fastened just above the sink, bare metal, with a slight haze of rust at its bent corners, and he set the razor there. No sense in alarming Gloria if whatever moved behind the shower curtain was only imagined—just like that face in the mirror. But what if it wasn't? What if someone was standing in that shower stall, just waiting for him or Gloria to be alone?

"Well, I almost slept through it, till those pipes started screaming at me through the walls. When are you getting that fixed, anyway? Sounds like a banshee living in there."

Ren's mind turned to thinking about how the house was too remote for them to get quick help if there was some kind of trouble. Few who lived up in the hills considered that prowlers might attempt to do their business in such an inaccessible location. And Ren had never thought of them either until recently. Several troubling events had left him unsettled.

About a month after he'd returned from service and started back in his old job with the force, there was a night when he thought someone had followed him up from town. There was an old black sedan, late thirties, it looked like. It was a Nazi officer's car. Those he'd seen at a disturbingly close range. He'd never forget. He'd first noticed the headlights tracking him up the lonely hillside in his rearview mirrors. Once he'd pulled to the right into his driveway, the sedan's twin lights had dimmed to black, and there it had sat on the graveled side of the road, like a spider waiting in its web. Ren couldn't see the driver, as the dark of the hills and the moonless sky shrouded the car. Still, he could sense the eyes in that darkness, watching, waiting in the hush.

Ren had watched back for a while, but nothing had happened. Then he'd realized that it might be a pair of lovers trying to find a quiet spot away from prying eyes. Up in the hills, this was a regular occurrence, however, around Griffith Park was 'the' spot to be. He'd walked down the flagstones to his front door, eyeing the sedan, then he'd turned around and bolted the house shut. That was that. On his way to work the next morning, he'd seen that the automobile had already left. So he'd chalked the whole thing up to his frame of mind. He'd forgotten the incident, and things were normal for a while.

A few weeks later, it happened again. The headlights had tracked Ren up the hill. But this time, he had with him a battery-powered floodlight from work. It was in the front seat, ready to switch on. He'd flung the car door open with his foot and swung the floodlight upward. It had painted a broad section of light that only seemed to intensify every shadow in its path. Trees became taller, potholes dropped to unknown depths, rocks in the road cast back long strips of black, and it all only complicated what he was seeing. He'd braced himself, drawn out a pistol from his chest holster, and approached.

"Los Angeles police," he'd said, but the car sat mute.

"Open the door." He'd inched closer, still pointing the clunky box-light in his shaking hand, and with his right thumb, he'd cocked back the hammer.

"Police. Take your hands off the wheel and step out of the vehicle." He'd heard his voice take on a pitch that sounded like hysteria, and he tried to get a hold of himself.

No one had responded.

Ren had realized that he had no way of backing out of what he'd set in motion. He'd lowered the gun he had initially pointed skyward for safety, and taken aim toward the driver's window. The glare of reflected light off the windows had obstructed Ren's view into the vehicle. The driver might have had his hands up already, and because Ren had a gun drawn, he might have been afraid to make any move at all. It could happen.

Ren had shifted the floodlight down at the ground and stared into the guts of the vehicle. Nothing there. Ren suspected the driver had already slipped out the passenger door and lurked somewhere in the weedy hillside. His heart had tightened, and his breathing had slowed to a stop.

He'd aimed the lantern beam upward. The tall pines had cast their slim shadows back. It would have been hard to know if someone was there, hiding between the lonesome streaks of dark and light. A creature, quick and silvery had darted off from between two bushes, and Ren had let off a shot that rang out across the high banks. A coyote had loped out across the road, all long legs and tucked back ears, and had slipped off into the forest thicket on the opposite side.

The battery must have been fading because the light had sputtered on and off. In a final flickering spasm, it went out. Ren had tapped the box then slapped its hollow sides like a conga drum, but it wouldn't re-light.

That was when he'd seen her. She was little more than a dark shape lurking by the side of the road, bowed at the shoulder, but squared off to him and posed like a small statue set far too close to his house. Black cloth had draped over her from head to toe except for a half crescent of white at the neck that caught the dim moonlight. Gray, skeletal hands clasped at her waist, reflecting the moon too, only less so, but enough to know it might be the form of a nun… a praying nun.

He might have missed her dark draping silhouette altogether, except that from behind, the yellow porch light had given her an eerie outline.

"Hello?" Ren had called out.

The figure stood, a brooding sentinel, and he'd felt her secret eyes boring into him from behind that shadowed veil.

"Is this your vehicle, Ma'am?" Ren had hoped he sounded unshaken.

She'd glared back.

"Ma'am… can you hear me?"

The floodlight had turned back on, and the old sedan had rumbled to life. The car had skidded in a sharp U-turn, nearly tipping over on two wheels. It had squared up with Ren and blinded him in the headlight glare. There was no time to use his gun, at least with any sense. He had to run.

The engine had roared in place, only for a moment, then he'd heard the metallic brake ratchet and release. The car had lurched forward like a dog at the racetrack and shot off its mark toward Ren. He'd looked back over his shoulder, and the driver's seat remained vacant.

He'd dove off headlong down the steep pine needle bedding that sloped down from the side of the road, missing his own driveway by only a few yards. The car had skidded to a standstill on crumbly asphalt at the edge of the pavement, and then it had idled there.

Ren had laid low to the ground, huffing in the dirt. By then, he could have reached his .38 Special, though using it would be a problem, given the dusting of topsoil and pine pollen in his eyes.

All four of the vehicle doors had opened. Ren had tried not to huff too hard and watched up the hill. He'd seen no feet drop from the vehicle to the pavement. The car had idled for a good while, giving Ren an opportunity to wonder, of all things, if his life might end in a gunfight next to his home. All four doors had shut. The car had edged away, taking its time, then had sped down the winding road toward the city.

The car never came back. But several days after the incident, Ren, Gloria, and Molly were all asleep when a small knocking at the front door had startled them awake.

"Ren," Gloria said. She spoke like she was telling him a secret. "Ren, wake up."

He started with a snort. "What? What happened?"

There were more taps at the door. They were faint ones—almost like those of a child off selling cookies for a scout troop.

"Jesus Christ. It's three in the morning. Who the hell is that?"

Gloria sat up and paused before saying, "It must be a neighbor."

He swung his legs over the bedside and rubbed his face.

"A neighbor? Are you kidding me? Our nearest is Maxine, and what would she be doing over here in the middle of the goddamned night?"

Maxine Ganz was the widow of a Nebraska banking and railroad tycoon. The couple had used their place some six miles up the hill to winter away from Lincoln. Alone and eighty, she'd taken up permanent residency there, where she'd slipped bit by bit into reclusiveness. Her driver would tote her down to Larson's home on an occasional Sunday afternoon for company and for doling out homemade cookies to Molly. No, she wouldn't come by in the middle of the night unless there was some emergency. Even then, that wasn't the urgent knock of someone in trouble.

The front door then boomed with a barrage of knocks. Something—or more than one thing—scratched and clawed with desperation, tearing the wood to splinters. The sounds intensified then ceased, though the hinges continued to shudder. Then the house groaned as though the timbers—the entire house frame—strained under the push of an immense hand.

"Molly!" Gloria cried. She lurched from the bed and ran.

Ren trailed behind her down the gloomy hall to the last door on the left, past the bathroom.

Molly was half-raised on her elbows, her blonde hair rumpled around her neck. "Mommy, I heard a noise."

Gloria rushed to sit bedside, and she stroked Molly's forehead. "Go back to sleep, Molly. Everything's fine." She shot a look back at Ren, who was standing in the doorway. There were only seconds before whoever did this got away, so he rushed back down the hall, his bare feet slapping the hardwood as he went.

"Why is Daddy running?" was all he heard before he gripped the knob and whipped open the front door.

There was nothing there but the darkened landscape, the sage-scented air, and the crickets orchestrating their nightly symphony. Ren yanked open the entry closet, nabbed a flashlight from the top shelf, and paced down the flagstone front path. There was nothing to see, not even the old black sedan, which he half-suspected would be there, lurking in the gloom.

Ren made his way to the road and flashed the small beam here and there. An overwhelming and inexplicable sense of dread overtook him. He let out a throaty sigh to calm himself, but he couldn't shake the feeling that something was wrong. He glanced back at the front door, and there she was, the nun, or just the tail of her dark train, turning past the front door into the house and toward the inner hallway.

Ren burned down the walk, scrambling into the house. The starchy black train on the floor trailed around the corner into Molly's room. Ren's heart seized up, and he clamored down the hall like a madman.

Gloria was just turning off the light, kissing Molly's forehead and stroking her hair one last time when Ren burst through the door, huffing, drunk with adrenaline.

"Where is she?"

"Shh. Ren," Gloria whispered. She pointed to Molly, whose eyes were closed.

Ren swept across the room and launched the closet door open, wrenching it nearly out of place. He yanked on the overhead chain, and when the light clicked on, he rummaged behind the heaps of Molly's clothes all bunched up on hangers.

"Ren, what are you doing?"

"What do you mean? Didn't you see her come in here?"

"Ren, *what are you doing*?" Her eyes flashed with anger.

For Molly's sake, he needed to take a breather and think about what he'd seen. He couldn't be certain. What had looked like a dark train from a nun's habit could have been a raccoon's tail—more than it could have been a nun who breaks and enters. And wouldn't Gloria have seen a raccoon, much less a woman clad in black robes coming into Molly's room?

"I guess I thought I saw… never mind," he said.

Gloria watched him with no need to say a word. She knew him well enough to know this was a sign that he'd not taken his prescription. Or he'd been taking nips from his flask. He felt like a child standing there in a mess he'd just made.

"I haven't been drinking, Gloria. I kept my promise. Honest. It's just all that… that noise… what was it?" Ren asked. He gestured toward the front door. Nothing sounded reasonable, and he could tell by the look in Gloria's eyes. There was some line in the sand she'd drawn without him knowing it was there. Now he did.

"Maybe now would be a good time to drink…" he said. It didn't sound as funny out loud as it did in his head.

They'd gone to bed after that and never talked about it again, as was the usual case for times in their marriage when things went wrong. There was more unsaid than otherwise.

The strange incident never happened again. Ren tried to put it out of his mind. But the image of that dark trailing tunic, just dragging around the corner, kept flooding his mind. There was no doubt what he'd seen. That was no raccoon. But further upsetting and disappointing Gloria was the last thing he wanted to do.

The plumbing sounded up again with squealing and screeching, shocking Ren back to the present. "I'll have a look at the pipes on Saturday," he said. Gloria nodded and passed down the hall, not able to look Ren in the face any longer.

The light above the sink flickered and then went out. Ren felt his thumping pulse start up again when he saw whatever it was behind the shower curtain—perhaps only a flicker—move. His thoughts shifted into a tumbling overdrive.

"What's that smell?" Gloria asked from the hallway. She had no clue what was happening.

"My new shave cream?" Ren asked. He approached the trembling curtain clutching the open razor.

"No. Something else," she said. "It stinks. Stinking up the whole house to high heaven for weeks now. I'm checking to see if Molly slept through all this."

"Saturday… I'll get it fixed." Ren said.

Guk.

This was an unfamiliar sound. It was wet and gloppy, like an animal gagging on a hunk of meat. And it was coming from the shower.

Guk-guk.

Click.

Ren's gut clenched.

Gloria was probably already with Molly, stroking her hair, whispering to her about how they'd leave this place one day and be happy somewhere else. Maybe even New York.

Ren gripped the razor in front of him and took a step closer to the shower. He didn't care who it was. An intruder was an intruder, nun or not. He felt his nerves bringing a tingling fire to his limbs. Just one more step. With a quick burst, he clutched the curtain and ripped it across. No one was there, but there was a white pillar candle. Its flame lit and faltering, drowning in puddled wax, it sat on the tub floor.

Next to it was an unidentifiable root, gnarled and curved, still dusted with dirt. Someone had bound it within a complicated web of red thread. As Ren bent to reach for it, he caught an ever-intensifying rancid stench. The tied-up object might have been a piece of dried cat shit, for all he knew.

Gloria turned the corner. "Ren, what is going on? I've been calling you."

She found him facing the candle as though entranced.

"Ren, what are you doing with that razor?"

His pulse was still thrumming in his ears. He switched focus. "Sunnie left us another gift. This time it was dangerous."

"Leave Sunnie out of it, will you? She's done nothing wrong."

Ren walked to the shower and pointed to the lit candle. A thick river of wax had dripped over the hours, forming a sizable white glob that pooled and coagulated near the drain.

"What is this?" she asked.

"Well, unless you've been trying to save on the electric bill, it looks like the work of our housekeeper. She left this burning, for Christ's sake. It's been lit since at least seven last night when she left. You know what could have happened?" He blew out the short stump that remained and made the wax splatter.

"Do you hear yourself, Ren? Sunnie means nothing by things like this. It just looks like one of her customs. She thinks she's helping us, protecting us. It's innocent." She went to the medicine cabinet, pulled out the empty prescription bottle, and held it up for him to see. He knew she wanted to protest his refusal to medicate.

"What Sunnie did has nothing to do with me taking medicine or not, Gloria. This isn't some figment of my imagination. Do you realize what could have happened?"

"Well, nothing happened. It's just Sunnie's way. Can't you leave it?"

Gloria felt fatigued, and Ren caught himself in her sickened gaze. "I'll call the doctor. I'll go. I promise," he said.

Gloria responded by watching him with her tired, lonely eyes. She swallowed and turned just long enough to let him know how close he was coming and how far he had gone. She disappeared out the door. Ren followed her. "I'll call. I swear this time." She was already at the end of the hall, in the kitchen, making coffee on the burner.

Ren turned his attention to an object on the floor. It was slim, dark, and shining. The hallway was just too dim to see its distinct form, but it looked like one of those rosaries that Catholics would carry around. He could tell that the beads were like beveled black glass, and the cross at the terminal end was shining silver. Was it her? Did she get in? Or was this another of Sunnie's artifacts? He reached, but before he could grasp it, the thing moved, then it undulated from side to side. He backed up with a start as a gleaming black snake made its way down the hall and disappeared down the floor furnace grate.

Two

Germany, 1590

Nikolaus caught a toe in the gap between the wood planks of his shop, causing him to tumble and spill an armful of precious manuscripts. The wire-rimmed spectacles that pinched the bridge of his nose dove gracelessly and skated to a stop at the edge of a tall bookcase. There was no time to care for an object so relatively trivial. He could lose everything he owned or even lose his life if he stupidly stumbled and straggled for long.

His toe swelled up and grew hot and angry against the thin layer of shoe leather. No doubt he had broken it, and at his age, it might never heal. Another casualty to his desperation. He wished he'd thought to pay more for sturdier shoes.

No matter, he had barely a moment to breathe. Johann barely lived the distance of twenty dwellings from him, and he'd be there all ablaze before too long. Word had only gotten to Nikolaus just now. The first thing was to shutter the place, take what he could, then head somewhere where Johann wouldn't find him for a good long while. He'd wanted to visit family in Isles anyway. Wouldn't they be surprised?

It wasn't Nikolaus' fault that Johann had impulsively paid the named price for the old manuscript bound in wood and written on dried human skin—if the rumors were true. It was a curiosity that had no match, and he was right in naming the price he thought fair. True, he had heard at the time he procured it that the manuscript might be false. The trained eye could see through an amateur's duplicate, with its many critical omissions and substitutions. Some apprentice likely skimmed the original manuscripts and later sought to line his own pockets using a feather quill, some parchment, and a passing memory of what he'd read.

But what was the difference to a doctor like Johann? Undoubtedly, he collected such works for personal rather than professional inquiry. Surely he'd understand that the subject was purely speculative, and that regardless, someone like Nikolaus would have to go to great lengths to ensure that the authorities never discovered it. That effort alone was worth the coin. Booksellers sell books, not the truth.

Johann was a man of letters and degrees. It was only a matter of time before he'd discover a forgery. Most knew not to cross Johann, and it was foolish that Nikolaus had attempted this deception.

He reached a trembling, arthritic hand for a stool to boost him up when the door suddenly burst open. A patron browsing in a back part of the shop craned his neck, saw Johann with his cheeks burning and his gray beard flying in every direction, and quickly brushed past the brute out onto the purple evening street. Nikolaus shook to a stand. It was too late, for Johann didn't have a single word for him. But his fists had plenty to say.

First came a word from Johann's knee. It was a straight bolt to the groin. When Nikolaus bent in half at the waist, Johann gave him an uppercut to his jaw. Nikolaus stumbled backward into his bookcases and shattered them. He'd held the shelves in place with pegs he'd whittled from wood-rotted furniture. It didn't take much force to loosen the gates of hell across his body. Nikolaus' face was a bloody mess and his jaw hung low across his neck at an unnatural angle. He coughed up a runny red slurry that flicked out across his lips.

Johann tossed the manuscript onto Nikolaus' chest and stomped over to the till box on the other side of the room, where the shopkeeper stowed his silver and gold. Nikolaus had secured it with a padlock, but in Johann's state, that really didn't matter much. He smashed the box of wood and iron on the floor, sending up a spray of coins. He reached down and gathered what was his, then before he left, he thought of what he might say.

"You forget, Nikolaus, that I am in the employ of the Holy Fathers. I have informed the beadle and the bishop of your wares, and they'll be along soon enough. Try your best not to quake so much while upon the gallows."

Then he slammed the door behind him. Down the steps and to the right was a mothy beggar woman, and Johann poured the coins into her empty cup as he pounded back home down the snow-packed gravel.

It was the last score among many that Johann used the day to settle, and when he was through, he made his way back to his small stone quarters above the cobbling stall. There, he'd already set for himself a noose slung over a heavy beam overhead to the height of two grown men. Below that was a wobbly footstool, easy to flick away with a toe. When they found him, they'd say that at least he went by first balancing the scales, finding some small justice in the world. He knew all too well that few men had the luxury of finding that.

He gave one last look around at his paltry and somber quarters and contemplated what had brought him to the end like this. These unkempt chambers were the sum of his reward for reporting to church fathers on matters and discoveries from the Forbidden Arts.

The church retained him to read these blasphemous volumes, then to sort out which were demonic and which were not. Armed with this knowledge, men of the cloth might experiment with the Arts for their own purposes, when they saw it might be necessary.

Meanwhile, they would place on trial the poor and the illiterate for practicing village folklore and simple customs. Punish the cross made of milk and spread upon the household door, but nod in piety to the one made of wood placed above the hearth.

The priests insisted that Johann keep the manuscripts in his own quarters. He was a buffer between the pious, the faultless, and the infernal. They'd rather he sully his hands while they kept their own in prayer or on the whip.

This provided some advantages for Johann. When the books were not the direct subject of inquisition, he discovered that they proved to be an absorbing subject for his own investigations, scientific experiments, as he thought of them. Following the old rule of the alchemists before him, he knew that the forces behind stone and fire, water and wind brought promising results and the Almighty looked upon these with some favor. Despite this, those who turned the spinning wheels of the rack informed their subjects that nature was itself a corruption of *Diabolus*. So Johann knew to keep his personal experiments a secret.

Giambattista's *Magiae Naturalis* provided Johann his starting point, but after he'd learned to bind a wound and heal the gout with gemstones, he thirsted for greater miracles. In time, he discovered other books with wonders that required more straightforward alignment with forces that were, without doubt, unnatural. Johann saw such perils as necessary to unravel the mysteries of the universe. He'd also heard rumors that some who trod these paths before him had lost their lives along attempting these more scandalous procedures. But theirs were lives spent in pursuit of science, a benefit worthy of all mankind, Johann thought.

He had followed the formulae in the forbidden tome precisely, even though it took a goodly amount of time. The text was not always decipherable, especially that which the author had scrawled in the margins in a splotchy, blood-brown ink.

For all of this, he'd produced an unexpected candle flicker in a room when the air was as still as the catacombs. And once, the small fire in his hearth had turned a greenish shade of blue. The effect didn't even last long enough for him to show to another. He'd had dreams too. They saturated his mind in the deeps of night, twisting in his sheets about his throat. Some might better describe them as nightmares, but not he. All phenomena were a subject for study, including those insubstantial night visitors, whether horrifying or no.

In one dream, he watched flying insects form into a man—or a creature that resembled one—though its face was black and lacking a solid shape. The flies that made up the man's body gathered in through Johann's open window from the carcass of a dog rotting just outside in the alley.

The buzzing thing moved like a squid, taking on one bodily form after another. It hovered as a mass above his bed, parallel to his sleeping body, and watched him. Johann reached up to touch it, and as soon as his finger lighted upon one of the black flying crawlers, they dispersed. And that was that.

These small experiences, the fruits of his many hours' labor, were incomplete without the companion volume that taught an evocation of a darker sort. Bound in the same laundry were both light and dark, and to separate them was as fruitless as separating the drops in the sea, Johann reasoned. So when Nikolaus' volume seemed to be the one for which he'd searched, the companion to the *Clavicula Solomonus*, whispered by those in secret circles as the *Lemegeton*, he had to obtain it and know whether its shadowy promises of power were true.

The eventual discovery of Nikolaus' fraud brought him to the brink of despair.

He'd given himself to these workings at the expense of all else. He had no wife or child, nor was he company fit for marriage. He was old enough to no longer have relatives. And friends? He'd sooner call a passing flock of geese friends before any human. The promise of his long years of seeking had turned out to be a fraud, and on that, he'd spent the remnants of his bank account.

It was easier than he thought to fit the rope around his throat. He was a mix of trembling limbs and a dark heaviness of heart. If he failed, the pain and the infirmity of a botched leap could last for his final years to come. And if he succeeded, it might mean the lakes of fire for eternity. Or not. One never knew whether punishments and rewards of the afterlife might be a matter of Catholic fancy. His books never revealed that secret, and he didn't have the patience to sort it all out on his own.

He pulled the rope above his head to assure it would hold. Then, quick as a whitecap licking the sea, he closed his eyes and stepped off the stool while clumsily booting it backward and away.

While his toes searched for the floor, he felt no strangulation; he heard no snap of the spine. His body weight had not stiffened the rope. He opened his eyes; the rope's end slid past him, cut clean as though divided in one axe chop.

His body tingled and felt buoyant, like floating atop sea foam. He ascended higher and higher, as though borne to the heavens by small angelic hands. *Have I died?* Johann wondered. If so, there was not much ado about it. When his hands reached the splintery beam at the ceiling, he knew he still lived. The chambers, as he could see from above, were a marvel to behold.

An invisible presence pressed the wood and lace bindings of a manuscript into his hands. How it appeared there, he could not say. But he was certain it was not of an angelic nature. The cover alone, marked in glittering gold paint with the symbol of darkness, told him it was the damnable book for which he'd searched.

So there was something watching him after all.

Cat Island, 1947
Two Months Before It Happened

Old Nany Root had lived in her small pink paint-scrubbed place on Cat Island since time began. That was the local lore, at least. Her shop near Pigeon Cay Beach took up a thin slice in a short but colorful row—a bazaar—all clung together under a single roof on a dusty side street. She was between a salon where ladies got "American style" manicures with drugstore glitter and glue, and a shoe repairman who sang the day through.

She couldn't afford to have a shop off the square in Arthur's Town with its stain-caked fountain and gravel-topped roads, right alongside the islanders who had more appealing shops. That was where the handful of daring tourists each summer might feel safe enough to venture and open their pocketbooks. She couldn't even afford to live near the secret market over by the Boiling Hole, where they'd sell forbidden things, which she needed to make her living.

Nany's place had to walk the line between being hidden away and available to the islanders. Doing what she did was an open secret. She had to be inconspicuous enough so that the police would leave her alone. It wasn't her fault that the police would involve themselves and meddle in her doings. It was the fault of Taja and women like her who made a spectacle of themselves, who made ridiculous claims and invited undue attention.

Taja lived north on the island. She had a small seaside hut, more modest than Nany's shop, and it was remote from the towns. Her women-kin or even a godmother who might have adopted her never trained her. But she knew how to bring in the crowds. She'd dress the part with her coconut husk and sea-grass mask and her hooting and hollering and falling to the ground like she was having some kind of conniption. No one knew for sure whether Taja's work was genuine or whether the ancestors empowered her at all. But over time, Nany came to hear that Taja couldn't do anything that would mark a woman of power, like heal or take a fix off someone. For that, she'd come running to the other women who knew of such things, begging for a secret or two.

But they'd not give them up. Not everyone translated the spirits for money. Last Nany heard, Taja had made a cure-all concocted of toilet water, rat pelts, and cheap cola that she'd boil together and sell to her customers, saying it was from Lourdes in France and blessed by St. Lazarus. Those who followed Taja were eager to have the wool pulled over their eyes, it seemed to Nany.

Doing such shenanigans got Taja into a lot of fancy clothes—right from the rack. She also drew the police into matters of all the island's healers and spirit workers when people reported getting sick from her dirty water. Despite all of this, people still went to Taja and paid top dollar for her service, swearing that she was the real thing. But now and then, someone would get the cramping squirts enough to realize she had duped them. The victims of the con would hold that grudge, which was rightfully against one woman alone, and sought to take it out on all the women of the island who worked with unseen things. They'd call the police whenever they could, or just spread a nasty word, even if it had no truth to it.

Nany had no time for Taja's foolishness, nor for thinking much about what that woman was up to. She had no interest in drawing a crowd, either.

Like Taja, the residents of Pigeon Cay knew Nany. What was different was that Nany's works were famed and somewhat feared. So folks would avoid Nany and her shop. People from her town would change their walking path just to sidestep the old woman if they spotted her ambling about in the dust with her limp and her cane, her headscarf pulled tight. They'd do so just in case she'd set something untoward and unforgiving upon them. They avoided her until they needed her. Then no one seemed to remember what the fuss was all about.

Nany was shorter than most women, and thinner than a lot of them, too. But her face was round, and her skin was tight. "No one stayed lookin nice as Nany," she'd boast to customers nosing around about her age. "Not one Nany's age held up. Not a one. They're all shriveled. Look like the devil himself dragged their faces down on his way to Hell."

The women of the island didn't care much for Nany's portrayal. "She's got no reason to brag," they'd say. "She's thin as a cardboard.

Bag of bones, if you ask me."

Nany was sick much of the time, and she hardly had anything to fill her mouth. Still, unlike Taja, Nany would not use "what God gave her" to summon up a meal or even a penny just for her own satisfaction. She tended to the basics, and that was enough. "And who needs a doctor," Nany would ask, "when I got me everything afforded a woman to live? Why, it's my mother and grandmother, and all the grandmothers before them that keep me here, so long as I'm needed."

The townsfolk also knew that Nany kept herself going with the collection of strange herbs and resins stowed away in big pickle jars that lined the walls top to bottom in her shop. Not to mention, there was a world of unseen helpers that fetched what she needed and took care of what she wouldn't put her own hand to. Rumors cut both ways. They'd kept folks away, and they'd fueled legends that kept her place running all these years.

Nany was probably darker-skinned than a lot of folks, too. Aside from the rumors, that presented another reason people on Cat Island avoided her when they could. They'd say she could stand in a midnight graveyard just a few feet away, and you'd only see the moon. People would say that invisibility at night would give Nany enough time to blow a little graveyard dirt on you. Or she could get close enough to whisper a word or two that could change your destiny—and not for the better if you'd crossed her.

"Sit up, damn you," she said. She used whatever strength she had to help the man on the floor who wore a thin, blousy, sweat-stained *guayabera.* White candles outlined his body, and it took more than a few of them, given his sizable midsection. Nany took a swig from a bottle of rum and spit it over his head, then she did it again on either side of him. Only a little got in his eyes.

She took two hand-bound broom whisks the length of her arms and clacked them together above his head and around his neck. She mumbled words in a language that only her unseen helpers and the ancestors knew, until she felt as though something inside of her shifted. She didn't know how to name this shift or what it was that changed. But she knew it came on her when she felt more substantial than the world, larger than life itself. And once that happened, she shouted at the top of her lungs in the man's ear, "Get out!"

He shuddered like someone dunked in ice water, but he didn't get up from where he sat. He knew that there was still more for Nany to do. She took the broom bristles and thwacked him on his beefy back, each time shouting, "Get out!" She made a few more sounds like cricket chirps and a dog's growl.

The man began bawling in a booming voice, and Nany stopped to gaze at him in disbelief. Two onlookers sat nearby in metal fold-down chairs, waiting for their own turns. Given the
big man's response, the two were reconsidering. Nany grabbed him by his rubbery shoulders and looked him in the eye. "Shh! Shut up! There ain't nothing wrong with you, damn fool," she grumbled.

The man stopped crying and looked as though someone had taken away his dinner plate.

"I'm only doing this cause there's something heavy on you. Your hands are too fast in town. Everyone's seen you take what's not yours—here and there. And they talk about it, too. So don't play dumb for Nany with your boohooing."

The man sniffled like a little child, then she helped him to stand. From the wall she then took a bottle she'd filled with a mixture that smelled like urine and strong pepper and instructed him to hang it on the tree outside his house—and to paint the front door blue. "You'll be fine now," she said. Then she gave him a little reassuring slap on the cheek. "Go apologize. And pay back whoever needs it. And stop being a snake," she said. With a new resolve, the man wiped his eyes and marched through the cascading strands of red and black beans, out to the sunbaked road.

She turned toward a girl who sat in the folding chairs and watched the scene develop. After what had just happened, Nany could see by her look she thought she, too, might face the same doom. The child, dark as the leather on a Sunday hymnal, knew her turn was next, and she stood, though she couldn't lift her eyes. Nany thought she was maybe only eight or nine years old, smaller and more emaciated than was healthy for a child her age.

"Come along then," Nany said. She motioned for the girl to take a turn lying amid the candles. Her moon eyes fixed upon the candles, then shifted to the likenesses of saints scattered about and chickens scratching in their cages off to one side. She seemed unable to move, her feet rooted to the floor. Her mother sat in her yellow flowered dress, a pattern that Nany found a bit too enthusiastic for a woman her size. She had the hem of her skirt folded and tucked under her rump, as though trying to be proper. Still, it hugged her, making her legs look like tree stumps, and her breasts flopped over her distended belly like two dead crabs caught in a fisherman's net.

"*Higo faddah*, Nany. Go on, child," the woman commanded. Then she stared at the girl with an intensity that Nany recognized and understood to mean more than, "It's your turn to speak." It wasn't the loving glance of a mother concerned for her child, but a mother concerned for her own reputation, or perhaps someone who hides a secret. The child stood out of reach in her frilly Sunday dress stained with red dirt on its bottom fringes, and she gawked at the wall of jarred herbs.

"Now what was I telling you before leaving home?" her mother said in a bit of a shout. "Don't be keeping old Nany Root waiting for you. It's disrespectful! Now answer to the lady, or you'll be getting it from your father."

Nany tapped the top of her head several times and rubbed away some sweat from her upper lip. "What's your name, child?" she asked. But it didn't seem like an actual invitation to speak, the child thought. The mother sat with her lower lip hanging like it somehow got detached.

"Child!" Nany called out. "Are you deaf?"

"The child's not right, Nany. It's not her hearing's the problem," her mother said. "The child won't proper speak. Been living that way for some time now, and believe me, we're all up to our gills in it. The devil's got her tongue and needs him cast out if you're asking me."

"Well, is that so?" Nany's voice softened. She pursed her lips and squinted at the child, then observed her mother's antsy movements.

"And what says your father?" Nany asked the girl.

Neither the mother nor the child would say more. The room filled with the soft hum and whir of the floor fans.

"Don't go poking no more, Nany. I'm telling you what's fixing the child. You hear me asking for your advice? I came so you'd clear the girl—take the bad thing away. If you can't, we'll push out to Taja."

Nany looked over at the child, whose dark, worried eyes became pendulums swinging back and forth between the two women.

"Peh! Plenty coming in here asking for a cure, but unless I know what ails the child, it's like laying ropes round a boat and thinking that will stop it from drifting," she said. Nany untied a polka dot rag she had around her neck and wiped her whole face. The girl stood with her big eyes glued to Nany, all the while trying to figure out if she was a witch just like everyone said. And if she was one, was she a wicked one? Or was she the kind to turn her into a lizard or a frog that she might squash?

"I'm neither nor," Nany said to the girl, answering her thoughts. The child took a quick in-breath and stepped back. "Doing good, doing bad—take the same action, get a different result. All depends on your state of mind, child. Where you're aiming, now that's important. You come with me." Nany turned on her calloused feet and slipped through the beaded curtain, out to the street.

The girl looked back at her mother, who seemed ready to erupt into flames. "That old crank left!" the mother said in a volcanic burst. Instead of waiting to find out whether her mother would combust for sure, the girl took off after Nany. Her black patent leather shoes slapped the concrete as she trailed along.

She tried to keep up, but Nany was nimble, more so than what she remembered of the old woman with her walking stick and her unsteady gait. Nany strode like a twenty-year-old man across the dirt road and then disappeared into the dense jungle greenery. It was a place her mother had told her repeatedly not to venture into alone. But she felt bold watching Nany, and she knew that following the old woman into the forest was what she had to do.

"Get back here!" her mother shouted from inside the shop. The child glanced backward in time to see her mother charging, fists clenched, looking like a rhinoceros ready to stomp her into the ground for taking off like that. The child decided not to wait for what her mother might do, so she sped across the road and down through a thicket of fanned-out banana leaves where Nany had trailed off just moments before.

The mother stood at the edge of the forest, shouting with a voice so resonant that it shook the air. "You hear me? It's a good licking for you once I get my hands on you!" Her words sent a small flock of parrots squawking over to higher trees. The girl wasn't that far into the jungle density, but she smelled it all, thick and heavy, around her—mushrooms and raindrops, earth and dung. She held her breath and wished that she could be invisible, just this once.

"The devil with you, then. You won't like what happens when your father finds out!" she said. Then she slapped her flabby hands on the flats of the banana leaves and grumbled, stomping her overgrown legs as she trudged away.

But neither Nany nor the child was in the jungle at all. Together they stood in the shop's doorway watching the mother trample dirt clods with her elephantine feet. Nany placed reassuring hands on the child's shoulders. The child looked up at the elderly woman and could not form words. The best she could manage was a croaking noise. Nany held a finger to her lips, and the child knew to remain silent or else this wonderful thing, this miracle might somehow go away—or it might turn into a nightmare. The girl blinked at the spectacle of her mother, and it occurred to her that this old woman might change things for the better.

Once her mother was far out of earshot, the child asked Nany,

"How come my mother thinks I ran out of the shop?" Her voice was like a thin wisp of smoke.

"How come you think you're in the shop? Don't be too sure of nothing." Nany raised her eyebrows and gave a punctuating chuckle. "Now, you go on and tell me your name, child."

The girl pulled her lips with her fingers for a second. "Justice," she replied. A mouse might have said it, the words came out so small and hesitant.

"No use talking as quiet as that with me," said Nany. "Might as well have said that to the wall."

"Justice," the girl repeated with more resolve.

"Well then, Justice. Come sit on the floor. I'm going to give you a good blessing. Ain't no more bad things happen to a girl, not in her own home."

Justice looked up at Nany with eyes that had seen terror, and she wondered if she'd be in for more of the same. "World's seen enough of that. Time for it to end," Nany said, again responding to what Justice thought. Then the old woman touched the side of her nose with an index finger.

The child nodded. She took Nany's hand, and she stepped over the dancing candle flames and sat down on the flaking concrete. The candle flames quivered in unison, but unseen by the child, they shot upward, stretching an inch or two taller than what Nany might expect. Even if the child had seen, she wouldn't have cared. Everything Nany said and did entranced her too much.

It was an important sign to Nany, though. She set the child down and fussed with the little one's clothes while using her peripheral vision to scan the back of the shop. Nany didn't want to seem particularly interested, but she was aware that something from the Unseen World lingered there. It surprised Nany, as her many amulets and devil traps, her washes, herbs, and oils surrounding the space should have kept things like this where they belonged. It seemed like a filthy and vile presence, and someone who had visited earlier in the day might have left it behind.

Nany knew not to look directly at the Unseen thing, or she might scare it into hiding. No, she preferred such things to be out in the open, even if they were lurking in that unlit back part of the shop. That's where she had laid out her mattress and blankets and an old gooseneck lamp. Things from the Unseen hated being watched, being known. That's how they might get trapped by a woman of Nany's abilities. Trapped and then used as a sled dog.

Nany fixed eyes on the child and then spoke some nonsense, trying to keep the thing from hiding, from embedding itself into a wall or even in the unsuspecting girl. In her side vision, though the detail was fuzzy, it appeared as a kind of wretched and broken body made of shadow. That shadow seemed to be drinking in the darkness with each of its restless, unsatisfied breaths. As it did, its form became more substantial and defined. It produced a kind of clicking noise. It also made a wet, squishy sound, like an infected throat choking on pus or thick mucus or blood.

Click.

Guk… guk, guk.

Nany had witnessed all kinds of Unseen things once she'd exorcised them from folks. She had her ways to get these Unseen things out, too. She could pray, spray blessed rum from her mouth, or call upon the saints to do the work. If all else failed, she might just wrap a rosary around a client's neck and choke what was foul out of them. As they took their leave, spirits might look like steam vapors vanishing, others like animals with more limbs than they ought.

But this creature seemed more malevolent than what she'd encountered before. This was no steam vapor. The other Unseen things she'd met were more like the tormented and lost ones, souls crying for their squandered lives. But this thing hadn't lost its way. It came with a purpose. She could feel it trying to turn her mind, to darken it and fill it with thoughts of destruction, desperation, and fury, each in its turn with every inhaled breath.

"Why don't I just slice this child's throat and put her out of her misery? Her father uses her for his own, anyway. She's become garbage to him, and she'll live her life in utter regret and horror. So why not end it now? Might be the kindest thing to do."

No matter how she pushed them back, the same thoughts occurred. Then, with an instantaneous slip of her attention, the destructive thoughts took over her mind and even seemed reasonable. She wrenched her focus back and tried to push them away from where they came. Doing so made the creature in the corner seethe with anger. She glanced from her peripheral vision again, so that the spirit wouldn't know what she was about. The eye gaze drew spirits from the shadows, and it was how they knew about you.

The form it took had long boney limbs and a neck just the same. Its face was a long blur, with dozens of milky white eyes set on its face where no eyes should be, and a black, gloppy mouth opened and closed, snapping in the air. Its skinny arms ended in withered claws that dug into the back wall. It heaved its emaciated chest as though intoxicated with hunger, having spotted a morsel it craved, and it let loose a long, thick string of drool.

Nany carried on as was usual for her, making protective gestures around the child so as not to frighten Justice nor provoke the creature toward them before she had time to prepare. She lit a cigar and placed it in a rock bowl on the floor, and she took out a large bottle of rum. She felt the thing watching, searing the room with its cancerous rage.

Nany whispered to the child that she should lay on the floor while she ground up a mixture of powders and dried herbs in a mortar. She poured the concoction a little at a time around the perimeter, making a barrier. The thing creeping in the darkness moved forward, but only to the edge where light and shadow met.

"Child, close your eyes and don't open them till Nany says so."

Justice nodded and closed her eyes, though she had no intention of keeping them shut for long, not with Nany doing so many exciting things.

Nany had a crate next to the floor candles that she used as a table topped with Catholic saint cards scattered about small candles, fruits, and coins. Inside the box was shere she kept her rum, some bones, and a box of her cigars. She dabbed a few drops of rum on her thumb and rubbed them in the shape of a cross on Justice's forehead. Then she recited a prayer that sounded Catholic, praising the Virgin of Mercy. Still, she called her by her proper name, *Obatalá*, a name her godmother once told her in secret. Her granny said never to waste other folks' magic, even if it was Christian and seemed like sheer nonsense. As long as it worked, she should use it.

This dark presence seemed unaffected by the prayer and continued to lurk in shadow. The creature must have been older and more corrupt than what simple prayers could reach. Nany wished now that she hadn't sent her helper, Charlene, on an errand. Charlene knew this kind of magic, the kind concerning older things, things that came from realms where Nany had no dealings. Charlene knew the dark arts from overseas—the fancy kind you'd find in old handwritten books on dusty library shelves. But she wasn't here now. Nany would have to use what was on hand.

The creature scuttled up to the ceiling as fast as an overgrown spider sensing fresh meat ensnared in its web. Just then, Justice's eyes opened wide and rolled back so that Nany could only see the whites. The child gasped like someone was choking her. When she finally got some air, she rocked her head back and forth like an invisible hand moved it. She threw it backward at an angle so extreme that Nany worried it might fracture her spine, if not snap the neck.

A wood crucifix sitting on her altar dropped into a crumpled heap of gray ash, while another metal one attached to the wall began wilting. The small metal Christ appeared to gasp and twist away from the little nails that fastened its hands and feet. The cross beam bowed downward, and the figure's arms snapped off, exposing small broken bones and gnarled gristle. The figure's mouth twisted in silent agony.

The whole crucifix melted together as a slimy black mass that drooled down the wall. But once it puddled onto the floor, it kept moving, like a black squid that found itself out of the water, slapping its inky, slippery limbs about in a wild search to latch on to whatever was nearby. The mass then sprouted spidery extremities and a face with shining black eyes, and the creature crawled on its eight jointed toothpick legs. It clicked along the edge of the circle like a poisonous insect.

Nany's godmother had told her strange tales of creatures such as these, and how she might catch them like a frog at a pond. But it was dangerous, maybe the most dangerous thing you could do. If you trapped it, her godmother said, you'd make it your own, so it could never harm another soul.

Justice gurgled, and it sounded to Nany like she might be drowning in her own spit, then her head lolled to one side, as though someone had removed her spine. Her head rolled forward and dropped, looking no longer connected to anything except her neck-skin, and it rolled back and forth on its own from weight and gravity.

"Sister." Justice's mouth moved, but she took on the voice of an older woman—someone familiar.

Nany eyed Justice. "Who's that?" she asked in a hush so quiet that she couldn't hear herself say it. She knew who it was, but there was always room for a creature like this that took multiple forms to fool her and lead to trouble.

The spirit on the circle's edge scuttled sideways like a crab, looking for a way past Nany's barrier. It hissed in a fury, showing a mouth full of pin-prick metallic teeth, top to bottom.

"Sister, you come quick." Justice's lips formed the words though her teeth clenched and cracked, and she foamed froth and flecks of spittle to the floor.

"I won't do nothing till you say your name, damn you," Nany said.

Justice opened her eyes, and they were black and shiny as new tar. Nany opened the bottle of rum, took a swig, and sprayed it onto the child. The creature lurking outside the perimeter flattened into a shapeless black puddle and roiled along the floor like a boiling chancre, still searching, searching for a way in.

"The mister's done something. Something awful. It's too late, but you still must come." Justice's lips contorted around her tongue, and the words sounded sloppy and ill-formed. Justice drew back her head, flexed her jaw muscles, and rolled her eyes back. Nany cradled the child's head as it continued to fall in any direction like a ball attached to the end of a rope. She tried to pinch together the child's cheeks to loosen her jaw.

"I asked you to say your name. Now do it, before I cast you back to the fiery place where you belong," Nany said.

Justice formed more words between her grinding teeth, and a bloody drool crept from the corners of her mouth. "Who else would know to find you this way? Who else knows to call on you in your shop? Who else knows I work for the American *Conchy Joe*?"

Nany laid the child on her back; her head rolled all the way over to one side. She arched backward and contorted her fingers while the knuckles and the bones cracked under the intense pressure.

"I won't say more," the visitor inside Justice said in a hoarse voice. "If that *thingum* there knows my name, it can trap me and eat me. It likes a soul with more sin to it, but it'll eat me just fine if it ain't got nothing better."

Nany kept track from her peripheral as the blob sprouted legs and a face once more. But this time, the face resembled Justice. Nany turned her head toward the horrible little thing. She knew it was a risk, but she locked gaze with its soulless eyes.

"Please help me," the creature said in Justice's voice.

With a sudden burst of bravery, Nany sprayed the creature's face with her rum. It hissed and then flicked out a long blue iguana's tongue and lapped at the air. Justice opened her mouth, and from it extended a similar long, blue, forked tongue. The tongue then acted as a separate entity as it trailed around Justice's soft, bent neck like a serpent, and it continued downward, exploring, looking for Nany's hand. Nany realized that the creature on the outside had figured a way into the circle, using Justice's body.

Nany grabbed the cigar, puffed smoke onto Justice's face, and formed a blessing sign on her forehead with a powdered root. Justice shrieked with a thunderous cacophony of voices and sounds, many of which Nany had never heard before. The shape at the edge of the circle then prowled backward, shrinking into the shadows of the shop as though she'd injured it. There it sulked in the dark. Its black eyes glittered in the flame flicker, like something that might catch the attention of the very young or the inexperienced, much to their regret. It shuddered and shook apart, then reassembled itself into the standing figure that had earlier clutched the wall and wheezed in the darkness.

Nany knew from her godmother's tales that to do what needed doing, she had to make use of the rum bottle. But it was almost empty when she started. A newer bottle was on the floor several feet away from the protective perimeter. She would only have one chance to grab it and make it back to the safety of the circle.

As if responding to her thoughts, the shadow-thing was already hunching and clawing. She could feel its trembling cold death-breath stuttering and its hungry eyes fixed on her neck. She dared not move—not yet.

The rum bottle trembled with a restless glass-tinging vibrato, then it scraped along the floor by itself until it was up against the powder barrier. It was a trap. She was no fool. But she also had no viable options left. The child might die under the influence of this spirit. She might also survive just fine, but she couldn't take the chance.

She doused the child once more on her forehead, and it caused Justice to cry at first in her own voice, then like a barrel-chested man. Her fit ended in a small giggle and a flood of ripe upchuck. Nany turned Justice's head to one side, and the stomach's contents slid out, a slurry both yellow and putrid. With the creature thinking it was distracting Nany with these horrors, she made a quick nab at the bottle. Still, a cold black clawed hand, as slippery as sin, was ready, and it reached out from Justice's mouth, running her tongue out beneath. The hand clutched Nany's with an unshakable grip and crushed it against the bottle's neck. With her free hand, Nany peeled the bottle away and stuffed its long amber throat past the slippery arm into Justice's mouth. The girl choked and gurgled on the liquid. Her eyes sped back and forth and bulged from their sockets as the blessed rum singed the foul spirit that had found a way into her.

Nany recited rhythmic strands of words in a language unknown to most islanders that her godmother said she should only use in an emergency. Then she shouted, "In the bottle you go. You're mine!"

The hand withdrew back down Justice's throat, and she opened her eyes in full surprise. The child nabbed the bottle herself and forced the neck of it down her throat while she gnashed her teeth against the glass, as though the damned spirit wanted the child to cut her mouth to ribbons. There was a terrible sound of glass scraping and teeth cracking.

Nany closed her eyes momentarily and caled upon all that was good to end this. "In you go!" she sang in a voice that trembled the cement. Justice rocked her body in fury. The child stood up as though following some unheard instruction, and spewed into the bottle a mixture of blood, rum, and a pitch-black tar-like substance. A lot of it missed the bottle, too, spraying down its sides and leaking onto Justice's white Sunday dress. Then she fell backward onto the floor, pushed by unseen hands.

Nany pulled the bottle out of the child's hands, and into its top she stuffed a cork. She turned to tap Justice's cheeks and tilted back her neck until the child gasped with the frantic inhalation of one drowning in a rip tide. She opened her eyes and threw her arms around Nany. Then she sobbed and sobbed, forever it seemed.

It was over. There were no more moving shadows in the room. Nany swirled the bottle around and knew she'd trapped the *thingum* in there. She set the jug down and helped the girl to stand.

"What's that you do with my girl?" came a deep, commanding voice from behind them. In the shop's front door stood two figures, outlined by the orange light of the setting sun. On one side was Justice's mother, fists propped on her hips. And next to her, her father, veins bulging in his neck.

"The poor thing got sick. She let go all over her party dress," Nany said. She reached with her neckerchief and wiped the child's chin and dabbed here and there on the skirt.

"What makes her sick, Nany Root?" the man asked. Nany could see him tightening his fists.

"Probably what makes her sick came from her home."

"What do you mean by that?" the man asked. He took a step toward Nany. "I didn't do anything. The child's a liar. Always has been." His face was stone, but his eyes told another story. Too many awful secrets there, as far as Nany could tell. "She lies about everything," the man continued. "Got to whoop the truth out of her."

"She looks like she's sick of something," Nany said. "Anyway, her mother left her at the shop, so I had to take care of her this whole time. Nany can't be a sitter for free, you know."

The man looked at his wife and squared his jaw. She looked back at him, weary and sad of what was likely coming once they got back home. He strode toward Justice, brow folded onto itself, his gait wide and stern. He knocked over several floor candles with his muddy shoes and wrenched Justice by the wrist. She whimpered at his touch, but bit her lip instead of satisfying him with a cry. He yanked her up, and her body went as slack as a broken doll.

"Goodbye, Nany Root. That's enough for one day."

"Now wait," Nany said. She swirled the rum bottle and waved it a bit. "This is for any trouble old Nany caused."

"What trick is this, old woman?" he asked. He dropped the girl's hand and grabbed at the bottle.

"No trick," Nany said. She tilted her head and smiled. "Old Nany thinks you have a bad fix on her, and she doesn't like it. So take. And come back one day when you need her well and true."

He squinted and inspected her face for signs of mischief. She blinked back and smiled like the Holy Mother offering a chance to hold her newborn. He uncorked the bottle with his teeth, spit the cork out onto the floor, and sniffed the contents. Then he looked down through the bottle's neck, like a pirate peering through a telescope.

"I gave you the best one I got," Nany said. "If you don't want it, I'll take it back."

The man gave a half-smile and acted like he'd won a great victory, triumphant and gloating. He hugged the bottle to his chest and took a step back. He glugged down a throat-full and let out a wet, satisfied sigh. He wiped some black dribble from his chin and raised the bottle for a toast.

"To Nany, a wise woman who always knows to serve a man proper." He glowered at his wife and slurped down more, which Nany suspected must have tasted delicious to him, as he filled his cheeks and swallowed it down hard.

"Come, child," Nany said. She led Justice toward her mother and patted her hands with a knowing smile. "Time to go." Justice looked up at her mother, then back at the old woman. Nany whispered, "No more harm will come to you, child. Not by his hand, at least."

Three

Los Angeles, 1945
Two Years Before It Happened

The man at the bulbous chrome microphone looked left and right before he widened his grin.

"Good evening, ladies and gentlemen. Is everyone enjoying the main course?" He slicked his black hair back and tugged down on the lapels of his tuxedo, making sure everything was just so.

"The chef tells me that when they bought the chicken for tonight from the butcher, there was a bit of a problem. It turned out that some hens had one leg longer than the other. When the chef complained, the butcher said, 'Hey, what's the problem? You gonna eat them or do a samba with them?'"

There was a drum and cymbal crash to punctuate his gag, and the audience gave up a small murmur, but he wasn't sure it was laughter. Others groaned outright.

"Wow. Brutal. I guess I'll stick to doling out traffic tickets," he said. The audience picked up the laughter.

"Tonight we have a bit of an unusual program," the man said. "But this year's program was influenced by unusual circumstances. In most years, we have one recipient of this prestigious award, but this time out we have a duo. Let's call it a tie. Between these two, there are forty years of loyal service. They worked side by side before one was taken away from us, and now, reunited, they've managed to continue their service to the force as an unbeatable team.

"They're more than workmates. They're friends. Known each other since childhood, and still, they get along. So without further ado, may I introduce the recipients of this year's Officer of the Year Award—or rather Officers of the Year—Glen Haddock and Ren Larson." The announcer bowed, and his black mop of slicked hair flopped forward, while with one hand he gestured to the two men. Then he stepped to the side, next to the velvet curtain.

The spotlight pointed toward the center table draped in white and glittering with bubbly champagne glasses. The two men wearing formal officer's uniforms stood up next to their wives while the attendees stood along with them in a cascade of applause and whistles. Ren and Haddock left the banquet table and lumbered up the auditorium steps. At the microphone at the center of the stage, they shook hands.

The emcee scurried beside them and handed each his award.

A photographer in the audience shouted, "Hey fellas, gives us a good one for the *Times-Mirror*." The men leaned in and smiled dutifully, holding up their prizes.

Los Angeles 1947
Three Days Before It Happened

When Ren pulled up to the incident address, six black and white cruisers were already scattered front to rear, sideways, long-ways, on and off the sidewalk to enclose the dilapidated hotel. Ren knew to expect blood when members of the "gun squad" showed up. The new chief wanted to clean up the streets of Los Angeles, evidently at any cost. He'd made it clear—if not officially to the press, then to the officers behind closed doors—that they should hold court on criminals in the streets. "Bring em back dead"—his unofficial motto—drove out many officers who didn't have the stomach for it.

From the middle of a dead sleep, Ren had picked up the phone receiver and without a moment's hesitance, his Sargent had crammed in rapid-fire details about some lunatic holed up in a downtown hotel. He mentioned a captive family and neighbors reporting screams and crashes from the hotel room. Ren's three o'clock in the morning mind had trouble sorting out the details, and he'd likely missed more than a few. To make matters worse, some woman listening in on the party line kept horning in with her own cockamamie commentary. Once he'd arrived at the incident site, he'd get his clarifications. Whatever the original situation, it had worsened in the short time between the call and Ren's arrival, judging from the hefty police presence.

Ren recognized the place as soon as he drove up. The *Downtown HOT*, he called it, because at night, the last two letters blinked out from the word "Hotel" on the faded neon sign.

"So, where are we with this thing?" Ren asked. One of the young patrolmen who stood under the weather-whipped awning stretched out in front of the gray stone apartments extended a hand to shake Ren's. He exhaled in visible relief. "Jeez, buddy. What took you so long?"

"What are you talking about? Sarge called not twenty minutes ago," Ren replied.

"Sure thing, Ren. Whatever you say. You better get up there. Jeez, he's a fucking fruit basket. No one knows what set this thing off either—or why he's even here."

"Jeez," Ren mumbled. His brow ran cold with perspiration. He lifted his tight black police cap and wiped his face into the crook of his coat. Even though it was still early morning hours when the city had time to cool down, someone had turned on Ren's personal furnace.

"Do we know this guy?" Ren asked.

"Better get up there. Fiorelli's up there and been waiting for like—look, hurry."

Ren picked up the pace and started up the stairs just inside the lobby with its cracked, gum-stuck terrazzo and brass-lock mailboxes hanging at a sad tilt. Stained flowered wallpaper curled and spread at the seams, exposing walls that hadn't seen fresh paint since the Great Depression. The whole place smelled like damp shoes.

This hotel was a place someone went when they had no place left to go. After this, it was either a shelter run by the Bureau of Public Assistance or a dank alley. Though it may have had its glory days, maybe forty years ago, the Downtown HOT had found its final glory as a joint for stewbums between halfway houses, low-level ex-cons, and biddies on the public dole. Ren and Haddock made regular police rounds here for domestic disturbances, prostitution, and drunken brawls.

The city should have torn the place down decades ago. The building next to the Downtown HOT had already fallen victim to the wrecking ball. An emergency had stopped the first attempt at demolition. The engineers hadn't emptied the building completely when the iron ball slammed the upper floors to smithereens. Workers discovered an elderly couple, naked and pulverized, among the wreckage. After that, the city scrambled to install new policies to assure the vacancy of knock-downs before demolition.

About two zig-zag flights up, Ren discovered that his legs no longer operated like his own. He'd lost direct control. His lungs compressed like something squashed them. He struggled to gulp down air. And the stairwell walls appeared to close in on him. Walls didn't move, did they?

Ren realized the dark-between was close. As soon as he closed his eyes, he stood within a shape-shifting landscape. The twilight sky loomed heavily with clouds, and beyond that, those crazy stars glittering in strange constellations. In a shift of his gaze, Ren found himself no longer in that twilight country, but in a rust-dripping jail cell.

"Try that again, Yankee Doodle—." Müller stood above Ren,

baring his crooked yellow teeth, his flabby face spread wide into an awful, sinful, almost elated smile. You'd never find a man like him acting alone in any other circumstance. Outside of his post, he was the kind who'd blend into a crowd, worsted wool suit and all. He was the *Invisible Man* standing behind you in line at the druggist, sitting in the row behind you on a city bus, breathing too hard, and making the air stale. But you wouldn't see him.

He probably spent his whole life flying under the radar, which was often more manageable than attempting to fit in. But now thanks to Ren, the jig was up. His fellow officers saw him, all right. They saw him for what he wasn't. He knew that they spotted a fraud, that he wasn't officer material, someone of intellect or cunning. The others would laugh and trade cigarettes and slap each other on the back as they guffawed at how he was no man of mettle, undeserving of his post. Heck, he probably shouldn't be in charge of a bratwurst cart. They'd hush thėir voices and add that Herr Müller was a nincompoop placed at the stockade managing foreign prisoners—likely by a relative in a higher post.

Müller would allow no one to disrobe him from his cloak of invisibility, at least not twice. He raised his long black rifle and bashed the butt into his captive's face.

"Try that again, and you'll dine on your teeth," he said.

Ren lurched forward and bent in half, smelling his dysentery-shit wet pants, putrid and sharp. The irons around his wrists dug in deeper as he hit the floor. The blood tasted like a warm summer brine, and the structures around his mouth became mushy. He knew he'd be in pain later. Herr Müller's eyes gleamed like someone had just brought him a double slice of strudel.

This wasn't how to treat prisoners of war. But Ren had now become Müller's toy to parade out to the other officers when he wanted to show off or justify his position. Ren was an American in a distant land. Even if the war ended and they sent him back home, how would he prove anything? Müller could just disappear into the crowd along with thousands of other citizens.

Ren blinked and found himself back in the Downtown HOT stairwell. He steadied himself before finally bending down and buckling to the floor on his knees. His innards bubbled up, hot and tart.

The door to the second-floor hallway swung open, and what was once indistinct, muffled shouting became as vivid and urgent as a red hot poker up the ass. Men shouted over one another with words of warning, directing this barrage toward the suspect inside a hotel room.

Ren climbed up the rest of the way, bracing on the handrail and lurching out toward the landing. He found himself in a dim hallway that was illuminated by a row of wall sconce lights made to look like pairs of candles. The flame-shaped bulbs sputtered from faulty wiring. At the far end of the hall, a group of uniformed men, guns drawn, crowded in front of a busted-open apartment door. Flies flittered about and speckled the stained hotel walls. Ren thought it odd they'd gather like this, as though there were a dung heap in a pig stall nearby.

Fiorelli turned around. "Detective Larson. Glad you could make it. We're almost done here." Ren straightened himself and forced down whatever weakness remained in his limbs.

Fiorelli was slender and precise, younger than Ren and willing to use his dark looks and his practiced charm to influence others. He was tucked, tight, and crisp, sleek and tidy as stainless steel. That was, except for his divot-marked face. Ren thought that was the one honest feature about the guy. Fiorelli couldn't mask that imperfection with his pomade and layers of shoe polish.

"Put it down," one officer howled out.

"Nooo," a man moaned back. His voice sounded muffled, as though he was somewhere further in the apartment.

Ren's pulse slowed to a halt. That was Haddock's voice, the whining child-like voice that he heard coming from the inner room. It was a sucker-punch in the gut. What was his partner doing there?

"No! No! No!" He heard Haddock bellowing and beating

something rhythmically in time to his words.

The weeping and wailing came from the bedroom, just off the beaten-up main sitting area, if anyone called it a "sitting area" at all. The walls were once wet-stained but now dried into puddled pond-scum markings, and the hardwood floors were the same. The place was lit by a bent floor lamp with a dented shade that sat at a broken slant. Someone had pulled the bedroom door off its top hinges and swung it wide into the room. Two officers crowded in, jaws clenched, eyes fixed, and guns lowered to their target.

"I can't." Haddock sounded heavy and hoarse. "It wasn't me. You don't understand. How could you? It's true! It ate them. It ate them!"

Ren's intestines did a squirming dance, but he steadied himself with the thought of how grateful he was the Sarge called him to handle his friend. The whole room wasn't yet in his view, but in glancing down he noticed an extensive blood splatter soaking into the slivered floor.

He couldn't reconcile this situation with the man he'd known for so long, the man with whom he'd partnered for decades. It was the two of them who talked other guys into dropping their weapons and out of jumping off ledges. Haddock dropped other men's defenses by sitting with them, calm and steady, talking about baseball or the weather or the moving pictures, while they all stood at the precipice of disaster. He'd say reasonable things so they'd feel understood, and he'd talk to them as though he was asking for the mayonnaise at a Sunday picnic.

Ren peered around the corner, hoping Haddock wouldn't glimpse him just yet. The officer sat in his underwear atop a dented mattress, sobbing, pounding his fists on a bedspread saturated with a deep ruby puddle of blood. There were blood crosses and other weird patterns smeared across the walls and ceiling, formed of geometric shapes and concentric circles. All around the patterns were random letter groupings. Nonsense words. He'd seen plenty of weird things, but he'd seen nothing like this.

Ren allowed his eyes to travel back to the bed to absorb the shock of what he couldn't—he wouldn't admit initially. There, Lily's limp body lay across Haddock's lap. The meat of her neck yawned open and exposed the trachea and other gristle that Ren wished he'd not seen. Haddock had split her from one ear to the next, and a deluge of red sickness bathed her dress. Her eyes and mouth were wide open. Worst of all, fresh blood and traces of torn flesh caked Haddock's mouth, as though he'd chewed them to death.

"Crap almighty," Ren muttered. He pulled his cap and pressed his back to the wall. "What in goddamn Gehenna happened here?"

No one responded.

"There's someone here to help," an officer shouted to Haddock. He sounded like a hospital orderly holding a long syringe behind his back.

"I don't want to talk to anyone!" Haddock boomed.

Behind everyone came a startling flash, then a crackle of a camera bulb.

"Jesus H. Christ! Who in the damn hell let the press in?" Fiorelli hollered so loudly that his bass voice reverberated through Ren's rib cage. Two officers from the hallway yanked the photographer by the back of his overcoat and pulled him out backward, slamming the door on him.

Haddock snapped up a revolver lying on the bed, and he whipped it up under his sweat-dripped throat. "I have to do it," he said. Then he began a deep sobbing that bubbled up from a well of regret. He leaned forward and propped himself up with his free hand. A squish of mattress-blood flooded between his fingers. He draped his hulking chest across Lily. Further into the room, on the closet floor, a small, pale arm lay as cold as flap-meat in a restaurant fridge—Haddock's daughter.

As soon as it all sank in, Ren gagged, and he choked down whatever planned on coming up. This was beyond his imagining. He tried to conjure up words to say, but none came. Then Fiorelli whispered, "Larson's here, Glen."

Haddock's eyes, unfocused, red, and bulging, seemed to soften for a second. His brow creased up, his cheeks quivered, and his convulsive weeping became torrents. He pushed the gun in deeper beneath his chin.

"Glen. Glen, it's me." Ren kept his eye on the weapon, and that kept him from letting loose in his drawers. "Glen, you gotta give up the gun. It's too dangerous. We can sort this all out." Ren held out a hand.

"They can't come back now. They can't!" Haddock shouted. From his lower lip dripped a long saliva string. "It *made* me. I didn't want to, but it *made* me." He nodded assuredly, like a cult member who had surrendered all doubts. "It got in, and then, I don't know. I don't know. It, it...." He made a gesture as if he wanted to extract something from inside his skull. "It made me."

"Yes. It did, Glen," Ren replied. He tried taking a step closer to grab the gun. "That's why we've got to... to work together. So we can stop it."

"Stop it?" Haddock's gaze darted wildly around the room following what only he could see. "You can't. *It gets in.* And then it..." He pressed his finger to his temple like a corkscrew digging in.

"We know all about it, Glen. And believe me, we can stop it." Ren took a bolder step toward Haddock, who reacted by repositioning the gun to his temple and cocking back the hammer.

"You can't! You can't. It knows too much. It knows everything. You think it's not watching you right now?" Ren took a step backward.

"Glen, we've got it under control. I promise you. I don't want to convince you of anything. I just want to sit down. They don't have elevators here, you know. So I walked up five flights. Do you mind if I sit?"

Haddock's eyes bulged, and he stared past Ren's shoulder. "*There.* Oh God, no. What do you want? You can't take anything else!" He heaved his mass upward off the bed, shoved Ren to the floor and charged toward the door with his bloodied revolver pointed.

The officers on either side of the door made quick work of it in a rain of bullets that echoed like fireworks being set off in the building, and dropped Haddock before he could do more. A red ooze eagerly seeped through black holes, and his dead eyes still watched something just beyond the dark hotel hall.

Ren pulled himself to a stand and eyed the other officers, their faces drawn and pale.

"Nice work, Larson," Fiorelli said.

Ren couldn't speak or move, so he stood among the carnage, unable to weep.

Fiorelli switched mechanically to procedures. "All right, boys. We've got a lot to do."

Four

Los Angeles, 1947
Several Days After It Happened

"You know, Father, some sin is intentional, while the rest of it we stumble upon and come upon it honestly, if that can even be allowed in the eyes of God. After our first intentional sins, we all tell ourselves that there are some transgressions worse than others. Later, we change the story and tell ourselves that we needed to do some of them out of necessity," the nun said.

The priest was still listening, she knew. He was breathing on her, and his breath smelled of garlic and communion wine. It cut through the incense. Worse, it mingled with it. He was listening, yes. So the Good Lord hadn't taken him from her, too, as a punishment that she'd never receive some kind of absolution—if even she might accept it. She wondered, in a pause, if she was beyond caring about such a thing, really. But she continued.

"I sat at a long table next to a magistrate. He seemed like an angry fellow, wearing his black robe and a scowl. Some people are born with such permanent facial features, an affliction from their sorrowful lives. Then I spotted him there. Johann. They had him seated at the rear of the chamber, behind a row of benches used for the spectators."

♦

Johann had two men beside him, arms folded across their chests, and neither of them seemed any happier than the magistrate. The guards had shackled Johann with thick iron rods above and below the wrists, fastened by iron pins. They had chained the whole thing to the splintery dais before him. His once-fine garments were soiled and ripped front and back, top and bottom, from spending months in a rat-and-feces-infested prison. His gray beard had grown fuller and wilder than Margurite had seen it before. She played a small game to see if she could spy his pout of red anywhere beneath the draping mustache. She watched his eyes, the eyes that had once seemed to ensnare, now drunken with regret and uneasiness. How ugly the man was, once she thought about it more.

"The jurors for our sovereign King John the Third present that the doctor who goes by the name of Johann Faust, husband of Margurite Faust of Stockholm, in and upon the thirteenth day of October, and on diverse other days and times, performed certain detestable arts called Witchcraft and Sorceries," the solicitor said.

Margurite enjoyed watching the solicitor's caterpillar-like eyebrows rise and fall seemingly of their own accord, though she noticed the man had no recognizable chin, and this bothered her most. A solicitor should have a proper chin, she thought. Instead, he had a prolonged neck connected to his mouth with skin loose as a turkey's, and he'd cluck, so his gullet wobbled. His name was Philipe. He was French. Margurite thought he looked so much more German and like a man she had once known named Hans. Hans was dead now, and they had never found his body.

He continued, "And on these many days and times, Doctor Faust, in the employ of the Church no less, wickedly, maliciously, and feloniously has used, practiced, and exercised these blasphemous arts in the town of Hamburg against Margurite Faust of Stockholm, by which said wicked arts he caused torture, affliction, and consumption so that the victim pined, wasted and tormented."

He pointed to Margurite, and she realized that was the signal to cast her gaze downward. She intertwined her soft fingers across the folds of her bodice. She thought the demure look was convincing and easy enough to manufacture. It was like play-acting in the mummer's pageant at Christmas time.

"The book of these wicked arts was found within Doctor Faust's premises in Hamburg and was purchased from one Nikolaus VanDyke who owns a shop of curiosities within walk's distance from Doctor Faust's home."

Philipe reached for the volume laid before the magistrate with an elegant and theatrical gesture and then held it aloft. The onlookers gasped and adopted haunted and shocked looks, like dogs that Philipe had suddenly splashed with cold water. They cupped their hands to whisper about how terrible it was to have such a man in their midst, and wouldn't it be just fine if they'd hang him? Philipe set the book back down as though the mere act of holding it were a sin upon his soul. "Is that a true account, Mister VanDyke?"

Now was Nikolaus' chance. Johann knew he'd have to pay. He hadn't thought it would happen this way, nor so soon. The spirit that had buoyed him up into the heavens that day, that sweet day in his chambers, lifted him with all the flames of a darker source, and while doing so, made such alluring promises that he was powerless to resist.

His Margurite, for example: he had longed for someone like her. He had yearned his whole life, and that had come to nothing until he met the spirit. The spirit had a name, but he dared not think or speak it, not now. He, with his high-strung voice like a violin concerto humming tunefully, arrived with promises of angels and delivered something much worse.

Had Johann known better the terms and the loopholes, the machinations of such damned spirits, he'd not be standing before the magistrate. If only he had tossed Margurite and that blasted child growing inside of her into the fire that Michaelmas past, as the demon had instructed, none of this would have played itself out. That was Johann's bargain—and his price. But he had refused to take it.

Margurite was ready with a beguiling smile and assuring words that all was well and right, that he should hold no fear in his heart. She told him that the damned spirit was a figment of his imagination. However, all of it—from beginning to end—was trickery inspired by the demon, a realization Johann came to far too late. Now the price was the gallows, he presumed.

Nikolaus arose, holding his hat. He pushed the bench back with his calves, causing an awful trumpeting, as though Robin Goodfellow himself and all his imps had come to announce the end of times—or Johann's end, at the very least.

"Yes, sir. I'd not known what the book itself was when I acquired it. And it sat for those many months gathering dust on my shelves before Doctor Faust purchased it, knowing what it was, and having a keen interest in the subject. I was happy to be rid of it once he informed me of its nature, and I prayed long to our Lord and Savior after he and that book left my shop."

"So you've already noted in your deposition, Mister VanDyke, that you'd no supposed knowledge of the book's subject. The court has made a record of your account, and your strenuous attempts to clear your name on the matter. I am certain the Church would like to press it with you at a later date."

Nikolaus looked as though his face had turned to wax. Sweating wax. He melted downward and sat with eyes gleaming like sharpened knives for Johann.

Margurite suddenly looked pained, and she bore down in half with a scream sharp as nails. The onlookers collectively caught their breath and huddled against one another.

Philipe rushed to Margurite's side, as did the armed guards flanking her. They gripped her by the elbows to straighten her out, but she seemed locked in her folded position, and all they did was extend her elbows beyond her back, like an awkward stork. She continued to moan and gnash her teeth.

"What is this?" the magistrate demanded. He stood and stepped backward, regarding her as though she had the pox.

Philipe said, "She is with child, but it is not due until June, more than seven months from this day."

Margurite continued to moan, then she said, "It is the spirit, the devil himself sent to torment me. He wishes to take my baby as a punishment for my true testimony. See there…" She pointed to an empty window across from her. "A yellow bird, sitting on the sill. And there," she looked to a vacant spindle-chair in the corner. "A black dog. They have come at Johann's bidding. Lord in heaven, be merciful!" The guards' arms barely hooked her when she finally dropped to her knees and clapped her hands in prayer.

The magistrate pounded his gaveling stone upon the desk to restore order among the onlookers who began to become hysterical from Margurite's display.

"Spectral evidence," Philipe said. The magistrate nodded. There was a wanness about him now.

"Stop these lies at once!" said Johann. The armed men on either side of him forced him back into his seat, though they seemed uneasy about handling him after what they'd witnessed.

♦

"I began to wail out the Lord's Prayer, but I grabbed my sides and heaved all the louder, as though I was being kicked by an invisible boot," the nun behind the screen said. She laughed a little to herself, not because what she'd done was funny, but because of the folly in it, because it took so little to convince others of wrongdoing.

The priest said nothing in response, still.

"I told the court that Johann was calling upon his master, the Dark Lord, and summoning him against me. Then I screamed and forced myself to vomit over the long table. It was a nice touch, I thought. Theatrical. And it was all the magistrate needed."

"I knew the consequences of my actions. I knew the damage to my soul, and I didn't care. The Lord can forgive all things, isn't that so, Father? It wasn't as if I had taken the rope and tied the noose myself. I only lied, which is a much smaller matter."

"Anyway, I had seen Johann conjure the thing, and I tried it myself. Struck my bargain with the horrible creature, a better one than Johann. The price seemed so little. My son was only an infant, so his suffering wasn't long in that fire. Besides, the dark spirit told me that my son would pass on as a martyr and go straight to heaven. I suppose it would have been true if I'd had him baptized. But I saw no need for it since he was only born just the month before. And I'm certain the conjured thing made me forget that detail altogether."

She paused and licked her lips.

"That was my only slip, Father. They say that only a woman has enough cunning to outsmart the trickery of the devil. Men have a hard time thinking beyond the length of their manhood, or what might please them at the moment. But a woman, they say, thinks ahead to what may please them tomorrow and for many tomorrows beyond that. And what I'd done had worked. At least for a while."

Los Angeles, 1947
Two Months Before It Happened

It was nearly eight o'clock that night when the last garbage truck sighed and sputtered its way into the city dump for the day. Old George didn't like that much. Latecomers always had a thing or two—mostly unapproved—going on the side. There might be a mistress in the picture or someone stealing daytime naps. A few of them hauled oversized furnishings and appliances privately, using the city truck, always for an under-the-table fee.

Old George preferred it when everyone did things just as the city liked, namely with honesty. That quality alone would give the profession and everyone in it a measure of integrity. There'd be no need for late drop-offs. If everyone did things as the city billboard out front told them, Old George could open the junkyard later and close earlier. He had even tried hinting at the trouble to the city manager, but he didn't get too far. Fat chance if anyone would take seriously some on-the-sly whistleblowing from a middle-aged, colored junkyard man.

Still, Old George had a hard time shaking his sense of responsibility. At a great personal cost, he'd learned about duty and obligation. Keeping secrets, too. All of it was dead weight in his life. He wanted to toss that anchor over the side of his ship. He'd had enough of encumbrances; he'd had enough for an entire truckload of folks who never had to think about the same burdens as he did every single day of his life. Though he wanted to drop them by the side of a long stretch of desert road and just drive away, something held him back. He knew what it was, too. Loose lips sink ships. Better to just hold on and keep everything locked in.

After never ridding himself of his inner burdens, the old albatross became familiar company. How could he expect anyone to understand? Least of all, the deaf ears down at City Hall. Another lazy civil servant, they'd think, trying to make life easier for himself. But that wasn't it. He knew the consequences for not following rules.

He grew up in the Furlong Tract, more than a bit to the east of well-scrubbed Hollywood and only five blocks long, between 51st and 55th Streets. The Furlong had a few small neighborhoods where things happened that a child probably shouldn't see—nor anybody, really. But it was safer for folks like his momma and him to live and congregate without there being much trouble from the police. You always knew your neighbor's business in the Furlong; there just wasn't any question of it. Everyone took a turn in need, and everyone helped out, knowing that their day would come, eventually.

His mother, Birdie, washed and ironed the neighbors' clothes to make ends meet. The neighbors said she could take the stains out of a soul if she had to. It was just a skilled hand with bleach, hot water, and lye soap. But whenever someone said that to her, she was so tickled that she'd laugh till her bosom shook. He could see that she was proud of doing things right. That's where Old George learned it or at least aspired to it. And even though she'd never really gone much to school, she'd figured out the secrets to a spotless sheet and a starched collar well enough to win her independence and a life for her child.

His father was a part-time Baptist minister down at the church on 50th Street. The rest of the time, he was busy minding a bottle or tending to the long-legged women who polished the pews and arranged the church flowers. Neither of those interests contributed much to the home, except that it kept him away, and Old George saw that as a blessing.

So when Old George came home from school one day, he wasn't much surprised at all to figure what was happening.

"Old Georgie," his mother said. "Old Georgie, sit down right here." She patted her hand on the couch with the worn-out hand-sewn patch where heavy bottoms so often planted themselves that they took the fabric right down to the nubs. He put his schoolbooks on the table and obliged her.

"Yes, ma'am," he said.

He noticed that she was wearing her Sunday clothes, even though it was a Tuesday. It seemed out of place that she'd get her best clothes all mussed and rumpled before she needed them.

She looked him up and down as though deciding on what she might say. Then when it all seemed right in her mind, she stood up and walked to the kitchen. "You want a lemonade, Old Georgie? It's hot today. I think we need a lemonade." She set two sweating glasses on the table beside the couch, and he watched droplets glide down the sides, making chocolate brown rings in the unvarnished wood. She held his hand and squinted at him, looking through only one eye. "Do you know why I named you Old George?" she asked him.

"Because of my granddaddy, that's what you always told me," Old George said.

"And because I always knew you were an old soul," Birdie said. Then she nodded at him.

"What does that mean?" he asked.

"Well, an old soul is someone born into life with a certain kind of knowing. They're wise. They know what's what. They know when to say something and when it's not the right time. You always had that in you. I could see it in your eyes the moment the doctor handed you to me."

She grabbed him with both arms and pressed him into her side, then sat him upright and straightened out his clothes. It was only right to let him sit on his own with as little fussing as possible. He wasn't a boy anymore, not now. "I just want you to know how proud I am of you. And I know you're nearly nine, but you're still the true man of this house," she said.

"Okay, Momma," Old George said.

He knew it was true, though he didn't much like it. He'd learned how to take care of whatever needs there might be, many times without worrying his mother with the details. She had enough to worry about. She glanced out the window with a weighty sigh and a gaze that looked as though she might never find peace. Old George thought maybe he'd seen that kind of look before. It never suited her. Her face was broad and open, and there were so few times he could remember that she didn't have a ready smile. But this far-away look always came after she and his father had words. The man was so big and mean, and Jesus was still on his side, or so he said, anyway.

"Now Old Georgie, you're going to have to take up more responsibilities at home. You know what I mean by that?" she asked him.

"I think so, Momma," he replied.

"Sometimes you have to do things that you won't like, or you might even have to do some things that don't seem quite right, but you still have to do them anyway because you have to take care of the family," she said. She watched his eyes for understanding. He just blinked his long black lashes that curled upwards.

"Now, for instance," she said. "Momma needs you to haul the small trash can out to the dumpster. Not to the one out in the alley, but to the dumpster behind the market on 52nd Street. You know which one I'm talking about?"

Old George knew. It was the black one with rust spots on its sides, almost as tall as a full-grown man. It had big dents, too, like someone had taken a baseball bat to it, crumpling up the corners and such, but no one really knew how it got that way. He also knew not to ask why he needed to walk down a block and turn down an alley just to take out the trash.

She walked into the kitchen and tugged a knee-high trash can across the floor.

"Momma, why do you have the trash can in the house?" he asked.

"Now, I want you to be real careful. Dump out everything in the can and don't look at what's inside, you hear me?" Birdie said. "Now you use your old red wagon to take it there. Don't spill it by accident and don't stop for anything. Just take it and toss it out real quick. You hear me?"

Old George felt like the blood in his face was draining all out to the floor. He didn't want to know what she had in that silver trash can. But as the man of the house, there were responsibilities, just like Momma said. He loved his mother, and he knew she wouldn't do anything that might harm him. So he nodded, even though the back hairs on his neck stood up and a tightening in his stomach made him feel like running into his room and shutting the door.

"Then when you come home, I'm going to make you pork chops, just the way you like them. That's your favorite, right? Pork chops?" Old George nodded, and together they hauled the can out the back door and down the steps to the alley where Birdie had already set up the wagon.

"It's six o'clock, and darker out than a boy should have to walk by himself," she said to herself. She looked up into the sky. Stars were already gathering above, while there was a thin line of red and gold on the horizon. "Can you do this real quick for Momma?" she asked him. Old George still said nothing. Instead, he took the handle and pulled the wagon down the bumpy pebble-strewn alley, hoping the can wouldn't topple. The whole way, whatever was inside rolled and clunked from one side to the other.

It didn't take long to get to the dumpster behind the market, but it was just as dark as it would be at midnight when he arrived. It was no big deal to use the dumpster behind the shop. Everyone used it to toss out things that were too big or irregular or smelly for the usual garbage pail. Mr. Johnson, who ran the store, was just like everyone else in the Furlong Tract, helpful to the neighbors in any way he could be. So he never seemed to care what folks tossed out behind the store.

Old George tried lifting the garbage pail by himself, but the dumpster opening was too high up, making it awkward for him to not only boost the garbage can but to raise it over his head and empty it out.

"Need some help with that, son?" Mr. Johnson asked. Old George felt his limbs freeze. Mr. Johnson came out the back screen door of the market wearing a green apron that covered him from chest to knees. He'd smeared red and brown meat drippings across it, and even his white uniform beneath had those ominous-looking splotches. Mister Johnson knew the boy was eyeing the stains.

"Don't let this scare you, son," he said, then he laughed. "Today was butchering day. Had to slice up all those nice juicy steaks for folks, didn't I?"

He rubbed Old George's head. "You're Birdie's boy?" He nodded. "Old George, right?" He nodded again. "Well, let me help you out with that," Mr. Johnson said. He bent down and helped lift the can with its scalloped sides.

"No, I can do it," Old George said.

"Now, don't be silly. That dumpster's twice your height. How are you gonna do that all by yourself?" he asked. "Now come on. You take off that lid, and I'll dump it in."

Old George stared as though looking through Mr. Johnson rather than at him, but only for a minute. He reached for the lid and placed his hand on top as if trying to keep a snake in a basket. Mr. Johnson laughed. "What are you worried about? Something private in there from your momma? It's okay, son. I won't look."

He closed his eyes to play along, while Old George lifted it off with caution, as though he was picking up a porcelain figurine. He squinted his eyes because he didn't want to see whatever was inside. Mr. Johnson shook his head and laughed again. He grabbed the can by the top lid and its bottom and tilted it up. Whatever was inside offered a heavy thud as it landed on a week's worth of dumpster layers. Then a small, hard object, no bigger than a wad of dried gum skipped to the ground and landed near Old George's shoe. He studied it carefully, trying to be sure of what he was seeing. It looked like a bloody tooth with a gold crown. He stepped on it and looked up to make sure that Mr. Johnson wasn't watching.

When Mr. Johnson set the can down, Old George noticed a red gloss slicking his fingers. His pulse began to jump, and his face went hot, then it went cold, and his breathing got rapid and shallow. He licked his lips and started saying a prayer under his breath. It was one he learned in church to keep the devil away.

Mr. Johnson took no account of the tooth. It could have been the sound of a pebble as much as anything else. Besides, plenty of things—unusual things—fell into the alleyway behind his market.

Nor did he pay much mind to what was on his fingers. Instead, like a good butcher, he wiped them off on his already bloodied apron while he flashed a brilliant smile at George. "All done, son. See? Teamwork," he said. "Now you go on home. A boy like you shouldn't be out after dark." Mr. Johnson loaded the wagon with the empty trash can, then Old George grabbed the handle and started running. The hollow trash bin bounced and clanked like a steel drum, but he didn't care, and he didn't stop until he got all the way home.

As soon as he arrived, he heard a scrub brush whooshing and the smells of bleach and laundry soap coming from the bathroom. He saw a cloud of steam from boiling water roiling upward from the door, a secret his mother used for difficult stains. Old George knew it wasn't Saturday, cleaning day, and she didn't have any neighbor's laundry. He wandered down the short hall and found his mother kneeling and bent over the bathtub.

On the floor, she had arranged all of her usual supplies. The boy watched her frantic elbows flexing and extending as she labored. She mopped her brow, then sensing his presence, she turned her head. "Old Georgie!" she said. "You scared the daylights out of me. I thought you'd be gone longer. Don't come in here. You listening to me? You go on out to the living room and start on your homework. I'm finishing up, and I'll be out in a minute."

The police came around asking questions once a few of the churchgoers began missing Old George's father. They held Birdie at the local police station for a few days, and Old George hated thinking of his mother in a jail cell. Then those few days turned into weeks.

He wasn't so sure his mother had done anything—at least so far as he'd seen. Now that time had passed, he was having confused thoughts about what had gone on that night. His mother had asked him not to look in the trash can. There wasn't much to hang a hat on. All the same, he was grateful that she'd told him not to look to see what might be rolling around in there. All he knew was that his father went missing, and no one seemed to care except for the skinny ladies from church.

He had to stay at his Aunt Florine's house in the meantime. One day, the police came to visit Old George at Florine's home. It was a Sunday evening when the officer, a young, well-set-up man with a strong jaw and a massive dark brow, knocked on the screen. His aunt tried to turn them away, saying Old George wasn't feeling well, and anyway, he was just a child of nine and the police should do their job without involving children. That was how Florine talked. She was a schoolteacher down at the neighborhood elementary school, and she was full of strong words for anyone who she thought was crossing a line.

The officer was polite enough but still found his way into the living room where Old George was sitting, listening to a radio show.

He took off his cap and sat on the couch next to the boy.

"Hello there, son. I'm Detective Griswold from the Los Angeles Police Department."

Old George just stared at the radio. He wasn't sure if he should say anything, and he knew for his mother, saying nothing was better than saying anything at all.

"You ever see a real live detective before?" Griswold asked. Old George looked up at him with his big eyes and shook his head.

"No, he hasn't, and he shouldn't be starting now," Florine said. Then she crossed her arms.

Griswold pointed to the carved wooden radio. "What are you listening to there?"

"*Uncle Don*," Old George said.

"That's a really nice show," he said. "Real nice." Griswold waited for a long moment of silence that made Old George's mouth run dry. "Now son, you know the difference between the truth and a lie, don't you?" he asked.

Old George nodded, his eyes wide and glowing.

"Your momma said you saw something, is that right?" The officer asked.

Old George shook his head. "I don't know what you mean."

"You know, the night your daddy disappeared, she says you saw something you shouldn't talk about," he said.

"I didn't see anything," Old George said. His chest was on fire with the lie. "I didn't even know he was gone. Daddy went out a lot. Ask Miss Washington. She works on down at the church, putting water in the flower vases. She saw him more than we ever did. Miss Sonya, too. Maybe even a couple more of them church ladies over there."

"Well, now." Griswold gave a short laugh. "That's not exactly what your momma already told us."

"My momma didn't see anything, and neither did I. All I know is you took her away, and now I got to live with my Aunt Florine. It's like being in school every day, even on weekends," Old George said.

Florine heard this and huffed a bit, but then she interrupted. "The boy said he's seen nothing. Now I think your time here is over. He's a child, for God's sake. He's got to get up early tomorrow morning, so you best leave him alone now."

Florine was a thin lady; mostly, a big floral dress hanging over skinny bones is how Old George saw her. In moments like this, her protruding shoulders would hunch up around her ears, and she'd lift her hands as if in utter surprise. Her voice was low and rattling. Maybe that was from yelling at school kids too much or from smoking all those cigarettes. But when she got upset like this, the pitch was up, and the officer could tell that his welcome had ended.

"Well, if you think of anything," he said, "you be sure to let me know." He handed a business card to Florine. "Why, you can even come down to the station, and I can show you around. Wouldn't that be fun?"

"Now I don't mean to be rude, but I said goodnight already, Detective," Florine said. She put both fists on her hips.

After he left, Florine sat next to Old George on the couch. She held his hands in hers and looked straight into his eyes like no adult had ever done before. He thought she might hurt him with that stare. "Can you remember what you just told the detective?" she asked him. Old George nodded while watching her with side-eyes. "Good," she said. "I want you to remember everything you said and say it over and over in your mind each night before you go to bed, you hear me?"

"Am I in trouble, Aunt Florine?" he asked.

"Not if you remember everything you just said, word for word. You understand me? Word for word," she said. She held his hands up and kissed them. "They may have my Birdie, but I'll be damned if they get you, too."

Old George never saw his momma much after the court ordered him to live with his aunt for good. His momma died in that prison somewhere up north, and he never knew about it the day when it happened. It seemed like word got to them a few days after the fact.

Florine got the letter—not even a phone call—and she didn't have much strength left after reading it. She just fell to crying softly on the couch.

Now, Florine was probably just being protective, but she said she didn't enjoy traveling those many miles, not to see her sister locked away. And it wasn't right to take a boy there. He guessed that Florine was thinking about that decision now that Birdie had died. Over time, he noticed that she never spoke of his mother again, even if he asked about her.

But Old Georgie never forgot Birdie. There were a lot of things he couldn't forget, like her broad, welcoming smile. Nor his momma fretting away at the bathtub, scouring something away with her cleaners and solvents, working harder than she'd ever done before. It was a wonder she didn't scrub right through the tub, he thought.

He also couldn't forget the lie he had to tell, even though doing it didn't save his mother. He liked to think that whatever he'd said helped her to live as long as she did. He saw some things, sure he did, and maybe that was why he was tormented over what he'd told the detective.

But everyone just jumped to conclusions about his mother without there being much proof. He saw nothing except for that tooth. To be honest, though, that could have belonged to anyone in the Furlong. Plenty of people went around with bad teeth because there were just more important expenses on their minds. Old George felt terrible often because he knew he was just as guilty as the police for carrying the question of blame around in his heart.

Florine said Birdie had gone to prison because the police didn't have any proof other than that she was colored. That's all they'd need sometimes, she told him. And it seemed right, too, from what he could see. Old George learned over time that the world didn't have the same rules for everyone. So he came to expect that things wouldn't be exactly fair, at least outside Florine's home. Or within the Furlong district. And maybe the police and all the adults had their own agendas rather than looking out for kids. Old George figured that since folks outside of Birdie, Florine, and the neighbors in the Furlong weren't really minding him, he'd have to mind himself.

And as time went by, his distant memories felt like they were miles away and just too hard to bring to mind. Other things took importance. There was a stock market crash, and Florine lost her job after that, then a war broke out. And as he got older, he started to understand that some folks came to blows, especially when a man and a woman came to live under one roof. Not that he wanted to believe that was what happened to his father.

But it affected how he thought about women and marrying one, and he decided that he wanted no part of whatever could lead to some terrible ending. So he lived his life tucked away in the junk heaps. He didn't mind it most days. But on others, on the days when he felt stormy inside, he wondered if his life at the city dump was all because he was still at the trash bin behind the market on 52nd Street, looking for the mysterious thing his mother threw out that night so long ago.

"Which side?" the trash truck driver asked.

Old George pointed to where the road forked, off to the right. "We're almost done for the day," Old George said. "I'd like to close up, so do your best to hurry along now."

"Sorry, mister. This comes special delivery from Hollywood. Probably full of empty movie reels," the driver said. "Anyway, we got caught by some road closures along the way. You know how it goes." The driver gave a wink, and he lurched the truck forward with a spitting hiss from the brakes.

Old George went back inside the small shack that he stayed in most of the day. It had a toilet closet, a desk for his ledgers, and a small table so he could have his lunch. Exposed electrical wires and pipes tucked right up along the corrugated tin ceiling were his decorations. He snapped off the lights and the table fan. Just as he was locking the door behind him, the truck zoomed past. "Goodnight," the driver said out the window. Road dust picked up.

It wasn't long after that when Old George heard a noise coming from the garbage-pile mountains. Probably rats, he thought to himself, and he stuffed his keys into his jacket. On his way to his truck, he heard it again. It sounded like tin cans rustling. But if they were, they were doing so in one of the garbage heaps away from his immediate view.

"Hello?" Old George called out. The sounds stopped.

He waited a few moments just to be sure that the noise had stopped so he could go home. He trudged a few paces toward his pickup truck when the rattling started again.

"Hello? Who's there?" he called out. Still no one answered. "Junk yard's closed for the day," he shouted. Then even louder, "When I leave, I'm locking this gate." More silence. Then the sounds came back, more frantic, as though someone was digging through the heaps.

"Goddammit." He knew the rules, and he couldn't leave someone locked in there overnight, even if it served them right. He marched down to where the road split off into the various heaps, and he stood still, listening for a more precise location. More cans and scraps clanked together, and he could tell that it was coming from the heap on the right, where Hollywood had just made its drop off.

"Hey, you need to leave. We're open in the morning," Old George said.

Out from the side of the pile, a raggedy mottled dog lurched out and barked at him.

"Oh, it's you, Jackie," he said. "Don't worry, I left you dinner."

The dog yapped some more and then ducked behind the pile.

Old George felt the back hairs prickling up his neck again, sensing that familiar and dangerous tightening in his stomach. He tried to ignore it. He'd seen Jackie act like this whenever there was a raccoon or something else he could chase. "Jackie, where'd you get to?" he said. Then he started around the heap. It smelled particularly awful that night. Whatever those fellas dropped off had been rotting for a while, meat or eggs or old soiled diapers. He spotted Jackie lying down low in the heap, chewing on what he'd found.

"Jackie, you know you're not supposed to eat what you find. You want to get sick again?"

The dog stood up, licked his chops with his long red tongue, cocked his head at Old George, and then trotted away, leaving his prize in the junk pile.

Old George was a child again at the market on 52nd Street, seeing sights that he ought not. What he spotted made him queasy and flushed like he'd just gotten off a roller coaster and maybe needed to sit down so he wouldn't spit up. But then he remembered that one of the big department stores had closed recently, and they tossed out all of their extras. It had to be off of a lady mannequin, with its fake-looking shiny red fingernails and all.

He planned to toss it to the top of the heap where Jackie would be less likely to nab it again. "What are you eating this for, Jackie? You got a thing for wood and paint? Gonna get real sick that way."

As soon as he reached down, he couldn't fool himself any longer. Where there should have been a wrist-bracket, he only saw a crusted darkness, oozing and severed. Where there might have been a peg, a bloody bone and some gristle spilled out beyond the wrist in dark red ribbons. The moonlight sparkled onto a silvery band with a small white diamond on one of the inert fingers.

Old George realized that no matter what he intended on seeing, some things were as clear as a full moon on an August night. Just like his father's stray gold tooth.

Five

Los Angeles, 1947
Two Days Before It Happened

Ren sat up in bed with a clutching gasp at some dark and unknown hour. A dream, yes. A nightmare. That must be at the root of his sense of doom. He scoured his mind, but all he recalled was a solid blackness. Sleep typically eluded Ren, but tonight he slept with some never known depth. With a suffocative oppression, the weight of a dozen saturated sandbags, and unable to catch his breath, Ren struggled to sit upright to gasp down some air. A sudden and prickling sense overcame him that something in his life, something in this house seemed unwell… cancerous, even.

He glanced down in the hush of their bed. The moon crept in through the window, a silvery-purple glow that spilled across Gloria, who slept on her back, arms up around her ears. His gaze followed the cascade of amber tangles and loose curls that poured across her features. She sighed with soft, full breaths.

Ren thought his wild heart-thumping understandable because of the many unusual and bizarre circumstances of late—the shocking loss of Haddock amid a storm of madness and bloodshed. Ren had seen the cruelest of conditions during his stint away. And what had happened to Haddock, as horrible as it was, at least came to an end. He had to keep living with his exhausting demons of anguish.

We're all so vulnerable, he realized, studying his wife. *We're all going to kick off one day, like Haddock—and like his family.* Where these thoughts came from, he couldn't tell. But it branded his mind with a red-hot awareness, and he wanted to scream, to lose control and beat someone to a pulp. Instead, he swallowed it all and forced his mind to settle.

It had only been a single day since it happened, and he hadn't told Gloria anything about it. Not yet. Too awful and too raw. And the two couples, such good friends. He blamed himself for not noticing signs of a work partner who had a lethal frame of mind brewing beneath that plastered-on jovial exterior. Ren had witnessed full-blown hallucinations—Haddock seeing ghosts or what have you. Jesus Christ. A lunatic murderer. His best friend. Tracking criminals together, staking out in parking lots, sharing meals, vacations, bowling, even heading to church a few times, only to please the wives. And all the time, Haddock had a sickness growing, and he'd soon wipe the lot of them out in a roach-infested hotel that couldn't even afford to fix the letters on its flea-bag sign. The words he'd need to tell Gloria, he did not have. And even if he had them, they might make him puke.

Ren supposed it didn't matter now whether he told her or not because the story would hit the papers today. He'd have to talk about it soon enough. Best to rest his mind, he thought. But his ruminations kept returning to what he could not un-see. Haddock's wife and daughter slaughtered and lying there like carcasses in the back room of a meatpacker took Ren's breath away. Haddock had smeared their innards everywhere. The bits of flesh at his mouth. Celeste's pale arm lying so still in that closet. And that stench—that stench from the goddamn bowels of hell.

He'd been doing this job a long time, but he'd never forget what happened in that rotten hotel room. And he had to come home and put on a face, pretend a business-as-usual day down at the precinct, and eat meatloaf and mashed potatoes with Gloria like nothing had happened. He wasn't sure if he'd be able to shut his eyes peacefully ever again.

He gained some sudden clarity about the pain Gloria must have experienced spending every day alone in this house, far from everyone she'd loved. A blistering, uncontrollable surge of guilt and remorse rushed forward. Someday he'd lose Gloria—or God forbid—she'd lose him first and she'd be…. He didn't want to think about it.

Or perhaps something simpler, more immediate and dangerous echoed from the bottomless pit of his soul where he thought he'd dropped memories to disappear and die. These lost things, these people and these experiences he'd had while gone from home—they seemed to fight their way back to the surface so he'd have to remember them all over again. They were rising, digging their angry, filthy fingernails into the pit's edge as they clawed their way back out….

Click.

Ren held his breath. It sounded like sharp dolphin clicks, or maybe it was metallic. The noise came quick, outside of his immediate attention, and he missed it. But soon came another sound arising from underneath the house's blanketed stillness. Mumbled, rhythmic, and light, it sounded like a prayer whispered to the dark.

It almost sounded like the voice of Molly, his five-year-old.

No, Gloria had bathed and tucked her in early. She'd be asleep by now. The mumbling continued as though the whisperer had no real concern of being discovered. It seemed like a chant being spun out in single staccato notes.

He stood beside his bed and peered down the hallway. It seemed much longer and darker than usual. Then Ren saw a shape move in that blackness, and he began drowning in a helpless panic that a child might have when lost in a crowd. The moving thing seemed massive—too large to be some wayward wildlife that had come in through an open window. It stood perhaps four or five feet tall—and it had a kind of flowing shape. A black dress. A robe.

She'd come back.

Ren tried to rationalize for a moment. Any object at all in the hallway would make a sound. The episodically dewy climate in the hills made the hardwood and everything else in the house loose, warped, and squeaky. This thing didn't make a single sound.

The shadow glided out of his view, and Ren heard a springy, mechanical door latch that caught as it closed on Molly's room. He tiptoed, trying not to step on the worst of the floorboards that crisscrossed the hall like a checkerboard. He'd practiced skip-stepping the boards many times before this. Though it started out as a game with himself, he realized it might be tactical, a rehearsal for some future date when—well, who knew what might happen?

If those creaky boards sounded when they shouldn't, he always had a pistol hidden high out of the way in just about every closet.

Click.

Guk. Guk-guk.

He stopped and held his breath, balancing on the center three boards in front of Molly's room. The sound was real, with dimension and location. It was verifiable. It came as small consolation to Ren that he hadn't slipped into the dark-between and was hearing things because of some episode.

Molly whispered to someone—yes, someone had entered the house; a stranger was talking with his child in the deeps of the darkness. Ren glanced down, and he noticed neither light nor movement from the small gap below Molly's closed door. He tried the knob. It turned all right, but an unseen force pressed with great strength from the opposite side, holding the door like a solid wall. A panic cold and wild arose within his chest, and he wondered if he had control of his body any longer.

"Molly," he said in a sharp parental tone.

The mumbling ceased.

He pressed the door again, but with a dry snap, it pushed back and cracked down the center. Ren staggered backward in disbelief.

"Molly, open this door."

The room became hushed and tense. Ren rushed at the door and rammed his shoulder into it, but it held like a steel girder.

Click… guk.

The goopy, gagging sound came again. But not from Molly's room. It was behind him, at the end of the dark hall near his bedroom. Only a few yards away. His breath burned, his heart ripping through his rib cage. He turned, but nothing was there—absolutely nothing. His bedroom door had disappeared and sealed up in the black. Some force plunged him into suffocating darkness that had no sense of up or down, left or right. He hissed out a dense and quivering breath through his clenched jaw while he pressed his hands along the walls for a way out.

Guk… guk-guk…

The goopy throat-choke sound neared him in the dark, lurching its way forward. A cold breath clouded on his back. His neck muscles strained as he kept pressing along the wall where he last saw Molly's door. His pulse pounded, and his throat closed with an all-encompassing tightening, and he wondered if he might implode.
A cold hand reached out from behind him and clutched his shoulder. He whipped around to face the horrible thing.

"Ren?" Gloria stood there, and she withdrew her hand, taken aback by his jolting reflex.

"Oh crap, Gloria!" Ren said through a breath that he'd been holding God knows how long.

"Ren, what are you doing?"

He made out her figure as she pulled the gauzy white robe to a snug fit around her soft silhouette. As he reoriented, he plainly saw that the hallway doors were in place as before.

"Didn't you hear that?"

"Hear what?"

"I… I don't know..." He realized he'd not be able to explain what happened. Not now, after the nun. And the car. "…Mumbling in Molly's room. And her door got stuck." He glanced at where the door had cracked in half and saw it now mended.

"Ren, we're out in the goddamn sticks. There are noises here."

Gloria twisted the knob and pushed the door wide. She whisked to the other side of the room, past Molly, who was fast asleep, to the gaping window which someone had left wide open to the hillside. A chill filled the room, and Ren saw Gloria's breath on the mountain air. The lacey, sheer curtains on either side of the window arose with a moonlit breeze and looked like a banshee's arms reaching, reaching. Gloria locked the top and bottom panes and clutched her arms across her chest.

"Ren, how could you forget this?" she asked.

"Me? You put her to bed."

"Yes, but you must have opened it after the fact."

Gloria's internal thermometer would bust the mercury if he dared deny, even though there wasn't any truth in what she thought. He paused and whispered back. "Molly must have done it. I heard some weird… I don't know… clicking and…. I thought maybe there were also voices."

"Voices? Ren, just stop it. There are no nuns that run into the house or cars that appear out of nowhere. We're up here all alone."

"Mommy?" Molly asked, propping up on her elbows, her eyes barely opened. "Is that you, Mommy?"

Gloria went to sit on the edge of the bed. Molly turned on one side to face her. "Mommy, what was that noise?"

Gloria's head whirled toward Ren. "What noise did you hear, sweetheart?"

Molly laid her head back down and closed her small eyes. "I don't know. Someone saying something."

"That was your daddy. See? He's right here." She lifted her chin toward the doorway.

"Oh," Molly said. She gave a wide yawn. "Where's the lady?"

Gloria's face melted, and her innards wrenched. She shifted her gaze to Ren. Molly's question overtook his whole mind; his muscles seized across his face.

"Honey, what lady?" Gloria asked in a controlled calm. Ren wondered how Gloria formed these words. He had gone numb, and she had to be as well.

"The lady wearing black. She was talking. She was standing in the closet," Molly said. Her eyes began closing, but she kept speaking with soft sleepiness in her voice. "She wanted me to read prayers."

Gloria swallowed at the air like a gutted fish. "You were—you were only dreaming, honey." She paused and looked out the window. "There's no one here except us," she said. Ren thought Gloria saying so might convince them all and quell the upsurge of puke rising from his clenched gut.

"I know," Molly said. Her words escaped like a little song. "She had to go."

Ren saw the closet door ajar. It was a narrow walk-in closet that would have plenty of room for someone to hide. He strode decisively into the bedroom, gripped the wobbly closet knob, and paused. Gloria stood up and placed herself between whatever might be there and her child. She clasped her hands across her pulsating throat. Ren flung the door so hard that it jumped on its hinges and his heart pinch closed.

Nothing unordinary was there. Molly's clothing hung in a single file and rippled a smidge in the air current when Ren swooshed the door wide. A few games lay scattered and stacked with the box lids askew. Three small pairs of shoes dutifully lined up. Ren swept everything aside but found no one hiding.

"What's Daddy doing?" Molly asked, rousing heavy-headed again.

"He's… he's…" She ran out of comforting lies. Gloria pointed to the window. On cue, Ren rushed out of Molly's room and fled to the front door, first stopping for his pistol.

He dashed in bare feet and boxers, crunching on twigs and prickly scrub oak leaves. In his haste, he began to wonder if his single-minded urge to protect his family might endanger them more. Whoever had broken in, now hiding in the woods, might also have a gun and might be well-practiced with it. The intruder remained unseen among the oaks, and Ren stood in plain sight. He didn't care. He had to put a stop to this. If he didn't, it might happen again, and maybe the next time, something terrible might happen to Molly.

He pointed the gun ahead of him and locked back the hammer. Hugging the side of the house with his back, Ren side-stepped his way toward Molly's window.

Click.

Guk, guk. Click.

"Step out. Put your hands where I can see them," Ren shouted to the trees and to the low-lying brush. "Police officer! I have a gun." The only response was night sounds; a cold breeze stung the hillside and pulled across the treetops.

A twig snapped in the near-brush, and Ren shot off a round in a fiery blast that echoed through the neighboring canyons. There came no further sign of movement or sound. Ren's hands shook with electric energy. He could not unlock his arms. His muscles seemed to have hardened to stone, and it made him ache all over.

"Ren!" Gloria called. "Come quick!"

Her voice kick-started his movement back on track, and he somehow found himself at the front door, though how he got from one point to another was a blur. Still holding the gun in front of him, he charged down the long, dark hall to Molly's room. Once he reached it, Gloria stood next to the child's miniature rocking chair that occupied the space below the window. She held out the Bible Molly would take with her to Sunday school, the one she kept on the seat of the small chair. Gloria shook her head, mouthing the word, "Why?"

She held the shredded thing up for Ren. He set the gun on a dresser and held the tattered remains between two hands. Whoever was there with Molly had sliced up every page, shredded them cruelly, but first scribbled upon them in black crayon. Ren paged through, and it made him nauseous. Toward the front of the book, there were only erratic scrawlings. But what began as erratic eventually took form with each passing page. The lines formed into vulgarities and abominable statements. Among the words was the phrase "Murder-fucker," scratched in crayon, the letters made bold by multiple angry strokes. The same strange words and symbols he'd seen before in Haddock's hotel appeared scribbled on the Bible's pages too.

He leafed through, and further on in the torn-up pages he found crude sketches of weapons and of stick figures stabbing one another, and what was supposed to be blood drawn across one's poorly scribbled mouth. Another figure held up a bloody hand severed from a body.

Gloria covered her mouth, and tears fell. Ren looked over at his daughter, not even old enough to understand such words or acts, or to have lived long enough to hold such a dam of rage like this or to act so…unhinged.

"This is it, Ren. We can't be here anymore," Gloria said. She wiped her eyes with the backs of her hands.

He knew it was right, and he nodded.

♦

Ren walked into Griswold's file-crammed office, and all he saw was the back of Fiorelli's grease-stuck head. That was the last thing he wanted to see on a day like this—when likely he'd find his name peppered into the columns about the double homicide and police shooting. The *Times-Mirror* called it "The Family Murder." Like it was some kind of cozy affair. They showed the picture, too. That goddamned photographer—that was Fiorelli's doing.

The two officers had been chatting when he walked in, their lit cigarettes dangling by fingertips, and the room was filled with smoky, guffaw-filled confidentiality. It seemed clear to Ren that Fiorelli had had the sergeant's ear for some time before today's meeting.

When Fiorelli first joined the force, he was the life of the party. He yucked it up with everyone, including Ren. He cozied up to the key players, the heavy hitters, and wheedled them with knee-slappers and nights out for cold ones at Shamrock's down at the corner. Once he'd checked that box, he had little use for the department nobodies like Ren who might offer him little professional advantage.

Ren tried not to overthink all the reasons for the chafing between them. It might have been because of Ren's sterling reputation. Guys who wanted to skate by on their looks and personalities hated men who achieved their status through hard work. Or perhaps Fiorelli didn't like it that Ren had snagged such a beautiful wife. A divot-faced creep like Fiorelli would work that angle as soon as he had the slightest opportunity. Ren had seen him make subtle moves on other cops' wives. The grease-ball had a wife and a kid of his own. But no. Someone like Fiorelli always wanted more—even when it meant trashing other people's lives.

Over the years, a quiet, mutual disdain had developed and become part of the work routine. It was like a bothersome chafing, and Ren couldn't find a good way to rid himself of it. It seemed as though somewhere along the way, Fiorelli had flipped from being passively to actively contemptuous.

And now the Sarge, who had known Ren for nearly twenty years, was slowly changing. He started acting more official. The laughs and shared battle stories began to be a thing of the past. And worst of all, now that Haddock was dead, Ren wasn't so confident who had his back any more.

"Ah, Larson," Fiorelli started. He swiveled his seat around with his back to the boss, who couldn't see his satisfied smirk. "Glad you could make it. We were just talking about you. My condolences."

"Have a seat, Larson." Griswold gestured to the chair beside Fiorelli.

"Sure, Sarge. What's this all about?" He knew. He tipped up his police cap at Sarge and didn't give Fiorelli a single facial twinge.

"Well, it's like I told Sarge," Fiorelli said. "After you finally got there—what was it? An hour after the call?—it seemed like whatever you tried only made poor Haddock worse. That's what happened, right? He got worse? Went into some kind of butterfly-net situation with you there talking to him? Well, it doesn't really matter anymore, because, well…. such a goddamn tragedy."

It was like getting belted, but good, right in the mouth. Ren didn't have anything to say in response that would meet him measure for measure, at least not in front of the Sarge. He had to eat Fiorelli's hearty serving of crap for now. But it seemed like any minute he might pop a vein or burst an eye with all the pressure that was building.

Griswold spoke up. "First off, Larson, I'm sorry about Haddock. It's not your fault he was a fruitcake and right on the edge of… well, you understand. None of us had any idea about what he might be going through. So you can't blame yourself. I've seen plenty of good cops go south blaming themselves for the things that happen."

Ren nodded. "Thanks, Sarge, I appreciate it." He flicked his eyes toward Fiorelli, trying to watch him burn up with rage that Sarge ignored his digs.

"That said," Griswold continued, "we do have us a situation." He lowered his heavy brow, and his jowls dropped another inch as he jutted out his lower lip. "Look, fellas, I like you both. But whatever this is between you is eating at everyone. People are starting to take sides. Hell, some of them are even placing bets. I can't have that in this precinct, in this division… under my command. You hear me?"

Fiorelli's bass voice boomed out, "This freak don't know how to tell time. Look what he did! Yeah, you heard me. This is your fault, Larson."

Ren didn't waste the opportunity. "Well, this pus-bucket called me when it was already too late!"

The two men stood, their heaving chests touching, arms back, as though some invisible force restrained them.

"The hell are you two doing? Sit down, both of you!" Griswold shouted. "You both nuts? This is the goddamned Los Angeles Police Department, not Goldbrick's Boxing Gymnasium. Is it not getting through to you, the magnitude of what's happened?"

The two sat down again, both looking straight ahead like

naughty kids sent to the principal's office. "We're gonna solve this situation once and for all. I am assigning the two of you to investigate this Haddock case—and everything that may be connected to it. Are we on the same page, fellas?"

"What?" Fiorelli complained. "You can't do that! Besides, this isn't an unsolved crime. The guy was a dry twig that snapped. And no wonder it happened. Look who he had to work with. End of story."

"I think this crater-face held off calling me, knowing the seriousness of the situation and setting it up so that something bad would happen."

"Fiorelli, Larson, you two better get a hold of yourselves. And no, this case is not exactly solved. We have no motive. But what we do have is a blood-decorated room. Haddock was as steady as they came—at least up to the end. No, this wasn't some guy who suddenly went to the dairy farm with no sign of any problems up to that point. No hanky panky. He was rock-solid. We would've seen something before this. Any one of us would have seen something out of the ordinary."

"He was fine, Sarge. I can vouch for that. I can't get it out of my mind how incoherent he was when I saw him just before he…. He barely recognized me," Ren said.

"A lot of what we see here so far doesn't make sense," the Sarge said. "And if it makes sense to either of you, then you shouldn't be detectives. Have you seen what's in the papers? The *Times-Mirror* splashed some shot of Haddock's blood-smeared room on the front page. They've compared it to the picture *The Seventh Victim* because of those goddamn blood-painted occult symbols. In this day and age. People believing in this shit like it's the Middle Ages. And now I'm getting calls from way up high in the food chain. Christ almighty! Haddock's kid was in the closet all cut up like a paper doll, and the damn photo shows her arm sticking out behind him like she's waving to everyone from the goddamned grave. Does either of you know how he and his entire family wound up in this crap-bucket hotel in the first place? We all knew the guy. He wouldn't set foot in a place like that."

Griswold turned darker shades of red with each sentence, and he stopped himself to reel it in.

"When I got there, a photographer was behind me taking shots. Fiorelli was the commanding officer."

"The guy snuck in. I had nothing to do with it."

"We got a mess of this, gentlemen," Griswold said. "As I see it, there's some shared responsibility. So the two of you are working as partners on this investigation of someone we all knew and appreciated. Are we speaking the same language, fellas? I have a meeting with the commissioner today, and I'm already planning a song and dance for the two of you. You're welcome. So, while I'm sweating it out with the big boys, you two are gonna clean this up."

The two men slouched.

"Now, fellas, there's some good news here. Depending on how you both do, one of you will move up to my position as sergeant. Now don't go spreading it around, but they already handed me my promotion. They're waiting to announce it until I find someone to take my place. Hey, it's a raise, boys."

Ren's thoughts shifted to Gloria, who, after last night, rightfully pushed for a move "back to civilization." With a raise, they'd be able to afford one of those lovely little new houses in Orange County and change things up for good.

"Now, I want you to shake hands and put whatever's gone into this bullwhip in the past where it belongs." Fiorelli and Ren looked sideways at one another. Griswold paused and pressed his protruding lips together, looking like a sea creature. "Okay, then. I guess we're all in agreement, gentlemen. That's just peachy."

Fiorelli extended his hand to Ren while squaring his jaw and sucking in a noisy breath through his tomahawk nose. He wasn't the least bit interested in burying the hatchet. The two shook on it, with iron grips, too firm to be an apology. They turned away from one another, ready to go.

"Larson, hold on. I need you for a minute," Griswold said. He looked down. Ren felt an upsurge of fire, and he clenched his stomach. "And I'll see you at the funeral," Griswold said to Fiorelli.

Fiorelli shut the door with a touch more force than he needed, and the reeded glass with the gold foil lettering on it rattled an echo of his displeasure. Griswold ran his hand through his sparse hair and clasped his chunky hands. "Larson, I heard you were out in the apartment stairwell, heaving up your guts."

"Coming from him, Sarge?" Ren said. "Come on."

"I got reports that you sat on those stairs for nearly ten minutes. The other officers said they called your name and shook you, but you seemed... dazed. That was the word, I believe. Dazed. So they left you there and ran back inside the hotel room. All the while, Haddock was getting worse."

"Dazed? Come on, what are you talking about? Sarge, it's me. You know me."

Griswold and Ren went back at least twenty years. Griswold knew Ren. And if he had soured because of Ren's stint away? That detour wasn't voluntary, and Griswold understood it. Fat feet can keep you from wearing tight boots, and Griswold should have been grateful that someone went off to foreign lands when he couldn't. It would be unpatriotic to turn on a veteran.

"Look, Ren, we all know what you went through... I mean, before you made it back home and all. I'm sure you didn't face anything easy, and I want you to know we're all rooting for you. I am...." The Sarge nodded several times before finishing his thought. "...rooting for you. I really am."

"Sarge, whatever happened before I got back home is of no consequence. Yeah it was miserable...but I survived it and I'm fine. Honest. And whoever told you that story about the stairwell? You got a beat on how things work around here. Listening to every snip of gossip around this place? Come on. Jeez, half the guys here are doing crap that's probably deserving of some of this attention. Anyway, I had to catch a little breather by the fifth floor. I've been packing on the pounds with a little too much butter and mashed potatoes since I've been back, that's all." He snorted and patted his belly. "And you know as well as I do that the outcome with Haddock would have been the same, whether I arrived one minute before or after. When a guy that's lost his mind like that.... nothing can bring him back—not me nor the goddamned Pope. After all of this, I can't believe you'd make things worse by listening to hallway rumors and believing them out of hand like that."

"Now come on, Ren. No one's thinking anything yet. Not seriously, anyway. But I need a clean bill of health on you. Okay? You're not in any trouble. But since the commissioner's gotten involved with this mess, I'd recommend you go get that today."

Ren felt like he melted in the chair. "Well, sure thing, Sarge. I can go, but I'm not sick. Just packing a bit too much around the gut is all."

Griswold had a gaze that Ren thought might be pity, and it steamed him that Fiorelli was the cause behind it.

"Great. It'll be a nice short visit, then," Griswold said. He sipped coffee, grabbing the mug with those sausage fingers of his.

"With Georg?" Ren asked.

No one wanted to visit that head shrinker, let alone get sent by your superior. Just setting foot in Doctor Georg's office was enough for anyone to develop a crackpot reputation. Guilt by association.

Ren thought about it from another angle. The guys all said that Georg was just another government hack doing the paces with only a few years before his Big Florida Retirement. Ren heard that all a guy needed to do for Georg was recite the Pledge of Allegiance, tell him who won the last World Series, and name the sitting president. Georg might be his easy ticket out of trouble. If Ren just took his lumps, this time anyway, he might come out of it with a slightly bruised ego and some bad press that, after some pub time and darts, the fellas might forget. In the end, he'd still have his job.

He'd have to get a better hold of the dark-between episodes, too. If Ren couldn't stop them, he'd at least need to figure out what brought them on. Predicting them would help him make quick getaways, like to a bathroom stall or a locked car.

Once he got back in Griswold's good graces, he'd still have to stomach Fiorelli just long enough to piece together what happened to Haddock. And when the other guys called him Sergeant Larson, when he found himself in a stronger position, then he'd see what could be done about that pock-faced climber Fiorelli once and for all.

"No Larson, not Georg. Commissioner wants a bill of health from your guy—what's his name again?" Griswold spread his chubby hands through the mounds of loose paper on his desk and fished out a brown file folder with the name "R. Larson" written in bold across the top tab. "Oh yeah, Dr. Kelly. Dr. Edward Kelly."

Ren felt like a falling log slammed him in the stomach. He'd have to eat this, too, so he smiled and nodded.

"Whatever you say, Sarge."

Six

Los Angeles, 1947
Three Days Before It Happened

Ren eyed one sitting right across from him. She definitely had a coin-purse full of loose change. She was gaunt and crinkled like a long-time tippler. She tried to cover it up with thick, uneven makeup that stopped halfway down the underside of her chin. The woman had a monstrous lump at the center of her forehead, which she alternately squeezed and then camouflaged with her thinning brown bangs.

And she was the most normal one of the bunch.

In the corner, sitting as far away as the room might allow, sat a man who looked like a living skeleton. He had a face pale as paper, with purple swoops beneath his eyes. He had bitten through most of his fingernails. Done with the appetizer, he started on the main course, which appeared to be flesh on his fingertips. He cupped both hands together at his mouth like a rat gnawing on some guarded last crumbs. They must have been tasty based on how he gobbled them up.

A girl with unwashed hair and crumpled clothes sat on the floor, chewing on her lips, which had become a mess of scabs. She bit more when her mother, in the adjacent chair, reached down and patted her head like a dog.

A man with wild white hair wore clothes that might have accommodated two men of any size. He sat holding a little gold-embossed Bible with hundreds of paper bits stuffed between the pages, as though he needed to mark that many critical parts.

Ren tried not to watch. Or listen. But he found it hard not to overhear the old man's list of recited names. The words had an Old Testament ring, like Ezekiel or Esau. Maybe the old-timer was simply mumbling the random sounds running through his head. "*Zagan, Voso, Orobas, Caim, Andras...*" The list went on rhythmically. With each utterance, the man rocked forward and ran his tongue out.

Ren had learned a thing or two about neurotic tendencies, Oedipus complexes, and Reaction Formations from college. And even before that, living with someone in his childhood home who wasn't quite right, he'd learned about the terrain firsthand. The daily, nerve-fraying tightrope walk at home became routine after a while. Then, at ten years of age, Ren stumbled upon his father dangling and blue-lipped from the end of a red necktie in the bedroom closet.

After Ren had grown and had a life of his own, he spent a lot of time washing away regrets with a bottle of bourbon. He wished he'd at least understood that something out of the ordinary was wrong with his father, especially on that particular day. A degree in psychiatry seemed just the ticket for easing the strain on his boyhood soul.

But when that motive wore thin, he dropped out of medical training. During one summer, Ren nabbed a job with the police force, at the urging of his high school buddy Haddock. And if Ren were perfectly honest with himself, the fit seemed fine—it was right, in fact. He hadn't considered that he might be cut out for more than one thing, and this discovery was both a revelation and a relief. He hadn't given up on his ideals. As an officer, he'd still make things right in the world, one way or another.

A lot of good his few years in college did him, anyway. Knowing unconscious drives and syndromes didn't ease his discomfort with having to sit among the string-eaters and the handsy hunchbacks. He wasn't one of them, he had to remind himself. Ren got drafted into a war that shot his nerves to hell, that's all. His nervous condition didn't evolve from repressed urges, overbearing mothers, or a desire to compete with his father. In fact, the only repressed urge he had was for a few belts from a shot glass, and it was too bad the nearest bar was a couple blocks away. No, he didn't need the same help as one of these overripe peaches.

"You're next, you know," the praying man said. He broke with his repetitions long enough to make the announcement. He resumed his task, nodding and waggling his throat skin like a sunbaked reptile.

Ren considered whether he should respond. It might be impolite to interrupt someone's fixation. "Thank you," Ren said. He kept it curt, hoping the man might figure out that a lobby conversation would not be in his immediate future.

"You're next, and *it* knows. It's waiting," the man said. He nodded and winked as though he'd told Ren some insider information.

"I'm sorry. What?" Ren asked. Now he wished he'd been a bit choosier with where he sat. He imagined how much more pleasant it might have been if he'd planted himself next to the finger nibbler crouched behind the umbrella stand.

"Well, it's more of a *them*, of course," the man said. He held a steadfast gaze and leaned as far forward as possible, smashing his prayer tracts into his lap. "*Zagan, Voso, Orobas, Caim, Andras—them.* Seventy two of them. Watching you right now."

Ren remembered that Haddock had uttered a similar phrase just before his death. And those same words scrawled on his wall. "Excuse me, sir. What's that?"

"It keeps the score. They do. But that's all I'm saying," the old man whispered.

"Oh, right. Yes. Of course," Ren said. He monitored his tone, trying not to come across as though he believed or disbelieved. "It…

them..." No sense in lighting a match around dynamite.

The man stared at him once more. "Them? Who said anything about that?"

The random shift caught Ren off guard. He hoped the interaction was over.

"Remember you're next, that's all." The old man glanced away with a satisfied smirk, as though he'd done his duty. Immediately after, he acted as though he were avoiding being noticed by some invisible entity.

The reception window slid open with an icy skid. "Mr. Gray," said the nurse. She had an over-powdered face that caught the eerie green waiting room light, and her white cap folded just so, with upturned corners. "The doctor will see you now."

The old man wobbled to a stand and shuffled past Ren, first checking that he still possessed the Bible and his bits of paper. Ren caught a whiff of toilet-stink, fermented wine, and cigarettes. The door to the exam rooms shut behind Mr. Gray, and the frosted window skated open again.

"Mr. Larson," said the nurse. "Doctor will see you now," she said. Then she slid the window shut.

When the door opened again, Dr. Kelly in his lab coat stood with a broad smile. "Ren Larson." His voice was warm and sure, better than any medicine he peddled. He extended his firm, thick hand to Ren and led him to one of the small examination rooms filled with a pronounced tang of disinfectant. He sat on a small swiveling stool, lit up a cigarette, and offered one to Ren. "No, thanks, Doc. I gave that up long ago. Molly—that's my little girl. If you remember—she's got asthma."

Kelly pocketed the pack and strapped a mirrored device to his forehead. He gestured for Ren to sit atop an exam table with a thin, translucent runner of white paper skimming the top. Ren obliged though in doing so, his heart began to do acrobatics. To him, sitting on the exam table was the first small but greased step down a slippery slope.

Kelly took a long drag and flicked the drooping embers into a cut-glass ashtray next to some hypodermic needles. "So why don't you tell me why you're here, Mr. Larson."

Ren shrugged.

"I could tell you myself, but I'd rather hear it from you." Sitting on the low stool, Kelly had to adjust his horn-rimmed glasses to peer upward at Ren, who sat like a kid on the exam table.

"Well, to be honest, I feel just fine. The boss wants you to clear me. That's all," Ren said.

Dr. Kelly nodded and put a finger to his lips before speaking. "Your boss called earlier and said you're not altogether yourself. Said that during a dangerous situation, officers found you strung out in a stairwell, unresponsive. Griswold seemed to think that delay might have cost a man his life. Does any of that ring a bell?"

"Come on, Doc, sounds like you got an ear full." Ren laughed, but the doctor didn't.

"I also saw the *Times-Mirror* article," Kelly said.

Ren replied, "I was just out of breath—and after five flights of stairs, even a kid would need a breather. And you know as well as I that short time couldn't cost a life. Haddock—the guy you're talking about—was my partner. I worked a beat with him for decades. And before that, I knew him when we were kids. I went to school with him, for God's sake. I knew this guy from the inside, if you know what I mean. He was solid his whole life. And when I saw him in that hotel room… Jesus Christ, it wasn't him anymore. He was just—well, he must have been wrong in the head, Doc. That's all it amounted to. And when someone's like that—I don't have to tell you—you can't stop them for nothing. If they want to jump from a building or run in front of a city bus, you just can't stop them."

"Mmm-hmm," Kelly hummed. He set up the little chrome shield on his forehead and snapped on the small light at its center. He looked into Ren's eyes and pulled the lower lids down to get a better look.

"And besides, Doc. The real reason I'm here is that some guy at work's giving me the runaround. Trying to make me look bad. He's probably having a good laugh right now."

"You sleeping at night?"

"Like a baby. Every night. Do you sleep every night?"

Kelly raised his brows. "Your eyes are telling me a different story." He pinched the patient's wrist with his fingers resting atop the veins and looked at his watch.

Ren shrugged again. "Wow, Doc. You're serious? Okay, yeah. I mean, sometimes I wake up because it's so damn quiet up in those hills. Sometimes all you can hear is the throbbing of your own pulse. But I sleep."

"Pharmacy says you haven't refilled your prescription in six months now."

"Oh, really? Because I take it every day, twice a day, just like you told me."

"Why don't you lay back? Stretch out for a minute."

A young nurse dressed in a white smock with a stiff nun's veil entered and quickly made herself busy without saying a word. It amazed him that she kept her uniform in such pristine condition. She hadn't a speck of lint nor a crease in her outfit. Her skin seemed too smooth, and she drew her lips upward, nearly what you'd see on the face of a porcelain doll.

She rolled up his sleeve, placed a blood-pressure cuff on his biceps, and started pumping it until his lower arm began to darken and ache. He huffed a bit and gave her a look that told her she needed to stop. She lifted her head and showed him that disconnected plastic-mask smile. Behind the smile, her eyes betrayed an inner revelry, like she enjoyed causing discomfort.

"Are you all right, Mr. Larson?" Doctor Kelly asked.

"Yeah, I'm… I'm a little uncomfortable."

The nurse listened with a stethoscope at the fleshy bend of his arm. She let the air out a tiny whisper at a time, tormenting him with the cut-off circulation. Ren felt the blood back up into his arm and up to his shoulder like a wave of pressure.

"So why don't you tell me a little about what you've been doing since you've been back," Kelly said. "It's been, what? Over two years now. Has anything changed at home? I know that you moved a little while ago, as you mentioned." Kelly distracted himself with the contents of Ren's file filled with notches and numbers and indecipherable scribbles.

The nurse maintained her gaze on Ren with that synthetic half-smile. He began to anger at her apparent amusement.

"Jesus!" Ren said to the nurse.

"What's that?" the doctor asked.

He felt a flush of heat as she let the final air escape from the cuff and his arm rushed back to life. She slid the equipment off and left so silently and sleekly that she could have been gliding on roller skates. Ren shook his arm and squeezed his fist to get the blood flowing.

Kelly stared a moment. "Is there something wrong, Mr. Larson?"

It was dawning on him that Kelly was indifferent to the nurse. He was too busy with his charts to notice what she was doing. Ren didn't want to complain about her to Kelly either, especially since he needed him to fill out Griswold's forms and put this business behind him.

"Yeah. I'm just fine. Gloria's fine. We're all sleeping fine. Everything's *fine*."

"I see," Kelly said. He was gazing through the bottom squares of his bifocals. Then he made more marks in the chart. "Mr. Larson," Kelly said. "You seem a little pale. And might I add, a little out of sorts—perhaps defensive. It's quite understandable, given the circumstances. But I will recommend an increase in the medication for a short while. You must follow doctor's orders. Do you understand? The medicine you take is standard and recommended for men in your situation. You've only been back in circulation for a short while. And for God's sake Mr. Larson, you're living all the way up there in the hills. Do you have a plan if there's some kind of—well, emergency?"

Ren sighed in frustration. This was the same flak he got from Gloria.

Kelly went on. "It's not that there will be one, Mr. Larson. But what if symptoms become more pronounced, more serious?"

Ren looked like someone shoved a spoonful of castor oil in his mouth. "What do you mean, more serious?"

"I mean like delusions. Hallucinations—hearing and seeing things. Paranoia. Mr. Larson, the aftershocks of what you've been through can be quite serious if not managed on a daily basis."

Ren shrugged and laughed. "Doc, you're just being dramatic. I'm telling you, everything's fine."

"Mr. Larson, may I be frank? Your type of trauma takes a good while to heal. Now, it's good that you're back to work. That's important, and I'm glad Sgt. Griswold provided you with that opportunity. But it's also important that you don't isolate as you have, and you don't refuse treatment."

"Well, Doc, I agree with you. I want to move down off that hill, just like you say. See, I'm up for promotion. I'm investigating this case, in fact. And if all goes well, I'll be promoted. Then I can afford to sell and move the family someplace else—someplace where there are real neighborhoods and families and kids for Molly to play with. That's why I need the note from you saying everything's okay."

"Well, Mr. Larson, I'll see what I can do. Meanwhile, I'd like you to take your prescription and meet me again next week. There are other options, of course. There's an east coast neurologist who has been showing consistent results with a procedure called a lobotomy. I hear they've been using this procedure over at St. Cyprian's Hospital just down the way. Perfectly safe, I assure you. But I need evidence of greater consistency from you so we might avoid any future need for, well, steps that might be more intrusive than medication."

He paused and scribbled more in the chart. "I need to make a phone call. Let me get this set up for you. Just wait here for a minute."

He stood, and the swivel stool scraped away from him beneath his knees. As soon as he left, the nurse with the mask-face entered again, this time with a rolling cart. Atop it was a long syringe and a rubber tube placed neatly inside a stainless steel tray.

"The doctor will need a sample," she said. Her voice was startling and not what Ren expected. In his mind, a nun who was a nurse might sound angelic. Instead, she was raspy, like she was speaking with sandpaper vocal cords. She drew the blood efficiently, silently. There wasn't even the expected sharpness of the needle stick. She had Ren hold a cotton ball to the puncture when she finished, then she floated away with the cart in tow. Ren held down the cotton ball with a finger, and he watched a fly float in and land on him. Then another came, and another. It made the place seem unsanitary.

Another nurse from the front office swung around the corner into the room. "We're all set, Mr. Larson," she said. "You can pick up your prescription at Hoot's Druggist on Hollywood Boulevard. It should be ready for you in about ten minutes." She noticed Ren holding the cotton ball against his arm, and she pushed her glasses up. "Did you hurt yourself, Mr. Larson?"

"What do you mean?" Ren asked. He held up his arm. "Aren't you supposed to have the patient hold a cotton ball after drawing blood?"

The nurse stood gazing at Ren with a blank stare with her steely gray eyes. "Did the doctor draw blood, Mr. Larson?"

"Yeah. That nurse—you know, the one wearing the nun's veil—she took my blood. Why?"

"May I see your arm, Mr. Larson?"

He removed the cotton ball, and together they inspected, but there was no puncture mark, and no blood on the cotton. "That's peculiar. There's just me and Angelica, who runs the front office. Angelica makes appointments, and I file the charts. Dr. Kelly does all of his own lab tests and draws his own blood."

Ren felt himself sinking into the floor. He didn't know how any of that was possible. She was real—flesh and blood. She was no figment of his imagination. And he wasn't in the dark-between.

"I'm sorry," Ren said. He tried holding his breath steady and forced a Sunday morning tone. "I have a confession," he whispered. "I just wanted to hold the cotton balls. I loved em as a kid. Didn't you?"

"Of course, Mr. Larson." She twitched a thin, wan smile. "You exit right here." She pointed to the end of the hall. Then she stepped through a separate door leading to her reception area.

"Psst," Ren heard from behind him. Smelly old Mr. Gray poked his head out from an exam room. "Watch you night and day, that's what they do," he said. Then he slipped back and shut the door.

♦

When Ren finally arrived home, Gloria was there in the driveway, pacing, with a tight clutch on the newspaper. Her eyes and nose were red and puffy. She stood in the remainder of the burnt lavender dusk—nothing but their small cottage behind her, flaxen weeds on either side, the stars just beginning to make an appearance.

He knew already what she'd read. Everyone knew, so there was no sense in attempting to misdirect only to buy him an hour or two of not having to tell her the news that was so ugly, so revolting. Gloria was just as much friends with Lily and Glen Haddock as was Ren. Molly and Maybelle got along so well that everyone who didn't know them assumed they were sisters. And this was how Gloria had discovered the sickening details of what became of them. When Ren saw her face as he drove up, it felt like he was taking one last gasp before slipping beneath quicksand. Christ, she'd probably been waiting and watching for Ren by the window all day, worried sick.

Ren parked the car and hastened to her. She collapsed into his arms.

"Yes," he said, because he hadn't anything left but to accept it all. He grabbed Gloria around the waist, pulled her close, and held her with as much strength as he could. "Yes. Yes…."

"But you were there," she said through the sobs. "You saw them dead."

"I was hoping you wouldn't find out just yet. I wanted to find the words so I could tell you myself. But I didn't have any."

"I don't understand how this could happen. The Haddocks were all so good. Things like this don't happen when people are good. They don't. I refuse to believe it. And their little girl—who would kill an innocent child? What kind of monster…?" She couldn't contain the storm of tears.

"I don't know either. So you understand why I—I just couldn't say anything to you, Gloria. It was just too awful to say. I was afraid that if I said it, something bad would happen to us. To all of us. Like it would jinx us. I know it sounds stupid, and it's no excuse, but I couldn't break your heart over this. I just couldn't."

Gloria dropped the paper and walked senseless, as though drugged, back into the house. Ren stood in the driveway for a while longer, just holding on to the hood of the car, staring straight ahead. "Christ, Glen," he said and looked around as though Haddock could hear him from wherever he was now. "Your shit just keeps getting shittier." He slammed his hand down, snapped up the paper, and then ventured into the house.

Gloria sat in the living room, her dress all fanned out and smoothed across the floral print couch, her hands folded neatly in her lap. She seemed as though she'd run out of tears. Or the damages were being replaced by something worse. She had a blank, stupefied look.

He sat down next to her, and she collapsed into his shoulder, shaking and weeping once more.

"I know. It's just terrible. And I'm so sorry."

She shook her head, and her hair fell over her face.

"What?" Ren asked. "What is it?"

"It's Molly, Ren."

"What do you mean?"

"You have to see it." She took his hand and led him into the house past Sunnie, who stood watching, moving only her eyes with her lips pursed. She made a sign of the cross over her full abdomen and shoulders, then clasped her fingers across her apron.

Sunnie held many superstitions, and when things went wrong for the Larsons, she was quick to offer her beliefs and a whole host of concoctions to boot. Herbs, powders, and hand-drawn charms were among them. Several times, Gloria had found disturbing collections of artifacts like hair and fingernails, iron filings, and roots all bound in small linen bags tucked here and there, beneath pillows or in drawers. Sunnie called those "hex-breakers," and she didn't understand that they were unnerving for families not from her hometown. Gloria knew Sunnie meant well, but she had a hard time with the more exotic customs, especially with a child in the house. And sometimes Sunnie's artifacts were dangerous things—like jars full of nails, or like the candle left burning in the bathroom.

Sunnie had a whole range of practices she insisted upon. For instance, Gloria had never wanted Sunnie to wear a uniform when working. She preferred a more relaxed feeling in the home. Nonetheless, Sunnie wore one anyway.

"Are you paying me or not, Misses?" she would ask. "If you're paying, I ain't showing up wearing a housedress and slippers, if that's what you're thinking. That would put me in a mind to lounge on the porch and drink a sugar cane rum. Sunnie's not here to fiddle the day away." So she wore her navy blue one-piece with a flat white apron every day.

Ren followed Gloria to Molly's room, and his stomach churned when his gaze fell upon the marked-up wall. Ren held up Gloria's newspaper turned to the front page, to that horrible photo snapped at the scene. Just like in Haddock's hotel room and in Molly's shredded Bible, scrawled in an angry blood-red crayon: *Zagan, Agares, Baal, Caim*, and others, right above her bed.

His whole body buzzed with a lightning jolt of adrenaline. Molly woudn't have known any of this. Someone had broken in again and was alone with Molly. A nun, or some basket case dressed up as one. His mind had gone numb, and he couldn't come up with any further explanation.

"Where is she?" he asked.

"Playing."

"She's all right? Not hurt or scared?"

"She doesn't seem to remember a thing about it, Ren. It's so odd. Why would she do this?" Gloria asked.

Without responding, Ren bit a lip and slipped through the kitchen. Peering out the connecting doorway, he spotted Molly wearing her mother's hat and pearls, setting up a little tea set. She was deep in her imaginary world, humming and pouring for her unblinking toys. The cathedral-style upright radio atop a nearby table was lit up, playing a raucous, static-speckled episode of *Baker's Broadway Smash*.

"Please, Ren, we have to move from here…." Gloria followed him from behind and touched his hand. She seemed determined this time and rightly so.

"Well, this news isn't coming a moment too soon. Griswold put me up for a promotion. His position—he's moving up the chain of command. If I can get it, we'll have enough to move and get a new place. Wherever you want to, this time."

Gloria clasped Ren around the shoulders and buried her face in his chest. "Really, Ren? Really?"

"Yes, really. Don't cry anymore, honey. We'll be out of here before you know it. I promise. I know things here are giving you the creeps. And I can't explain half of it. But there's an explanation for everything. Right? You know that, right, honey?" He didn't want to bring up the nun again, so he had to generate another plausible reason for the wall-writing.

Gloria shook her head and wiped her eyes. "Why would a child write these horrid things?"

"Gloria, when did you get the paper?"

"It came earlier this afternoon," she said.

"By any chance, had Sunnie already collected it from the porch?"

She wiped her eyes more. "Well, yes, but what does that have to do with anything?"

"Don't you see?" Ren said. "Why, she could have brought that paper and left it anywhere while she was helping you around the house. Molly probably saw the picture and was just copying what she saw, that's all." He hoped Gloria bought it. He'd need some time before they could leave this place.

"But what about the lady in the closet? Molly said she saw a lady there. And her Bible was all torn up and, and… I don't even know the words to describe what happened to it... I know I said I didn't believe you about the nun before. And I'm not sure what I believe exactly. But now that things keep happening, I'm just so—so scared."

"Gloria, think for a second," he said. Then he laughed a little. "Kids have nightmares. Don't you remember?" He tried his best to backpedal his concerns. He wasn't sure what to believe any longer, and he even wondered about the reality of what he'd seen that night. Maybe it wasn't a nun. Maybe he'd slipped into the dark-between again. He certainly didn't want Gloria to know about that.

"I still have them, to be honest," she said.

Ren looked down and took in a long breath. "I think maybe we're both getting a bit spooked up here all by ourselves in the hills."

"Just promise me again that we'll move from here and never have to look back," Gloria said.

"Of course. We'll go. I'll get promoted, and we'll leave just as soon as we can."

She wiped her eyes with the back of her hand and sniffled a bit. "Oh, thank God. Thank God. You're the most wonderful husband in the world." She threw her arms around his neck and kissed his cheek. "Let's just try to put this behind us and have dinner, can we? We're all here, and we're all safe. That's what's most important, right?"

Ren nodded. She hugged him again, and he bit his lip.

Gloria handed him the newspaper, and she left for the kitchen, trying to act like nothing serious had happened. "We have pot roast," she said.

"That sounds fine." Ren cracked open the paper past the front page to the photo spread set up in the middle like some kind of sick centerfold. He studied the photos and used a pencil in Molly's room to underline the words that were exact matches between the two rooms. Then he noticed a disturbing anomaly in one of the over-exposed shots, faces all washed out by the flash. The image looked like a dark shadow, though it had form, substance. He could make out a head and a shoulder if he looked at it just right. It hunched there in the back of the closet, just behind the dead child.

Ren had been there that night. No one else had been in that room except Haddock and his family. And if Ren hadn't seen anyone, then Fiorelli and the other officers would have found someone lurking in a closet. He took a mental note that he needed to speak to the photographer at the *Times-Mirror*, and he stuck the paper in his overcoat pocket.

"Sunnie," Ren called out.

"Yes, Mister?" she called from the other room. She met Ren in the kitchen.

"How are you doing today, Sunnie? Sorry that I rushed right past you. You understand."

"Oh, no offense taken, sir. Your wife, she was in a terrible state most of the day after she read that paper and saw those pictures," she said.

She busied herself helping Ren take off his coat.

"Sunnie, would you mind helping me get that crayon off the wall?"

"Of course, sir. Better not to have a thing like that in the house. Horrid thing!" She made the sign of the cross again and then left to get warm soapy water and two sponges.

She met him in Molly's room, and together they wiped the walls. The red crayon smeared like blood at first. They did the work without talking. But after a while, Ren said, "Sunnie, by any chance, did you pick up the paper from the porch?"

"Why, yes, like always."

"And did you leave it where Molly might have found it?"

Sunnie's face became as serious as a fresh grave. "I left it where I always leave the paper, Mister. The child can reach things on the coffee table."

"You know, Sunnie, Gloria and I just think the world of you."

"Well, that's nice to say, Mister. Sunnie loves your whole family right back."

"I know you want what's best for Gloria, right?"

She suddenly stopped wiping the walls. "Of course, sir. What we all want, isn't that right?"

"Would you mind, for a while, not mentioning anything about devils, or hexes, or omens? Just don't mention things that could frighten Mrs. Larson, okay?"

Sunnie looked like someone took the nickel out of her. "Why, yes, of course. But Mister, if you just look at these walls. Something ain't right."

"Sunnie, please. Your stories are just making her upset."

She regarded the wall she was sponging down. The letters of the word *Andras* were so aggressively scrubbed onto the wall that chunks of red crayon clung to the markings. She looked down at the bucket and started scouring again. "I promise, Mister. But as long as you let me say my peace. Then I can leave it."

"Sunnie, I've heard you talk about curses and hexes and fixes before."

"No, sir. This ain't about no fix. Sunnie knows you don't want to hear about it, sir. But this… this is different. I've seen it before in my life." She crossed herself and kissed her clasped hands. "There's something come after you. After the whole lot of you. Mr. Crooked." She said it in nearly a whisper but then covered her mouth, as if saying the name alone was like rubbing a genie's lamp.

Ren consciously tried to control his face. "Mr. Crooked? Well, this is a new one."

"No, sir," she said. She locked eyes on him, and she seemed immune to any dismissive tone. Her face, usually as cheerful as a Christmas wreath, was doleful, and the corners of her mouth drooped. "This is an old one. Very old."

Ren wasn't about to inquire further. He sighed.

"He makes things happen. Terrible things," she muttered. "But it's not him who's done them. He made you do them."

"Was that it?" he asked. "You're done with campfire stories?"

She nodded, but it was a nod the executioner gives before he throws the electric chair switch.

"You won't bring this up to Gloria, right?" he asked.

"You can't stop Mr. Crooked. Least not on your own, Mister. No matter how big the gun you carry. Someone's got to help you now." Ren realized she'd waited for this moment, and she'd gotten herself good and foamed up about it, too. Sunnie pulled a slip of paper from her apron and handed it to Ren between both of her hands, as though making an offering. He slipped it into his shirt pocket and flashed her a dutiful smile.

"All right, Sunnie, thank you."

"Yes, sir…." She slopped the sponge around in the red soapy water, then watched him leave with eyes that pronounced judgment.

Seven

Los Angeles, 1947
Nearly Two Months Before It Happened

Old George never left the Furlong district, not for long anyway, even though he tried. For a while, in his early twenties, he ventured to the more central parts of the city where neighbors in Furlong told him he'd find his way. Old George realized that over time he'd become like that grocer on 52nd Street. He was one more Furlong fixture, full of secrets, and a lot of bloody trash out back. Old George needed a place where folks wouldn't whisper about him and anchor him to what was over and done.

"Isn't that Birdie's boy? Such a shame. I heard he knows what really happened, but won't ever tell." They were right about that. Old George was smart enough to know a man couldn't outrun his past, but he could find somewhere else to build a future.

Once he settled and found a room to rent, it wasn't long before he made friends with a girl who had bright green eyes and skin like hot cocoa. They met while washing clothes at the corner Laun-Do-Mat. Her name was Serene. She was a night student at the community college and studied forensics. Her dream was to land a job with the city's new Crime Lab one day. She had the mind for it and the mind for justice, too. Until that time, though, she taught institutionalized children. "Nervous and feeble-minded," she'd heard neighbors call those children. Serene thought the sound of that was simply wrong-headed. She found most of the children worthy of love rather than being cast off by their families, as happened in most cases.

In time, Old George and Serene got engaged. They even picked out an apartment they might live in after the wedding, close to Normandie Avenue, so they would both be within a reasonable distance of their work.

Every day they'd ride the Red Car together into the downtown, Serene to the Hospital at St. Cyprian's, and Old George to his work driving the trash truck and delivering its payload to the city dump. Getting to sit next to his green-eyed girl for the ride every day was the cure Old George needed. As the months passed, he forgot about his old life in the Furlong and the troubles he'd had up to then. This was the life he'd dreamed of, and Old George thought for a time that any man could give his past the slip, if he just put his mind to it.

When pains in her knees and shoulders began plaguing Serene, Old George could still see through them to the happiness on the other side. But the pains came upon her every day, sometimes for the whole of it. Over the months, the pain crept up all over her body. In time, she was bedridden, so much so, she couldn't think of how she might ever work in that forensics lab.

Old George didn't pay much attention to those worries. He knew she was strong and she'd get better in her own time. So Old George would make her soups and rub liniments into her muscles, and ointments onto the ulcers on her legs. He'd draw hot baths and put her to bed, then he'd walk with tears in his eyes to his place around the corner, and pray in the night for her to get better.

One day, the time came, and Old George walked in to find her lying in her bed, staring straight up, as though something sudden and frightful had occurred. She'd gone cold. The doctors told him it had to do with her condition, and what took her was her heart. Serene's heart was always so open and vulnerable. Maybe that was it, Old George thought. Maybe she was just too much heart.

Old George returned to the Furlong after all that, back to the community who knew him before his life with Serene. All he wanted to do was put it all behind him and go someplace dark where he could disappear, right along with her.

Though years had passed since her death, it was really Serene who brought Old George into Mr. Porter's shop this day.

Old George would come visiting Mr. Porter's with his momma since childhood. She'd take him there with jewelry his daddy bought her, hoping for a price and a way out of some debt if she could manage it. Mr. Porter was always fair, but he didn't seem swayed by people's circumstances. "Got a business to run," he'd tell folks who came in with a sob story and a ring or necklace worth half of what they thought. He'd even give them full price for whatever they paid sometimes. Old George once overheard Mr. Porter telling the Mrs. in the back room, "It just wouldn't be Christian to turn them away when they need help the most." She fussed about it, but he still ran the shop how he saw fit.

It seemed everyone in Los Angeles knew Porter's jewelry for its high quality. People traveled from all over the city. If they were looking for a fair price, they'd find their way to Porter's after they'd gotten a gander at some of the price tags in the fancier shops.

The brass bell at the top of the door sang in a high-pitched frenzy as he entered Mr. Porter's jewelry shop. "Well, Old George!" Mr. Porter said. When Mr. Porter grinned like that, showing off those teeth that looked too big for his mouth, well, it got everyone else smiling. Old George figured Porter's protruding smile was because the false teeth were once his daddy's or granddaddy's china choppers, but they definitely did not look like his own.

"Hello, Mr. Porter," Old George said. He noticed how aged Porter had become in the intervening years. He hunched forward, and his back curved in a swing to one side. His head nodded around now, as though he agreed with everyone. He made his way around the counter, and Old George noticed Porter marched now with high knees, and even with that, he made many mistakes in his footing along the way. His gait was like someone who was avoiding roller skates lying in his path behind the counter.

"Where've you been for the last half-decade?"

The two men laughed. It had been much longer than that. Mr. Porter wouldn't have asked such a question, if only he'd known.

"If I remember right, you came in to buy a ring—a small diamond, but a good one. It was for a nice girl you'd met and planned to marry. What was her name? Selene? Was that it?" Mr. Porter's voice sounded like a toad now, if a toad could speak.

"Serene. It was Serene, Mr. Porter."

"That's right, Serene! How is the old gal doing?" he asked.

"Oh, she's just fine, Mr. Porter." There was no sense in saying more.

"They always stay with you, if you give em one of Porter's Jewels," Mr. Porter said. Then he flashed his toothy smile again. Old George wasn't sure if Mr. Porter could see things all that well anymore. He had swollen eyes, puffed forward with a slit to see through.

Old George thought about what Porter had said, and he supposed he was right about Serene staying with him. He knew it was strange, and he hadn't conjured up nonsense out of sentimentality. He could honestly feel and hear her at important times. The night he found the hand and the ring in his junkyard, for instance, he felt her close by. *"Don't be afraid, Old George,"* she'd said to him. *"Take the ring to old Porter. Let him tell you whose it is."*

The night he found the ring, he dreamt of Serene's funeral down at St. Vibiana's Cathedral.

It was one of those vivid dreams that seemed real and took a long time to shake.

Old George sat in the front row, distracting himself from the awfulness of the day by looking around at the flowers everyone brought and the statues of Jesus, Mary, and the saints who could not care less. They'd seen plenty of flowers for funerals and weddings alike. Nothing special about one more death for the ones up there on pedestals. The statues all posed with beatific expressions frozen to their faces, eyes gazing heavenward, no matter what horror the world held or what deep sorrow might be right there in front of them.

Old George wondered what made them so special. There were plenty of good people in the world, as far as he could see. Plenty of bad ones, too, pretending to be good. He wondered why the Church saw fit to remember some of them in gold leaf, pedestals, and halos. He couldn't see how it was right when his Serene, who did no wrong, who helped people in need, would soon be buried in the municipal cemetery. Unlike the saints on the pedestals, the world would forget her after today.

That was when he thought he saw the wooden statue of the Virgin Mary swing her starry-crowned head around to him. She had faced forward when he first entered the church, he was sure of it. Her eyes, like all the other statues, were searching the celestial bodies and the heavenly hosts. But now they bore straight through Old George in a way that caused his pulse to quicken and a sense of dread to creep from his belly.

It was almost as if it had noticed him in particular, and now it stood there on that pedestal watching him with a look of rancor. He knew that grief and distress could cause the mind to play tricks. His Aunt Della had once told him that his dead Uncle Theo visited her at night, floating face down over her bed. But Uncle Theo's floating corpse was a product of her tears and regrets, and an old confused mind.

Remembering all of that, Old George ignored what he thought he saw in the statue, thinking he hadn't really seen it, and he put some effort into what the priest was saying instead. He got a twitching feeling in his gut, and he glanced at the statue again. Mary's mouth gaped open in a silent scream. Her lips peeled back to show her wooden throat. He reassured himself that carvings couldn't move any more than Serene could now, and that someone must have carved the statue that way to begin with, for some godforsaken reason.

He closed his eyes so he wouldn't see it anymore. What forced him to look again were the wild screams echoing around the church walls, just as though the place had caught fire. Everyone at the funeral was in a panic, running from their pews.

He turned his head and watched them, not understanding what could have caused such commotion. When he turned back, he couldn't see Mary on her pedestal anymore, and it sickened him. Old George squeezed his eyes shut and pretended he was praying.

He felt a rigid wooden arm, and he heard it crack and splinter as it clasped his shoulders, but he kept his eyes clenched and his head hung low. A small object, like a pebble, clattered onto the bench next to him. He didn't dare look, but it felt like an invisible force compelled him. He opened one eye and saw the tooth—the one with the gold cap—lying on the polished wood. It looked as though someone had just ripped it from his daddy's head, and it dripped with bright blood.

A fly landed on the tooth, then it buzzed around Old George's ears.

He tried not to flinch or to scream and run, even though he thought the thing might rip his teeth out, too, for all he knew. Old George felt his heart freeze, and he couldn't move even if he wanted. His breath came in uncontrolled pants.

"Now's when we see if you really are a coward," the statue said. It spoke with Serene's voice. But Serene never had a harsh word to say, and neither would the Virgin Mary.

"You saw what fell on the pavement that night your mother sent you to the store, Old George, and you never told me about it. You never even bothered," the statue said, still mimicking Serene. "In all that time we spent together, you never said a word. You didn't tell the police, did you? Someone needs to pay for what happened. You never came clean for your father. And look at what happened. You didn't save her after all, did you? No. You just lied, and you made her die alone in prison. She died thinking of you, sorry that you lied like that. I keep track of who fills their heart with lies, Old George. And liars burn in lakes of fire. I take them there myself, take bites from the running wounds of their decaying souls, and dance at their perpetual agony. But now is your chance to redeem yourself. Throw that ring back in the heaps and walk away. If you do, I'll just turn around, and I won't devour your soul."

Old George shuddered with such uncontrolled dread that he felt a string of drool slip from his bottom lip. Then other words bubbled up from his heart and sounded above the words of the torturous mimic—the fake Mother of God. *"It's only using my voice. It wants to harm you, but it can't. So much fury that it would burst into flames if it could. Just stand firm. You'll need courage now. Find who owns the ring. You'll know what to do next."*

Then he woke with a terrible, wall-splitting scream.

He couldn't sleep after that. He had to turn on all the lights and play music from the radio just to get the awful feeling out of his mind, his room, his house. But he did what the second voice told him, and he fished the ring off the nightstand and looked it over with a magnifying glass. That was when he saw the imprint of Porter's Jewels inscribed on the inside of the gleaming band.

"I brought something for you," Old George said.

"Oh?" Mr. Porter asked, "is that so?"

"I found this and wanted to take it back to whoever bought it. I saw P.J. on the band, and I knew it must have come from here."

He reached in his pocket and laid the ring on the glass.

Porter's fingers fussed and fidgeted as though he was grasping at things no one else could see. Then he reached for a jeweler's loupe too small to fit into his puffy eye, and he examined the ring.

"That's my logo, all right," he said. "White gold. Very expensive. You know that if you bought this somewhere else, you'd pay full price. But I don't do that to folks. I say fair is fair. Say you wanna take the ring back to someone? Mighty big of you to do that. Most folks'd keep it and hock it for the money." Mr. Porter shouted to his wife so she could hear, "You see, Tilda? Still some good people in the world."

"Oh hush," she said. She smiled at Old George, and a fly landed on her front tooth.

Porter turned back to Old George. "Where'd you say you found it again?"

The fly swooped from Tilda to Old George. He swatted at it and remembered the intense dream. Old George swallowed hard, feeling his Adam's apple dip, and he felt his collar tighten. He lied again, even though Serene, and the Virgin Mary, or whatever it was, told him not to lie anymore. "I found it on the sidewalk, I said." The fly landed on his hand. He watched it crawl around there. Then it fell on Porter's enlarged earlobe, crawled into the hairy canal, and burrowed deep out of sight.

"On the sidewalk? That's impossible. A woman doesn't let her wedding ring slip off like that. She may take it off to wash the dishes or to wipe a window, but she'll always put it right back on," Mr. Porter said. He was still examining the diamond with the telescopic lens. "You still work over at the junkyard?" he asked. Then he took out the pointy metal sizer, slipped the ring over it, and inspected the fit.

Old George laughed. "How'd you remember that?" Another fly came in, a big one with red eyes, and just like the first, it zoomed down Porter's dark ear canal.

"Oh, I remember everything. Matter of fact, I can tell you who bought this ring. White diamond set in a white gold band. That's a special order. Naw, you didn't find this on any sidewalk, son. It didn't slip off any woman's finger. This was custom sized. You must have found it in your junkyard's what I expect. The lady who wore it must have taken it off on purpose, just like I told you, and it fell into the garbage."

He turned back to his wife. "You hear that? Woman took off her ring and lost it in the trash. Just like I told you could happen." She made a gesture like she was slapping him.

"No. I'm sure I found it while walking," Old George said. His collar felt hotter and tighter.

"Still being a coward?" Mr. Porter said, but in Serene's voice.

Old George looked away just before he heard it. But there was no doubt it was Serene's voice. He stared thunderstruck at Porter, who glared back at him with a look that only criminals waiting in dark corners give when they see their next victim. Old George watched four more flies land and tunnel into Porter's ear. Old George realized that hearing Serene's voice from Porter was absurd. He was just making that up. But what he couldn't dismiss what was the fact that Porter didn't feel a whole nest of insects crowding inside his skull.

"Walking? Where was it?" Mr. Porter asked. It was his normal croaky voice.

"Oh, over on Wilshire."

"Another lie," Porter said in Serene's voice again. He was growling out the words now, and he had a contorted smile twisted onto his face. *"Keep this up. You'll be ripe and taste as good as the others."*

"What?" Old George asked.

Porter changed his voice again, sounding like his old shaky self, and his facial muscles fell back to their droopy position.

"I said, in that case, the woman who owns this must have lost some weight. Twenty pounds, if I were to guess it. This kind of thing happens from time to time. When you lose enough weight, a ring like this slides right off. Wouldn't even know it happened, neither."

Old George wondered if he'd lost his mind. How were these bizarre changes in Porter possible? He eyed Tilda sitting on a stepstool not far behind Porter, and she didn't seem to register the changes. She kept on swatting at the many flies filling the shop. The air was alive with them now.

"So, who do you think owns it?" Old George asked. "I'd sure like to take it right over if I could. Woman must be worried sick by now."

"I may not know the name off the tip of my tongue, but I can sure look it up in my records. Special orders are easy to find. Don't get many like this one, I can tell you that," Mr. Porter said. He high-stepped into the back room, where his wife handed him a ledger.

Old George felt a tickle on his ear, and he heard buzzing. He slapped a hand to it and tried to keep it from entering.

"Are you all right, son?" Mr. Porter asked.

"Oh, I'm fine," Old George said. "I think I got a fly on my ear."

"Well, don't let it get in, son. Next thing you know, you're hatching baby flies out your head," Mr. Porter said. He laughed an old man's laugh, then opened up his ledger. "Well, anyway, here it is."

He set the ledger on the glass, then he shifted his personality again, staring with a kind of red-eyed malice that Old George had never seen in his life.

"You do this, and you'll burn with the rest. I'll eat your soul and dance," Porter said. But Porter no longer spoke with Serene's voice. There was a cacophony of voices merged into one mouth. Porter widened his grin, and from between the gaps in his teeth, dozens of flies crawled out and covered the man's face. He never flinched. One by one, the insects shot off and zoomed out a frayed hole in the shop's screen door.

Old George backed up and took a sharp, inhaled breath.

Mr. Porter looked up from his ledger and gave another one of his toothy smiles. "The name here says, Larson. Ren Larson. I can give you a copy of the register slip."

Eight

Los Angeles, 1947
Two Days Before It Happened

Ren pulled up in front of the hotel where Haddock and his family had died. His throat closed up, and it was like choking on a peach pit. He felt a feverish tide building inside, and he wondered if it might melt him down completely, right there in the squad car. Fiorelli sat beside him, drumming his fingers on the passenger door.

"Larson, for the last time, we combed the room for evidence. Crime Lab says all the blood types were a match for Haddock's wife and kid. The residents on the fifth floor already told us they never saw anyone come in or out of that room. The manager… what was his name… Degrassi? Well, he didn't see anything either. He wasn't even aware there was a family in that suite until there was a commotion. So what exactly are we looking for?"

"Christ, Fiorelli," Ren said. "You think I like this? You think this is my idea of a good time?" It surprised him that the question hadn't triggered a volcanic eruption.

"Just give me one good reason we need to be here. Shouldn't we be interviewing Haddock's brother or sister? Get something to verify the guy's mental state?"

"You want a reason? You said it yourself. No one can account for Haddock entering the building, not the neighbors or the front desk manager. Don't you think that's worth looking into?"

"No, I don't. At this point, we've got a cracker-case of a guy who lost his peanuts and nothing else. How'd he get in? Just like everyone else. He held the door after a resident opened it with a key. And managers leave their desks unattended all the time—especially in well-run establishments such as this one, only a hair's breadth away from the wrecking ball."

"Fine. Wait in the car."

Ren's heart ticked up a few beats, knowing he'd have to face those enclosing stairs again. An elderly woman wearing socks and work shoes, carrying a full bag of groceries, approached the hotel door and unlocked it. Ren caught it before it closed. He glanced back at the car and noticed that Fiorelli had watched it happen, just like he said it could. He slipped in behind the woman and disappeared inside.

Again, as Fiorelli had predicted, the gum-stuck checkered floor tiles led to an empty reception area. Ren stepped up and smacked down on the domed brass call bell. No one answered. He rang it a few more times. Still, the only activity was the sound of a pendulum wall clock's rhythmic ticking on the back wall.

"Ain't no one there, copp'r." Ren turned and spotted a thin black woman standing on the shoe-scuffed stairs behind him, across the seedy lobby. Her hair was all covered up by a colorful head-wrap made of strips of fabric. "You a copp'r, right?" she asked.

Ren tipped up his hat and approached. "Yes, ma'am. I'm here about the disturbance in the building the other night."

She chuckled low and put her hands on her hips. "Disturbance here every night, if ya ask me. What happened last night ain't nothing out of the ordinary." Ren noticed that she had a particular lilt in her voice, similar to that of his housekeeper.

"Is that so?" he asked.

A voice came from behind. "Can I help you?"

Ren whipped around to find an old man in a dirty tank shirt with crescent sweat marks beneath each of his saggy pecs. He chomped on a wad of chewing tobacco, and it gave off a noxious odor.

"Yes. I'm Detective Larson from the Los Angeles Police Department. I'm here about last night's incident."

"I already told that Fiorelli fellow what I know. And that's a whole lot of nothing."

Ren turned back and discovered that the woman from the stairs had vanished. There didn't seem to be any footsteps trudging on those rickety stairs as he would have expected. She seemed to… evaporate.

"I'm sorry, didn't you notice an old woman on those stairs?" Ren asked.

"Look, are you gonna be here all day, detective? I got a business to run."

Ren looked around the empty lobby and figured he'd interrupted Degrassi's nap. Then he said, "I'm here to inspect the hotel room again, if you don't mind. It shouldn't take long at all."

"Be my guest." He reached back, nabbed a key for the room, and slapped it down on the desk. "Fifth floor, across from the stairwell. You know…."

Ren slid the key into his pocket and started up the steps that groaned beneath him. The hotel manager shouted after him, "And be sure to leave that room clean. I don't want any telltale signs left for someone to discover. I'm already gonna have a tough time finding a renter." Ren touched the brim of his hat and gave a short nod.

Degrassi waddled through the door behind the banged-up counter, and Ren gazed upward, taking in the length of the stairs. His stomach tumbled, and he lost focus. A cold sweat broke on his forehead, and he steadied himself with the handrail.

"Hey, you don't have an elevator somewhere, do you?" he shouted. All that came back was more from the pendulum clock.

Ren focused his gaze down and he started up the steps. To his surprise, he didn't have any trouble with the climb at all. He was thankful for avoiding any difficulties that might get back to Griswold. He reached the fifth floor, and he looked down the hall in both directions. There wasn't a soul in sight. He unlocked the door to Haddock's suite, and it swung wide. The officers had scrubbed the walls before they left the scene, but deeper stains penetrated the wallpaper, and the seams looked like someone had dragged their long, bloody fingernails down them.

They'd stripped the bed, and there was a depression in the center of the mattress. There was a brown, irregular blotch where the family blood had puddled. Flies gathered on the walls and on the windows. They were big, red-eyed, hungry flies. The stench of the dead, difficult to clear away from closed-in spaces, drew them. The room was empty, but Ren couldn't erase the sight of Haddock on that bed, bodies scattered everywhere.

He trudged across and pulled back the edges of some cheerless green curtains, cranked two vertical windows open, and light flooded in. But that didn't relieve the oppression Ren sensed somehow lingering in the very air. The incident had stamped the room with the madness and carnage of that night. Degrassi was right. Anyone with any sense at all would catch on that death remained in this room.

"Not natural, what happed. No one's asking an old woman."

Ren turned, and the skinny woman with the colorful head wrap who had disappeared from the stairs now stood in the doorway, her arms akimbo still like she was angry about something.

"I'm sorry, ma'am. You'll have to go. This is an active police investigation."

"The place is thick with them, don't you feel it?"

"I'm sorry, what?"

"The spirits. Don't you feel them?" She inhaled with a whooshing through her flared nostrils and allowed her eyes to gaze upward, as though she were seeing the very floating ghosts to which she was referring. "Mystery, isn't it? How'd they get here and all?"

"Did you see something?" Ren asked.

"I always see something. Question is, did you see something?"

"Ma'am, really, unless you've got concrete information about what happened last night, you really need to leave."

She didn't budge. "You a man looking for some peace."

"What?" Ren shook his head.

"I'm looking for it, too. But you looking for a special kind of peace."

"And what makes you say that?" Ren asked.

"I know things. It's my job." She pointed out the door and down the hallway. "Madam Zolva. Past, present, future. I know things. Only two dollars. Room 55."

"Yeah, well, if you know things, can you tell me who did this?"

"Maybe." She shrugged. "Maybe not. You ever have someone throw you the bones?"

"Bones? What? Lady, please go back to your room if you have no information that will help."

The woman turned to leave, but hesitated at the door. Ren paid no attention and returned to searching, this time heading toward the closet.

"You the kind of man who looks in the mirror and see something… something not natural… something that scare ya."

Ren whipped around, astonished by what she'd said. It was impossible that she'd know anything about the strange dark shadow in the mirror.

She raised her eyebrows, satisfied. "Only two dollars. Room 55." She turned around and left in the direction where she'd pointed earlier.

It felt like a shock of electricity coursed through Ren. He suddenly remembered the name Sunnie had written on that slip of paper for him. It was the name of a person who might help, she told him. The name was *Zolva.*

Ren considered the foolishness of pursuing it. It was a common medium's trick to lure the foolish and the desperate by making general statements that had a broad meaning. Still, what she'd said about the mirror seemed more specific and uncanny. Besides that, it was more than a bit coincidental that the woman Sunnie had recommended might occupy the same hotel as Haddock on the night he died.

He crossed the room and looked out the door, but Zolva was out of sight now. The hallway was dim. Only one narrow window allowed a slim shot of light at the extreme end. He padded in the direction she'd gone, found her room number, and rapped on the door. He couldn't believe what he was doing. There was no such thing as real fortune tellers. But maybe she had a lead she'd divulge for her fee.

She swung the door wide. "We throw the bones now?" She did not smile anymore, but chomped on a thick cigar. She stepped aside and gestured for Ren to enter. She wore two bracelets made of small cowrie shells, and there was another set of them woven between woody red berries dangling down the front of her shift.

She'd filled her suite with strange objects that reminded him of an old museum or a carnival freak-show, which must have appealed to the table tipping and spirit-board crowd. The air was a stuffy haze of sweet-smelling smoke and dim lighting. In front of him was an old table covered with candles tall and small, and something decayed and dried in the middle of it all. It couldn't be a human head, Ren reassured himself. Not really.

There were odd things strewn around the decaying furniture: a stuffed owl tipped over on its side, some snake skins, the horns of different animals, and a curved knife prepared in some arrangement around several black bowls. Ren wondered what use they might be to a fortune teller. A doorway in the back of the room looked like it adjoined to another suite.

Once among these oddities, the whole situation seemed more preposterous than ever to Ren. It was as if he had a microscope and could see the smallest parts of his experience. The moment's heat was an alchemical fire that burned away the dulling lead of his mind until he saw the shining truth beneath. There were a myriad of reasons and possibilities accounting for what Zolva had said, and what he thought happened in his mirror—let alone the odd things happening at his home. He was getting carried away. He hadn't slept well in God-knows-how-long, and maybe he'd been drinking a little too much. Those elements alone could make anyone lose their perspective—see things, hear things, imagine them. Believe them.

He tried to pull himself together.

"You know a woman named Sunnie?"

"Many women come see me. All right copp'r, go on, take the bones, throw em!"

"You said something about a mirror…" Ren said.

Another woman, younger and shapely, with pale, almost translucent skin emerged from the adjoining door in the back of the room. She had the demeanor of royalty, like a Duchess from another era. In fact, she wore clothes fashionable about twenty years ago, along with multiple layers of jewelry stacked upon her fingers and between her small breasts. Ren spotted among her lavaliers a five-pointed star that rested upon her flat-ironed chest.

"Is everything all right, Zolva?" she asked. Her initial, unsure steps into the light became firmer, more resolute, and she stepped forward with a theatrical flair. "I sensed the presence of authority. A man of the law. And, well, it seems my premonition was correct." She wailed the words like a Shakespearean actor.

"Everything fine, Charlene," Zolva said. "Go back to your own room."

"Are you sure, Zolva? I can whip up a quick protection spell if it's needed…" She said it in a stage whisper.

"Charlene. Go back! Do I come barging in on ya when you reading cards? No. Now go on and get back there!" Zolva said. She didn't even bother to turn around when addressing the other woman.

"Very well," Charlene said. "But before I go, I will say, I sense a deeper mystery unfolding. And great danger…" She swept her arms in the air as though dispelling ghosts that stood in her way. She seemed to think there was a full house to the play going on in her head, even though only two people sat captive in the front row.

"Charlene!" Zolva said.

The woman whirled around, causing her black chiffon to fly up and then flutter back down. Then she disappeared through the darkened back area, miffed at the lost opportunity to share premonitions and to take a bow for her sure-fire second act.

Zolva eyed Ren with one shut. "She don't mean no harm."

"Christ, this is ridiculous," Ren said.

"Nothing is ridiculous. You come in my place. This means you look for answers. What's your name, copp'r?"

"I'm Officer Larson." His pulse throbbed at his temples.

"Come over here, Larson, the copp'r."

She approached her candle-lit table and blew cigar smoke across it, then she blew more onto Ren. Upon closer inspection, Ren noticed that the tabletop was a hodgepodge of saint statues and framed pictures of them fitted between candles. Also among the artifacts were a collection of feathers, red berries, and different colored powders spilled across the feet of virgins and martyrs alike, all with their eyes turned heavenward. A chicken clucked and pecked in a wooden crate below.

Ren's eyes got glassy as he blinked in disbelief. "What is…? Look, ma'am, I'm not sure what you've got going on here, but I'm certain that not much of this is legal or safe. Leaving burning candles? Livestock?"

"Only one time there was a fire from candles. Burned me good!" She laughed and touched the side of her head.

"I made a mistake by coming in here. I should go…." Ren said, and he turned to leave.

"Nonsense!" She said it in a way that made Ren feel small and scolded. "You sit there. This only take a minute."

She pointed to one of the scratched-up wooden chairs near the table's edge. Ren eyed what looked like a dehydrated monkey's paw, stiff and curled at the foot of the Virgin of Guadalupe. She gestured to a pile of white bones that looked like a complete set from some long-deceased animal, and when he handled them, they were light as air. From a bird, he guessed—maybe even from one of her chickens. "Careful now. That's from my beloved Fifey. Never begged at the table. She still serves me well now—maybe even better. Take what you want of her bones, then throw them. Throw them like dice in da casino." Then she gave a wheezy laugh.

He held them, but he found he couldn't do it. The old woman demonstrated for him with imaginary dice. "Snake eyes!" she cried. Then she laughed and slapped her knees. "Throw them!" She no longer sounded jovial, but strict and commanding, an undertone of warning in her words.

Ren just let them fall onto the table in front of him. He stood up and backed away, as though he'd let loose a handful of tarantulas. The old woman came up close, putting her nose almost on the table, and she moved a candle to help her study the outcome. She closed her eyes and sang a song in a strange and lilting language.

Her eyes opened, so they looked like she had them spring-loaded. She didn't turn her head, but her gaze drifted toward Ren. She glanced at him in suspicion, as though he was the kind of evil spirit she was used to expelling, or having coffee with, or whatever it was she did with them.

"You leave Nany's place," she said. Her teeth ground down on the words, and the corners of her mouth drooped as she spoke. She looked like she had never seen Ren before this moment. Her tone was steady and sure, like a pile driver getting ready to slam down at any moment. "Don't you ever come back here. Get out! Get out!" She opened a jar and blew some powder at Ren. He coughed and closed his eyes. It was definitely an effective powder. It made him want to leave. And maybe give her a citation.

He decided not to provoke her further, so he raised his hands and began backing away.

"Not you, damn fool," she said. "Sit back down."

Ren looked over his shoulder, but no one was there behind him. Apparently, the Madam was a few cowrie shells short of a reading.

He sat back down.

"Get out! I'll bottle you back up and sink you to the bottom of the ocean to rot for a thousand years!" she said.

"You know there's no one here besides you and me, right?" Ren said, trying not to laugh.

"Of course there's no one else here. Don't be stupid."

Ren wanted to congratulate her on her recent grasp of reality.

"But there is some *thingum* here. One from your mirror." She paused, sniffed the air, and closed her eyes as if trying to feel for vibrations. "It knows old Nany is the boss, so it leaves now." She nodded and sniffed again, cocksure.

"Who's Nany? You mean you?" Ren asked.

"It's what they call me."

"Then, who is Zolva?"

"American ladies don't let an old colored woman named Nany do a reading for them. But they do if she called Madam Zolva."

Amid Nany's yelling, neither of them heard the door open, even though it had some time ago.

"Holy shit, Larson." Fiorelli stood in the doorway watching the scene before him, his eyes all lit up and leering like a judge at a bathing beauty contest. "What's all this?"

"Looks like you got another divil on your tail," said Nany. She gave Fiorelli the once over and looked as though she'd just licked an ashtray.

"Thank you, ma'am, for your cooperation. We may call on you later once we know more." Ren tried his best to sound official.

"Wow. Boss is gonna be awful interested in this, Larson," Fiorelli said.

Nany approached him with her arms across her chest.

"Who have we here? Ain't no one say you can come in! Now get out."

"Okay, old-timer," Fiorelli said. Then he postured himself as though she were armed and dangerous. "Why don't you just take a breather? Go back to your snake charming or your crystal ball."

Nany closed her eyes and held a palm out toward him, then she moved her hand around as though she were somehow sensing something beyond him—through him. She tilted her head and raised her eyebrows. "Man of the law, are you? Nany seen it. A lady friend. Blonde. She's not the wife. You paying her not to tell." Nany opened her eyes. "Now, who's charming the snake?"

"What the… how'd you..? You looking to aggravate an officer in the line of duty?" Fiorelli asked. He looked pallid, and his eyes shifted left and right.

"No one is aggravating anyone," Ren said. "Jeez, Fiorelli. Lighten up. Can't you see she's just some old kook? Come on, let's get out of here. She was a dead end, anyway." Ren tried, but Fiorelli would not let some old, black woman get the best of him. Ren knew that this guy couldn't take the slightest insult, even when everyone realized he had the upper hand.

"Dark thingum already got the scent of you now. Hanging close to this one, it got to know you. It likes the taste of lies, and you're ripe with them," she said. "Gonna just eat you up, it will!" She growled.

"All right, that's it."

Fiorelli turned the old woman around and snapped his handcuffs around her thin, loose-skinned wrists. He fitted the key in the double locks to make sure she couldn't loosen them and do something foolish, or tighten them to hurt herself and claim he did it to her.

"What are you doing? She hasn't committed any crime. You gotta let her go," Ren said.

"Are you kidding me? Threatening an officer? Disorderly conduct? Let's see if she's so willing to sass off once she's behind bars at county."

"She's no threat, Fiorelli. Come on, let's just get out of here," Ren said.

Nany squirmed, but Fiorelli held her by her thin shoulders.

"You hear that accent?" Fiorelli asked. "And look at that headdress. Probably isn't here legally, anyway. Not from around here, are you, honey? Even if she's not a threat, she's perpetrating a public fraud with this whole spiritualist set up. So maybe some jail time will cool this old bitch down."

"You watch your mouth," Nany said. "Nany didn't do nothing! More lies from a liar. The thingum is gonna find you nice and juicy."

Fiorelli shoved her forward, and she stumbled. Unable to balance or brace herself, she fell onto her knees. The old stained carpet took a good share of her baggy skin, leaving her with shiny red kneecaps that oozed red streaks down her shins.

He dragged her down the hall and all five levels of stairs. She shouted for help the whole way, but no one came out of their rooms.

The bright sunlight hit them all like a blazing headache as soon as Fiorelli wrenched open the hotel door. There was a strong scent of water evaporating from the sidewalk and date palms over-ripening in the last of the late November sunshine.

It took a moment for Ren to adjust his eyes. But as soon as he did, he spotted the husky black sedan with silver trim on its curved, snouted hood. It was the same one that followed him and nearly ran him over in the hills. There it was, parked right across the street, with the morning sunlight glinting off the vehicle's mirror finish. An elderly nun dressed in a black and white habit stood watching with a skin-crawling intensity. She slipped into the car and shut the door. The engine purred to life, and she peeled off toward the downtown. At first, Ren thought his mind was playing tricks, but in the back seat of the sedan, face and hands pressed to the window, was Haddock. He seemed to be screaming and then pounding on the rear oval window as the car sped away.

Ren ran out to the street, following the vehicle as far as he could. He shouted after it. "Hey! Hey!"

"The fuck you doing, Larson?" Fiorelli shouted after him.

Ren jogged back and put his hands on his knees, huffing the whole time.

"Did you see that?"

"What?"

"Didn't you see that nun?"

"What damn nun, Larson? Come on, let's take this old bat in."

"It was—didn't you see that car? The nun in that car?"

"Jesus H. Christ, Larson. We've got a live suspect in custody, and you're chasing down vehicles on foot. You're a real piece of work."

"No. In the back seat. You didn't see…?"

"I saw nothing. Got that? Nothing."

He flopped Nany like an old onion sack into the back seat of the vehicle and didn't bother with whether or not she might have hit her head. But despite her stinging knees and the disgrace of being hauled off like a mongrel, she held her face like stone.

Nine

Los Angeles, 1947
Sometime After It Happened

The priest shifted in his little shadowed cubicle behind the screen and thought about moving himself further away from her.

"I am penitent, Father. There's a place in my soul that fears what I've done, so I am penitent. And I feel shame. Yes, I think I might feel a bit of that, too." She took out a pack of cigarettes, popped one between her lips, and snapped a lighter until it torched up.

"Sister, what are you doing?"

"Breaking one more rule won't change the outcome. I know where my soul will go. Penitence of the heart can't erase indelible stains or change the damage that's already done to others, can it, Father? So what's one more transgression for a doomed woman? One last smoke before the firing squad…." She took a long drag and puffed the fumes through her nostrils.

"Sister, please. This is a church."

She took one last puff and snuffed the coal out on the floor with her shoe. "Fine, Father. It wasn't improving the stench of 'holiness' anyway. Unburdening my soul didn't turn out as I expected. I thought I'd be feeling lighter by now, you know? Instead, this is going like surgery without anesthesia. So forgive me if I need a little bracer before I describe some of the… less savory details."

Germany, 1591

The cold seemed unbearable and bone-crushing that winter's night. The air was a misty blackness, a mix of frost and new-fallen snow. It was not a night anyone would be out wandering unless there were some urgent need. Yet there Philipe stood in the doorway of Margurite's place. It was formerly Johann's, but he'd been gone for months now. He'd met his end at the hangman's noose. Philipe shivered and seemed to have lost control of it, despite being wrapped from head to toe in thick black woven woolens and being heavily heaped across his broad shoulders with furs. In his frostbitten hands, the knuckles and the webbing between the fingers cracked and bleeding from the cold, he held the wood-bound book.

"I… I don't know why you should have this. I don't know why I brought it," he said. The words came out as a staccato between bouts of chattering teeth. His face, blueish in a particular light, was a picture of confusion. He seemed unable to believe his own hands, or his own words, as though each were foreign and wrong.

Margurite stood in the doorway, dressed in nothing but her loosely draped undergarments. She exposed one of her soft white breasts. She had rehearsed the move before so it would look accidental. She held a candle in one hand and guided it close enough that he might inspect her flesh for himself. He only noticed the candle briefly, as though it were part of a dream, and in it, Margurite had carved the candle from top to bottom with a knife. The carvings were strange words and peculiar shapes. He didn't care much about what she carried while she illuminated her bare nipple in the candle's glow.

Philipe's gaze turned to artless want. He knew the sin he was committing. He knew the word of God by heart, and as he licked his dry lips, he tried to speak passages of prudence. But instead, his tongue burned and dried in his mouth. It felt to him as though he'd become sodden from too much drink, though he could not say why.

"Why, Philipe," Margurite said, "have you brought me a gift?" She shrugged at her white shift, and her breasts popped back inside with a small bounce. Her nipple probed against the thin broadcloth, and Philipe realized he could not think of anything else. His lips parted slightly with the barest tip of his tongue.

With her free hand, she snatched the book from his slacking grip. "Goodnight, Philipe. Time to go." Then she blew out the candle and shoved the door closed.

He turned, dutifully strode back down the steps, and began trudging his way through the icy night, still confused by what had made him steal the book from the magistrate, and even more, what had made him cut the man's throat and leave him to bleed out. It was some sorcery, yes.

As he waded through the new snow, he watched his hands move, as though they were under a control not his own. They removed his garments, one layer after another. Still, he pressed on, bare black-footed and bleeding, until he marched utterly naked. By then, he was a field away from Margurite's door. He turned back to look for her face, for her bare breasts. She might have been in one of the windows. Just then, Philipe fell to vomitus fits, projecting quarts of dank gut blood into the snow until he could neither see nor move anymore.

Los Angeles, 1947
Two Days Before It Happened

Dusk began to make its presence known in the hills, with all its ghostly sounds and soft, wild fragrances. Ren buckled beneath the full weight of what had happened earlier while he parked his old two-door automobile down the street, just out of sight from the house. He popped open the glove box and thumbed the prescription bottle from Hoot's Druggist. What had happened today in Griswold's office—that he'd found himself on thin ice—he'd keep from Gloria.

He considered spending the night in the car, hoping she wouldn't miss him. He should never have told her about the possibility of promotion because now that chance seemed nearly impossible—for either of the men. Ren needed that carrot to dangle, especially after all she'd been through with him lately. He wouldn't snatch from her the promise of a promotion and a fresh start away from their Hollywood Hills nightmare until the option had been good and snuffed out.

Ren took some consolation in having witnessed Fiorelli catch grief from Griswold, too.

Both men had taken the Sarge to the very edge of his patience. Fiorelli's account of Ren cavorting with some old spirit-trumpeter for a tea leaf reading then chasing a church vehicle on foot seemed at first like a blatant smear. It might have been, if Fiorelli had made the same complaint about any other officer. But given the recent reports about Ren, the Sarge found it hard to dismiss entirely.

Griswold found it equally troubling to conclude that "the old genie"—as Fiorelli called her—plausibly posed a threat enough to provoke him. Griswold strained to understand Fiorelli's rationale to go rough up an old woman half his size and twice his age. He confirmed his suspicion that Fiorelli was both a hothead and a loose cannon.

Because Ren and Fiorelli had generated this incident in public, and it had resulted in a citizen's injury, they both received official warnings—just one step away from suspension. Griswold released Nany without a record.

Meanwhile, Griswold's secretary had received word from Dr. Kelly about Ren, but he didn't have a mind to address that matter just yet. He still had to calm down the broader situation with the higher-ups. And to make matters worse, he now had to handle ordinary citizens who'd read the papers and wanted to learn what actions the police were taking to stop the "Satanic murders."

Ren scrunched down in his front seat and allowed his neck to lie on the leather backrest. He swallowed one of Doc Kelly's pills. Then another. He fished more through the glove box, found his flask, and downed what he'd left swirling at the bottom. He guessed it might have been whiskey at one time, though it now tasted like rubbing alcohol from too many days left in the California heat. The leftover dribble burned and numbed while passing down, which was all Ren needed.

After Griswold had chewed him and Fiorelli out, Ren had left to find Nany in the station lobby. She was plopped on a flat, institutional wood bench and held two cold compresses on each bloody knee. He'd offered to take her to a hospital or back to the hotel. After what she'd been through, he realized it was the least he could do. She had refused the hospital, saying that she had "better things to do" back in her room.

So he took her back to the Downtown HOT, and they drove along in an exhausted silence for a long while. She watched out her passenger window with a finger to her bottom lip, and to Ren, she seemed antsy and conflicted. Finally, she seemed to have decided about something, and she spoke.

"You tried to do a good thing for Nany. Yes."

Ren shook his head. "What thing?"

"For one man to tell another that's he's done something wrong is hard to do. Sometimes dangerous, man to man."

"Well, it wasn't right, what he did. It wasn't right."

"Nany saw blood in the man's eyes—a blackness. Not for me, but for every woman who ever stands in his way. Not the first time he take a fist to someone—and I don't need no throwing bones to tell me that. Hard for Nany to say it, but thank you."

Nany nodded, and her face drifted back to looking at the passing city scenery. Ren withdrew the folded-up newspaper from his coat pocket, and it opened up on the seat between them to the photo of Haddock's blood-splattered room. She only skimmed it briefly with a passing curiosity, then returned to scanning the scenery.

"You seem to know a lot about strange things," Ren said. "I'm still having a hard time imagining you wouldn't know a single thing about this."

Nany made a short hissing sound and shook her head. "You're not blaming an old woman for this, are ya? You expect an old woman climbs the walls and paints blood on the ceiling?"

Ren gave a short sigh. "No, I didn't expect it was you, specifically. But I hoped you'd noticed a few details—anything about the incident, or the night. Like how that whole family got into that room with no one seeing or hearing them."

"That night was quiet—until the hallway full of screams. Charlene was in her room and come see Nany when the screams start. No one else live on the fifth floor. They all move out. Building's comin down with the wrecking ball, they say."

The drive continued in silence until Nany spoke. "He was a good man?"

"Yes, you might say that."

"Someone you cared for? A friend?" She looked out of the corners of her eyes.

Ren nodded.

"Hard to lose someone close to ya, isn't it?"

Ren had to look away. The sting of tears he'd held back for a full day began to surge up. Now that a bit of time had passed and the events had sunk in, he began plunging through the void of his loss. All he had left of Haddock and his family was some lousy funeral. The brutality and ugliness and inexplicability disturbed him deeply. Ren swallowed hard, trying not to let the floodgates loose in front of his passenger.

"I can tell you this. The thingum in the mirror—you see what it is, don't ya?"

"What?"

"Don't play a fool, copp'r. You know the one. It watches you from the glass. You listen to me?" she asked. Her sudden words sliced through the car's insular stillness. She didn't look at him but continued to hold a gaze on whatever passed outside her window.

"What?" Ren asked. He understood her, but admitting so might mean he agreed with her ghost stories, and that wouldn't do.

"Only one thing brings a divil round like that," she said. "A terrible sin. Only you know what ya done, isn't that right, copp'r? A divil smells a terrible sin like chum in the water. It comes to eat it. And if you haven't come to rights on what you done, if you haven't got the terrible thing out of you, then it eats you, too."

She'd pushed Ren into silence. He didn't want to respond either. If he did, he'd veer dangerously close to insulting her. How could he hold anything against an old woman with a glowing imagination and an unstoppable tongue full of fanciful tales? Neither Haddock nor Fiorelli were at the root of his upset, either. He held himself accountable for what had happened—for not knowing his friend better—for not noticing anything that would have warned him Haddock was on the edge. He should have had his partner's back, just as much as Haddock would have had his. A dreadful sunken hollowness radiated from his stomach, and he considered that might become a permanent feature—and maybe he deserved that to happen.

Nany's words rang through him like the clang of an enormous bell. The echo would not stop. Once he drove up to Nany's hotel, she got out and marched away without so much as a backward glance.

♦

Ren plunged through the night sky, along with all the rest. Jetting through the night air, there only existed weightlessness that put his stomach in his mouth. He was surprised to realize the awful appeal of zooming through the darkness, no sound save for the rush of air. Ren once learned that from afar, death was a fearful specter. But once upon you, death had a magnificence to it. He realized the truth in it now that he could taste his funeral so close at hand.

Moments before, inside the aircraft hull, chaos had ensued. Sparks and bullets flew. Men shouted all at once, different commands, none of which seemed right, and all of which might have been. The engines finally sputtered and stilled. The plane glided, but everyone sensed the ocean rushing up to meet them.

They'd have to leave a couple of men behind, like luggage on the Titanic. Bullets riddled them, and their bodies slumped on the punctured aircraft floor. The rest of the men took their chances jumping by parachute, falling amid the stars. The sky was sick with them. Polished and sparking—there were more of them hanging in that sky than he remembered seeing as a boy. Instead of fear gripping him, he marveled at the universe—such a pretty thing to see before he met his end.

He wasn't sad. At that moment, emotion evaporated. All that existed was falling, falling, and the sound of wind rushing past, pulling on his uniform and his cheeks. Then there came the sound of the plane smashing into the waves.

Ren saw that the others had ripped their cords already, and one by one their chutes puffed open. Mushrooms in the sky. He had a passing thought he might not pull the cord. That way, he'd keep on soaring, and then things like bullets that spray into airplanes just to wipe out faceless men might no longer be so.

He fell past a soldier. He didn't know which one.

"Pull it," the man shouted. Did the other soldier say this, or did Ren call it out in his own voice to awaken himself from this trance? Then Ren got dragged by a sudden and unseen violence. It came as an up-jerk that squashed his testicles and forced him to catch a frozen breath. He sensed a deeper coldness welling up. He recognized the reaction as fear, finally catching up and ballooning open like a parachute deep inside his guts. The sensation made him yack up sour chunks of something, even though he hadn't eaten a single thing that day.

Ren thought the air slowed, then there came a polar plunge into the water so cold it might burst organs. The chute settled atop the churning sea, and the agitation caused it to take on water. Ren unhooked himself in that underwater; his face felt like it was frying and peeling beneath the frigid white caps. He could not find his way from beneath the undulating tangles of silk. They clung to his face and found their way around his forearms. They swallowed him and pulled him into the darkness, but little else told him whether he moved up or down.

He hadn't taken a breath before his plunge. His lungs seared and jerked forcefully, urging him to take a breath. Still, in his world, there was only infinite ocean darkness on all sides.

In a strange and sudden shift, Ren found himself in the light, sitting in Dr. Kelly's waiting room with the wincing greenish fluorescent above. The glass slid with a somber frosty scrape. No one sat behind it. The nurse wearing the nun's white veil opened the door leading to the exam rooms. Her head lowered, and she folded her deathly pale hands across her abdomen in silent prayer.

"Mr. Larson," she said, but her mouth did not move. Her voice had a reptilian rasp to it. "Follow me, please."

She turned and went down the hallway with its black and white checkerboard flooring and its pressing walls. Ren followed, but he didn't know why. He walked past an exam room on his right. The door stood open. He saw another nun, also dressed in a white veil and uniform, but blood drenched hers. She hunched behind an exam table with Haddock's mauled and mangled body writhing atop. She unhinged her jaws like a python, and she flashed her top row of spiked fangs while she gnawed on one of his ripped-off arms. Blood drooled down both her chin and his lopped-off stump, and it pooled past her fingertips onto the table. She had already torn one of his legs off. Ragged bloody tendrils of muscle, skin, and flesh spilled out from what was ripped away. Haddock writhed in torment, and his eyes pleaded for help while he mouthed words Ren could not hear. "Watch you night and day." That's what Ren thought he said.

But Ren saw no particular urgency to help his old friend. Already done for, that's what Ren thought—but the detachment seemed out of character. Even more so, there was a growing pit of rage, intense, cold, building up like a hydrogen bomb compressed to an explosive degree and ready to detonate. He realized this animosity wasn't his own. This pain was transplanted like an old, dried-up patch of sod plopped down in the middle of a dew-kissed lawn.

Haddock deserved this was Ren's first thought. He had killed the innocent. His soul was ripe with sin, and now he'd feed the damned with his juicy, blackened soul. Along with these thoughts, a flood of fury burst through Ren like an untamed, fast-moving river. It troubled him that the experience started to seem natural. And comfortable. More than that, he began to sense a form of power mingled snugly between these troublesome thoughts and feelings—unlimited, dark, and dangerous power—a rush of it, though he could only taste the honeyed tip. A twisted strength arose in him from this rage, enough to defy the order of the universe.

He passed another door on the left. This, too, was left open. On the table sat the old bum with his Bible and his bits of paper. Mr. Gray. His head lay severed from his body, and another nun in white garb held it up and fed on the flesh from the bloody part. Fresh red drippings smeared her face like a wolf that didn't concern itself with how sloppy it got when it devoured a carcass.

While she held the head, its eyes opened. They were milky, the iris covered over by a thick, creamy liquid that began to run down from the sockets. "Watch you night and day, they do," Gray said. Or he tried to, through a gurgle of blood and the fluids that form with decay.

An awful dread overcame Ren. A pulse began thumping in the back of his neck and at his temples. His limbs felt immobilized. Against his will, a force drew him forward, as if by a conveyor belt, drawing him further down the hall to the door at the end. The door shook by an unseen hand, then it ceased. It creaked open inward, and Ren could see that inside, beyond the door, was a more welcoming, softer light. He heard rollicking men's laughter that rolled and boomed. Glasses clanked together, and the room stank of cigars and armpits. The men spoke in some other language, but it sounded familiar.

He pushed on the door, and inside was a round table covered in cards and beer mugs. Four men sat around the table, while one stood and slammed his hand down. He yelled at the other men in that other language, and they all laughed at him in an explosive chorus. Two of the men threw their cards at the one having the tantrum, but they fluttered away in all directions. Then there was more raucous laughter.

Most of them wore thin, sweat-stained t-shirts. Cigars and cigarettes clung to their bottom lips. Several legs stuck out from below the table, and Ren could see the crisp creases of an officer's pants, and shining military boots, all black. One, who had removed his shirt altogether, wore a black military hat with a short, gleaming brim and white piping. At the center front of the hat, there was a silver eagle perched atop a laurel wreath surrounding a bold black geometric figure. It was the hooked cross the Germans liked to use to symbolize their party, their new war machine. The room was thick with a silvery haze of smoke and belched breath.

The sore-headed soldier drank the last of his beer and banged the mug down. He slid a revolver he had lying casually on the tabletop over to another seated soldier. That one, fat and greasy, looked pallid, like someone had asked him to shoot a dog. But because the others watched and jeered, he pretended he wasn't afraid, and loaded the gun with the single bullet that the shirtless officer threw at him amid the ruckus.

Ren lay on the rough plank floor, his body restrained in a web of rope. Handcuffs restrained him behind his back, too tight and too sharp—slicing into his wrists. Then men had stuffed an old pair of ripe boxers into his mouth. The nervous, fat one scuffed over and snapped the gun's barrel into position. The shirtless soldier stood impatiently and knocked his chair back to the floor with a terrible wooden clatter. He nabbed the revolver from the fat one, spun the gun's barrel with a cold gleam, and held the weapon to Ren's head.

Click.

Ren could barely catch his breath. He writhed, and the shirtless soldier kicked him hard in the stomach. Ren struggled to remain alert. He sensed he might slip into that familiar darkness that he hated, but that might serve to protect. But he couldn't let himself go. He might die and be lost forever in that nebulous, purgatorial dark-between.

The shirtless soldier blurted more to the fat one, and he slapped him. This made the fat soldier huff and try to harden himself by grinding down on his teeth. He spun the barrel and held it to Ren's temple. His hands and face shook and dripped with sweat.

Click. Click.

The men roared again with laughs and threw beer at the fat soldier. He staggered backward into the table, sliding it a bit, and set the gun down with a clatter. The shirtless one stacked the cards, split them, and riffled them back together with a casino dealer's practice. He drew a single one out and held it to his chest. The others slapped the fat one on his back to encourage him to take his turn. Once he drew it, he turned it upright for the others to see. When the other soldier revealed his card, the men went wild, laughing and shoving one another. The fat one had to take another turn. The one next to him shoved the revolver in his hand again and spun the barrel one last time. He needed to use his arms to steady himself to stand. He reached down and placed the cold barrel to Ren's head.

Click… click.

Ren sat upright in bed as though struck by lightning. He was panting, and his sweat soaked through the sheets. He held a trembling hand to his mouth, swung his legs over the bedside, and reached for the bottle on the nightstand.

Sounds came from the bedroom, somewhere in the dark corners. Ren lay back and tried to reach for the gun—the extra one he'd hidden under the mattress in case of dangerous situations. He kept reaching, but it wasn't where he'd left it hundreds of times before.

Click… Guk. Guk.

"Ren, what's the matter?" Gloria asked. She propped herself up on her elbows. "Ren?" She sat up and watched him. "Ren, what's the matter?"

He said nothing more. The weird sounds suddenly died.

"Did you hear that?" he asked.

"Hear what?"

Ren turned to Gloria. She had a concerned look but smiled a little smile for him. From the corner of her mouth fell something small and white. The little object patted onto her pillow. Another fell from her mouth. He wondered if these were teeth.

"Gloria? What's that?"

"What's what?" she asked. A spoonful more of the small things fell downward, splatting in a pile on the mattress. "There's nothing, Ren. I don't hear anything." She froze, tuned in to the quiet, and touched his arm. "But if it will make you feel better, I'll go check on Molly. You lay back and relax. Okay?"

She pulled back the covers, noticing nothing else, and padded down the hallway.

Ren snapped on the lamp and looked at the pillow to know what fell from his wife's mouth. Maggots squirmed together on her pillow. Not only that, but flies swarmed the room. He jumped out of bed and swatted at the ones that had landed on the wall above the bed.

"Shit!" He swatted the maggots from the sheets, but they writhed in scattered clumps across that mattress. He didn't want the flies to invade the house further, so he switched from maggot-swatting to flinging open the window to shoo them out.

Gloria trotted back, hearing Ren's expletive. "What is it?"

"Jesus, Gloria. Look at this!" He swatted the sheets more.

"How did this happen?" She looked like she'd eaten rotting meat, and she covered her mouth.

"I turned on the light, and...." He gestured.

"We were lying in that?" she asked. She noticed that they were in her hair. She gave a short, disgusted cry, raced to the bathroom, and turned on the shower.

Ren gathered up the sheets, carefully keeping the vermin inside, and he shook them into the trash cans at the side of the house. He stuffed the bedding down and came back inside to find Molly standing on the other side of the door. She was in her flannel sleep-shift, and she gently rubbed her eyes with the back of her hand.

"Daddy? Why is everyone awake?"

"It's nothing, honey. Let's go back to bed."

He turned her around and guided her down the hall. That was when he noticed several maggots crawling through her hair, too. He took a steadying breath to calm a growing sense of urgency.

"Stay here. Don't sit on anything. Just stay here," Ren said. He left her next to a living room lamp that he clicked on for her.

Dead panic set in. The foul insects heaped onto Molly's bed. But worse, his pistol was lying in the center of her mattress. Molly didn't know where he kept the gun hidden, so the possibilities were few. If Gloria knew this, she would insist on leaving this nightmare right then and there. And she would be right, at this point. But he couldn't admit to her where he stood with his boss at this moment. He might not have a job at all if he didn't make serious progress on the case. If Gloria were scared enough, she might force the issue of leaving. That move would wipe Ren out financially. If that happened, he'd probably never see Molly again.

While Gloria scrubbed herself in the shower until her scalp was raw, he disposed of Molly's squirming insects in the trash. He changed her sheets, slipped the gun in the elastic waistband of his pajamas, and brought Molly back to bed.

"Daddy, why were you making the bed at nighttime?" she asked.

Ren sat down at her bedside. The light from the hallway cast a long, geometric sliver that fell across her bed and onto the wall closest to her.

"This is only a dream, Molly." He stroked her hair and hoped the lie would work. "Go back to sleep." She shifted to her side. Her eyelids fluttered, and soon enough, her breathing was deep and peaceful.

That was when a symbol on the wall stood out. The design

dripped down in crimson strings above Molly's head. It was similar to what he had seen in recent days, though this was decidedly more distinct—a double circle with the letters *A-N-D-R-A-S* around the outer portion. The inner circle contained a complex squiggle of intersecting lines, smaller circles, crosses, and arrows. A fly landed in the ring and fed on the syrupy blood.

He stuffed down his urge to scream, and his blood began to freeze. Of course this wasn't Molly's doing. So someone else was in their house again. Slowly he drew down Molly's sheets to determine whether she'd somehow cut herself, or whether someone did this to her. Far down the mattress, by her feet, he discovered a hypodermic needle; blood filled the glass barrel. The nun at Doc Kelly's had used one like this to draw his blood. This was his blood on the walls, he realized. Before Gloria finished and wandered in to witness the scene, he ran to the kitchen and wet a dishcloth to erase any evidence. He clicked off the lamp in the living room, and immediately the house filled with an inky darkness.

He started on the wall, scrubbing, trying not to wake his child. Red smeared everywhere.

"Ren?" Gloria called. Her voice sounded from the hallway.

He had to hurry now, or she might get a look at the mess. "Yeah, Gloria. I'll be right there. Just give me a second."

"Ren?" she called again without saying more.

He would have to step out of the room to block her from coming in.

"Just a second," he said. He hid the blood-stained wash cloth under Molly's bed and entered the hallway. The lamp in their bedroom was turned off now, and the house was too dim for him to make anything out at the other end.

"Gloria? You all done?" She didn't respond. "Everything all right?"

He took a few more creaking steps, and against the shadowy light coming in through their bedroom window, he noticed an outline. What stood there was a near-human figure. Ren initially

reasoned it was Gloria, but something rang out like a fire alarm in his mind, something that made him want to run. The shape occupying that darkness had a thin chest that heaved while it panted and gasped, like an animal that had spotted its prey, excited for the kill.
"Gloria? ...Are you all right?" The creature clung to the bedroom door with its wiry arms stuck to the surface, its claws gouging into the wood.

Click. Guk. Guk.

The sounds caused Ren's stomach to bubble up with a foul paste. This was neither his wife nor a trespassing nun. "Gloria?" He crept forward one more awful step, straining to identify what waited for him in the dark.

"Police," he said. The wheezing stopped. Even the crickets outside had ceased their eternal evening song. "I've got a gun," Ren said. He heard his voice tremble.

Click. Click. Guk. "Ren? Why? Why can't we leave?" Whatever this was, it spoke with Gloria's voice.

Ren stopped and glimpsed the horrid incarnation, the monstrous mutation that clutched the door with its long, boney fingers. Its back was a spiny hump that heaved with each of its stale, wheezed breaths.

Ren saw that face, or what the beast had in place of one. It was a mass of black blistered skin, putrid boils piled atop one another. It had no recognizable facial features, and the head looked more like a beehive or a melted blob atop a neck. Soon a hole developed where a mouth ought to be, and from that, a black, wet ooze dripped to the floor. The dark hole bore rows of sharp metallic teeth. Several dead-white eyes blinked open across its gnarled forehead, and it locked onto Ren with a hateful glare.

Ren turned and broke into a sprint the other way down the hall. A scream tried to form in his throat, but it could not find its way out. Something primal had overtaken his whole body, and the only objective he understood now was... run. He sprinted like a maniac to keep from being overtaken by the beast.

He boomed down the wooden floors and listened to the

monster in sickening pursuit. Its foot-claws scraped and slid for traction. Cold dribbling from the creature splatted on Ren's neck, and he knew he would soon feel its claws ripping into him. He slid into the kitchen and grabbed the doorjamb leading to the family room, using it to re-direct his forward trajectory. His gun skated away on the kitchen floor, into the darkness.

He knew he had to double back to the entryway closet, where he kept another pistol. The hall had gone silent. He stood, and there was the monster clinging onto the kitchen wall, watching him with those many eyes, heaving for its breath. Then it exploded into a cloud of flies that swarmed down the hallway back toward the bedroom. It seemed to have known Ren's thoughts, and it sped to reach the closet before him.

Ren ran around the other side, through the living room to the front closet—though he wondered in that short time whether the gun had bullets, or even whether they'd work to stop this monstrosity.

Ren grabbed a nearby iron floor lamp topped with a decorative spear-shaped finial. He charged toward the closet, holding the makeshift spear forward to wound the thing and give him time to nab the gun. The flies emerged from the hall and assembled into the unearthly beast, which then shrieked. It stood to the side of the closet as though guarding the gun beyond the door. It eyed Ren's weapon and tilted its head in amusement.

Click. Guk. Guk. "Ren, can't we leave?" it said like Gloria. Then it flicked out a long, snake-tongue while sizing things up with those scattered, inhuman eyes. It yawned open its fang-studded maw and hissed.

Ren did not wait to find out what would happen next. He charged with the lamp-spear and struck the beast in its abdomen. He heard a cracking noise, followed by a sloppy wet sound. Ren backed away and saw that he had pierced the creature clean through. But it seemed unaffected and licked the air with its forked tongue while withdrawing the long pole from its abdomen. A black ooze gushed from the wound. The beast dropped the pole and trembled as two more sets of arms sprouted from its sides. It tipped forward and scuttled up the wall like a scorpion. Then it clung to the ceiling.

While it repositioned itself, Ren lurched for the closet door, swung it open with reckless haste, and scraped the gun off the top shelf. He let loose several rounds into its body.

Just then, a light snapped on, and Gloria stood next to the switch plate in her nightgown.

"Ren?"

As soon as the lights were on, Ren saw that he had shot a series of holes in an otherwise empty ceiling. He slumped to the floor, tugged for breath, and the thought rang through his mind like a frantic whisper: *There's no such thing. There's no such thing.*

Ten

Los Angeles, 1947
The Day Before It Happened

"You're the only one I can talk to," Ren said. He tried to keep his voice low, but he was talking to her from the other side of the door in the hotel hallway.

Ren rapped with his knuckles again.

"Please. I understand now. You were right. I don't know what this is, but it attacked my family. Please. Please let me in."

He reached in his pocket and pulled out Gloria's wedding ring, wiped his eyes, and used the ring to tap on the door. Whatever this was, this creature, this *divil* as Nany called it, had taken everything from him.

"Nany, don't leave me out here."

The pain in his head was searing. How much had he drunk? How many of Dr. Kelly's pills had he taken? Ren had no recollection. He told himself he wasn't going to drink anymore. It wasn't right—Kelly had told him not to mix his medicine with alcohol. Now he was so tired. There was no sleeping after Gloria left with Molly, headed to Maxine Ganz's house.

It all began to make sense like it does to someone emerging from a deep, dreamless sleep. A renewed sense of sickness arose once Ren realized how all of this might look or sound to anyone happening by. Yes, it was five-thirty in the morning, and Nany had told him not to expect anyone on that fifth floor except for Charlene, her tarot-reading friend and neighbor. Still, he scanned the area to determine whether anyone might be around laying eyes or ears on the situation. He realized he looked—unraveled—and he didn't want anyone to witness. The last thing he needed was another public inquiry about police behavior making its way to the Sarge.

He tried the door, and it held against the lock. Nany yanked it open as far as it might go against a security chain. In her haste, she'd left her head unwrapped, and exposed as it was, Ren noticed one side was hairless and stretched with old burn scars. One of her ears was a melted spot with a hole in it. The other side of her head was a flattened mess of gray hair.

"Wait," she said. She slammed the door, slid off the chain, and a few moments later, opened it again. "Keep it down, you damn fool. You want the whole world to hear your business?" She held a white turban and fitted it snugly across the scars. "Anyway, I told you all I know, and I ain't got anything more to say to you. Now go home." She began to shut the door, but Ren stopped her.

"No, wait. You're the only one who might know… Aw jeez… who might know what's happening," he said.

"I don't know nothing, copp'r. You go your way, I'll go mine. You done enough already."

"Please," he said. But Nany shut and locked the door again. Ren thought for a second and tried a harder tactic. "I'll have to come back with a search warrant. More cops, too. Pretty sure you don't have a permit. Card reading's still against the law. Comes with fines and jail time if I ask for it…. The other day, an old lady set up with a card table and a bedspread in Echo Park got hauled off."

He heard the door bolt click from the inside, but Nany didn't open it any more than that for him.

"Come in. And make it fast," she said from inside.

Ren pushed the door open to find her standing square in front of the door with her arms folded and her brow lowered. "Looks like you finally seen it, then." She laughed low and menacing. "Can't turn back the time on what's already been, copp'r."

"I'm sorry, can I sit down for a second?" Ren asked.

"You here, ain't ya?" She crossed over to her table and created a ring of roots around a colorful holy card depicting Michael the Archangel. Ren followed her and noticed that everything was ritually placed, and the tabletop was aglow with candles. He recognized the root because of its familiar foul odor.

"Where did you get that?" he asked.

"That's my High John the Conqueror, and you leave it be!"

"No, my housekeeper placed that in our house—in a bathroom."

"Did she? Now ain't that fascinating? Did you come here at the spirits' own break of sunlight to tell old Nany about your roots problem?"

Ren sat on one of the chairs gathered around the table and sighed. "I came to ask you—God, I don't understand anything that's going on."

"How's this Nany's business?"

"You're the one who said something was after me. You said it was coming."

"You talking about thingums in the mirror? Things I already told you about? I don't repeat myself. Not my fault you got something in ya the thingum wants. Told you already what you need to do to stop it."

"There's no such thing as monsters or 'divils' or anything like that. There can't be, for Christ's sake. I'm not one of your customers looking for some island fairy tale!"

"Hmm." Nany shook her head and began to chuckle. "It's all in your head, right copp'r? Nany tells too many stories, isn't that right? Nothing a good bottle of whiskey wouldn't fix. Check your glovebox again. Now go home."

Ren stood speechless that she'd known he kept alcohol in his car.

"I can't... I can't..." he began to say. Then his words turned into sobs, and he hid his face in his hands. She noticed the missing wedding band and a white line on his finger where it used to be. Ren reached into his pocket and extracted his prescription bottle. He rattled it a bit in his hand. "Do you have any water?"

"You gonna take that and numb your mind? Be my guest. Only don't do that here," Nany said.

Charlene swooped through the back entrance between her and Nany's rooms. "Zolva, what in Endor's name is happening at this hour?" She eyed Ren and pulled her slinky black nightgown to hide whatever it was she though Ren might see.

Nany stood in silent regard for Ren's outburst. She limped over to a stained sink at a wall that had a small kitchenette, and she spooned ground coffee from a canister into a pot.

"No need for ya help, Charlene. Go back and lock your door—and don't listen from the other side either. Ya got it?"

"Very well," she replied. She swooshed back through the beaded curtain, first turning before she went. "But remember, 'he is like a villain with a smiling cheek, a goodly apple rotten at the heart,'" she said. She glared at Ren in a look of warning, then she shut the door between the rooms.

Nany went back to puttering at the sink with that limp. Ren noticed that her knees were much more swollen than before, thanks to Fiorelli. Making coffee wasn't the response Ren had expected. The silence gave him a moment to realize that he was lashing out in the wrong moment with the wrong person. He peered at the bizarre items and candles strewn across the tabletop and found his heartbeat slowing as he gazed into the flames. "I'm sorry," he said. "I'm just—I'm not myself."

"Hard to believe everything in the world, especially when some of the things in the world don't match up—quite right." She chuckled. The hot plate made an unnerving sound of electrical gyration when she switched it on. "You sure you're somewhere, and not nowhere at all? Flat Earth might be, too. And how's it things fall down rather than up? Ain't nothing to prove it else-wise, far as I can tell. Except going on what you see, what you touch, what you learn in a book, eh? Going by that, probably ain't no Mr. Crooked either, just as you say, copp'r. Just as you say."

Her words started to take root in the pit of his stomach and spread prickling tentacles of fear in his veins.

"Now, far as I can tell, Mr. Crooked is only an island story the old ladies like to tell. Copp'r ain't gonna be scared of no story, now will he?"

He forced his mind to calm by distracting himself. "What are you making there? Some kind of potion?" Ren asked. He needed to switch the conversation to anything—whatever might be more tangible and understandable.

She didn't fluster or bother to turn. "Could be. But at this hour, might as well make a cuppa joe," she said. "I make some for you, too."

"Oh, uh, yeah. Thank you," he said.

She puttered at the small counter and soon enough returned with a small white-enamel-coated tin mug and set it down on the table-altar within his reach. He used both hands to hold the cup to keep from trembling so hard it would shake out the drink. She sat across from him and sipped hers. She glanced at him from the corners of her skin-tagged eyes.

"Better check with your partner before you go off half-cracked about what you don't really know first-hand," she said.

"My partner?"

"Yeah. The man who tried to put Nany in jail. One who shoved Nany and bust her knees. That one. Fiorelli. How's he?" she asked. She raised her eyebrows.

"What does Fiorelli have to do with this?"

"Didn't say one way or the other," said Nany. She took another sip and hid her mouth in her mug. "Just that he may have more to tell ya about island tales right about now."

"What? What do you mean?"

"You really that stupid, copp'r? Or you already know what Nany says is true?"

Ren put the mug down. "I better go."

"You better. Go check your friend. Then you learn more about island tales, too. You have any more questions, you come back to old Nany. Only two dollars. Room 55." She laughed, sounding like the idling of a broken-down jalopy.

Ren wasted no time and sped through the pre-dawn streets of Hollywood. He'd been to Fiorelli's once before, so he was sure he'd remember the way. A few guys from the precinct had met there for a barbecue right around the start of last summer. He switched on the top lights of the car and held down the gas pedal with a furious foot. He crisscrossed several streets into the neighborhoods near the farming village of Prospect Park, which wasn't that far from Nany's hotel. Once there, he switched off the lights to reduce unwanted attention.

At the crest of the hill, Ren made out the glow of road flares. As he descended the slope, there were three official vehicles parked out front, some of them police, but an ambulance, too, and the coroner's vehicle. The top lights swirling at various speeds made the nearby shadowed trees look like slow-moving science-fiction creatures—men from Mars with their long tentacle arms outstretched.

He parked near the house and jogged up to the property. Ren's work buddies were keeping things quiet. The neighbors in their bathrobes and hair curlers gathered at the edge of Fiorelli's lawn to gasp, clutch their nightgowns, and whisper words to make themselves feel better. Things like, "Wasn't he a policeman?" "He seemed so respectable" and "Things like this don't happen around here."

He approached the tidy little bungalow's front door, dressed up with spiraling topiaries on either side. When he popped up the front steps, one of the younger officers stopped him. "Did they call you?"

he asked.

"You mean Griswold? Yeah, he did," Ren replied. "Can I get in yet?"

"Yeah," the officer said. "Guys from the Crime Lab haven't shown yet. So keep your hands to yourself for now."

The officer rapped twice with the back of his hand, and someone opened the door a crack. Ren slipped through sideways and entered the living room. The house was rank with the smells of death, and his pulse darted. When he turned, he faced a massive floor-to-ceiling blood-rendering of the symbol *A-N-D-R-A-S*. Other ritual markings similar to those he'd been seeing decorated the surrounding walls, dripping their syrupy crimson in long streaks. His blood went wild and throbbed a painful tempo in his neck.

"Bathroom," another officer said. He stood behind the opened door and pointed to another doorway with a bloody cross finger-painted across it. Ren paced across the room but felt there was a presence watching him. And that nauseating feeling intensified, the closer he came to stepping through the door.

The bathroom was neatly tiled pink and white, a suburban fantasy. The tub at the far end overflowed with a red-tinted brine. A delicate hand with glossy pink fingernails lay pale and still on the tub's rim. Ren approached and saw her mouth agape and the shocked blank eyes staring out at some last horror. Black swimming hair slowly twisted around her once-attractive features. Her hair flowed out of the way to expose the gaping flesh at her neck and the trachea opened. He looked down and noticed for the first time the shallow lake of bathwater on the floor that stained his shoes with her blood.

A surge of pinpricks shot down his arms and legs. All he could think of was to get out. And the more he resisted the urge, the more the pink-tiled walls seemed to squeeze in on him. The guys were all watching, and there would be talk if he did anything—anything odd at all. All he needed was to get over the hump, he told himself, only this once. He didn't have to slip into the dark-between, he reassured himself. But his insistence failed to overcome the cloudiness overwhelming his mind.

He braced himself by bending and propping himself with his hands on his knees. The officer from the front of the house spotted Ren crumpling. "Woah, hang on there," he said. The man splashed his feet in the blood-water, swooped a hand under Ren's armpit, hauled him across the living room, and ushered him out to the front porch. Ren leaned on the small white wrought iron handrail on one side of the front steps and took deep breaths until he sensed his mind dropping back out of the cloud of frenzy. The officer stationed at the front door spoke, but Ren heard nothing. Finally, Ren asked, "Where's Fiorelli?"

"That's what I've been trying to ask you," the officer said. "He's gone missing. Thought you might have some idea where he went."

"No. Not really," Ren lied. "Sorry, I… I need a breather." He caught his breath as though he'd been running a marathon. "Their daughter…" Ren said. He couldn't finish.

"Gone," replied the officer. He gave his head a slow shake. "You don't need to see the work going on in there either," he said.

Ren launched himself with his arms off the rail, and he lurched down the walkway, trying to command his muscles to obey. He wondered if he might be floating; he could not feel the concrete beneath him. His mind orbited the stratosphere. In his haste, Ren split the group of gathered neighbors in half as he passed through to a renewed round of gasps and pajama-clutching. He knew where Fiorelli might go, and he needed to stop him before anything more dangerous occurred. He stumbled into the patrol car and sailed away, siren sounding and twirling lights aglow.

♦

Ren felt as though he'd awakened from a deep sleep. His senses were sharp, and he felt urgency now that he'd snapped out of his benumbed state. He knew he had a good chance of slipping away, given he'd nearly done so at Fiorelli's. But he never imagined he'd disappear into that void while driving. The thought of it was enough to take his breath away. Now alert, he discovered that he was driving south on La Cienega, in the direction of the beach, which was an unnerving distance from where he had intended to go.

He pulled to the side of the road and tried to refocus himself. He glanced at his watch, preparing himself for the worst. Only thirty minutes had passed. Still, that was long enough for terrible things to happen.

It was still early enough that cars hadn't yet started pouring out onto the streets from the bungalow-lined neighborhoods. Only a few early risers happened by. Ren cranked the steering wheel as far to the left as he could and U-turned. He needed to head back to the downtown and make fast work of it.

He focused on each signal and street along the drive so he would not accidentally slip into those forgotten dark-between places. Just as he'd suspected, there was Fiorelli's beat-up 1930s four-door parked on the street at a deranged angle. He parked in front of the Downtown HOT and dashed in.

The lobby door was wide open, and he scrambled up the steps, taking two at a time until he reached Nany's floor.

"Get out of here, copp'r," she said.

"Just tell me what to do. Just tell me what to do." Fiorelli was like a whimpering dog. His arms looked as though he had dipped them in a pool of his family's blood, and his clothes were splashed and splattered with red. He'd drawn his pistol and held it low in one hand, pointed to the floor.

"Ain't nothing to do. I told you already. I don't know what you're going on about."

"Yes, you do. Yes, you do." His face was red, and his neck was bulging with blue and green veins. Then he caved inward and dissolved into a mess of tears.

Ren withdrew his own revolver and cocked back the hammer as gently as he could. But it still made a slight click.

"What was that? What was that?" Fiorelli screamed. He pointed his pistol all around, frantic and aimless.

Ren heard strange noises that came from somewhere in Nany's front parlor. *Glug. Glug-glug.* They were the sounds of something alive and submerged in water, air escaping its lungs.

"Oh God, oh God. Please make it stop!" Fiorelli dropped the pistol and clapped his hands to his ears. He stared upward at whatever seemed to be moving the room's dark corner.

"Stay where you are," Ren said. He tried to sound commanding. In his mind he was attempting to stabilize Fiorelli's incoherence. But he had lost more control than he thought. His voice came out as a shriek, and his face filled with unbearable blinding heat.

He was ready to take a shot, but at what, he wasn't sure. Then he spotted what had dropped Fiorelli to his knees. Hiding away in the depths of the room, in the shadows of the darkest corner, was the thing… that thing. It was pressed high on the wall near Nany's ceiling, suspended by nothing, and it changed forms. It started off with a nearly human shape, except horribly disfigured. Then it sprouted wings; it morphed into a spider big as a desk, and each of these was made up of hordes of buzzing flies, forming and re-forming themselves into the creature's different shapes.

Nany backed herself against another wall and made the sign of the cross over her abdomen while holding a bottle of rum. She clutched the strand of dried red-berry beads around her neck. Nearby, she found one of her stubbed-out cigars in an ashtray. She lit it up and then blew the smoke outward, and the smoke formed into a thin, undulating wall that separated her from the creature.

The flies formed into the dark, emaciated creature with the milk-glass eyes scattered across its head. It appeared to have an outstretched hand that elongated many times normal length as it clutched toward Fiorelli's face. Fiorelli tried shielding himself, sobbing, as the thing's arm burst into a jumble of flies that speckled the officer's head at first, then his whole body.

Ren watched as the flies crawled into his ears. Fiorelli's arms seemed frozen to his sides now, and he screamed in fiery agony and fell to the floor writhing. He struggled and gained control of his arms, then pounded at his ears with his fists. Then the flies re-routed and entered his mouth, his nose, even digging into the corners of his eyes. He arched backward in an unnatural bend that popped his spine in splintering cracks. His fingers curled into claws, and his eyes bulged, no longer white, but deep blood red. His neck muscles compressed, as though being choked by invisible hands.

His twisted fingers grasped his pistol that fell to the floor in his efforts to ward off the flies. Nany again puffed the cigar and blew smoke, and it fortified her protective layer.

"Oh God. Our Father, which art in heaven!" Fiorelli's prayer was choked out by the flies piling out of his mouth. But he kept trying to recite the awful, desperate prayer, as his arm shook against some invisible, fierce resistance. He struggled to form the words as he wrestled with something unseen. He stood up and barged past Ren, lurching down the stairs, falling and tumbling part of the way.

Ren and Nany followed him out to the street where Fiorelli fell to his knees and shoved the gun to his neck.

"Our Father, which…" Fiorelli's jaw clamped and blood flecked from his clenched teeth. He continued, though not with the Lord's Prayer. "*Zagan, Voso, Orobas, Caim, Andras,*" Fiorelli said, but not in his own voice. "*Baal, Agares, Marbas, Valefor…*" He vomited a gusher of flies.

Fiorelli observed the pistol from the corner of his eye. Someone else was doing this to him, and he struggled against an unseen hand. "Forgive me," he said. He thumbed the hammer back.

"No, stop!" Ren shouted.

Then Fiorelli pulled the trigger. Red sprayed out, then gushed down both sides of his neck, soaking onto the pavement. He flopped forward.

Nany stood at the front lobby door, holding the cigar, and she puffed out one last lung-full. The flies floated off, vanishing into the morning air as if they'd never been there at all. Fiorelli lay motionless, his head lolling to one side and his blood pooling in a brilliant red halo.

"Jesus Christ!" Charlene shouted. Ren could hear her heels clopping down the steps. She flew out of the door clutching her silk kimono. She gasped and put both palms to her mouth. "Call an ambulance!" she shouted as soon as she could collect herself enough to speak.

Eleven

Los Angeles, 1912
Thirty-Five Years Before It Happened

"To your room...."

Ren's mother wouldn't listen to the same complaint from him again. She pointed down the hallway as she commanded him. He'd already peeped his head out the door and tiptoed down the hall twice. The first time, the guests had started to arrive, and later, he snuck back when he thought they might be moving around the furniture.

"But it's early," he said. His mother chose not to register the protest. She put a red-polished fingernail to her lips and then pointed down the hallway again. Ren slogged and dallied back, and she followed until he closed the door.

He didn't want to miss out on *Tarocchi* night when all the women in attendance wore their most exotic perfumes and gaudiest jewelry. And the men boomed with raucous laughter and puffed cigar stubs until the whole house got lost in a blue haze. But that was only the first part of the night. After a while, they'd get quiet, all of them. He knew what they did after they'd moved furniture and emptied bottles of whiskey.

The neighbors said it once. They called his mother a "table tipper." At first, he thought it was an insult, believing that the term meant she had no manners at the dining table. But when he overheard a woman whisper that his mother had the ability to contact "the other side" and bring back lost loved ones for a final conversation, he recognized her special term evoked a sense of awe rather than slander. If what the woman said was true, then his mother was probably pretty good at it. He knew that because her sessions of Tarocchi increased from once monthly to five nights in a week with strangers and friends alike huddled around the candlelit hush of their living room.

As the word of his mother's talents spread and a demand for her services increased, the family began to travel to far-flung destinations. They stayed in hotels where maids and butlers attended to their needs. And they ate rare delicacies at dining establishments where his mother would require him to flatten his hair and comb it with a beeswax and mineral oil paste. But, when they returned home from their travels, and the sessions happened right in the next room of his own house, he didn't see how it was fair that he'd be sent to his quarters while mother did the task that brought her such fame and the family its good fortune.

"It's later than you think, darling," she said. "But I know what you're needing. Mummy forgot your treat," she continued. Then she handed him a cup of cocoa that she'd only make when he promised to stay in his room on such nights. Not long after that, he'd be asleep—a strange, dreamless sleep. By the next morning, the furniture would have returned to where it began, and all would be set to rights. His parents never discussed Tarocchi nights, nor the strange business of calling up the departed, not in front of Ren. If he brought the subject up, they'd suddenly develop an interest in anything else.

One time, when he'd not fallen all the way asleep, it sounded like the group of visitors were mumbling together. A whispered child's voice followed that and seemed to hang in the air, arising from nowhere and everywhere at the same time. The rapping noises began then. Whatever knocked did so all the way down the hall, closer and closer, until his doorknob twisted in the darkness. Ren fished out the spare key he had stashed under the mattress to lock the door so that whoever or whatever tested the knob could not get in.

He backed away and crept under the covers, layering them to leave only an opening for his eyes and nose. But within that relative shelter, he noticed that the bedding rustled, and not from anything he did. The sheets rose and fell on his shoulder, and he listened to the sound of someone wheezing—someone who seemed to be sick and lying in the bed with him. There was no use in watching the doorknob by the faint moon-glow any longer. Whatever it was on the other side of the door was already in the room.

Ren shivered in the dark with alarm, knowing that he was locked inside the room with this thing. The covers continued to rise and fall right along with the strange hissed breath. He shifted from where he lay, turning to one side so as not to disturb whatever made the noise. Though he was afraid, he felt compelled to turn, to see what had come from the dark hallway.

That was the first time he glimpsed the thing that would haunt him across his life. It reclined with its gnarled spine toward him. The creature seemed thin, with glistening, blister-piled black skin. Ren thought it might be roughly the size of an adult. The wheezing figure stretched out with one scraggly arm dangling along its side. The thing's sharp, cracked nails twitched to dig into something living, to rip its life to pieces. The thing looked emaciated. Its spine stuck out in lumps, and Ren watched its ribs expand and contract.

Ren heard it whispering odd words—the kind you'd hear a priest reading from the Bible at Sunday services. They were like those strange names that come from the book of Genesis, Ren thought. Perhaps the creature said prayers to the angels—and maybe the praying thing was an angel himself. After all, his mother would never call up anything less than an angel of God, would she?

"*Zagan, Voso, Orobas, Caim, Andras,*" it said. It rasped in a high-breathless voice, sounding like a broken concertina. "*Baal, Agares, Marbas, Valefor....*" The list seemed endless, and the thing sounded unable to stop its recitation.

Ren's blood turned to ice with the realization that this thing wasn't likely praying, not to the angels, anyway. Without ever having to turn and face Ren, the monster began to choke him with a fear that knocked the breath out of him. Either that, or Ren realized not to breathe, not to make a peep, or surely the thing would turn and devour him. The shouts for help Ren could not make paralyzed him further, even though his parents and their guests chanted just down the hall, only in the next room. His heart clung to his throat and thumped hard.

Using as much strength as he could, Ren covered his head with the bedspread, and he hoped the horrible thing would leave on its own. And anyway, such things couldn't be real, Ren assured himself, mainly to keep from screaming. So he lay in the dark with the uninvited guest by his side, rasping and reeling off its incessant words. And despite the numbing terror of the experience, the cocoa worked its magic and put Ren into a narcotic sleep.

That night, he dreamt in a series of nightmares, the kind that do not belong to a child.

Los Angeles, 1947
The Day Before It Happened

Ren zoomed through red lights and near-misses while Fiorelli sprawled half-dead in the back seat, his head lolling side to side with each turn in the road. His eyes twitched to stay open and rolled back; only the whites showed. His head rested on several torn towels from Nany's place, which had finally reached the limits of what they could sop up. She held another cloth to his neck, but his innards were bleeding through so that the bunched-up rag looked like a deformed extension flowering from his neck. Blood drained off the back seat and pooled onto the floor.

Once they pulled up to the hospital, medics fished Fiorelli from the car, laid him on a gurney, and wheeled him away. Ren filled out intake forms then took a seat next to Nany, who was plopped down on a waiting room bench along the corridor. Most detectives and the Sarge himself might suspect either him or Nany of shooting Fiorelli, each for their own good reasons. He'd watch his every word at this point, as whatever he said would likely make its way back to the Sarge.

After some time passed, an effervescent nurse with shining red locks spilling out the sides of her white cap leaned over the counter. She tickled the air with her index finger toward Ren. He scanned the area first to make sure that no one else was around.

The nurse curled her hair around her pinky and told Ren that Fiorelli was in critical condition and being transferred over to St. Cyprian's. "It's the hospital over there by MacArthur Park. We rarely transfer patients, but you see, they have a special treatment unit there," she said. "For people with his kind of difficulties."

"With 'his kind of difficulties'?" Ren asked.

"Well, I'm probably not the one who should tell you this, but seeing as you're a police officer and all…." She looked at him with her bright blue eyes and then looked away, demure. "You are a police officer, aren't you? Isn't that your big squad car outside?" Ren realized the come-on. Then she whispered, "Anyway, the doctor will tell you straight away, I'm sure. But the man had War Nerves. Worst case that I've seen, too—going by his records, anyway."

"What do you mean, War Nerves?" he asked. "The guy never served a day in his life."

"Well, the records say that Officer Fiorelli served in the 40th Infantry Division. The Sunshine Brigade, they call them. I think that name is just swell, you know, because of the sunshiny weather and all. It looks like he served time in Hawaii. See? Right there." She pointed to a line in a manila chart. "Looks like he'd come to this hospital before… something to do with too much opium…."

Ren felt his tongue swell up. "Op—opium?"

"He had a head wound back on the islands," she said. "Oh my. Well, anyway, Hawaii is a lovely place to visit, I imagine. Don't you, officer…?"

"Larson. Ren Larson." He extended his hand to her.

She blushed.

"Well, even though Hawaii is an absolute dream under any other circumstance, it's probably not so much for Officer Fiorelli. Terrible what happened at the harbor. I don't suppose any of those folks who live there will ever be the same, do you? Anyway, we see this kind of thing all the time. You know, some men just have a harder time adjusting back to civilian life. Oh, don't get me wrong," she went on, "St. Cyprian's treats mostly the mental cases. You know, the psychotics and the melancholia, and the ones who tried to rope their necks. Types like that. Poor things. But ever since the war, they started helping with the soldiers, too. I think it's real Christian of them since no one else knows what to do with them—so many of them."

She tilted up her black-rimmed cat's eyeglasses and placed a thoughtful finger on her cherry lips as if that were a method to stop them from going on too much.

"I suppose so," Ren said. "Well, thank you, miss. You've been very helpful." Then he propped Nany up to a stand, but she shot him a disapproving look. He gripped her by the arm and whispered to her. "We need to get out of here and stick together," he said. Nany didn't hear, or she chose to ignore him.

She finally stopped and drew her arm from Ren's grip. "And why would I be fritterin my day with the likes of you?"

"What? You got some kind of card-reading emergency? An officer nearly took his own life—and that's the second event at your hotel. You think there's not going to be questions? Reporters? More police?" Ren asked. "We need to keep this under wraps as best we can and stick together until we have more facts and know better just what's going on. And the only way that'll happen is if you come with me."

♦

It was about one o'clock in the afternoon by the time they rolled up to Fiorelli's home. The police had set up concrete cones to block off access to the house. An armed patrolman stood on the front steps looking grim. Neighbors no longer bothered standing outside to watch the activity. Ren figured the shock and novelty had turned to disgust and fear.

An officer stepped off the curb, put up a halting hand, and chirped his silver whistle.

"Get down on the floor," Ren said.

"You want me layin down in the blood?" she asked.

"Just get down, and cover yourself with this. Everything. Especially that white turban." He tossed his dark overcoat at her, and she did what he said.

Ren rolled forward and cracked open his window.

"This is a restricted area. You can U-turn here and head back," he said.

"Gil, it's me. Larson. You know Griswold has me investigating. Come on," Ren said. Then he put out his hand to shake Gil's, but he didn't return the gesture.

"Sorry, Larson. Our orders are to only allow Crime Lab personnel," the officer said. He kept his back to the sun, and Ren couldn't make out the officer's expression.

"Look, I have directives from Griswold, too," Ren said.

"Yeah, about that… I was told if you showed up to send you back to the precinct ASAP. Sarge needs to see you."

Ren swallowed hard and felt his hands on the steering wheel get slick with perspiration. He debated what he might do next. He cranked the wheel around.

"What the hell is he talking about?" Ren said.

It didn't take him long to make it back to headquarters. He

parked the patrol car in the lot and told Nany to wait where she was. "Just stay here and don't let anyone see you, you hear me? You're a suspect, just like me. You got it?" he asked.

She nodded, and he left her behind.

Griswold was heading into his office with a carrot in his mouth and fists full of paperwork in each hand when Ren found him. The sergeant jerked his head toward the office door, letting Ren know to come in and sit. Griswold stretched his too-tight pants into his gouged-up chair. He crunched on the carrot and set the remaining piece down on a pile of papers, leaving a scatter of bright crumbs and a wet orange stain. He switched a table fan on and gulped from a chipped coffee mug.

"The wife. Got me on some kind of plan. Says it's good for my heart." He held up the carrot, like Exhibit A, and munched down another mouthful. "Maybe it is. But I'm just starving all the time and cuffing my own wrists to the desk every time an apple fritter passes by." He slapped the carrot down into the trash. "Who am I kidding? What the wife don't know. Right?"

"Why?" Ren asked. He knew Griswold was just vamping. "Why was I turned around like that? Turned away from my own investigation like I was some kind of nosy neighbor?"

"Larson, come on. This isn't personal. I'm looking out for you. Can't you see? You know what the boys are saying about you now? Do you? I've got a whole precinct full of fellas who don't want to ride with you anymore. You getting it? No one."

Ren sat mute. Then he said, "It's only been a couple of days. Of course, things are going to get messy. It happens all the time."

"Yeah, and in those couple of days, you've managed to lose your partners—both of them. Don't you think these are some peculiar circumstances? Let me answer that for you—yes. Yes, it's fucking bizarre. And if you don't think so, you're gonna make a lousy sergeant," Griswold said. "Reasonable is what makes one good at this."

Ren thought about the tattered Bible, the weird words and

symbols reproduced at all of the crime scenes. He toyed with telling Griswold about the connecting evidence, but at what price? Some of this evidence was difficult for Ren to believe, let alone the Sarge, who already thought Ren was coming unglued. Or worse, the Sarge might take Ren's leads and turn them over to someone else who would get all the glory… and the promotion. Ren decided he'd solve this case with or without the Sarge's official direction. And if he did find out what was going on, he'd take that to the Commissioner, not to the Sarge.

The sergeant leaned back in his chair, and it tipped on two straining legs. He looked like a big adult baby-rearing up on a hobby-horse.

"Look, Larson, even if you wanted to take this on solo, you know as well I do that it's a much bigger case now," Griswold said. "We have five dead in two days, and there are clear connecting patterns. Christ, there's blood splattering everyone's fuckin walls right now. This thing's bigger than one guy, Ren. Much bigger. And think of how this looks to the boys in the big chairs. And everyone else who wants a piece of my ass right now." The sergeant paused and lipped his coffee mug again. "Like I said, reasonable."

Then he let gravity carry the chair back to four legs with a scrape and a boom. "Look, you're a nice enough guy, Larson. But you know as well as I do that you're part of this investigation now. You're a witness at the very least—you and Fiorelli and that crazy old genie, wherever the hell those two might be…."

"You're kidding, right?" Ren asked. He had to say something, even though it felt like he'd been sucker-punched.

"Larson, look, I'm putting you back on some kind of detail as soon as I can. Maybe one day, we can revisit the promotion and all that. But right now, I need your wife to come pick you up."

"I can't ask her to do that," Ren said.

"Whaddaya mean?"

"My wife has gone out of town… to New York. Family business."

He wasn't too worried anymore if what he said sounded believable. He twisted the wedding ring on his finger. She'd never come back to him with things the way they were now. In the note she'd left on the dresser, Gloria had said she'd stay at Maxine's as long as she could. She and Molly, that is. But he knew well and good that she'd probably be looking to ship out altogether sometime soon. Then Ren would be alone in that house, that goddamned house that had God knows what crawling around inside. He felt a cold pressure in his chest build into a panic and then drop into ever-expanding darkness that filled the pit of his belly.

"Okay, we'll get one of the guys to drive you back. Maybe Benson. I hear him always asking you about Gloria. Go out, the two of you, and get a few beers on me." Griswold lifted to one side, pulled out a weathered wallet, and slapped five dollars down on the desk. "That reminds me, the last time I saw Fiorelli, he gave me this for you. Said it was personal, and he didn't want to leave it in your locker."

Griswold slid open his top desk drawer, withdrew a small, white, unmarked envelope, and handed it to Ren. He inspected it and saw that it had been opened. "Again, don't take it personally. It might have been... something we needed… evidence." Ren slipped it into his overcoat.

He swallowed, but his throat had developed a tight lump, and he hoped Griswold hadn't heard the loud squelch. "So, that's it?" Ren asked.

"C'mon, don't make this harder than it already is. This is standard procedure, right? We just need to get some hard facts—enough to clear your name. So for now, I think it's best for all of us if you lay low at home. I figure about two weeks, and we'll have this sorted out."

"Sarge, I'm the guy who won our officer's award, remember?"

"Yeah. And now you're the guy who's got front row seats to a shit storm. Come on, Larson, you know how this rolls. It could happen to the best of us. Just remember, you can't leave your house during work hours. And don't talk to the press. Other than that, you're a free man till further notice. Hey, in some ways, it's not too bad with the time off, am I right? I could sure use some vacation right about now. Things keep going like this, I'll have it when I'm layin' in a hospital bed at county with my chest all stitched up and carrot juice in an I.V. bag."

Ren nodded. It was official. He would be a captive in that house for two weeks. And whatever it was, the thingum, Mr. Crooked, or even just his imagination, it would kill him.

"I'll just collect my things from the car." He slid the five dollars off Griswold's desk and slipped it into his pocket.

"Oh, one more thing." Griswold stood up to walk side by side with Ren out of his office, and it felt like a bum's rush. But Ren needed to act like everything was honkey dory—or at least not a complete disaster. "That old genie has gone missing. Fiorelli, too, though we know he's likely on the run. We got guys looking for him now. Anyway, a couple of the guys went down to the old genie's hotel. Found a bunch of bizarre things there. Occult crap. Dolls and bones and things like that. Seems to fit what we've seen so far. Not sure if you and Fiorelli were there talking to her the other day because you suspected her of involvement, or what. If so, good call. Of course, she's been gone a little too long, and it's looking awfully suspicious. You haven't seen her since you went there, have you?"

"Nope." Ren tipped his cap and tried his best not to break eye contact. Everyone knew the "tells." Sarge was likely baiting him, suspecting Ren might have an idea where the old fortune-teller was.

"She didn't try to leave the hotel or anything like that?"

Ren shook his head. "I wouldn't know."

"We'll find her, one way or another," Griswold said. "Just leave your keys on my desk," he said over his shoulder. He nabbed them as soon as Ren tossed them up. Then Griswold peeled off and headed down a separate hall where a secretary flagged him down.

Ren slipped out the door to the lot quick as he could and found Nany snoring in the back seat, her head wrap at a tilt.

"Hey, wake up," Ren said.

Nany snorted. "You scared me half out of my wits."

"Never mind that. There's an all-points bulletin out for you, and I can't help anymore," Ren said. He scanned the area for officers or anyone who might witness them together.

"Are you crazy, then?" Nany asked. "Nany don't need the copp'r's help." She started laughing in a low, secret sort of way.

An officer rolled into the lot and gave Ren a quick wave. He parked his patrol car several stalls down. "Don't sit up," Ren said. "And don't move. Just lay there."

"Hey Larson," the officer called out. It was Benson, who was quite the office gossip. He locked up the vehicle and sauntered over, but kept a safe enough distance that Ren felt Nany might still go unnoticed. "Tough break, Bud," he said. "Jeez, a real tragedy, ya know? What could have made both those guys go so damn nuts like that? You rode with them, right? Did they act strange or eat anything weird?"

"I just talked to the Sarge. It's just really confusing. Both guys seemed so normal," Ren said. He moved to one side, blocking Benson's view of his back seat.

"Yeah, it's always the so-called normal ones that turn around and hack up their families. Like I said, a real tragedy." He shook his head and leaned in to extend a hand to Ren. He stopped short, seeing movement in the back. "Who's that?"

"Hmm?" Ren asked.

"On your floor in the back. Who's that?" Benson said.

"Oh, that?" Ren bit the inside of his cheek. "Just some old drunk. I'm bringing her in to sleep it off."

"Oh right," Benson replied. He leaned in, trying to see around Ren. "Looks like she's dressed up for a Halloween contest or something."

"Ain't that the truth?" Ren said with a laugh. "Must have been on a real hum-dinger. Know what I mean?"

Benson rolled his eyes and nodded. "I guess we've all been there before. Don't be too hard on the old gal." He trotted along, and Ren watched him enter the building, making sure no one else was coming or going.

He helped Nany out, and together they skipped out through the walking gate, and with luck, they slid into a taxi parked across the street.

"And just where do you think I will go, copp'r? Thanks to you, I ain't got a business no more. All my things—my needed things—they're there, too. You made a mess of this real good." She crossed her arms and looked away.

Ren addressed the driver. "Take us downtown. 850 South Broadway."

The cabby eyed the pair with suspicion, but he lurched off into traffic without saying a word.

"Why are you taking me back?" Nany said.

"We need your things," he said.

"I don't know what you think, but I already done enough for you. I told you what you need to know, what you need to do. Leave Nany out of the rest of it," she said.

"I'll get your things, and you're coming to stay with me for a while," he said.

"Now I know you lost your mind!" Nany said. "I can't—I won't go to no place other than my hotel."

"Why? You afraid of Mr. Crooked?" Ren asked. It was an odd thing to say to her, seeing as they both knew the answer, except one of them wasn't willing to admit it. And he couldn't stand the thought of going back to that house alone.

She looked into his eyes with a soft, world-weary sadness.

"What other option do you have, lady?" Ren continued. "Way I see it, you can come along now and take your chances that we can solve this together, or go back, and you'll likely lose everything once you have jail time and they deport you. I doubt you'd even survive the long wait in the county jail until a judge could hear your case. You know how many months immigration cases are backlogged? You could be behind bars for a year. Maybe more," Ren said.

"I'll stay with Charlene," she said.

The cab driver shot another confused look at them in his rearview mirror and made a squeaking noise as though sucking between his teeth.

"Fine," Ren said. He had to lower his voice with the cabby listening in. "But I don't want you wandering around at night, or heading back to that room of yours, you hear me? It's only a matter of time before they come back and look for you."

"Why are you trying to be nice to Nany? I don't have anything for you." She nodded, satisfied with what she'd said, then looked away.

The cab came to a stoplight, and next to them rolled up the familiar black sedan—the one the nun drove, the one that ran him off the road at night, the one with dead people inside. "Christ almighty," he said. He felt a terrible gripping in his heart that would not let go.

Ren rolled down his window and squinted in the unforgiving sunlight to glimpse whatever or whoever he might. The traffic light turned, and the sedan took off at a clip that likely flattened its passengers. Ren stuck his head out the window and locked on, trying to glimpse the license plate, but the sun blotted his vision.

That was when two thin hands pressed against the sedan's back window so hard that they became a translucent white. A blurred outline of a familiar face emerged between the hands. It was Fiorelli's wife. Her head twisted to one side, her eyes wide with fear, and her mouth gaped in silent agony. Just as suddenly as she appeared, something sucked her back into the black interior.

Ren knew that this was not dreamed up—some awakened remnant from his trauma in a foreign land, no matter how cruel or terrible that might have been. No. This thing was parading about in broad daylight, and it was taking another of those it had somehow claimed. First Haddock, and now Fiorelli's wife. But what caused him to pause and restrain himself before he blurted out words that could send him to the booby-hatch, was that both of them seemed very much alive. The dead don't come back to life. He knew that.

But, then again, he also trusted his senses. What he'd seen—twice now—was concrete, three-dimensional, real.

"Cabby, can you please keep up with that car?" he asked.

Without a split-second pause, he pulled to the side of the road and turned to face the pair with a thick, creased brow and a scowl across his gray and black stubble. "Look, Mac, I don't know what you do for a living. You seem like a respectable enough guy. But, when you're in my cab, it's my rules on account of it being my living, see? I kept my mouth shut when you dragged some colored woman into my place of business—could be a streetwalker or some other kind of criminal, for all I know. But I says to myself, hey, it's none of your business. A fare's a fare. But I'll be damned if I go chase someone down. You get it? Now the two of you can get out, or shut the hell up and finish your ride."

Ren grabbed Nany by the arm, and the two slid out of the taxi. Ren gave the door a good slamming with his foot, leaving a nice door-ding. The cab screeched away, drawing up a stained old newspaper from the gutter onto Ren's legs.

Ren saw Nany give a small smile, and she adjusted her head wrap just a smidge, touching the back of it as though primping a full head of hair.

"What have you suddenly got to smile about?" Ren asked. He was still feeling pulsating hostility from the encounter.

She said, "Nany nearing eighty years old. The man say I'm pretty enough to be a working girl."

Twelve

Los Angeles, 1947
Three Months Before It Happened

The evening was gray, and a thick curd of clouds crowded away the stars. They were always there, Gloria liked to remind Ren. "Even though you can't see them, there's always a star shining on you," she would say to him. He held on to those little bits of hope. His job took him down some dark roads, and little things could quickly alter his mood and affect Gloria.

Gloria's black velvet opera cape swirled back and forth as she walked ahead of Ren. And he watched her, mesmerized by the subtleties of movement and how it hooked him every time into loving her as though today was the first time. Ren wore his best wool suit and a pair of too-tight wing-tipped shoes. That's about all of the evening he remembered, with any clarity, at any rate.

Haddock and his wife were equally as groomed and attired. The pair proved a well-coordinated unit of pomade and black leather shoes that mirrored the streetlight shine, pearls, and slicked-back hair. The four of them hadn't gone out together in a long time, but tonight was like old times.

"That was something else," Haddock said. He walked in lock-step with his best buddy. They could have set their strides to music. The women stayed together ahead of the boys, linking arms.

"Oh, Glen," his wife said. "Enough. We get it. It wasn't your cup of tea."

"Leave him alone, Lily," Gloria said. "Men don't get art. You're not going to knock it into him. They're all alike."

He laughed. Ren kicked his opinion in. "Now wait a gosh-darn minute, honey. You think I didn't appreciate that… that show?"

Gloria stopped Lily, and she turned around with that annoyance women feel when men forget how to behave. "We weren't at a circus, Ren. So it wasn't a show. It was an opera."

"Well, that explains the tights," Haddock said. The boys laughed but tried to contain it a bit so as not to further provoke.

"The men wore tights because… oh for goodness' sake," Lily said. "We should have just gone by ourselves, Gloria. Try to uplift these little boys with a bit of culture? Forget it."

Haddock suddenly leaped in front of the women and spread his arms wide. "I am Metropolis, King of Hell, and I've come to make a deal—how about for this mink stole?" He grabbed Lily around the waist and tugged at the fur around her shoulders, and she squealed.

"Knock it off, Glen," she said. "We're with company. Besides, it was Mephistopheles. And bargaining for someone's soul is a serious subject—or I guess it was back in the day. Who invited him, anyway?" She shrugged and giggled toward Gloria.

Haddock laughed and fell back to walk with his buddy. Ren lit a cigarette and offered one to Haddock as they all strolled down Wilshire Boulevard, blocks away from the theater, toward the all-night diner.

"Hey, wasn't it a couple of years ago that this same troupe of singers was doing shows out of a church hall somewhere in Beverly Hills?" Ren asked.

"Ren, not you, too," Gloria said. "This opera was your idea, if you'll recall. Lily and I had a wonderful time. So you keep your negative reviews to yourselves."

"Your idea, huh? I don't get it," Haddock said. "That Faust fella could have asked for anything he wanted. If he was making a deal with the devil, why does he go and ask for a wife, for Christ's sake?"

"And what's wrong with that, Glen?" Lily asked.

"Well, I think it's romantic," Gloria said. "Don't listen to him."

"What if his wife got the beat on him? You know?" Ren asked.

"How's that?" Haddock replied.

"Well, what if Faust's wife made her own deal? A new deal. A better deal. Beat the old man to the punch. Did it all behind his back. Made a deal so she could live forever. And what if she had to do a lot of bad things to keep it all going? Just to keep from having to face the music." Ren had the right amount of steam under his ideas to give Gloria a familiar sickening dread.

"You mean, like double-crossing him?" Haddock asked.

"Exactly," Ren replied.

"Now, that's a good story. I'd go see that opera, tights and all."

"Someone like that would have to be pretty clever to hide her tracks," Ren said. "Have to change identities, maybe even join the Church to hide out."

Gloria turned backward. She watched him draw his overcoat collar up across his neck and puff on his cigarette, head hung low. Her muscles clutched at her chest, so stifling that they threatened to pulverize her heart.

Haddock suddenly exploded with laughs. "A deal with the devil and hiding out in the Church? Brother, you are a twisted son of a bitch."

The two men laughed.

"Well, you know women and their beauty treatments. I guess they'd try anything once—including consulting with the damned," Ren said.

"What an imagination," Lily said. She asked Gloria, "Has he always been like that? You should send that in to the mystery magazines."

Gloria smiled back, but she had to force it. "Well, you know men. Always in their heads about one thing or another," she replied.

"This is the place, right, Ren?" Lily asked. She stopped in front of a big bay window that curved around the corner like a bulging wave. The sign read Durst Diner. Ren and Haddock busied themselves smoking and laughing about things they didn't want the girls to know.

"Oh my goodness. I'll gain twenty pounds," Lily said. She tapped Gloria on the shoulder to look at the pie carousel spinning with its temptations. But her friend looked lost in a private world of pain.

"Honey, are you all right?" Lily asked.

"Huh?" Gloria asked. It was like she snapped out of a hypnotic state. "Oh, I'm fine… really… I'm fine." Her words seemed far away.

At that moment, another couple crowded up to the door and passed the women on their way in. The man, a sturdy, black-skinned fellow, looked at Gloria and tipped his hat to her and smiled as he passed.

"Hey there, hold on a minute," Ren said. The couple continued on inside.

"Jesus Christ, did you see that?" Haddock asked. "We were right here at the door. Where are people's manners?"

"Yeah, and that guy just gave Gloria the once over," Ren said. He took off his hat and handed it to Haddock. He snubbed out this cigarette on the sidewalk and marched past the women.

"Ren, don't do anything foolish," Gloria said as he passed her. "He was polite." Her stomach clenched. *Not in front of guests*, she prayed to herself.

The diner was warm and dressed up in tinsel, green and gold, for the holidays. The waitress behind the counter told Ren that she'd seat them as soon as she could. She went back to counting change for a white-haired gentleman and his wife, and poured coffee refills for the counter guests.

Ren scanned the small room and spotted the couple who had pushed through. They were taking off their coats and hanging them on the hooks at the end of the booth.

"Excuse me," Ren said. He strode with the force of an officer in pursuit of a suspect.

The man stood and watched Ren approach. His arms hung loose at his sides, and his back was bent with years of labor and crushing life circumstances. He had an expression of sad familiarity in his eyes as a white man approached him with a tone of rancor.

"Excuse me, but did I see you making eyes at my wife?" Ren asked.

"No, sir. Being neighborly is all," the man said. He averted his gaze.

"What's your name?" Ren asked.

"Only reason a man wants to know another man's name is when he's got a bee in his bonnet and wants to start a fight. I ain't interested," the man said, and he started to sit.

"Old George, just ignore him. Can't you tell he isn't right? Something wrong with him," the seated woman said. She placed a hand on his arm and gave him a look of encouragement.

Ren grabbed the man's other arm. He felt his thick biceps flex beyond his grip. He thought twice of provoking, though the man seemed to stare a bit too long at Ren's hand on his arm, and he thought it might already be too late. Old George then stood to his full height, which was an inch or two above Ren, and his shoulders were broad enough and well-armed to handle such situations.

"Sir, I'm going to ask you again to leave us be," Old George said. Ren removed his hand.

"Well, Old George. Did you know you're talking to an off-duty officer?" Ren asked.

Haddock stumbled in and squeezed past between the patrons at the counter who were turned around and deciding whether they should leave.

"Larson, it's not worth it," Haddock said.

"I'm not going to let some boy come on to my wife," Ren said. His face flushed, and his neck strained with the words.

"Ren, stop!" Gloria shouted. The folks out for an evening meal murmured, and she bit her lip, looking around the room at their disapproving faces. Gloria walked past Glen and put her hand on Ren's chest. "Ren, he was just being polite," she said. She turned to Old George. "I'm terribly sorry, sir. He's just a bit worked up."

The waitress wasn't going to allow such nonsense on her shift ruin the holiday atmosphere, and maybe some of her tips. She raised her voice from behind the counter. "I'm going to have to ask the four of you to leave."

Ren wouldn't budge while he locked eyes with Old George.

"I've already called the cops," the waitress said. "Go now if you want a head start."

"We are the cops," Ren replied. He stepped in closer to Old George.

Old George stared back at Ren with his dark brown eyes, drinking in all the details so he'd not forget.

"Come on, buddy," Haddock said. He grabbed Ren by the shoulder. "Let's go. Nothing here for us."

Thirteen

Los Angeles, 1947
The Day Before It Happened

It was a struggle to find a cab willing to stop for the two of them. It was a decent prediction from the cabby who tossed them out. Instead, they took a bus and a Red Car for several miles. Plenty of passengers stared at them along the way. Folks returning from work in their suits and wool coats gawked at the woman in island attire. Nany acted as though the attention was because of her newly discovered youthful look. The last leg of the journey gave Ren time to read the contents of the envelope Griswold had passed to him. After reading, he decided to share the other contents of his overcoat's inner pockets.

"I want you to look at this," he said. He withdrew his daughter's desecrated Bible.

"What is this?" Nany asked. She studied the crumpled and defiled thing before she realized Ren wanted her to take the book from him. She was no fool. Nany could tell when evil was contaminating an object. Using two fingers to grab a cover edge, she allowed it to fall on the seat between them. The pages opened to the vile crayon scribbles written across the endless words of Christian holy men. The waxy red lettering seemed drunken and full of rage.

Nany nodded in acknowledgment of what Ren showed her, then her brow deepened, and she shook her head.

"This is yours?"

"We got it for my daughter for her baptism. It just sat on a table in her room until… this. We found it like this a few nights ago." He pointed to a symbol on one page. "The same thing on these pages, and even more showed up on her bedroom wall, and at two other murder scenes, including at Fiorelli's house. My daughter is only five. She couldn't have written this."

Nany peered out across the bus, out to the passing streets. She flexed and released her jaw several times and seemed preoccupied.

"No child done this," she said, "if that's what you gettin at."

"What do you mean?"

She closed her eyes. "Once it comes, it don't go. Not till it eats you all up. The sin it sniffed out is what it wants." She shook her head. "It come from the in-between place you go." She closed her eyes and touched the air. "The world goes dark there, but not quite, and the sun tries to, but never sets. Sits there right out of sight."

He gawked. She opened her eyes and gave a solemn, careful nod as if making sudden moves might shake away the dream she had spinning before her eyes.

Ren didn't want her to say any more. If she did, his entire world might unravel. "Look. I just thought maybe you could see—" he started to say.

"Thingums notice you—study you in this place. They get the whiff of your sin." She was nearly in a trance. She gazed downward, as though her fortunes lay in her lap.

He felt locked in a clutching dread that kept his mouth shut. Finally, he forced himself to speak. "I don't know what you're—" he tried to say, but before he finished, she snatched his hand. In the shock of her sudden move, he tried to pull free. But she placed her other warm, weathered hand on his heart, his guard dropped, and his grip relaxed. She explored the skin of his palm as though she'd lost something there. She closed her eyes and snapped up an in-breath in a way that was sure to draw the attention of onlookers. Ren glanced around the interior of the Red Car, and sure enough, a woman in hair rollers and a shopping basket draped across her arm frowned at the two of them.

"There it was. In your bed," Nany went on. "You were only a child. Summoned up from down below, it was. Knock, knock, knock on the wall. Can't scream. Can't run." She opened her eyes a peep to connect with Ren's wide stare. "That dark in-between is a place where the thingums go and are lost. They're tired and hungry in that place—mostly hungry and looking for a good meal. Don't care the cost, neither. Lure and follow—that's what they do. Find them the ones who are easy prey first, like the lost, the weak... and the already damned."

Ren's silence was honest and as vast as the desert plains in the dark-between. Maybe he'd never speak another word. Palmists and fortune tellers were good at reading between the lines, and that kind of trickery duped lots of folks out of their hard-earned money. But Nany's insights went far beyond that parlor trick.

"Nany thinks you do know who writes, who draws these things in the Christian book," she said.

The bell clanged for the next stop as if to draw them from the world unhinging before his eyes to a more concrete moment. One with signals and train stops and even murderous people. Yes, even that would be more comprehensible than Nany's uncanny feat.

"Eastern Columbia." The trolley driver had a steady, practiced voice that sliced through the din of the car. With that, Nany opened her eyes and directed her gaze to Ren. It seemed like that allowed her to more directly bore into his mind, if that were possible. And once she found a way in, she recognized things, the things Ren thought he'd hidden away from the world.

He finally tore his gaze away and looked down. Nany was the first in his life to say anything about his dark-between times. They'd haunted him across his whole life, the darkness creeping up at unexpected moments, though usually when he was alone. And then he'd find himself in that murky twilight landscape. Those dark shadowy things were almost everywhere. But he didn't have control over his comings and goings. And his compulsory visits had increased in frequency since his time away, when he was subjected to terrible things, and he had to do things just as terrible to survive.

He held up the envelope Fiorelli had left for him and slid out its contents. He passed the handwritten note to Nany. She pressed her tongue between her front teeth while looking at it, as though she was trying to solve a complicated math problem.

"It's a license plate number," he said. "It's a damn license plate number. He saw it and remembered that car we chased into the tunnel. The same car we saw when we were in the cab earlier. And Fiorelli wrote it down. Look here, beneath he wrote St. Cyprian. St. Cyprian! Jesus. If it weren't for him, we'd have nothing, and now it's a damn miracle. Don't you see it? All I have to do is follow this. That's it. Then I'll have a much better idea of what the hell is going on. You'll be in the clear in no time, and you can go back to your life."

She nodded, but she seemed even more worn by the world than before. The trolley lurched to a stop. Nany passed back Ren's things, and she stood up.

She pointed a finger at him. "Watch yourself," she said. Then she hobbled away.

Los Angeles, 1947
The Day It Happened

Ren left the next day dressed in civilian clothes, a gray suit and a red tie, pressed and crisp like a paper airplane. As the taxi pulled up, he drew back the gathered sheers from the narrow vertical glass that ran along the side of the door, taking care that undercover officers who might monitor his activities didn't observe him. Ren knew he was hanging by a thread, but he had to get something tangible. Something useful. He needed whatever he might find to explain these deaths. He'd clear his name and maybe even get back in the Sarge's good graces, and get his family back.

While getting dressed, he thought of various excuses should anyone from the precinct call or visit while he went out to Fiorelli. The tied-up party line was always an easy out for missed phone calls. And if someone came snooping in person, he was asleep or in the bathroom. Easy.

The cab driver smelled like goat cheese and unwashed gymnasium locker. His eyebrows joined across his brow, and he barely managed a grunt when Ren gave his destination. He was good enough for driving, though. He sped with expert crisscrosses through the Hollywood streets and arrived at St. Cyprian's by nine o'clock. After Ren tossed in his fare, the driver looked up at the place, shook his head, and sped off in haste. Ren understood the response.

The hospital took up the whole block. It was an imposing dark-brick edifice that loomed over the surrounding neighborhood with its squared turrets and its stark slate roof like a vampire's castle from an old movie. It surely robbed the nearby residents of comfort as it loomed over their homes. It didn't give the feeling that someone could recover in a place like this. Instead, it seemed soot-slathered and unclean. Once you entered, you'd certainly not be well ever again, Ren thought. He took one final hit of his cigarette and snuffed it out with his heel.

Fiorelli knew. He saw it, too. Haddock—in that back window, even though the man was dead and gone. He saw him in that back window clawing at it while that crazy nun drove him off. That was why Fiorelli wrote down the license plate. He wanted Ren to know he saw it—and it scared him, too.

Once inside the hospital vestibule, Ren glanced upward. A dark blue painted dome loomed above him. Gracing the ceiling's curvature was a nighttime sky dotted with gold stars. In the center of that ominous sky was an old bearded man in white robes. His arms outstretched to those below, and in each hand were lightning bolts.

Ren crossed to the reception desk, feeling a bit dizzy from the display above him. It was hard not to look at that haloed man floating on soft pink clouds, his eyes boring in with an unforgiving glower.

"That's him, you know," a dark, stern sentry nun said. Her voice carried and echoed in the cavernous vestibule. She wore her starched habit suitably. It fit her charms.

"Him?"

"St. Cyprian, of course," she said. "One of our beloved martyrs."

Ren removed his hat. "I'm here to visit with Officer Fiorelli." He showed his police badge, which he'd pinned behind his lapel. The nun looked at him in an odd, familiar manner. Like a schoolmarm, she bunched her wrinkled lips, and she paged through the roster of patients, every now and then glancing up from her ledger at him.

"I'm sorry. Mr. Fiorelli is unable to have visitors today. He was only recently admitted."

She closed the book and stared ahead at him with her ice-blue eyes. Ren figured she had to be seventy or eighty years of age, given the folds in her neck and the droop in her eyelids. Though, remarkably, her gaze was full of fire.

"I'm sorry as well, ma'am. But this is an official police matter." He locked his gaze back at her and let her know he wasn't going anywhere. "And if I can't see him right now, I can be back within the next couple of hours with a warrant and a team of officers who might take an interest in your operation here."

She moved her jaw around like she was trying to dislodge a nut from a tooth. She watched Ren with her watery eyes, as though trying to determine whether what he said were truthful. Or was she looking at him as though he was a child, dressed up in some Halloween costume, looking for leftover trick-or-treats? Why she might gaze at him with mild amusement was bizarre and unsettling.

She excused herself so she could speak with another of her order who stood near an inner gate. She, too, was eyeing the exchange with suspicion, like an old busybody who sat on a porch watching what the neighbors carried out to the curb on trash day.

"You can see him for five minutes, but that's all," the first nun announced. She adopted an expression of warning that she was perhaps used to giving elementary school students.

"I'll try to remember," he said.

He passed by her, then the other nun who watched them took the lead, hands crossed over her abdomen, covered in heavy draping sleeves. The dour thing clopped in her sturdy shoes as she strode, and the lonely sound of it echoed throughout the sterile white hallways. She carried a large metal hoop of a dozen or more iron keys that dangled next to her sparkling obsidian rosary.

The whole thing rang like fairy bells with each step. It might have been almost pleasing to anyone else. Still, it stung in Ren's ears like a hundred pinpricks that bored into his skull until he lost his center of gravity and felt as though he was falling, falling, falling. It took concentration to keep from dropping to the floor. An inexplicable and sickening sense of terror sprouted like a wild mushroom, and he vibrated with involuntary trembling. His panic had become a runaway train.

"Are you all right?" the nun asked.

"Yes—Yes… I'm perfectly…" He couldn't finish the sentence. His tongue lost control, and words sounded thick and stupid.

She turned back and continued down the sterile hallways until they arrived at a large arched door made entirely of black iron. She fitted the key inside, unlatched it, and heaved her practiced shoulder into the entrance to uncouple the lock.

From where they stood, Ren saw dozens of torch-shaped white-glass light fixtures hanging low from the two-story arched ceiling. And high above on the wall—well out of anyone's reach—were a series of rectangular windows. There was just enough of the afternoon sun filtering through to keep the place from feeling like it was perpetually night.

Rows of hospital beds stretched out along the broad block walls, men lying in them in various stages of disrepair. Some were bandaged, yes. But others had more profound wounds. They were jabbering, squawking, madmen rocking back and forth in their own messes. The place smelled both like charring skin and a recently used toilet. A slim, sheer curtain of haze hung in the air.

"Come along," the nun said.

They continued down the central aisle from the door, passing patient after patient. Ren realized now that what seemed like injured men was something else altogether. Yes, they may have sustained injuries, but many had thick leather straps tying them to their beds, either belted across the chest or with leather cuffs attached to the frames. There were others who the nuns hadn't shackled. But these seemed incapacitated, unconscious, or unable to walk. Now and then, a man's shriek cut through the silence. Nuns in starchy black tunics attended to the men—the screaming ones had first dibs—holding cups to their lips, applying cold cloths to their pale, shaved heads.

Ren followed his guide as she switched between long rooms. The nuns watched the pair with quiet unrest and darting eyes, nodding one to another in some silent conversation. Ren's tour came to a sudden stop.

The nun gestured to a bed. There Fiorelli lay flattened on the thin mattress, strapped from neck to toe like a monster in a mad scientist's laboratory. Someone had tipped his head back against a pillow, and it made the gauze and cotton bandaging across his neck seem all the direr.

Another nun approached with a slate and chalk and laid it across Fiorelli's stomach. The chalk rolled back and forth with each shallow breath. It appeared they'd given him too much of whatever they provide someone to stop them from trying to shoot themselves in the neck. His eyes were out of focus. Even so, Fiorelli lifted his head and grimaced, fighting to see who came to his bedside.

"It's me," Ren said. He hoped that the interaction would distract him from his riotous heartbeat. Fiorelli ran his thick tongue out and used it to wet his lips.

Ren knew he might not want to say anything in front of one of them, so he turned to the nun glowering from behind.

"Can we have a moment alone?"

She crossed her arms over her chest.

"You're gonna look just lovely in a striped jumper," Ren said. She flexed her jaw and sniffed loudly at him. Then she clopped and jangled away, looking over her shoulder at him. The other nuns watched in dreadful, suffocating silence, but they continued their duties like drones in a beehive.

He slapped Fiorelli's face lightly, trying to sober him up. Fiorelli inhaled sharply, almost like a gasp, and his eyes rolled around until he focused onto Ren's face. His eyes began to well up, and a tear rolled down to his neck bandage. Ren recognized a man in a state of remorse and grief. He'd seen it many times before, but usually after a judge's sentence.

"They're not going to let me be here long, so we have to work fast," Ren said.

Fiorelli tried to swallow. He grimaced as the inside of his throat moved.

"I'm gonna ask you some simple questions, and here—"

Ren picked up the chalk and the slate.

"We can use this." He placed the chalk in Fiorelli's hand, though the arm was strapped down. Below the elbow, Fiorelli could still move, so he could write. Ren placed the slate under that.

"Something is going on. Something that made you do this. Right?"

Ren looked down to watch for a response. It required Fiorelli's considerable effort with a hand that seemed to have its own response to gravity to shape the letters. He fought back the mental blur from whatever they'd given him, and he willed himself to print a reply.

Ren took the slate.

What Fiorelli had written looked like the work of a very young child who was just learning to trace. Nevertheless, he had spelled out Y-E-S.

Ren used the bedding to erase the word. He glanced around, but no one was close enough to overhear his question or see the response. The nuns tended to beds on either side and seemed dutiful to their tasks, though their tense eyes locked on to whatever they could and would dart away whenever Ren caught one of them.

"You left me the license plate of the sedan we chased. It belongs to this hospital. Did you see him, too, in the back of the sedan? Did you see Haddock?" Ren asked.

Fiorelli's eyes became puddles again. His mouth ran red and bubbled up with blood and saliva. He strained to lift his head but gave up after grunting with pain. Ren placed the slate under his hand again. Fiorelli struggled still, eking out, with considerable strain, the letters H-E-L-. But that was as far as he got before he fixed onto Ren's eyes with such intensity that Ren might have believed he was in some danger, right there in his bed. And to Ren, it looked like Fiorelli shook his head, ever so slightly, then shifted his gaze to whatever was just behind Ren.

Ren felt a hollow sickness in his gut and a chill clung to his limbs. He erased the board and backed away from the bed. When he turned, he faced another of the sisters. This woman was much older than the others. Her face crinkled around the edges, at the jaw and cheeks, where the white skull cap pressed into her tissue-paper skin. The headpiece elongated into loose white cowls down her neck and lay like an elephant's skin atop her dark robes. Her eyelids drooped with the weight of time, but her eyes were clear and alert. Ren also thought they seemed careful, crafty.

"Excuse me, Officer Fiorelli seems to need something," he said to her. He hoped he could account for whatever Fiorelli was writing.

She pointed off, and it was plain that the other nuns knew her signal. That seemed to mean "mind your business." So they did. When she pointed, Ren noticed a marking in the webbing between her thumb and first finger. It looked like a symbol, like a hand-drawn tattoo, in blue-green ink. It was odd, a nun with a tattoo. He wondered if maybe he just hadn't seen it long enough to distinguish it from, say, a vein. A fly zipped off from her hand, and Ren watched it dart off into the vastness of the great hall.

She scuttled her hands beneath her robes, then probed Ren's eyes with an authoritative stare that he was sure would have worked well with keeping order among the nuns. Whatever it was unsettled him, made him think about running, hiding. But he knew it was unreasonable. She was a frail old woman in a robe. Why should he be afraid?

Yet the sense of disturbance kept layering, like a winter frost that becomes a thick, immovable layer of ice.

"Officer Fiorelli is in our care now. Are you in need of some assistance?" She narrowed her eyes until there was not much to see except slits.

"I'm—I'm an officer—Los Angeles Police Department." He knew his language decayed in his mouth, and he showed his badge, hoping that would compensate. "I'm here to—Officer Fiorelli is a crime witness."

He felt like he was shrinking. It was almost as if the nun had some power over him, which was ridiculous. He hoped that his practiced police officer tone might bring some grounded sensibility to the situation and hopefully tamp down his growing and inexplicable sense of panic. But it did nothing for him. Or for her. She maintained her inert stare.

It dawned on him that he shouldn't have come alone. He was inside someone else's world, behind a locked iron door. Who would know he was there at all? With his wife and daughter gone, and the people of his life disappearing one after another, it occurred to him he was quite isolated now.

"We admitted him only yesterday, Mr. Larson. I am certain that he is in no condition to act as a witness to anything except his own recovery."

As she spoke, the loose skin around her face pushed and pulled, stretching across her old bones like it was once an over-inflated balloon that lost all of its air.

"You—you knew my name," Ren said. "I never said my name, but you knew it."

The nun stretched her crinkled mouth into a yellowed smile. "Of course, Mr. Larson. Sister Francine told me you were here."

"Oh, yes. Right," Ren said.

He noticed Fiorelli was becoming increasingly red-faced. His blank eyes fixed on the ceiling, and he trembled as though he was having convulsions. A second nun arrived with a squeaky cart. Atop it was a gleaming metal tray with a bottle of antiseptic and a long hypodermic needle. It was the crazy nun from Doc Kelly's office. Ren found his voice had shut off completely.

The body of the syringe lay on its side, and it dripped a yellow liquid onto a white lining paper atop the tray. The nun wiped Fiorelli's arm with the antiseptic and then plunged in the needle. Nearly immediately, he fluttered his eyelids, and then he drooped them shut. His head sprawled to one side, and his jaw went slack. A string of bloody spittle wetted the white pillow. The nun wheeled the cart away with what Ren thought was a secret smile.

Trying to hold in check his impulse to shout and bolt from there, Ren got busy digging up the slip of paper that had the license plate number on it from his overcoat. "Is this vehicle registered to this hospital?"

The elder nun glanced at the slip of paper and gave the slightest hint of a smile that reminded him of a snake's mouth. "Yes, it is, Mr. Larson. But I'm a bit confused. Are you here to elicit testimony from one of our patients, or are you here about a hospital vehicle?"

Ren thought for a second. But then realized that even a single beat of pause might confirm any suspicion, and he needed to assure his safety in this locked ward, far from prying eyes. "Whatever I am bringing to your attention is a matter under investigation. So—so this isn't a vehicle belonging to the hospital? Sister?"

"Reverend Mother," she said.

"What?" Ren asked.

"Reverend Mother Margite. You may address me as such."

"Margite?" Ren felt more fluttering in his chest, and his head started to throb on either side. He tried to swallow it down and explain it to himself. There was no need to be afraid of a nun. And perhaps he felt unsettled because of so many stresses. Obviously, he'd have some reaction, given everything that had happened. Doc Kelly said it could happen. Too bad he had a delayed reaction until this very moment, he thought.

"All right. Reverend Mother Margite," Ren said. "I will."

She watched him with a cat's eye, as though thinking about a mouse she'd like to trap and play with before swallowing in a bite. Maybe two.

"So, Reverend Mother, we've received complaints about this vehicle. Speeding. Running people off the road. We have reports of individuals inside the back of the transport, seemingly in a state of distress. Not exactly the kind of thing we like hearing about. Wouldn't you agree?"

"Mr. Larson, I'm afraid you've used up enough valuable time with foolishness. You are aware of where you are, sir? These are very sick men. Do you realize that you've caused one to lapse into distress, so much so as to require sedation?" she asked. She swallowed and bore down on her words, as though she was practiced at steadying her voice in aggravating circumstances. A skill no doubt developed from working with this clientele. It took a very different type of person to work in a place like this. Usually, it was someone who had a few loose screws themselves, or so the story went.

"This is a church vehicle," she said. "So I'm assuming you've come here with some proof of these allegations? And, may I ask, who have made such complaints?"

"We don't make it a business of sharing who's made complaints. That's left up to the courts if it comes to that. But I can tell you that Officer Fiorelli here reported your license plate and confirmed one incident."

"A man who in a fitful state slashed the throats of his wife and daughter, and then nearly shot himself to death? This is who you've relied on for information?"

She looked left and right and seemed to give a signal.

Without a sound or a hint of warning, Ren found two of the larger nuns flanking him. He turned around, and two more of them were behind him.

"I wonder what Cardinal O'Shaughnessy might have to say," Ren said. "You know he's a friend of the commissioner…"

"I'm sure he'd tell you that matters of church and state rarely intersect, Mr. Larson. In any event, before you take your leave, I'd like to share some words of wisdom. Tread lightly, Mr. Larson. Be careful what you seek. Sometimes what we think we want to know can be our own undoing."

"What's that supposed to mean?" Ren asked.

The nuns placed their guiding hands on Ren's body. "Get your hands off me," he said. He shrugged them off, but they began assisting him between the rows of beds towards the exit.

"God be with you, Mr. Larson," the Reverend Mother said. He looked over his shoulder and saw her make a sign of the cross in the air as if giving him a benediction.

"You think I'm not coming back? With a warrant? And a team of officers to shake this place down?" he shouted. "I'll come back, Fiorelli. I'll get you out."

But before he could finish his words, they'd led him through the iron doors and shut them with an echo that boomed through the halls.

Fourteen

Germany 1790

Margurite sat in the musty chapel vestibule. A pungent stink of damp and rain, an odor that seemed years in the making, hung in the hallway air. She didn't want to raise her eyes to identify what might be the smell's origin, lest she somehow sin again.

Our Father, which art in Heaven.

Margurite sinned a lot, and she didn't want to add to her growing list. Giving it a second thought, she supposed it really didn't matter much anymore. She'd gone against God's laws so often now in both big and small ways that doing so was like so much passing scenery. The odor overpowered her, and she just had to look. She flicked her gaze upward and saw the wood slats and cross beams upholding the roof stained with perhaps centuries of rainwater.

"I hoped those corroding beams would collapse on me," she told the priest in the confessional booth. She wondered if he even listened. Maybe so. Old men always made time for gossip, even under the guise of expunging sin. She suspected he hadn't nodded off. "Because, if those beams fell upon me, once and for all, the whole thing would be over," she said.

Thy will be done on earth as it is in Heaven.

"I'm not sure I believe in God because I could never find him in any of this. Only his dark twin, and perhaps he was all that existed for me, all that ever wanted me, in the end. I prayed to whoever was in charge of roofs caving in. But I remembered what might come next—after death—and I realized I wasn't ready."

"It's not that I ever really forgot what would come next, after I died and all. But I worked hard to put such thoughts out of my mind so often that they stayed in some permanent place somewhere off in the blurry and wild sidelines. After so many decades, taking expedient shortcuts seemed tempting, even if wrong-minded. They were like the fruit of the tree. Low hanging fruit. But that's what the dark thing wanted. It wanted to tempt me toward my doom, so it could collect on its deal. I knew it needed to feed."

Give us this day our daily bread.

Margurite found a monastery near the Dobbertiner See, a lake not far from the bustling cities. The weather in that region had been unusually stormy that spring, and bitterly cold the season before that. An attendant nun made her wait on the bench outside the Abbess' quarters. When vespers finished, the Abbess might grant an audience and speak with her. If only they'd been specific about the time. Vespers occurred both morning and night, Margurite recalled—or she'd learned somewhere along the line. Margurite realized that the nuns might make her wait in that bone-chilling hallway for longer than she'd expected. Days, perhaps. The Church was in no rush to admit a new novitiate, she'd heard. Another mouth to feed. Another veil to mend.

Except for the biting cold, she didn't mind the wait, not really. She considered it part of the penance she felt she must pay. She'd start with small contritions like this and work her way up.

Forgive us our trespasses.

She wanted dearly to change, to remove that which she'd done up to now. To outrun what she'd left behind—at least for the moment.

Here, inside the cloistered walls, she'd be safe. Here someone might give her absolution, after which she'd vow to live within the holy strictures of the Church. She'd have a godly life. She'd even change her name to *Margite.* And maybe, just maybe she'd experience a deeper forgiveness, not just the kind offered by some man in a robe and a hat. But by those who'd met their fates at her hands. None of this was her fault, though, was what she kept saying to herself. A small voice, a knowing of sorts told her she must keep sinning. All these many ages, she had to keep doing it. Otherwise, the bill would come due.

Forgiveness—God's mercy—would supersede all of that in the final analysis, wouldn't it? A whole lifetime of secrets and trespasses and blood—so much blood—she would expunge it all with a few Hail Marys and a lighted votive. But the dark powers that rose against her were crafty. So to assure her safety, she'd have to stay within the monastery walls.

It couldn't reach her here. That's why the Abbess had to accept her plea to stay, to work, to pray with the other women of God. That's why she needed to wait, why she needed penance and forgiveness.

Bargains, especially for souls, were made to be broken. Piss on the rest.

Deliver us from evil, amen.

Los Angeles, 1947
The Night It Happened

The terrain of the dark-between appeared darker than usual this time around. The perpetual vague purple haze of light was at least some illumination while Ren traversed its endless landscape. When he was a boy, the haze was brighter, and he saw vast plains of mud-cracked soil stretching out in all directions. But as time passed, he found he could only track what was right before his feet. He was always moving—toward what, he could not tell.

He stumbled on an object with substance, more so than anything else he'd ever encountered in this place. It felt like hefting hundred-pound barbells for Ren to lift his gaze enough to know what blocked his way. A dark knowing told him, *No, don't glance up. Just turn around and find your way back.* But he knew that there was no leaving just by willing it, at least not that he'd ever discovered. He summoned the strength to lift his head.

He was before an imposing structure still assembling itself from the surrounding murk. But from what he could see, the structure was like a church, with twin spires that stood like two soldiers on either side of the towering, riveted entry. He had stumbled on stone steps at the base of the chapel, and he forced his strength again to step up until he reached the landing and felt heavy with immense gravity. The structure solidified now, and he was in front of the iron-hinged doors of St. Catherine's Catholic Church. His mother and father—long since gone—stood behind him in their crisp Sunday best.

With a clank and a groan, the church doors widened inward, and he felt compelled to enter. A row of candles fitted into shoulder-high candelabras took the edge off of what might otherwise have been a murky blackness.

He heard music up ahead, the sounds of a choir comprised of high and low voices—women—singing in a foreign language, Latin he presumed. His feet no longer touched the floor. An invisible force suspended him in the air and sped him on. Or he was borne upward by unseen spreading wings.

Ahead was the altar. The cloth was white, like a hospital bed. A body lay upon it, disrobed, unmoving. As Ren floated closer to the scene, the more unsavory details clarified. The Reverend Mother Margite appeared from a side vestibule, her hands pressed together in prayer. She ascended to the high place behind the altar where only priests should stand, and she raised her arms to the darkness in silent benediction.

She raised a silver chalice and said, "Then *it* took the cup. Again it gave thee thanks and praise saying, 'Take this cup and drink. For this is the cup of my blood. The cup of the new and everlasting covenant.'" She lifted the chalice, and bells chimed. She drank with greedy haste, and blood drizzled from both sides of the cup, down her pale neck, saturating the white bib of her habit.

His body, the one lying on the altar, convulsed. His eyes locked back, and his teeth clenched down. Nuns from the choir intensified their singing, and some broke ranks to assist Margite by loosening Ren's jaw and inserting a flat rubber oval into his mouth.

And then it was dark.

♦

The pulsating neon red announcing HOT startled Ren back. He was just standing there in the dark in front of Nany's hotel, staring up at the neon sign. How he got there from the hospital was a blank spot in time, filled with little more than images of the Reverend Mother Margite. He checked his watch. Nine-twenty. But how much time had elapsed? It wouldn't be the first time he'd slipped into the dark-between for more than a day.

The last he remembered, he was leaving St. Cyprian's. That was in the afternoon, January sixteenth. He spun around and searched for the nearest trash bin. There was one of rusting metal just at the corner, so he rummaged through until he found the day's newspaper. The headlines were as he remembered from earlier. Either the paper was old, or he was still in the sixteenth.

He eyed the tavern across the street. There was a straggling group of vagrants leaning up against its sides. Most of them had planted their upturned hats on the sidewalk, in case they could snag a few contributions. He licked his parched lips and considered taking the sting out of his experiences on a barstool—just for a few minutes. That's all it would take. He fished into the lining of his overcoat, found his flask, and downed the last few sips. A few gulps of whiskey weren't enough—but he'd rather drink it, than not.

The flash of red neon blurred his vision and seared his brain, urging him forward to the hotel's call box. He knew more than ever that he'd need Nany's help, whatever form that might take. Something sinister was happening to him and to those around him. Whatever it was involved the occult and that Reverend Mother, he just knew it. Nany was the only one who'd had any answers up to then. He wasn't exactly up for her bizarre countermeasures, like taking some noxious root or the butchering of some helpless chicken. But he didn't know what else to do.

None of what was happening would make sense to any rational person. Logical steps now would not prove useful. He presumed that he might be next in line for whatever was making a path splashed in blood. And his family, too. He'd have to track them down, Gloria and Molly. They'd fled to Maxine's, and now he couldn't protect them until he had them back.

Ren skimmed the directory posted behind glass for Nany's name. She was in room 525, but someone had removed the tiny white letters spelling out "Zolva," leaving a dusty outline in the felt board. He verified the address on the shredded awning, in case there was another hotel with neon signage and blinked-out letters.

No. He had it right.

It wouldn't be the first time a potential suspect had fled once the heat turned up. It wouldn't be much of a loss to the Downtown HOT. If Charlene remained, she might fill in the blanks. He searched the short roster for her name, with no luck. He figured she likely used an alias, like her friend Zolva.

Ren peered through the doors to see if the clerk minded the front desk, but, as he suspected, the place looked deserted. He tested the door, in case it unlatched, but it held firm. That was when he saw the official notification from the city of Los Angeles taped to the glass, informing residents of the building's demolition. Nany had never told him that detail, but she must have known. The wrecking ball would smash the building in a few days. He wondered if anyone at all remained inside any longer.

He tapped on the glass and pressed the buzzer for an attendant, but no one responded. On the off chance that Charlene remained, he had to get in. He had to talk with her. He loitered in the dusk and the cold, tugging up the collar of his overcoat so it stood up straight to meet with the wide brim of his hat. For a Los Angeles evening, this was an odd one, with its damp and chill that smarted on the cheek.

After an hour, a woman passed out from the building. Ren nabbed the door with his fingertips, and after she'd walked around the corner, he slipped through. So, he stepped to the side, out of view of the front desk, and lightly trod up the worn steps.

He tried focusing on his footsteps, rather than on how snug the stairway was likely to appear. Or the constriction of his breath that made his lungs pull in asthmatic strains. Each step he took fell heavier than the last. He ascended halfway up the first flight before he needed to stop and lean on a wall to keep from buckling. He doubled over to put his hands on his knees, trying to steady his churning intestines, drawing in a few short huffs. When he straightened up, he saw the top half of a large oval mirror in the second-floor landing. A shoddy gold-leafed table stood beneath it. He'd stop there to gather his wits before finishing up the last four flights.

The hallway was dim, lit by a short line of bare-bulb wall sconces made to seem like candelabras. The shadows beyond them swallowed up the far ends of the corridor. Ren caught his face in the mirror, and it looked unwell. His eyes were sunken with dark circles, and his cheekbones protruded amid gaunt features. He realized he hadn't faced a mirror at home in a long while, to keep from seeing disturbing things.

A fly landed on his cheek, and he swished it away. Another replaced it, and then another. Ren realized what was coming—what the flies meant. They set his nerves on fire, and he was not sure that he had complete control of his limbs as they began swarming, clotting into some ghastly form in the darkest part of the corridor. He forced himself to step backward to re-enter the stairwell.

Click. Guk. Gukkk.

The sounds the thing made… the sticky bubbling reverberated throughout the hall. Its gurgles started from the dead-end hallway, past six or more doors. The wall sconces dimmed, and the screws that bolted them into the walls unscrewed with no visible hand at work. One after another, the candelabras flopped forward and dangled from their dusty inner wires. Bulb by bulb, they flickered and popped out, until there, in the deep shadows at the hallway's end, the formed figure skulked. The darkness of the hallway outlined the even darker figure, but Ren saw its claws twitching to clutch, to shred, to kill, just like they did before. The thing shambled down the hallway, thudding with a slow, dead limp. It plodded as though it had no concern whether or not it might snatch Ren's soul; it was just a matter of when.

Ren felt paralyzed, knowing that it would come for him, no matter what he tried. It found him no matter where we went. The creature stopped and widened its mouth into a grotesque smile with hundreds of jagged teeth before it busted open into a thousand swarming black flies that buzzed at record speed down the hall toward Ren. He didn't know whether they might reach him, but he also didn't want to find out. He scrambled back to the stairwell, stumbling and slamming his head and shoulder into a wall along the way.

Ren struggled upward toward the fifth floor, cramming each step beneath him as fast as he could, or else he might pass out from the walls closing in. He kept racing upward for three more flights. But his lungs stung from gasping, and his legs began to give out.

Click. Guk-gukuk.

The thing moved behind him.

Ren had a handful of steps to go. But he felt forced to his knees, and he spewed his innards onto the stair treads. He tried to crawl upward, but he slipped in the puke puddle and banged his knee on a stair. It seemed to him as though his body became heavier than his muscles would bear, and his vitality wilted. Even though he wanted to press on, his body was surrendering.

"Help…." He wanted to scream so loud that even strangers passing by on the streets would hear him through the walls. But the cry stalled and died in his throat. His scream got stuck there. Deep, relentless distress spread across his whole body, dragging him downward, downward.

Click. Click. Guuuk.

The creature had re-assembled itself into its grotesque many-eyed other form, and it thudded up each step. Ren heard its mucous-wet talons trudge upward, like a creature long-dead trying to re-discover the act of walking. Ren wanted to lift himself up and crawl. But the creature wrapped its sharpened claws, clammy and constricting, around his shin, and it crushed through his bones. Ren struggled to release his leg, but his ankle cracked and popped to pieces. The pain was intolerable, but he had to shake free. As he struggled, it felt like the creature took his life energy and used it to fortify its own malicious vitality.

Ren looked up the steps and saw small feet in sensible black heels appear. In his mixture of pain and fear, he knew his strength was almost gone. Whoever stood there puffed smoke at him that smelled of ashtrays and dark nightclubs. A colossal roar filled the building as the stair treads popped loose from their nails in a loud series of shots. Whatever had gripped his leg before disappeared, leaving only the sting of ripped skin. Then everything went still.

♦

The first thing Ren saw was the uneven circles of a water-stained ceiling, yellow and brown. There was scratchy, warbling music from a Victrola, too—opera, though he didn't know which one. Then there was a woman's voice, soft, pleasing. He'd heard that voice before, and he tried to recall where. She was humming. His head throbbed, and he reached up with a weak hand to inspect the damage. He slipped it beneath a cold cloth that someone—this woman—had laid there. But instead of feeling the lump he expected, his forehead was smooth and cool. He checked his ankle, the one grabbed by whatever was chasing him. It stung, but there was no blood, no wounded flesh, no swelling.

"Oh, you're awake," Charlene said. It took him a moment to recognize her. He was stretched out on an overstuffed couch with brocade fabric like he'd seen in photos of old European estates. It smelled grubby, as though she'd left the place undisturbed to gather dust for a long time.

He sat up—maybe a bit too quickly—because the movement made him almost vomit. It took a minute for his tongue to cooperate with his thoughts. "What the hell?" He heard the high tone of panic in his voice, and it was unsettling to hear.

"Is there a problem, Mr. Larson?" Charlene asked. She sat at a nearby table she had covered with a Spanish shawl.

He stood up, but his legs buckled, and he dropped back onto the couch. "What was that…that thing?"

"What thing?"

"The thing… the thing that chased me up those steps…"

She crossed the room in her sensible low heels and reached for the doorknob.

"Jesus, lady, don't open that door! Are you crazy?"

She swung the door open and looked down the hall. She turned back towards him and shrugged. Leaving the door wide open, she returned to the table, where she continued doling out cards one by one and squinting at them through a pair of small spectacles. The soprano singing from the crackly record seemed unaffected by his jitters.

He propped himself up and staggered over to inspect the hallway for himself. It was clear, and the light sconces were all in their places, as though nothing had happened.

"Mr. Larson, you've been here for nearly three hours. If you're feeling better, I really must move on. Packing to be done, you know. I'm the last one here. And the building comes down any day now.

Any day," Charlene said. She sighed. "It's too bad. Nothing ever seems to last, does it?"

"Three hours? What? You mean to tell me you didn't see that thing… that horrible thing coming after me up those stairs? Why, you were standing there, watching, puffing that cigar and it scared it off."

She placed another card down and then took out a magnifying glass to inspect it more thoroughly. "I'm afraid you have me at a disadvantage. I haven't the slightest idea what you're talking about. You came to my door, white as a snake's belly. Sweating and speaking in some foreign tongue. That's all I know."

"Foreign tongue? What are you talking about?"

"You were saying things. Odd things like…Zagan… Voso… Baal…. honestly, you might as well have been speaking with a mouth full of marbles. I don't know any foreign languages myself. Except for a bit of angelic, which, of course, is also a bit demonic. But that isn't much of a language at all, is it?"

"What? Angelic… what?" Ren asked. He thought maybe he was hallucinating this conversation.

"Well anyway, you were prattling on and on with that twaddle, and you just wouldn't stop. Seeing you in that state, I naturally invited you in to sit down. Then you just…passed out."

"Passed out?" It was a possibility, Ren realized. But he didn't want to talk about it to Charlene in case she'd think he was drunk.

"Yes. Passed out. Maybe this will help you remember how it happened." She held up his silver flask and set it down on the table near her cards. "It slipped from your coat as you lay down. You know, booze is a nasty habit, Mr. Larson. It leads one down life's darker corridors." She held up one of her tarot cards and squinted.

"Where's your friend?"

"I don't have any friends, Mr. Larson. You'll need to be a bit more specific."

"Nany. Zolva. Whatever her name is."

Charlene laid out another card. "The Fool!"

"What?" Ren asked.

"The Fool. You got the Fool as the card crossing your path, of course." She looked through the magnifier to inspect. "Well, that doesn't surprise me. You must feel quite foolish, having come back only to find that Nany's flown the coop, as they say. And right under your detective's nose." She gave a small laugh.

"What do you mean? She's gone?"

"Yes. Gone. Like *With the Wind*."

"Gone where?"

"How should I know? Although I suspect she's headed back to her home in the Caribbean. Where was it again? Cat Island? There are so many of them. Islands, that is. Well, anyway, they're all the same to me—balmy. All year round, hot and sticky. So hot. All year round. Can you imagine?"

She smiled at him and then snapped down another card.

"Anyway, she came to fulfill one purpose, and that's what she's done. So now she's…." Charlene made a gesture like a bird flying away. "You know, I haven't yet drawn another card, but maybe it shows travel in your future. I do hope you like hot… and sticky."

"What do you mean, purpose?"

Charlene went on after positioning another card. "Oh my! This one says there was something under the mattress."

Ren caught his breath but tried not to act like she'd struck a nerve.

She closed her eyes and pressed the card to her lids. "Yes, its coming in clear... Yes. Under a child's mattress. Something quite foul. A book of symbols... spells? Demons. Seventy- two of them—and yet, just the one. But then again, it's been with you since you were a boy… your parents—no, wait—your mother. Yes, herself a conjurer of sorts." She put down another card and gasped as though she were on stage. "Give me your hand."

"What?"

"Don't be a child. Give me your hand."

He stood and approached the table where he saw a black-handled knife laying alongside the card pile. Before he could stop it, Charlene nabbed the blade and jabbed it into her palm.

"Jesus, lady, what are you doing?"

"Oh shut up!" she snapped.

She pinned his hand down to the table with a strength he could scarcely comprehend. She smeared the gathering blood from her hand on his open palm, then forced it down onto a waiting piece of blank parchment. When he lifted his hand away, he saw the symbol there, drawn in fresh red. It was the symbol he'd seen before, painted on the walls where they all had died. Fiorelli's wife and child. Haddock and his family.

"Mmmm. Yes. Andras. That's who it is."

"Andras?"

"Andras. Andras! Yes, you idiot. That's who's come. One of the seventy-two. A demon. A real nasty one, too. *Mr. Crooked.*" Her eyes lit up with elation.

Ren staggered backward and went around the other side of the couch. He eyed her knife and tried to think of ways to stall. He tried to change the subject.

"You said Nany was here for a purpose. What was it?" Ren asked.

Charlene clutched at her neck and kept on, ignoring his question. "Yes. Andras. It knows you. It follows and waits. Ooh, you're good and ripe with sin now." She laughed, but it wasn't the kind of laugh full of lightness. It had secrets behind it. Secrets and wickedness.

"Charlene, what the hell is going on?"

She turned her whole body in the chair, then rose with the grace of a trained dancer.

"Charlene, Charlene…" she taunted and laughed. The voice had changed. It was husky and low, like a chorus of men. There was bite and malice in her eyes. "That bitch is long gone. I took her myself. Now she's just… dying… again and again… right alongside your mother. One death is more painful than the next. But let me tell you—Ren—she was one hell of a conjurer. And thank you,

Charlene!"

Ren backed away from her.

"Don't be stupid. Not now. Of course, you should have known that Nany would be on her way. Especially since there was only one thing left to take. And that she left for me alone."

"Take?"

The door—his only escape—shut on its own, and the lock clicked into place. Ren turned to witness hands, white as the walls, sprouting from the door and gripping onto the jamb to keep him from leaving.

It was too late. Too late. Ren realized he would die here. But he couldn't allow it. He had to fight.

"Yes. Take." She took a step closer to him, and she turned her head to one side. There was a loud cracking sound, as though her bones were breaking inside her neck. Her shoulder dropped, as though no longer connected to her skeletal frame. A black smoke-wisp appeared and stretched out from behind her. It formed itself into a shadow of a wing. "Your best friend? Taken." She took another step with a smile, and likewise, her other shoulder dislocated. Both arms hung, dead, and another shadow-wing budded from her back. "Your job? Taken."

Ren backed up and smacked against the door. The disembodied hands clutched and clawed him into place. He reached down, but there was no longer any knob, any lock.

"And where is your wife? Your child? Anyone? Everyone? Taken. *Guuk, click.*"

An eyeball popped out and rolled across Charlene's cheek, dangling by the bloody optic nerve. A dark, clawed finger twisted from the hulled-out eye hole. Another split open the flesh from a nostril as it pushed through, and a third reached from her mouth, longing for whatever was beyond the toothy opening. The three hooked talons locked together and ripped everything to one side. And when Charlene's face opened like the skin of an overripe pomegranate, bloody juices and gristle gushed forward, revealing what was beneath that façade.

Ren turned back in time to catch the black, shining eyes twinkling with a murderous joy from beneath the torn carcass. The skin sloughed off completely, an unfastened costume. And there stood the boil-infested creature, covered in a viscous afterbirth, bearing its claws and a ragged row of fangs lining the depths of its red, open throat.

Like a hawk diving for its prey, it darted at its target with unerring precision. Ren struggled against the hands holding him and covered his eyes with his forearms to keep the monster's talons from gashing them out to sample the small filets.

When he did not feel the sting of claws sinking into him, Ren uncrossed his arms.

He was standing outside the hotel entrance once again. This time, though, the hotel doors were wrapped in thick layers of chain, and prominent *Condemned Building* signs were affixed in plain view. Next to the structure stood a towering steel crane, equipped with an enormous black ball that dangled from a thick cable. Ren backed away from the scene, his sense of balance and comprehension gone. He was trapped inside a city block of wooden fencing surrounding the property, but, like the rest of what he'd seen, none of it was there earlier. He hoisted himself over the wall and ripped his coat as he fell to the sidewalk.

Fifteen

Los Angeles, 1947
Nearly Two Months Before It Happened

Old George sat at the corner, near the blue mailbox so sun-washed it was the color of faded blue jeans. He thought of dropping this envelope off at the central post office. Some delivery men there knew Old George, and they might take good care of it. But he had second thoughts. If he sent what he had anonymously, he wouldn't mix up a bunch of federal employees in events as gruesome as this.

He felt the envelope, making sure he hadn't forgotten the most crucial part. The paper bent only partway because the insides were stiff with photographs. Plenty of them—from all angles. Also, a copy of the sales slip from the jewelry shop. It was only a matter of time now before Griswold knew the truth, or he'd at least have enough to investigate. Then it would be over for Officer Larson.

He dropped the letter in the box and walked away, pulling his hat brim down so no one watching might know it was him for sure.

Sixteen

Los Angeles, 1947
The Night It Happened

Ren had flagged down a taxi in the dark, and by the time he reached the Hollywood Hills, a dense fog had begun midway up the hill. Nothing seemed real any longer. Nothing at all. Ren had a vague, disembodied sense, as though wandering through a dream.

Right before he got into the cab, he used the telephone booth across the street from the Downtown HOT over at the Vegas Room, the wino-pub across the street. It was there he tried phoning Maxine Ganz's house. He'd persisted with that over the past several days, but no one ever answered. The phone buzzed for several pulses, then someone picked up.

"Hello?"

"Hello, Maxine?" Ren asked. He realized this wouldn't be easy. There wasn't any way Maxine would let Ren through to his wife if she'd given that order. But he had to try.

"I'm sorry. I think you have the wrong number," she said.

"Is this Granite-five, two-two-one-eight?" he asked.

"Why, yes, sir. But there's no one here named Maxine. You must have misdialed the number," she said.

Ren's breath quickened. "Please, Maxine, I know that's you. We've met a hundred times before," he said. "I need to talk to my wife. Do you hear me, Maxine? Now, I don't know what she's been telling you, but it's not true, you hear me? We can work anything out. Just me and Gloria, you see, Maxine? We can work anything out." He listened to his voice as if from a distance, breaking up and weeping. "Oh God, I miss her. I miss Molly. Please, Maxine. Please get my wife to talk to me. I'll do anything to get them back."

"You must have misdialed the number." She sounded vacant, as though she'd missed everything he'd been saying.

Ren wiped his nose. "Huh? Maxine, it's me, Ren. Can you hear me?"

"Why, yes, sir," she said. But she said it exactly like before, like a skipping record. "But there's no one here named Maxine. You must have misdialed the number."

"What's going on? I want to speak to my wife. Maxine, please!"

Ren saw the street lights from the window flicker like they had in the hotel hallway. One by one, from the most distant to the closest, the lights fizzled out.

"Why, yes, sir. But there's no one here named Maxine. You must have misdialed the number."

The street darkness grew heavy and flattened against the window. There was some static on the phone, and the sounds on the other end began. "*Guk, click, click, guk.*" He dropped the receiver, flung open the phone booth door, and staggered out to the street.

The sedan from St. Cyprian's rolled by just then. A small set of hands pressed against the back seat window, and a face emerged. It was Molly. And behind her, an adult hand. It was Gloria. Her eyes streamed with tears, and her mouth gaped open in a silent scream. Black-clawed hands wrapped around the two of them and dragged them back into the dark. The vehicle reared on its metallic bulk and sped away.

"No, no, no!" He chased after them, his shoes slapping the

pavement. "You're not… you can't be… You can't be!" He lost all awareness of his surroundings, and his legs fell out from underneath him as he slid stomach-first onto the pavement.

"Oh God, no."

He wept and crumpled to his knees while watching the sedan blaze down the street until it was gone. "Oh God. Come back!" Ren sobbed into his hands. The vagrants sitting along the gutter knew to keep their distance. Ren eventually pulled himself up to a wobbly stand, and he lurched toward the curb. A cab rounded a corner, missed him by inches, and skidded to a halt.

The cab driver stuck his head out the window. "You crazy or something?"

"Please. Please, take me home."

The cabby looked at him and his tar-blackened shirt, his tear-streaked face. Ren noticed the man's expression, and he realized he must have seemed like a lunatic.

"I've got money," Ren said. "I'm not crazy. I'm a cop." Ren dug into his coat pocket and flashed the driver his badge.

The cabby wetted his lips and looked around. "Okay, look, Mac, I'm gonna get the fare up front, ya hear me?"

Ren pulled out about ten bills and waved them with a trembling hand at the driver. "Yes. Yes. Okay, sure. I have money, see?" Ren opened his wallet and showed the driver.

"Sure, sure, pal. I can see," the driver said. He looked at Ren again and assessed his options. "You say you're a cop?"

"That's right. A detective."

"Where you headed?"

"To my home. Up the hills past Woodside. Past the Village and go on about 20 more minutes," Ren said.

"Look, I don't want any trouble."

"No. No trouble. See?" He opened the door and slid inside. "How much is that?"

"Two bucks. But honestly, Mister, I think you need to get to a hospital," he said.

Ren pulled out five dollars and held them out for the driver. "I'm all right. Only a little shaken up. The wife and I are having some trouble. That's all."

"I get it. I don't need your life's story," the driver said. He slipped the cash from Ren's fingers and screeched away. During the length of the drive, he eyed the suspicious man in his back seat. He monitored his rearview mirror every few minutes in case the backseat stranger killed himself, or pulled a hatchet out of his overcoat.

The cabby slowed as he reached the gathering mist. The lack of street lighting in the hills made it difficult for him to notice the edges of the road. He had to make a series of sharp and dramatic steering adjustments to avoid the places where the pavement met the sides of the downslopes and the sharp drop-offs. The lights from the taxi blurred into the hazy white wall of mist that seemed to go on forever. Ren knew how dangerous the roads were in the dark, even in broad daylight, so he figured the driver would likely pull over any minute.

"It's around the bend in the road here," Ren said.

Maxine's house was much older and statelier than Ren expected, though it was decidedly a place of decayed opulence. They pulled up the semi-circular gravel driveway toward the plaster-chipped, red-clay-roofed estate. Ren counted six paint-peeled windows across the second story level. They were all connected by a fragmented and mold-infected balcony that exposed the underlying brick structure every few feet. Three Spanish arches supporting the upper gallery served as pillars for the expansive front porch, and the entry lay buried deep beneath. Not a single light shone.

"Wait here," Ren said to the driver.

"This your house?"

Ren fished for his wallet in his overcoat and threw down several more dollars. "Just wait here. I've got one thing to do."

The driver ratcheted his head around in all directions with sharp, uneasy movements, as though he were looking for potential crime witnesses. He reached down and swiped the cash into his pants pocket. "Sure thing. Whatever you say. But be quick."

Ren took the stone staircase two steps at a time, and when he reached the door, he gave it a knock that resounded with hollow echoes throughout the house.

A few moments later, the porch lit with a dim amber glow, and Maxine cracked the door open enough to establish who it was coming around at such an unusual hour. Ren noticed that the door only opened as far as the safety chain would allow.

"Where's my wife?"

"Mr. Larson. What in heaven's name are you doing here at this time of night?"

"I found Gloria's note. Where is she? Where's Molly?"

"I couldn't rightly tell you." She adjusted the thick, round-framed spectacles that made her stare more like an owl's than ever before. She clutched at the neck of her bulky black nightclothes.

Ren took out the note he'd stashed in his overcoat. "This is her note. Says she came with Molly." Ren showed it, and the old woman's watery eyes peered through the gap, not at the note but at the man in his street-soiled clothes and his drunken sweat that beaded on his tear-streaked face.

"I haven't seen Gloria lately," she said. "I've tried to come around, but she said she's been busy. With what, I can only imagine." She gave Ren the once-over from top to bottom.

"That's her handwriting, isn't it? She says she came over to stay with you. She's been gone a couple nights now. So if she isn't here, then you tell me where she's gone. She only knows a handful of people. Most of them moved on since she got married. Like I said, the note says she came here. Where else would she go?"

Maxine glanced down to inspect the note. "I couldn't rightly say if that was her handwriting or not, Mr. Larson, seeing as she's never written me anything."

Ren shoved the door, and the chain held it fast. "Goddamn it, Maxine. I know she's here. And you're hiding her from me."

"Fallow, Ditch, come!" she called out. She unhooked the door chain and widened the gap. On either side of her sat two black

Dobermans, rumbling with a low and menacing snarl, baring fangs, restrained only by Maxine's immediate command.

"I'd suggest you leave, Mr. Larson... before there's any serious trouble."

"I'll give you trouble, lady. You're dealing with a flipping police officer."

She raised her doughy chin. "Mark!" she commanded. The dogs stood on all fours, and their pointed ears dropped back.

"Did you know your wife told me on more than one occasion that you frightened her? She once mentioned going back to her family in New York. Have you checked the train stations, Mr. Larson? Have you checked with her family?"

"That's not true," he said. He tried to control his tone, given his situation.

"Take your leave while you can, Mr. Larson. And don't come back."

The dogs began snapping their fangs and taking small steps toward him. He backed away.

"You tell Gloria she needs to come home. You hear me? Molly is my daughter, too."

"Goodbye, Mr. Larson," she said.

When Ren got to the edge of the steps, he glowered and flexed his jaw.

"Storm," the old woman said. The dogs scrambled their paws on the stone, trying to gain traction. Ren rushed down the steps and slid into the back seat of the taxi. The dogs sprinted after him, barking, thick strands of saliva flying as they pounced on the closed car door.

"Jesus, Mister. What the hell did you do to cheese off whoever lives there?" the driver asked.

"Just go," Ren said.

Ren recognized a mile marker on the side of the road reflecting in the headlights and saw it as the right opportunity. No sense in anyone catching him taking a taxi late at night.

"I can take it from here," he said. The driver halted in the street with a short skid. Ren hopped out, and again, the car squealed off.

Ren popped up his coat collar and fitted his fedora down over his brow. He trotted along the street, his mind in an unfocused and chaotic state. It was like a lens blotting out everything in the periphery while focusing on the safety of his wife and child.

None of this should be happening. None of it. And maybe it wasn't. The whole thing might be a nightmare. Though this was the story he'd kept alive since he first encountered the unexplained events, it was now upstream swimming in a rough current. The only reasonable option left was for him to believe in what Nany had told him. Mr. Crooked. He'd come for Ren.

A sparkle of light came, reflecting in the mist behind him. Though he noted nothing else worrisome, he was alone on the road after midnight. Things had happened here before. So he picked up the pace. Who knew if it would be the hospital sedan again? With that crazy bitch, Reverend Mother Margite, driving it, and whatever else she had going on. That murderous lying bitch who'd made some kind of pact with the devil. She was in league with it. Why didn't he see it before it was… too late? Nany must have run off in fear. Despite her own occult practices, she couldn't control this thing or Margite. She'd tried to warn Ren, but he was too thick to listen.

Margite was hunting his family; demons were her hunting dogs. She had already taken Fiorelli's wife, Haddock, and his entire family. All of them bathed in blood, unwitting sacrifices to Satan. He tried not to think about the vision he had of Gloria and Molly pressed to the glass in that car, screaming, screaming in unheard voices.

And that bitch in clerical clothing, conjuring demons. Prowling around taking innocent lives for herself, as though the blood of his loved ones was cheap roadside gasoline. That's what was going on, despite his efforts to deny it.

He saw the flicker of light again. Then it vanished. But he didn't hear the sounds he expected. There was no squeal of tires on wet pavement or a motor purring or a clutch being released.

His house was only a couple of city blocks away from where he was now, so he doubled his pace, trying to outrun whatever or whoever this was.

He ran, but when he turned around, the twin headlights from a car pierced the night and the murk. The strange thing was that the car made no sound. The lights grew stronger, but still, no engine putter came. It had to be the nun. Sister Margite. He ran at top speed, huffing and wheezing to stay ahead.

His strength was gone after a short while, and he had to prop his hands on his knees. The outline of his house in the darkness was just up ahead. But the headlights now beamed in front of him. Out of thin air, the vehicle had somehow passed him and pointed straight at him. He put a hand to shield his eyes from the glare.

"Hello?" he said. There was no response. The lights darkened with a hush.

"Hello?" he said again, but his voice had weakened. From the blackness of the vehicle emerged the outline of a woman in dark robes. She was a faceless black blob standing in front of the car. "Reverend Mother?"

The nun became airborne, at least a foot from the ground. Her limp feet dangled below her robes. She advanced toward Ren, gliding in the mist. Her hands were clutching claws, reaching out toward him.

"Oh shit," he said. He took a few steps backward and ran with whatever he had left for the house. In his blind panic, he slipped on the pavement, wet with the night mist. His leather soles slid like ice skates, and he fell forward, breaking his fall on his hands and knees.

Ren took just a second to study his palms, shredded and studded with black pebbles. Where the rocks had fallen free were deep, meaty holes overrun with blood. The specter continued to advance, arms outstretched. He reached for his gun but realized it wasn't there. He steadied himself and sprinted toward his front walk. Just a few yards left, and he'd lock the door and lock her out. He'd opened his door to her sometime back when it knocked with the thunder of hell, and the house tilted under the weight of the damned. He wouldn't make that mistake again.

He reached the stepping stones to his door, but it was too late. Claws sank into his neck, and he fell to his knees. Her fingers penetrated through to the bone, and he let out a sound, primal and raw—that of a farm animal knowing it was on the slaughterhouse floor.

"Larson!"

Griswold stood watching from the porch. He'd parked his police vehicle next to Ren's in the driveway. The headlights exposed everything in their white glare. Ren continued to shout as he fought off what he figured were Margite's claws, or Mr. Crooked's. As he reached around, he punctured his hand on a long, thorny bougainvillea cane that was growing from an oversized bush along the walkway.

"Larson, what's going on?"

"Sarge?" Ren asked. His voice shook, and he tried to control it. Griswold would never understand any of this. Ren didn't understand any of it. "Is that you?"

"Larson, what are you doing out of your house?"

"I, uh," Ren started. He laughed. But that laughter became hysterics, a mixture of crowing and crying. "I thought I saw something pretty bad." He hoped he was passing it all off pretty well. He stepped up to the front porch. The Sarge took several steps back, and he looked like he was trying to find a quick way back to his car.

"Jeez, Larson, you look terrible."

"Yeah, I'm just… yeah, not feeling too good." Laughter rose up again, and Ren cupped his hands to his mouth. He couldn't help it. How could he think someone trying to grab him? And where was the sedan? Just vanished? It seemed so ridiculous now that the Sarge was standing there.

"Is that what you do out here in all this… isolation? Scream your guts out?"

Ren had no response. He looked down at his bloody hands, which were blazing with an oven-hot pain now.

"Did something die around here? It stinks to high heaven. What in damnation is that stench?"

"You know, Gloria said the same thing. It's been going on for days now. Must be a dead skunk. We get those out here from time to time…. in all this isolation." He took a step toward the Sarge. And the Sarge took a step back.

"I haven't had a chance to check it out," Ren said. He shoved his hands in his pockets, hoping the Sarge hadn't seen the bloodied palms. But the wet red stains in his pockets grew without control, and the Sarge couldn't stop staring.

"Okay, well anyway, I came out here to check if you were home. I got reports earlier in the day from St. Cyprian's about you visiting there. Is that right?" Griswold said. He stepped down off the porch and walked toward Ren.

"I'm not sure what you mean, Sarge. I've been here all day. I just stepped out to take a walk, that's all." Ren said.

"In the dark? You were walking in the dark? In the hills? By yourself?"

"Yeah, I do it all the time. Not sure what that has to do with your visit, though."

"This lady, the head of the hospital, says you were there today interviewing Fiorelli, and they couldn't get you to leave."

Ren took another step closer to Griswold.

The Sarge stepped back again. He continued, "I says to myself that Larson's a smart guy, he knows better than to walk out of the house the day after he goes on a leave ordered by the department. I thought this smart guy wouldn't actually go against a direct order, especially given his situation."

"Well, like I said, I… I just went for a walk. You can see my car right there. I haven't moved it," Ren said.

"Yeah, I saw the car. But the report came in from earlier today in the afternoon. Benson said the old genie was in your police vehicle. And he found blood on the car floor. A lot of it. I didn't want to send one of the guys up here to check this all out, seeing as this is a kind of sensitive situation. Thought I'd check things out for myself, you know, keep things private—for your dignity and all. So I came up here when I could. And here you are, out of the house."

"What do you mean, sensitive situation?" Ren asked.

"Look, Larson. You know....everyone knows that I did Gloria a favor by taking you back right after... She said you were fine. And you were, for a while at least. You made it for two years. That's not too bad Larson, especially given.... Anyway, after you had your breakdown, I thought, well, we all thought you'd never really recover. You know, that's how come me and the boys have been looking after you. Making sure nothing tipped you back over, on accident. Just like Gloria and the doctor told us. But once I asked you to.... I should never have asked you to handle Haddock. Jeez. What was I thinking? But I figured since he was your buddy, it would give you some—I don't know—time to work things out in your mind. Settle you. You know?"

"Breakdown? Tipping me over? You got to be joking," Ren said.

"You think a year at Cyprian's was a joke, Larson? Convulsive treatments a joke?" Griswold asked. He mopped the sweat gathering on his brow, and he sidestepped toward the walkway.

"Convuls—wait a minute Sarge... what are you talking about?" Ren said. "You're mixed up. You're not talking about me. Yeah, I went away, but I was in the war. I was a captive in Germany. I had to—." His voice trembled, and he decided not to say more.

"Sure, Ren. Like you said—the war. No one's gonna argue with you, buddy." Griswold paused and grimaced. There was a long silence between them. Their eyes locked, and Ren sensed the Sarge's fear. He'd never seen that before. "They said this might happen again," Griswold said. "You can't keep going on like this. You need help, Larson, not a job," Griswold said. "I'm sorry, buddy, but this is over, effective immediately. Now, I'll give you the night to settle down a bit. But come in early tomorrow. That way, you can miss almost everyone, so when you bring in your badge and gun, it'll be more private-like."

"My badge? Gun?"

"Be reasonable, Larson."

Ren pressed his hands on either side of his skull, and his face reddened. "Okay, never mind that," he said. "I have information. Good information that could break open this case with Fiorelli, his wife, and Haddock. The whole damn thing. You got to believe me," Ren said.

Griswold said nothing, but took a pace to his car that gave away his sense of alarm.

"What information, Larson? What? Huh?"

Ren realized that his pieces were only fragments—and not even reasonable ones—about devils, card readers, and the occult. And that somehow it all seemed to tie to Sister Margite. He knew now that if he said a single thing, he really would sound like… like what Sage was saying.

"It's just that… Sarge, it's complicated…." Ren started following his boss, who was walking sideways, trying not to lose sight of Ren. "You can't be serious about letting me go. I got leads. I'm telling you, I do. And they're all solid."

Griswold shook his head, slipped in the vehicle, and backed out.

"I just went for a walk. I didn't leave," Ren shouted. He followed the Sarge into the street and banged with his bloody palms on the window. More pebbles loosened from them and trickled onto the ground.

Griswold screeched away down the hill into the dark and the mist.

"I just went for a walk!" he shouted. But only the fog heard him.

♦

Ren sat in a kind of caged silence after Griswold left. All he could do was rattle around in his thoughts about what happened. It wasn't because the Sarge was right. No. He needed to keep his mind occupied to keep from choking with panic. Ren was alone in the house in hills, and that thing or Sister Margite would return in time. Nany said that he had some secret, some sin inside that attracted the creature.

Since Gloria left, he'd taken up sleeping upright in the den's wingback chair. He positioned it in the corner to maintain a clear view of the room. He had his holster with a loaded .38 Special slung across his chest. So if Margite or that thing showed up again, he'd see if they find it all that special.

He emptied a bottle of whiskey. And when he'd drunk more than enough, he let it clop to the floor.

The silence of the room was suffocating. Ren realized that it was in this kind of silence that things seemed to happen. Bad things. He took his glance away from watching the room long enough to extract Gloria's ring from his pocket, and he turned it over in his fingers. His grief of her loss overwhelmed him. In that flood of grief, he lost control of his body, and the ring slipped away with a knock on the floor. He couldn't muster the strength to pick it up again. But an unrelenting and uneasy thought told him to look down at it anyway. Instead of her diamond wedding ring, lying beside the chair was an ordinary flat washer the size of a nickel. Seeing this odd transformation triggered an awful sense of dread that washed over him, filled him up, and threatened to drag him down beneath its dark currents.

A nearby table clock tick-tocked with an insistent metronome, and the oval braided rug seemed to be spiraling, drawing Ren down, down. To anyone else, it might have been a trick of the eyes. But Ren knew the signs adding up, and these meant he'd soon propel into that unwelcome in-between landscape.

He was starting to lose his inner resolve to escape from this other-world. So instead of resisting, he focused his attention on the ever-growing understanding that Gloria would never return. Once she'd understood that he'd been sacked, she and Molly would hop the next bus to Brooklyn. Or wherever. She'd never loved him. It was difficult to admit. But it was time to stop running from the truth. His loss was tangible, devastating, and unstoppable. Tears began to flood his eyes.

His ruminations did nothing to stop the dark-between from engulfing him. The braids in the rug swirled, sucking him into that dark, vast, and perilous place. He slid from the chair through the winding coils on the floor.

He stood within that godforsaken endless desert, gray and black. Below his feet, the soil had broken into a million uneven jigsaw puzzle pieces. From the ground, just up ahead, arose a small wooden structure. Ren had no strength to resist. He had to walk. He had to reach whatever showed up in that landscape. There seemed to be a force of gravity now that he'd never felt before. It came as a dragging weight, pulling his muscles, his skin, his face toward the soil. It also stole away his thoughts, his words, so that all he had left was an unbearable horror growing in his gut. Nothing left but pure, raw fright.

Ren couldn't tell whether it took a minute or a month for him to reach the structure with its tooled and scrolling spires, its carved entrances. It had three doorways in all. He had enough words left in him to identify the thing standing in the middle of the desert as a confessional, the kind he'd seen as a boy.

A figure emerged from out of the right side door, clothed in the habit of the Reverend Mother Margite. Trapped in the choke of her black veil, the face seemed a black, shapeless blotch of boils. The figure opened a hole where a mouth should be, and where it parted, strings of ooze stuck together and sucked away down into the black hole at the center of its face. The abomination uttered a sound, an inhuman one, that Ren thought could be an animal lowing in pain or something else groaning in sorrowful agony. The creature pressed boney hands together in a mockery of prayer. It opened one, and Ren saw in its palm the strange design that had appeared at every death, the design Charlene had showed him in blood.

The left door of the confessional opened and out came Charlene. She beckoned Ren to come forward, and he did so without knowing how he might stop that from happening. He entered, and she locked the door behind him. The cramped space had only enough room to turn in place and kneel on a padded church-kneeler. A square panel the size of a Christmas card slid open. On the other side, in the shadows, sat Nany.

"Bless me, for I have sinned." Ren heard himself recite the formula he'd learned as a child, though he was confident his mouth never moved. "I don't know how long it has been since my last confession."

"Tell me, copp'r. Say what you done, or else. The sin is in you, good and ripe now. It's your last chance. Mr. Crooked waitin for you right now."

The confessional vanished around him, and he found that he and Nany sat side by side in the plush red velvet seats of a movie house.

A stuttering click from a projector began, and a screen ahead of him lit with a silvery glow. The image was scratchy and full of black blotches, the sound a warped recording as the film threaded through the projector high up somewhere in that vast darkness.

"This is how Russia battered their way through to Berlin in the last weeks of April," a narrator stated. He had a British clip to his voice that cracked and skipped along with a dramatic yet warping musical track. Cannons blasted buildings, and mortar blasts tore up the streets. Bewildered citizens emerged from smoking subway shelters onto the streets. "That's one way to make an entrance. British forces aren't going to make friends with Mr. Hitler that way." The narrator said it like he could have been selling soap or hair tonic. "St. Hedwig's Cathedral, Anhalter Bahnhof, the Brandenburg Gate, once Germany's pride, have been reduced to rubble as the price of Hitler's nightmare of world conquest."

The scene switched to Ren cuffed in thick irons, naked and bent forward on the floor of an unlit, filth-strewn cell. The broken skin on his forehead kissed the mucky floor, and bent low as he was, he mumbled incoherent words over and over. Flies buzzed around his face, but he seemed indifferent to them. One landed on his cheek and entered a nostril. He took no note of it, but kept mumbling.

"Look out. Here's a fellow in a bit of trouble," the narration stated. Ren glanced over at Nany, who fixed her gaze on the scene playing out.

"What were you saying?" Nany asked.

"It was a prayer I heard someone tell me," Ren said.

"Who told you?"

"I don't know. Just some night whispers. They said it to me again and again. At first, I thought it was gibberish. But then I came to love it. The whispering voices told me to say, '*Zagan, Voso, Orobas, Caim, Andras….*' I'd say that over and over, just to keep the pain from filling my mind."

"That's the talk you hear when you're taking the stink of evil out of someone. Callin to Mr. Crooked. Callin for it to help by its many names, that's what you done. You knew it all along. You knew it was evil since you were a boy, and you called for it when you wanted its strength. When you wanted it to do what you couldn't do alone because you were a coward," Nany said.

"Yes," Ren said. The admission stung. "The names sounded good in my ear. And tasted sweet coming from my lips. All the time, I wished that man was dead," Ren said. His face bunched up, and his brow lowered, heavy and dark. "I wished someone would cut his goddamn throat," Ren replied. He spoke through ground-down teeth, and he spat as he spoke.

As though in response to Ren, the narrator said, "Careful what you wish for, soldier."

The film showed boots striding into the cell at a stern pace. It was Müller, with his greasy hair flat, parted, and swept to the side to emulate his party's leader. He kicked Ren with his military boots and yelled at him in German. Ren trembled on his knees, bent forward to avoid any more damage. Dried blood covered his face, and he had a gash in his head, old, black, and clotted, to which his hair clung, all matted and thick with body-ooze. He'd been beaten so gravely that one of his eyes had swollen shut and seeped with a yellow discharge.

Müller shouted again, and Ren seemed to realize he had to stand, though lifting himself without his hands to brace his body left him shaking and staggering forward. Müller kicked him in the back, and Ren slammed into the grime-stained wall. The soldier shouted again and fitted a key into the weighty shackles binding Ren's hands behind his back, leaving bloody and bruised welts. He opened one cuff, and Ren's arms fell slack, making it difficult for Müller to open the second cuff. At this, he shouted again and pounded the side of Ren's head with his fist. Blood trickled out of Ren's ear and down his neck in a crooked line.

With a tremendous and sudden thrust, Ren spun around and whipped Müller's face with the iron cuff that swung from the chain link that bound the two together. The blow knocked Müller off his feet, causing him to clutch at his face and scream in agonized surprise. Something terrible overcame Ren. The opportunity presented itself; the wish was out of his control. A frenzy possessed him, overwhelmed as he was by months of brutality and hunger and hopelessness. Whatever had once whispered to him had now become his fury, and it would not stop until it had granted his wish.

His fists fell on Müller, over and over in an unstoppable streak of madness. His eyes lit with a kind of ecstatic, dazed satisfaction. And this pleasure grew the more his fists slammed down and withdrew ever bloodier than before. Muller's teeth broke out onto the floor along with a piece of his tongue. And with an awful grimace, Ren withdrew the dagger from Müller's army tool belt. He jammed the silver blade into the man's neck so deep that it made him howl. The Nazi's mouth gaped open and closed like a fish splatted on a deck.

Ren gripped the handle with both hands, stepped on Müller's head, and dragged the knife across his throat. Blood gushed out into a sad pool on the floor while Herr Müller gave his last fitful spasms. Ren pulled the knife away and observed what he had created. But Ren's face didn't reflect the remorse or even recognition one might feel after a fit of blind, bloody rage. Instead, his eyes betrayed a growing hunger.

The screen went black. A new scene flashed onto the screen.

It seemed to be a gathering of Nazi officers around a card table. A cigar haze filled the air, making it difficult to see the men's greasy sodden faces. But there was raucous laughter and the slamming down of shot glasses and the throwing of a bottle which smashed somewhere off-screen. A new soldier entered the room. He looked similar to Müller with his black, greasy, parted hair, but the face was wrong. The officers had no time to react. Ren had found a machine gun in Müller's office, and he sprayed the room with bullets in a frenetic rain of hot lead and blood. He dropped the gun when all that remained were clicks and empty rounds, and he slid Müller's bloody scalp and Nazi cap off his head. Then he proceeded, as he had done with Müller, to open up each officer's throat.

The men shot through were not entirely dead. It took time. But Ren looked quite satisfied with his work as the men choked on their own blood, making the terrible, sticky sounds of drowning in their throat-blood. *Guk. Guk. Guk.*

The film stopped in the projector, and on the screen, Ren watched it burn yellow, then brown. And the lights blacked out altogether.

"That's not how it happened, and you know it," Nany said. "It's coming to eat you now. So we might as well see the truth of it."

The projector started up again with a new reel. This time Ren flashed on the screen in a small white room with padding on the walls. He had leather cuffs around each of his wrists, and his head lay on the floor. He mumbled to himself. A doctor came in along with a black-garbed nun. Together they lifted him to his knees and pried his mouth open to force medication down. He dropped forward and thumped his head again and again on the soft floor. Within minutes, his body became rigid, and he convulsed. Flecks of foam formed on the sides of his mouth.

"No. It didn't happen like that," Ren said. His eyes filled with tears. "No, it didn't. It's a lie. It wouldn't lie like that. I gave it what it wanted. It wouldn't lie to me like that. Not about this."

The scene flashed to Gloria in the bathtub, her throat opened wide and her hands reaching out, pleading with someone who held an open straight razor. Then the reel switched to Molly, mangled in her small bed, her pillow flooded with blood. The same hands holding the blade, a man's hairy hands, dipped in the carnage and drew things on her wall. Terrible things.

The child was still alive, but drowning in the mess of blood and gore. *Guk, guk, guk.*

"No. It wasn't… I would never…." Ren could barely breathe or say those final words. "It's a trick. You're using me for something. I don't know what. But you're doing this."

"It liked what you done, copp'r." Nany whispered the words that seemed to awaken terror residing deep down, but Ren could not bear it. If he did, he'd crumble. He'd blow away into the dust of the formless desert. That much he knew. "It tasted the blood leavin em," she continued. "It tasted your sin. Like chum in the water. And now it won't go away till it takes you, too."

"You lie. You're a lying bitch! You and that Charlene. You're witches! Witches!"

Ren wasn't in the dark-between anymore. He could feel the substance of things now, like the cold porcelain of the bathroom sink in his hands as he leaned forward. A stream of hot water clouded up the air.

"It's a lie. It's a lie. It's a goddamn lie."

Ren sobbed and bent over, retching into the sink, with yellow strings of saliva coming up. He'd spent the contents of his stomach at Charlene's, and all he had left was dry heaves and bile. It had to have been some kind of nightmare. He wasn't in the dark-between. He'd never seen such an elaborate, sickening display in that place before this. He wiped his chin and heaved more, though not much came up.

The light above the mirror dimmed then popped in a quick flash and went out. He looked up into the mirror. Behind the condensation, not standing behind him, but there, inside the mirror, was the thing. Mr. Crooked. It stood in its blackness, looking out with a cold, dead eminence. It moved forward more. Through the cloudy water droplets, Ren watched as it drew up a hand, a bony, pointed, split-clawed talon. It touched the mirror from the other side and formed letters that squeaked across the glass. *Murderer.*

Ren backed out of the bathroom, first bumping into the wall next to the door. "You're all liars. Lying witches! Fucking demon worshippers."

The glass snapped into a spider web, as though the thing inside had smashed it to get out.

Ren backed away toward the hall and made his way to the living room. That was where he first saw the amber glow shining in through the shutter-louvers. He wondered if it was morning already, and if he'd slipped through to that land for so long. But what he perceived initially as daylight was moving, changing, now light then dim, orange and red.

He heard the pop of pine sap igniting, crackling right outside the house. He flung open the shutters to see the entire forest behind his home engulfed in twisting flames, flicking up toward the open sky. He ran to the bedroom, thinking to take what he could. He paused for a moment in the doorway, wondering if it was worth it. What if he stayed, he wondered. It wasn't as if he had anything left now—except for being chased down by that thing. And these lies. That's right, he told himself—these visions were Nany's lies. Gloria and Molly were at Maxine's house for now. They were safe, yes, but the sickening truth was that he'd never see them again. Nany'd taken care of that. He sat down on the edge of the bed and thought more about letting go. He wanted to lie down and allow the flames to consume him.

He stretched out, only for a moment. It felt good to stop running. A warm hand pressed into his palm. He turned to the side and saw her soft outline beneath the covers.

"Gloria! Oh God. Gloria." Ren said the words, but he lost all language, and he crumbled into sobs with his face buried in her breast.

"Ren. Oh, my sweet man, I'm so sorry. I shouldn't have left you like that. I shouldn't have. Please, please forgive me." Tears fell—tears of regret and anguish, and she buried her face in his neck.

"There's nothing to—can you forgive me?" He whispered the words and kissed her hands. "She lied to me about you," Ren said. He shook his head, and more tears fell. "That horrible old woman. She showed me terrible things. They were about you and about Molly—all of them lies—sickening and…. And I nearly believed them, Gloria. I nearly believed them. I was going to—just now, I was planning to…." He broke down more with an uncontrollable torrent of pent-up emotion and put his face in her hand. He was so overcome at that moment that he blocked out the fire. He opened his eyes and saw a lick of flame outside the bedroom window.

The blaze had progressed—and quicker than he thought. Like a spring lock snapping, he sat up and grabbed Gloria's hands.

"I need you to stay as calm as you can. We have to collect just a few things and get out of here. There's a fire."

"A fire?"

She sounded as though she were still asleep or under hypnosis.

"Yes, Gloria, a fire. Come on." He tapped her face with his hand to rouse her from her stupor. "Where's Molly?"

"In her room," she said. Once she caught sight of the flames at the window, she bolted from the bed, gasping.

"It hasn't made it to the road yet," Ren said. "Just get Molly."

Gloria stopped short of the closet, and she stood transfixed.

"What is it?" Ren asked.

"We're not alone," she whispered. She turned her head, and her eyes filled with panic. Ren looked past her, and through the tight louvers of the closet door, he could see the outline. The creature hid there.

His eyes met hers, and he motioned with a hushing finger to stay quiet and to back away, which she did with hands cupped to silence the scream ready to erupt from her mouth.

Once she was far enough back, Ren reached for the gun he had beneath his overcoat. But it was gone. In a burst of fire and smoke and flying bits of wood, the thing hiding in the closet fired the pistol that was once in Ren's possession. Ren shouted in agony and fell backward onto the floor, writhing and grabbing at a wound in his stomach. The bullet had punctured him clean through, and a warm red gush flowed between his bare fingers.

The demon threw open the closet doors, leaped over him, and dropped the gun in its haste. Ren scrambled to pick it up, but the pain in his belly was hot and sharp with each move he tried to make. He aimed the pistol from his spot on the floor and shot toward the door where the thing had run.

"This is why I left you in the first place," Gloria said. "You need help, Ren. You need help."

She marched out of the room.

"Where are you going—?" he shouted. "Gloria. Come back!"

Seventeen

Los Angeles, 1947
The Night It Happened

Old George slid a finger along the blade of a hunting knife he'd once found in the junkyard. It was real rusty and dull when he picked it up. But Jake, one of the trash truck drivers who had a penchant for knives and swords and such, took it because he said he could fix it up for free.

"It wasn't nothing," Jake said. He handed Old George the knife and smiled with pride.

"Well, you come to do a drop off any time, even after hours if I'm still hanging around," Old George said. He examined Jake's craftsmanship and care. Now it looked like it came straight out of the General Merchandise catalog.

"Like I told you, already got the equipment in my garage. I don't mind making things like this useable," Jake said. 'You gonna sell it?"

"Naw," Old George said. "I need this in my office. My Jackie is too old now to put up a fight. Never know when it could come in handy. Not that I ever had any trouble up to now, mind you. But you never know."

Now Old George held the knife at the ready below the dashboard of his faded 1939 pickup. He was there, just down the street, nearly a half-block away from the Vegas Room. Larson had gone in there last night and two more nights before that, always around the same time. Old George would watch Larson leave sloppy and staggering, and then he'd drive off in that state. He followed Larson's swerving car up into the Hollywood hills one night, where he parked at a house that matched the address on the sales slip from Porter's Jewels. It was an easy guess that Ren might show up yet again at the Vegas Room to get soppy on alcohol.

It was early evening when Old George got up the nerve to head by himself up into the fog-banked Hollywood Hills. He'd never seen anything like this fog before. Maybe a few times deeper in December or January, when the winter clouds were heavy and dark and they rolled up from the Santa Monica and Venice coastlines. You might see it then. That's when the clouds might sometimes press up against the expansive Heaven's Hills Cemetery, facing the north side. Then they'd creep over the tops, as though carrying with them a thousand souls trying to find their way home. If you were to look up from where Old George lived, you'd never know how high the hills were at times like this, when Mulholland Drive was lost to the sea mist.

It was danker up in the hills than Old George realized, as there was not much street lighting beyond the Franklin Village neighborhoods at the base. It made it even more challenging to find the house a second time without Larson taking the lead.

He knew this whole thing was foolish—he had no solid plan or any back up. But it had been some time since he'd sent Griswold that letter with photos of the severed hand and a copy of the sales slip from the ring on its finger. And from what he could see, that Larson was still on the loose. God only knew what that man had done. So Old George knew he'd have to do something on his own.

He had a tentative plan. He was smart enough to know he couldn't drive up to the police station and make an inquiry, not with his history. Griswold had never believed him as a child, and now the man was a high-ranking officer. And anyway, he'd heard rumors of how things went down at that police department. The papers disclosed all kinds of cover-ups going on there. The police were an impenetrable and silent crew. There'd be no chance for a black man to seek justice, at least not in an ordinary way.

It wouldn't be too hard for the police to turn things around and to pin the whole thing on Old George at this point. He had a human hand stowed in his junkyard, and he'd gone to find the name of the owner of the ring. It would be a simple connect-the-dots process for the police to place him at the center of whatever happened—or was happening. Old George realized he'd need much more than a ring to make his case, and that would keep him out of the picture.

He needed to see what was going on with his own eyes. But Old George knew that his own eyes weren't enough, so he had with him an old second-hand camera that his aunt had left him before she died. It looked like an old black leather box with a strap down the center. The edges had worn and the raw leather frayed at the corners. It worked just fine, though. He had the thing tucked away inside of a duffle bag along with other items he thought he might need, like a flashlight and his sharpened hunting knife.

He kept looking out the window for house addresses, but homes were scattered and sporadic out here. The mist and the gathering darkness added to the near impossibility of his task. He watched the headlights tracking only a few feet ahead as he swerved around tight hillside curves.

"Folks who see fit to live way up here all to themselves must have a reason," he said to himself. He listened to the words, and though they were right, they didn't ease his mind at all.

After one of the tight curves, there was a long straightaway, and off to the side, Old George thought he spotted Larson's driveway. Finding the place on his own without following a lead was trickier than he thought. He'd already passed addresses smaller than the one listed, so Larson's house had to be this one or maybe one more ahead.

Old George stopped off to the side, swung the door open, and kept it that way, just in case he needed to hop in and peel away real quick.

He slipped out and jogged up the hill to the driveway. His heartbeat was thunderous as he approached. And there it was—the bungalow he'd seen Larson pull into before, perched on the hillside slant. Larson's vehicle was in the driveway. He'd spotted Larson going into that bar, so he knew he must have taken a taxi down the hill.

The house was dark and ominous. It was too early for sleep, so if other people lived there, they must not be in. So he felt bolder in standing closer to the entrance where he might otherwise be spotted. That was when he smelt the strange odor coming from somewhere on that property. It was foul and far surpassed any stench he'd whiffed at the city dump.

He heard a twig snap and crunch under the weight of footfall. It sounded like it came from deep in the misty forest beyond the house. He squinted.

"Hello?"

The hills had a tense, unnatural hush to them. Old George's voice wouldn't carry far, as though the fog blanketed it and kept his words for itself. If his plans went wrong, he realized that no one would hear him. The nearest house wasn't any less than a mile down that hill.

"Someone there?" No one responded, but he wasn't sure he wanted to know the answer to that question anyway. He realized that in his haste, he'd nabbed the flashlight and camera and left the hunting knife behind, but he didn't want to waste time. He needed to do what he came to do and be quick about it.

Dried wood snapped again, this time somewhere behind him. It occurred to Old George that he might have seen someone who looked like Larson, and the man might be standing right behind him now. He felt an unsteady wave of flutters from his chest, and his limbs bristled with tiny pinpricks. He whipped around. There on the road was a coyote. It stared at him, then gave a lazy trot up the steep, weedy embankment on the opposite side of the way.

Old George kept fighting the urge to run back, shut himself in the truck, and drive away—not looking back and not regretting his choice to watch out for himself. He let out a breath and realized he hadn't been inhaling or exhaling in a while. He panted until he caught his breath and tried to settle himself.

There was no turning back. From what had wound up in his junk yard, he guessed someone must be dead or at least pretty well injured in that house. This Larson was a man with no soul, no life behind his eyes. He'd keep on doing whatever it is he'd done so far. Old George couldn't have that on his head. And he couldn't leave someone who might need his help.

He thought about his plan after he'd gotten evidence. He'd first go to the papers with his story, his photos, his letters, and the jeweler's receipt. And he'd let justice—a justice free from Griswold or Larson—take its course. That did little to ease his quaking nerves. What gave him some resolve, though, was the memory of his mother dying in that prison, nothing but circumstances and maybe the color of her skin to keep her there. It was true that he recognized the situation was off kilter that night when he came back from the grocer and the clattering tooth, but he might have been wrong about what he saw. The police and the judges could have gotten it wrong, too.

He took a breath and overrode the inner debate.

As he approached the house, he fumbled with his lantern-sized flashlight and switched it on. He hadn't thought to change his work boots, which sounded out in a dull, muddy thud no matter how he stepped on the wood-planked porch. He stopped after testing out some steps to see if that got anyone's attention inside. His heart was throbbing somewhere near his throat. Now that he was on the porch, the reality of having no escape plan hit hard. He realized that he'd be able to slip down the hill past the house as fast as he could should anyone stir inside the house. He'd be ready to spend as much time as it took hiding in silence after that to convince the Larsons they were mistaken and that no one prowled outside their home. He thought that he might also need to abandon his truck and find the road on a tier lower down the hill if he wanted to escape.

The stench was overpowering on the porch. He thought of the coyote he saw moments earlier and remembered that they left the remains of finished-off prey when they were done gorging themselves on its organs. The little thing must have made a kill somewhere nearby. Old George buried his nose in the crook of his elbow and tested the doorknob. It held in place. An officer knew better than to leave his dwelling unsecured.

Old George stepped off the porch and followed the downslope alongside the house, with its thick bed of pine needles and wild sage offering some relief from the odor. The flashlight beam reflected off the mist, giving him an arm's length of visibility and making his short hike a lesson in equanimity.

Whatever he stepped on next was softer than the pine needles. It crunched down under his weight, then his foot slid. He flashed the beam down and saw a pulpy, half-eaten opossum with a handful of flies buzzing around it in a chaotic halo. Maggots squirmed over its partially opened belly, and he knew they must be stuck to the underside of his boot. He raised it away and tried to shake off any of the slimy gore that clung to him and to rid himself of the crawling insects.

He shot the flashlight beam upward toward the windows. There was one just above the overflowing trash cans. He knocked one bin over, dumping its contents onto the decaying bed of pine debris beneath it. The stink intensified once the muck at the bottom of the garbage got racked up. He flipped the can over and stepped up onto its platform surface. It made a metallic pop that spooked him.

Inside the window, some frilly pink sheers framed the inner darkness. Old George pointed the narrow flashlight into the house. It was hard to make out the specifics amid the trash heaps inside. Someone had strewn garbage across the floor and furnishings. Chairs and tables had been left overturned. It looked as though the place was either abandoned or used by squatters that were hooked on something that made you lose your senses.

He set the light down between his feet and tried the window, but it was good and stuck. He held the beam up again and saw that someone had sealed the window shut with a thick layer of paint. He couldn't understand the point of a window way up here in the hills, if you couldn't fling it wide open to enjoy the fresh air.

Before he had a chance to think more about it, a car pulled up to the front of the house. It had to be Larson, he realized. Back from the Vegas Room.

He scrambled off the trash can and in his haste, landed in the decrepit animal carcass. Some of it gushed up his pant leg, cold and wet. He resisted the urge to shout in disgust. Instead, he hobbled down the slope to the lowest part of the house, all the while shaking his leg, trying to get off what he could. There, behind the house, was a double-story wall, and in front of him was a door. He remembered his aunt, who had a similar storage room behind her home that sat on a slope. She'd used it for garden tools.

The car door opened and shut. He clicked off the light and tried his hand on the basement knob. It wouldn't turn, nor would the door itself budge when he pushed in. His breath choked off and a wave of dizziness overcame him. If Larson caught him prowling around, it would be more complicated than a word exchange at a diner. With newfound adrenaline, enough of a jolt to fuel a small missile, Old George yanked backward, and the door piled up forest droppings as it scraped open.

Thick, dust-coated spider webs stretched and broke with the widening door. The air was rank inside that cellar, and the stench forced Old George to cover his mouth and nose once more, just to avoid vomiting. He gagged a few times, and his stomach lurched upward, but he forced it to be silent, lest he draw Larson's attention.

Heavy, striding footsteps made their way down the hillside. Old George recalled that Larson was a tall man. The steps matched. He realized he had no option but to shut himself inside. He held his breath and searched for an inner lock. There was a metal slide bolt at the top and a knob lock. He locked both, trying to do so without making noise. But once he twisted the knob lock, it clicked.

The footsteps stopped.

"Who's there?" a man called out.

Old George put his back to the wall and tried to control his breathing, which he realized was getting harder to restrain. The dark scent of death filled the room, and he had a hard time containing the raging upsurge from his guts. Flies swarmed all around him and explored his eyes, ears, and nostrils that flared with each nauseated indrawn breath.

The footsteps picked up again and seemed more determined. A hand tried the knob, then joggled it. The door pulled back just enough to catch the slide bolt.

"Someone in there?"

Old George struggled against the spew forcing its way out from his mouth. He made a small involuntary groan, then cupped a hand to his mouth.

"Come out, Larson. We need to talk."

With that, Old George realized Larson wasn't outside the door.

The slide bolt rattled more while the man on the other side rechecked it. Old George clenched his lips together and used all his strength to keep still.

The footsteps continued around past the door and faded. Old George couldn't see much through the gaps between the old door planks, except for the few strands of light that shimmered. Sweat trickled down his cheek. He knew he couldn't hold on to his stomach any longer. The man outside was probably out of earshot, so he backed up and retched hard, bracing himself with his hands on his knees. Now that he'd cleared his stomach, his mind produced a flood of panicked thoughts. He was in too deep now to get out and up to his truck.

More flies landed on him around his mouth and chin, where there was still some dribble. He caught his breath and tuned into the hum all around him. It sounded almost like there was a beehive inside the small room. He backed up more and then stepped on a soft and uneven surface. It felt much like the opossum outside. He tried to switch on the flashlight, but it only sputtered and then went black.

"Shit." He realized that he should have checked the batteries before he left home. He remembered that his aunt's basement had its own light source, an overhead bulb that switched on from a plate near the door. Old George scuffed toward the door again, trying to avoid where he thought he'd emptied his stomach, and he felt around the walls.

There it was, the switch plate. It was one of those older two-push-button models, and he knew he had to depress the protruding of the two buttons to activate the light. The bulb started on, flickered, then went out before he could glimpse a clue. He dropped the flashlight, and it switched on.

The beam stretched like white fire across the rough concrete floor, past the wet yellow chunks lying there to the thing just beyond. Old George picked up the flashlight and aimed it until he could see it better. Beyond the cloud of insects scattering in the light, he saw the leather sole of a woman's high heel shoe. It was upright, as though perched on a rack. But there was no rack. The shoe was on someone's foot. He traced the leg upward along the center of the body where horseflies with big red eyes scurried about. The woman wore a navy blue service dress and white apron. Curled-up dots and splats of dried brown blood caked her clothing.

His stomach churned again, but this time he felt like he might let loose in his pants. He shone the light further upward and saw that the woman had dark skin like his own. It was that, or the corpse had rotted so long that the hide was like an over-ripe banana. Her face was contorted into a scream that no one could hear anymore—if ever they had at all—and her eye sockets were empty, or nearly so, the eyeballs likely consumed by rodents. The upper part of her dress was a scabby mess of blood-cake that trailed down from the neck, gaping wide from an enormous gash, exposing a yawning chasm of dehydrated flesh.

Old George covered his mouth. He scrambled backward until he was pressed up against what he thought was a wall. However, the whole thing crumbled down and toppled stacks of heavy trunks and crates. They broke everything in their path with their rough steel edges. Old George took the brunt of it with his arm. The crates gouged open a deep slice that ran from his biceps to his forearm. A rush of deep, dark red flooded his shirt, and he gripped as much of the wound as he could with his free hand while he slid down the wall to sit.

The man outside likely heard what he'd done and would be back any minute. He glanced up at the doorknob and saw that the wreckage had snapped it clean off. Crates stacked up waist-high against the door. If that man came back, he'd never shove all that junk away just by pushing. Judging from his injuries, Old George suspected the crates contained heavy metal or machine parts. But by the same token, Old George wouldn't get out that way either, not with an injured arm and all.

He felt like a boy again, watching his mother scrubbing something awful away while he stood by, helpless to say or do anything that could make it stop. He was a boy, kicking that gold tooth like it was nothing more than a loose pebble, then realizing that something terrible had happened but that he was too late to stop it—if ever he could have.

A fly landed in his ear, and he tried to swat it out. But it crawled in deep until he heard Serene's voice again. "You'd better move on, Old Georgie, or you'll never leave this place alive." With that, the fly kicked out from his ear and joined the swarm.

Old George felt himself striving to hold back tears, but he wasn't very successful. He sobbed with his inhaled breath, and when he heard it, he thought it was the cry of someone who hadn't done so in a very long time. With great effort, he pulled himself to a stand. He felt around the floor for the flashlight, but instead he grabbed hold of the dead woman's foot.

"Mother fuck!"

In his reaction, he released his grip on the arm wound. A warm gush oozed, and he clamped it up again and held it, though it stung like slices made by red hot razors. He probed the ground for the lost flashlight until he felt a part of it stuck beneath one of the fallen crates.

He squatted and tugged at the handle until he reached the switch with his finger. It turned on, but the beam end of the flashlight was sandwiched beneath a massive crate and the floor. The glow was just enough for him to better inspect the damage to his arm. The cuts penetrated enough to see his body-meat. He knew the injury was too serious to ignore, and he'd have to get medical attention soon. He unbuttoned his shirt, pulled it off, and wrapped it around the laceration. He started feeling light-headed, so he sat on the floor while flies swarmed around the sticky-fresh meal.

The injury would slow him down, he knew. But the light beam provided some hope. He studied the crawl space in greater detail. As his eyes roamed, he noticed a new bullet shell lying next to one of the busted-out boxes. He leaned over and laid his cheek on the dusty floor so he could peer inside the wooden box. From what he could tell, the whole crate was a load of bullets.

Where there were bullets, there were guns. Old George forced himself to a stand by bracing his legs and sliding his back upward against the wall. He staggered around in the near-darkness, groping at walls, hoping to find a tool he could use to crack the crates open, starting with the one containing bullet casings. Fumbling along the wall, Old George stumbled against a crowbar. He dragged it over and began prying at the wooden coffer.

Wood split and splintered as he leveraged his body weight. There it was, as he suspected. Hundreds of cartons of bullets, but also an object wrapped in cloth. The thing had weight. He unwrapped it and found a .38 caliber revolver. His daddy had owned one for extra protection when taking the Sunday collection to the bank, so he knew it right away.

He found the chamber release on the side; he pushed the barrel through the frame. Then he loaded up all five chambers with bullets, and he snapped it all shut. He shoved it into his pocket, and in the other one, he stuffed a handful more of the loose bullets. Then he scanned the crawl space for some way out. Just beyond the dead body, where the floor inclined like the shallow end of a swimming pool, was a short ladder he'd not registered before. It led to a framed area with a separate set of planks across it. A trap door.

"God damn," Old George said. He knew he'd have to climb over the corpse to get there. There was no other way.

He looked around more, and he found cans of paint and a gray canvas tarp smudged with white paint streaks. He reached for it with his better arm and holding one end, flung it so it opened up over the crusted, insect-infested remains. He lifted it again, spreading more of the cloth over as much as he could. Once he was satisfied, he traversed across it, stepping between limbs to the best of his ability. He searched the floor for his camera and saw the little lenses popped out and the inner workings crushed and splayed by the falling crates. He'd never get his first-hand evidence now. All he had left was surviving and getting as far away as possible from this place.

"I'm sorry. I'm so sorry," Old George whispered to the dead woman. The corpse didn't seem to mind. He closed his eyes and braced himself to get past the torso. With his arm in bad shape, he'd not be able to get past without stepping where he'd rather not. He followed the outline with his tearing-up eyes as best he could before taking the step. Then he felt he'd landed on a semi-firm body part, probably an arm. As soon as he stepped, the tarp flooded with an oozing brown liquid, and it slipped from underneath him against the runny mess beneath. He lost his balance, and he fell flat on the maid's collapsing torso. The compression from the fall released built-up gasses, and more of the oozing innards that saturated the cloth filled the room with a foulness not even reserved for morticians.

He felt her squishing beneath his hands like an old bag filled with soft fruit, as he braced himself up from having lain flat on her cadaver. The room swam in front of his eyes, dim as it was, and what his stomach had wanted to spew up before made its way up and splatted out across the drop cloth. Despite this, the screaming pain from his arm kept him focused on his one task: to get out.

He righted himself and straddled over her reeking remains. Then using all of his strength and renewed adrenaline, he pitched himself forward until he collapsed onto the squat ladder. His arm filled the makeshift tourniquet with so much blood that as soon as he reached up onto the first rung, it rained thick, warm droplets onto his eyes. He turned to wipe his eyes on his shoulders.

He hooked his injured arm through the uppermost rung and balanced himself on the bottom one. With his better arm, he pushed on the trap door, and it lifted. He threw his shoulder and head into the task and pushed the trap up until he had it extended upright.

The room he was entering seemed to have the scents of clothes, shoes, and the waxy smell of crayons. It had rows and rows of hanging clothes, too small for an adult to wear. Having to peer through the dim light from outside the house made it difficult to discern what he was seeing. He scanned through the door connecting to an adjoining room. What caught his eye was what he thought was some bizarre wallpaper at first. But as his eyes adjusted, he could see that writing covered the wall from floor to ceiling.

He clambered up the ladder, using his stronger arm to brace himself. Once he was above the cellar, he flopped on the floor and lay there panting. He could tell for sure he was in a child's closet now. He'd lost a lot of blood, and he wasn't sure how much more he'd be able to do. He wondered if maybe he'd never get up, or if he collapsed, whether anyone might find him. The thought of losing his life in this place fortified him, and he rolled to one side. Then he got into a kneeling position and sat on his thighs, listening for sounds in the house. There was some ticking from a clock in another room, and beyond that, the house was hushed.

He spotted a string dangling from a lightbulb, so he reached and snapped it down, turning on the light. He was right. He was in a child's closet. But his eyes drifted again toward the connecting room, and he was right on that account, too. On the distant wall someone had drawn, scribbled, and written vulgarities. As he stepped further in, he saw the entire room was a stifling enclosure of mad, chaotic incoherence.

A scatter-shot of flies swarmed between a window and the bed. On the floor, beside the bed, was a book with a wood covering and lace bindings. It seemed like the cover was ordinary plywood that someone had smeared with a now dried-brown liquid. When he cracked the journal open and leafed through the pages, he found strange symbols, angry words, and violent drawings. The walls were a page by page replica. It was dizzying to consider the obsessiveness behind all of this, and it made Old George touch his trouser pocket to assure himself that he still had the revolver and the bullets.

Once he could take his eyes from the freakish mural, he noticed the child lying in bed. His pulse doubled, and he knew that if the child screamed, it'd be over. He crept past. Then he noticed in the dim, offset light, the dark stain around the top edge of the bedspread where the face might be. His heart took a nosedive.

The dark crust began in a bowl shape from the bedsheet's top edge, but extended off to the side of the body, and continued in a black cascade of sickness down off the side. Old George's eyes burned with tears, and his throat closed up with a dry, unyielding disgust.

"Hello?"

His voice was soft, as though he might startle the little dead thing.

"Hello?" he asked again. This time it was louder, as though the child were standing somewhere across a crowded room. Then he kept saying, "Hello? Hello? Hello?" He could hear in his voice a quaking mix of fury, fright, and revulsion. Tears streamed down his face as he gripped the coverlet and drew it back.

A little girl, only five or six, he figured, had her throat opened from side to side and her gaping eye sockets filled with twisting piles of insects. A fly landed in her open mouth, crawled around her blackened tongue, then buzzed away.

Old George clasped his hand over his mouth. He backed up and staggered against the farthest wall, next to a door. He lost track of how he might keep on breathing or going any further than this.

The same voice that he'd heard at the cellar door was now on another side of the house. But now two men were speaking. Old George forced himself to move. His legs would not cooperate, though he knew they should help him at this moment. He inched along the wall until he reached the door.

A fly dropped into his ear canal again. "Do what you came to do and get out before it's too late," Serene told him.

He staggered out the bedroom door, strode to the dark hallway's end, and to the left, just past what was likely the front entrance, was a big bay window with frilly pink sheer panels. There was a couch just behind the bay window, and he knelt lower than the sofa back to observe the two men outside. One was Larson. It took a minute to recognize the other. He realized it was an aged and husky Griswold. He must have come by Larson's place because of the evidence Old George had sent.

"Well, I… I just went for a walk," he heard Larson say. "You see, my car is there, parked in front of the house."

Old George watched Larson advance on Griswold, who took a step back and placed a hand on the gun in his holster. He hoped Griswold would just shoot Larson and end it all. If only Griswold knew what was going on inside the house. It was much worse than the evidence Old George had sent. He strained to understand what their muffled voices said.

He heard mention of a breakdown, and more about the mental hospital, St. Cyprian's.

He watched Griswold reach into the vehicle and show Larson the pictures and the ring receipt. Without even blinking an eye, Larson reached into his vest holster and shot Griswold between the eyes. Griswold dropped like an old sack of dirt on the side of the road.

"Jesus fucking Christ," Old George said.

Larson then pulled a large rock, nearly the size of a child's head, from the side of the road. He lugged it to where Griswold lay, just behind the car door. Larson lifted the stone and pulverized Griswold's head with it, smashing the rock over and over until there was only a runny pulp remaining.

"I just went for a walk…." Larson kept saying the phrase like a scratched phonograph record while he took Griswold's car keys. He swung open the passenger side door. Then with extraordinary strength, Larson lifted Griswold's body and laid it across the squad car bench. He went back around to the other side and dragged the sergeant by his feet across the seat. He turned the car wheel, inserted the keys, and the engine growled to a start.

He wandered to the side of the road, still saying, "I just went for a walk." He carried back the bloody rock he'd used and dumped it onto the floor of the driver's side, causing the engine to scream like a race car. He pulled down on the gear shaft, and the vehicle sped down the road until it veered off down the steep pine-needle-coated embankment. Old George heard it slam into something solid. Larson began shouting, his neck muscles straining, glowing orange, then red in the reflected firelight. "I told you, Griswold, it was just a walk! Goddammit. I told you. I told you!"

Still muttering to himself, he turned toward the house. That was when he stopped to observe someone standing in his living room behind the curtains.

"Oh shit, oh shit," Old George said.

Larson clenched his fists and strode at a determined pace across the fog-slicked, fire-lit asphalt, toward whoever was inside his house.

Eighteen

Los Angeles, 1947
Two Months Before It Happened

Gloria dropped her bags as soon as she realized the house seemed wrong. It was far quieter than expected given a husband, a five-year-old, and a hospital worker. The doctor had said that Ren needed to live up in the hills for the peace; he needed a place of serenity, where nothing would agitate his mind further. But this was a different kind of stillness, and it made Gloria's blood stop. Then she sighed with disgust.

Gloria had hoped her life would amount to more than this. Here she was now, married to an invalid husband with a young child, both needing a good deal of care and attention. Though it was tiresome, she told herself she would try—at least for a little while, anyway. But if Ren got any worse, her backup plan was to pack up and leave for her family in New York. She'd take Molly, too, though she'd considered adopting her out once or twice. She might have considered it a few more times than that. Maxine had asked about Molly, and Gloria realized she would have a home with her, if need be.

She relieved her guilt by remembering that Sgt. Griswold knew all about Ren's situation and he had promised to keep Ren around, give him easier assignments. Nothing with guns. Gloria recognized that even though Ren had days where he seemed in another world altogether, no matter what, the police force would take care of him. They always watched out for their own.

This eerie house-hush exceeded the doctor's orders. This was a mortuary stillness. She'd only gone for groceries to Bert's, just two miles down the hill. Thirty minutes was all it took to get there and back. Bert's wasn't the best, in Gloria's view. The small local grocer merely carried basics. She liked the more abundant food markets closer to downtown with all of their modern conveniences. But conveniences like that existed in her distant past. Ren would never change for the better, no matter what the doctors told her. Two years had passed since his last episode, and he'd never turned the corner like the doctors thought he might.

Luckily she had Sunnie. She used to work at St. Cyprian's, so she had extensive practice in their methods. She had a way with men in Ren's condition because she always understood how to sweet-talk and distract when Ren found it hard to self-soothe. And if worse came to worse, she was as big as a rodeo rider, and she had a lot of practice with pinning a man down if she really had to. She'd never found it necessary with Ren, though. He was always so doped-up and sloppy that she didn't need to do much at all, except bathe him and take him to the toilet to do his business. Out of boredom, Sunnie helped Gloria with caring for the household. She'd water plants and make dinners. She even started caring for Molly, assigning her chores and creating small activities, things that might occupy a child's time.

That gave Gloria a sampling of freedom. Maxine was the first to tell her she needed time away from such oppressive conditions. Gloria had to be free of these house-captors and the confining little dwelling with its narrow corridors and all of it's—illnesses and need. Gloria only felt the need for small breaks at first. Thirty minutes at a time was enough to give her some relief. But these breaks eventually got longer and more involved. She'd started at the Farmer's Market downtown. Soon, she found herself on road trips out to Santa Monica beach, where she'd spend the afternoons with her toes wiggled into the sand and filling her senses with fresh sea air and the sting of sunburned cheeks.

She met a few men along the way. Some of them younger. And it seemed good to be with men less downtrodden than her husband.

Gloria told herself that she deserved more than this little life on the hill. All Ren did was ruin her life and her expectations for anything better. She wanted to make the most of whatever time she had left in her youth. Her big plans all along took her far and beyond these dreadful Hollywood Hills. Now she was little more than a shut-in, helping to care for a patient and a tiresome, needy child. She needed these little escapades. As long as she still had control of the money, she would ride this until the wave petered out.

Afterwards, she'd be on her way. Everything good starts with the right timing. She had her eye on that wedding ring, which alone might give her what she needed to begin a new life. She wondered if she might even start back with dancing in the chorus line again.

"Sunnie," she said. The house continued to meet her with stillness.

"Molly?" Gloria picked up the pace down the hallway, hoping to find the child in her room. She peeked through a crack in the door. Molly lay on the floor, humming, coloring on the back of a ribbed paper plate.

Gloria stepped further down the hall to the kitchen. "Sunnie?" But the kitchen only responded with the tick-tock of the wall clock.

Past the fridge, Gloria spotted an ankle, thick and dull, the stocking bagging around it like a burlap sack. Gloria tried to shake off the chill that came over her. The further she crept, the more the sickening scene revealed itself.

Sunnie lay on the braided oval carpet in a dense, crusting pool of her blood. Ren had turned her head to the side, and Gloria saw that he'd gashed her throat wide open. Sunnie had other slashes, too, on her face, hands, and arms. She must have fought back, Gloria supposed.

Sunnie was in charge of Ren's daily dose of medication. The little white pills disappeared each day, all right. But Gloria suspected that Miss Sunnie had developed a penchant for opium herself. The woman should have remembered the role those little pills played in keeping Ren adequately controlled before she finished them off in her greed. And now, here lay Sunnie, her blood drained out to the floor. And it annoyed Gloria that Sunnie's mess stained the rug she had recently purchased. She saw the straight razor laying on the ground nearby, and she snatched it up, wondering where she might hide it.

Standing there looking down at the bloody scene, Gloria realized that she was accountable for supervising Sunnie. The doctors had asked Gloria, not Sunnie, to dispense the medicine and keep it safely out of reach each day. There would be questions. Too many people had witnessed Gloria traipsing about each day, leaving Sunnie alone for hours at a time. Too many fingers would point to her.

The doorbell rang.

Gloria took a shocked gasp of air. She stepped over the toy tea set and the doll with its perpetually horrified eyes that Sunnie had toppled during her fall.

"Mrs. Larson? Are you in? Is everything all right? I'm coming in, Mrs. Larson. Hello?" The door started to open, and Gloria caught it before the neighbor might see or whiff too much, and she blocked the door from fully swinging wide with her foot. She held the dripping razor behind her back.

On the front porch stood Maxine Ganz wearing dark sunglasses with a shining, detachable nose guard. Gloria placed her face in the small door opening and flattened her body against it to keep her from looking in.

"I'm here, Mrs. Ganz. How can I help you today?" Gloria gave a distracted smile.

"Now, you know I want you to call me Maxine! Go on—say it."

"Okay," Gloria said, trying to be patient. "Maxine." Gloria felt Sunnie's cold blood run down her hand.

"Well now, dear, I realize I came by unexpectedly and all. But I wanted to give Molly some fudge I made this morning." Maxine held up a tin with thick, dark brown squares stacked inside. "But while I was at the door I heard screams," she said, "and it sounded like Mr. Larson was shouting at someone."

"No, no hon. Not at all. I just got home, and everyone is napping." She put a finger to her lips.

"Napping? No, Mrs. Larson, I distinctly heard back-and-forth squabbling… and then a woman screamed."

"Screamed? I don't think so," Gloria said. She held her face as still as possible. "Oh, I realize what you must have heard. Molly loves her mystery radio shows. Sometimes our home is just… full of screams. Yes, that must have been it. I'll have her keep it down." Gloria began shutting the door.

"Well, I told the driver to wait," Maxine continued, "and I stepped down the hill slope to see if I might get in through your back cellar. But it was locked," Maxine said. "Then I listened to the sound of what must have been your car pulling up."

"Yes, that was me. Well, thank you again," Gloria said.

"Well, dear, won't you take the fudge? Molly would like it."

Gloria tossed the razor to one side. It clattered to the floor, and that caught Maxine's attention. Gloria reached for the tin with her clean hand. Maxine handed it over and looked down to see blood drips on Gloria's legs. She blinked, but did not react more than that.

"All right, Mrs. Larson, there you go. Are you certain you're all right? I'll leave if that's true. But I want you to appreciate that some things I understand, from one woman to another. I'm old enough to realize that at times we find ourselves in terrible situations where remaining silent is the safest thing we might do. Just tell me, you're not in any immediate danger, are you? I can call the police when I get home if you'd like."

"No. Don't call the police. I mean… Thank you for troubling

yourself, Maxine. If we didn't have good neighbors like you, we might be more worried way up here in all of this… isolation. There is no danger, and there is no need for police. Okay? I must drop by to your place soon and repay the visit. So kind of you, but really, we're all just… napping."

Maxine paused and began down the walkway, but turned back to Gloria. "You understand, dear, that my invitation remains open. If you need a place to stay, if you need a place of safe refuge for any reason, why you just say the word. You and Molly are welcome in my home. For as long as you'd like."

Gloria nodded. "Thank you again, Maxine. I really need to put my groceries away. Ice cream tonight."

"Of course, dear. I'm glad you're all right," Maxine said. She ambled down the walkway, loaded herself into the back seat, and her driver whooshed her away.

After Gloria shut the door, she understood that she would have to take action, and soon. What if Maxine called the police anyway? The cops would be up here in a flash, especially if it involved one of their own in untoward circumstances. She had to act now.

Sunnie had no family here in the states. She had a sister, or at least she thought Sunnie had mentioned something about that. Gloria vaguely recalled that she'd talked about her living on some remote island? Did it have to do with cats? Sunnie didn't read nor write, and the sister was likely the same. Probably dirt poor, too, so she wouldn't come snooping around so readily—at least for now. The sister wouldn't even have knowledge of where Sunnie worked each day, specifically. And even if she did, she wouldn't know what Ren and Gloria looked like. And if on the off chance she showed up one day… well, Gloria wouldn't be around for that.

"Ren," she called out. But he didn't answer. "Ren, come out. It's me. Everything will be all right. You don't need to hide."

The small trapdoor that led to the shallow basement squeaked open.

"Ren, come out and help me. I can't fix things alone. Shut

Molly's door first."

He clomped up the short ladder, leaden-footed, and shut Molly's door. Gloria walked into the family room and sized up how they might get Sunnie's cadaver stowed away. The immediate plan was to transport it under the house. But, after a while, when Ren forgot all about what he'd done—and he always forgot once he got regular with that blessed medicine—she'd start asking him to dig a shallow grave out back. Oh, she'd say they were planting roses. Easy. Then, once they'd buried Sunnie, Gloria would disappear in the middle of the night.

Nineteen

Los Angeles, 1947
The Night It Happened

Old George retreated from the widow and tracked back down the hallway only to find himself trapped in a kitchen with no door to the outside. He found only a slim rectangular window, enough to let in air and let out kitchen smells. There had to be another window. But he remembered that Larson had painted them shut.

Back he ran to the opposite end of the hallway, to a larger master bedroom. A big window there looked out onto the driveway. Flies converged on the glass, so many that it seemed impossible. A bed stretched out between him and the window—anyway, he figured, Larson must have painted all of them shut. A louvered closet door on his right was open, and he closed himself in. He pressed himself to the back wall through the clothes and the tinkling hangers, and he stilled them all with his hands.

The front door opened and slammed shut. Larson marched into the kitchen, and there was soon the smashing of glass—and the tiny tinkle of shards splintering about.

"Gloria," Larson said. His voice, cracked and hoarse, sounded like he'd been sobbing.

Old George tried to keep still. Even if he was able to get past Larson and escape this house, a fire was beginning to spread, and there was no telling whether the road would be passable by now.

Larson thudded across the floors, and his footsteps echoed hollow, as though he'd walked atop a wooden drum. Old George listened as Larson jabbered and hissed to himself. It sounded to Old George like the man was pacing. With a sharp break from the aimlessness, Larson's heavy footfall began thundering down the hall toward the bedroom where Old George hid.

Old George knew he'd have to be as quiet as he could, so he took one final, deeply inhaled breath. His bladder was busting, and he thought he might piss himself.

The footsteps halted mid-hallway. Larson shouted as though someone else were in the room with them. Old George peered through the closet door slits, and in the dim light saw no one else but Larson there.

"You followed me!" Larson said. His voice trembled and cracked more.

"I just wanted the pain to end. People want things all the time. You don't get what you want. That's not real. It's not real! I didn't do it. It wasn't my fault. You did it. You did it all." Something else in the room smashed, but Old George couldn't tell what. He thought about confronting Larson with the pistol he had, but the officer's job involved using one every day. He had much more experience than Old George. The gun had to be a last resort. But it might be his only chance to escape, with the fire closing in on them both.

The footsteps boomed again, now echoing closer to the bedroom. Old George tried to breathe shallow and soft, even though it felt suffocating and made him want to take big gulps of air.

"Gloria! Oh God. Gloria," Larson said. He sobbed and landed on the squeaky bed across the room.

Old George watched Larson unfold a bedspread to reveal yet another cadaver, nude, with dried black blood covering the whole bed below the neat top covering. He watched as Larson bent down and kissed the putrid corpse's lips, even though insects squirmed about, spilling from the corners of the dead woman's mouth, nose, and eye holes.

"There's nothing to—can you forgive me?" He lifted her wrists and kissed one hand, then the stump where he'd chopped the appendage off. "She lied to me about you," Larson said. "That horrible old woman. She showed me terrible things. About you and about Molly—all of them lies—sickening and.... And I nearly believed them, Gloria. I nearly believed them. I was going to—just now, I was planning to..." He put his face in the corpse's one intact hand and he caused it, like a puppet, to caress his face.

"I need for you to stay as calm as you can. We have to get our things and get out of here. There's fire."

"Yes, Gloria, a fire. Come on," Larson said as a response, as though the rotting body had somehow added to the conversation.

"Where's Molly?" he asked. Larson continued as though the conversation further developed. "It hasn't made it to the road yet. Forget that and get Molly."

Old George's eyes flooded with tears of regret for his life up to now, tears because he hadn't done more, tears because he never took the risks he should have. He'd die here in this den of sickness, and he knew it. Or he'd have to act fast. He'd need to use the gun, and if he missed, if he got one thing wrong, he might die at the hands of this monster.

One small movement on his neck did him in. It felt like a tickle, but Old George remembered that he'd been atop a corpse in the cellar, and the whole house crawled with them. A cold, squirming maggot inched along his neck—he knew it. It could have been more than one. Old George couldn't bear the thought of it. With care, he reached his injured arm behind the hanging clothes and sensed a whole slew of the insects clinging to the underside of his bloody cut.

He stifled a throaty yelp that wanted to escape, and he clenched his teeth.

"What is it?" Larson asked the air. No one responded. But he rose from the bed, focusing on the closet. "We're not alone."

That was when Old George heard the noises. Strange, inhuman sounds gurgled from Larson's mouth.

"Click. Guk, guk. Click."

The flies that were on the window, and maybe from the whole house, gathered in an enormous writhing ball above Larson's head. Some unseen hand tipped the man's head backward at an unnatural angle. Old George thought it might be impossible for anyone to survive with their neck bent as though the spine was missing. The gathering mass of flies shot down Larson's open throat. There was a moment of shuddering, as though the man had a seizure, then the head straightened back up with a robotic erectness, and he glared straight at the closet.

Larson shambled forward, his mouth contorting and his lips peeling back to show his clenched teeth. "*Click. Guk, guk. Click,*" Larson said. His movements jerked like a broken marionette. His shoulders raised and forearms leveled upward; his hands twitched, hungry to kill, exploring the air for whatever they might take next.

Larson reached the closet, gripped the door handle, and ripped it to one side, breaking the whole thing off its top hinge. Old George burst out from between the garments and shot Larson clean through his stomach. The injured man howled and fell backward onto the floor, writhing and grabbing with both hands. A stain of blood widened beneath his shirt. The flies poured back out from his mouth and scattered. But they reconvened in a ball above the dead woman's body, and they poured down her throat like a swirling black stream.

Without wasting a second, Old George stepped over the man writhing in pain. But to his horror, the corpse on the bed sat up with Larson's same robotic stiffness. Old George didn't want to see what would happen next, so he leapt past and sprinted out the door. Larson had fallen, but he managed to draw out his own pistol and fire a round toward Old George. The bullet sprang off the door jamb and splintered the wood. When Larson missed his target, he dropped the gun and continued to moan and twist in agony.

The dead woman's remains turned to the side as though unaware of anything except for some secret command. She stood with bones and ligaments cracking and went to the window, where she parted the curtains. She stared out at the glow and the falling fiery branches, then turned toward the fallen man.

Old George charged across to the front door and swung it open. A tree trunk like a stack of barrels, alive with flame, crashed down and blocked the door. Sparks and burning coals sprayed across the front foyer, and the pink frilly shears lit like oiled candle wicks. A gray haze filled the room from the ceiling down.

The injured man came out from the room and shielded his eyes from the smoke and the flames. He still held the pistol, and he waved it about. "You can't leave now," he shouted. Again, it seemed like he was talking to the empty air. His eyes, bloodshot from the smoke, couldn't see that Old George had backed away and disappeared into the family room, where the air had not yet become suffocating. "You can't leave now," the man cried again.

Another tree collapsed, this time smashing through the front porch and collapsing through the foyer. The man fell to the ground in the chaos. The walls had become solid barriers of fire that surrounded him, and the man raised up on his knees in prayer as the dead woman's cadaver twitched and shuffled out from the bedroom. Her hair caught fire and went up in a flash of orange heat, but she continued to shuffle toward him.

Old George thought of smashing through the painted-shut window, but the shrubs and trees surrounding the place were a fire-fury. Instead, he thought to escape through the floor-trap and out the cellar. That might be as big of a risk as any other, but he had no other choice. He charged back across the family room, smashing his way through the piles of trash left to accumulate. As he started down the hall, through the haze, he saw the dead child shuffling gracelessly in her blood-crackled night dress. She seemed to have forgotten how to walk upright. Old George gasped without realizing he'd done so, and the child corpse turned its head and locked eyes with him. The creature-child opened her mouth as if to speak, but a stream of liquid filth poured out like blackstrap molasses onto her nightie. She lost interest in Old George and resumed her shuffle down the fire-lit hall.

He rushed behind her and slipped into the child's bedroom. It, too, was filled with thick clouds of soot that stung his eyes and lungs. He shielded his mouth and nose and attempted to enter the closet when he met the standing corpse of the maid, staring out with pale, hazy, unseeing eyes.

He fell backward onto the body-fluid-wetted bed as the creature shuffled past him and out the door. Maggots stuck to his clothes, but he didn't care. As soon as the woman limped past, he rushed into the closet and opened the trap door. A roar of heat and smoke burst upward.

He'd run out of options. He would die here among these creatures.

Remembering that Larson and the corpse had evacuated the bedroom, he shot back down the hall to smash through the large bay window. As he passed the foyer, he saw the three corpses holding tight to Larson's limbs. The flames at the front door parted like blazing theater curtains as an old black woman with a turban and a simple white shift passed through. She stood staring at Larson, who seemed too stunned to struggle.

"An eye for an eye, copp'r. This is for what you done to my sister," she said. She kissed the maid's rotting cheek and raised her arms toward the group. The three corpses dragged Larson into the wall of flames that had overtaken the living room. Larson screamed in such anguish as Old George had never heard before, nor that he'd ever want to again. He smelt flesh charring, and he heard skin sizzling. He let out an involuntary shout, and the old woman turned to him.

"What you doing here, ya damn fool?" she shouted. He placed

his back against the wall and realized some unseen force pinned him in place.

"Don't look back and don't remember nothin. You hear?" she said to him.

He nodded.

She raised her arms again, and a tunnel opened through the smoke and fire. He saw that it led to the road past the flagstone path, and he saw the nighttime sky clouding up with a plume of ash.

"Go!" she shouted.

Old George entered the tunnel where flames surrounded him and smoke pressed against the confines of some invisible barrier that formed the tunnel.

He ran through it and watched the night sky alive with flames. The brightness almost seemed like the sunrise. The whole forest surrounding Larson's house raged. A hellscape. Flames licked the sky high above, and the pines surrounding the home began dropping blazing branches onto the roof.

Then came the sudden bursts, and the house detonated and into a million embers that climbed and dropped like Fourth of July fireworks. Old George fell flat on the fog-moistened road, and he covered his head and face. The ammunition, he remembered. That's what had exploded, the ammunition.

As soon as it stopped raining cinders and clumps of charred wood, he stood up. Old George didn't understand how he could run as fast as he did. The road was downhill, yes, but it seemed like another force guided his feet, guided his mind down, back toward the earth, back to a saner world. He'd long passed the inferno, but he still felt the heat on his face. It would never leave him. Not in a million years.

Lights, car lights, red lights, passed in a furious stream along the side of the road. Before the sirens and the swaying red truck passed him, he slipped behind a tree and watched them disappear around a bend in the road. Another one rushed up, and yet another came, curving upward toward the charring forest above.

Though his limbs had become numbed and rubbery, he walked. His mind was as blank as the night sky. If only there were some stars for him. If only there were something to keep the darkness from filling him up and taking him, too. He didn't see how that would ever be, not after tonight.

"Don't look back. Don't remember nothin. You hear?" The words echoed in his mind with each footstep that night and for many years after that. He didn't know if it was possible to not look back. Nothing would be the same for him. He heard someone weeping. Who was it, he wondered? Then he felt the tears wetting his cheeks, and he tasted them.

Twenty

Los Angeles, 1949
Two Years After It Happened

"Come on, Old George, or we'll be late," Sheila said. She fussed around that small clapboard office of his, packing up the last of his 22 years of service.

"I've still got one more thing I need to do," Old George said.

On October 31 they had first met at a church social. They billed the event as a Fall Festival because a "Halloween party" was against church rules. Such a party might invite the devil in, they all believed. And though most of the old biddies kept biblical notes in their minds about how wrong it was to partake in such a celebration—despite renaming it—the updated phrasing that centered on the changing seasons eased their minds in part. The guise of a seasonal change gave them some spiritual distance from evil and its special holiday. With that, only a few diehards squawked about it and kept from attending.

Black and orange crepe streamers twisted together overhead in the church hall, and a few carved jack-o'-lanterns flickered with their candle lights near the sandwiches and fruit punch. Old George dressed himself in tuxedo-tails and top hat. They once belonged to his granddaddy, a vaudevillian who danced for two bucks a week with a troupe called Madame Rentz's Tippy-Top Tappers, playing the Chitlin' Circuits across the Deep South. Old George needed such a costume now. It was time for him to dress up and pretend to be fine with the world once more. What better time to wear one, except at a Halloween party pretending not to be one?

He hadn't been out of the house much since the events, since that night. Except for work at the dumpsite, he'd holed himself up in his shoe-box apartment and made do for a good long while. Years had passed since it all happened, but it didn't seem that way to Old George. He couldn't bring himself to wander out to new places just yet. Every time he'd head to the door, he'd see those three corpses again shuffling, shuffling. He bought himself a good flyswatter.

A thin, shapely woman dressed as Cleopatra approached and stood next to him at the punch bowl. "You must be thirsty. You haven't left that punch bowl all night," she said.

"I, uh..." Old George went blank. "Plenty of reasons a man stays by the punch bowl," he replied.

He sensed sweat forming on his forehead, and his pulse tripled. He, for the life of him, couldn't figure out why he'd forced himself out that door to come here. Then he recalled that he'd had another dream of her. This time, she didn't come as some Holy Virgin or a horsefly that whispered awful things in his ear. This time, she came as herself. She came to say goodbye, and to tell him he'd reached his time.

"What time?"

She stood with a soft, silent gaze and a half smile. She'd sometimes give that look to him when he should understand better than he did.

Old George woke up that morning, his pillow washed with tears. He could feel it all now, and the tears flooded down like a terrible storm, for a good long time. He experienced all of what he couldn't since what happened to his momma, and since Serene. The pain, both unbearable and exquisite, seemed so terrible from afar. Now that he faced what he'd lost, there was a bliss in the release. And after the rain had run its course, and the sun glimpsed past the clouds, he felt that nothing dammed him up any longer. He realized, too, that there wasn't anything keeping him at that dump, or in his memories as a helpless boy, or anywhere at all.

He felt so brave, so sure of himself until he arrived at the dance, with another *her*—a *different her*—standing at the punchbowl. Bravery turned to tight collars and lumps in the throat.

"Besides," he said. He turned his head, and his heart softened by the sheer power of her gaze. She had a vulnerability in it, truth, too. She was all the things a woman should be to his mind, a woman who might fit well in the world, unlike him. "You're one to talk, Miss."

"And what do you mean by that?" she asked.

"Well, seems to me the Queen of the Nile would have far more men at her beck and call. You think I haven't seen you with your girlfriends, sitting over in the chairs alongside everyone dancing? Seems a real shame that all your majesty would go to waste like that."

She laughed and straightened out the glittery collar on her homemade tunic. "And just who are you supposed to be?"

"Who? Me?" he asked. "I can give you a hint. I'm a tap dancing fella on the big screen. You know, the one from Top Hat." He lifted his hat and gave it a stylish tip.

"Him?" she said. "Well, if you ask me, you're much better looking. Besides, I don't get out to the pictures much."

Old George dipped his head and tucked his lips. At first he wanted to smile—a smile he hadn't felt on his face in the longest time. He wanted to say clever words, like *Well, we should fix that.* But he held back. And that made him wonder—if only for a second—whether maybe someone had cursed him after all. He wondered whether the weight of that curse might doom him to live his life amid the city's vile refuse, looking for his father's fallen tooth.

"Well, Fred… it is Fred isn't it? Care to show an old Nile Queen how you foxtrot?" she asked. She held out her hand just like a queen might do to a subject so they'd kiss her royal ring.

"The name's George. They call me Old George," he said.

"You don't look so old to me," she said. "I'm Sheila."

She was lying. Old George, despite his age, looked a decade older after everything he'd been through.

He caught her hand, and the pair stepped out under the twisted streamers and twinkling candle lights. A prim church-woman stood alone at the phonograph and played *Moonglow*. After Old George and Sheila took a turn on the dance floor, the small crowd of princesses and beasts, fools and kings joined them.

Old George wondered if he should blame the dance, or the night itself, or the curve of her low back that fit so well into his hand. He might as well have blamed the song or the streamers. There seemed to be magic in these things. True magic. Those same arms that had bundled up Birdie and held his dying Serene now held another. The moment was tender, but it was also part fire, part gunshot, part severed hand and fallen tooth. In that turn on the dance floor with the Queen of the Nile, all the fragments seemed to fit together and lift into the heavens, past the stars, out where they could harm no more.

Old George made his way from the weathered clapboard office out to the gravel roads that twisted behind the piles of refuse. It seemed right, his walking away like this. He found he didn't need to stay like some prisoner. With each step, the burden of that place fell away as if the very earth beneath his feet slipped into some void after he stepped down.

There was one last place he needed to visit before he left this place to the void. It was a place where he kept special things. Old George had his share of searching the piles of rubbish only to strike gold, or at least a trove of unusual, special things. He once found a stack of forged twenty dollar bills all bound with a rubber band. They had smudged green ink on them, so whoever printed them decided it might be better to dispose of them than to spend bills with a smeary-faced Andrew Jackson. He also found beer signs, a magician's props, golf clubs, and the camera he still liked to use. In that special stockpile, he also kept things that weren't as nice, like the small dried-up alligator, its face sunken like a raisin. He also kept a painting with part of a woman's face cut out—and one more repugnant item that he kept from thinking about too much. Two wooden bins filled with these oddities and treasures stacked atop one another near the incinerator.

He uncovered the tarp and opened up the crate. He had come to visit the thing on top for the last time. He'd created a small wooden box for the terrible thing and lined it with some old remnant of purple satin that he found. Once he'd finished, he'd nailed the thing shut and stowed it away. He had a mind to walk away and never lay eyes on the foul thing again. The little container brought to mind those days and those events. If someone else discovered the box, the police would cart him off, and no one would think to ask twice. A severed hand in a box wasn't a thing you kept.

Old George considered that it was necessary to visit the box once more, despite his fear of standing in its presence again. He shuddered at the madness behind such wickedness. But he couldn't rectify the situation by blaming lunacy alone. Other things were at play, he came to recognize. Darker things. He tried not to remember them too often, out of fear they might happen again. At unexpected times, though, that old woman in the white dress entered his mind, and he'd remember how she stood like a statue in that burning fire. She was untouched and unflinching. And he remembered how she commanded the dead to walk. Old George didn't want to recall such things anymore, but they came to him repeatedly. So he made peace knowing that he'd live with these ghosts until his own death.

Old George brought with him an old rusty hammer. Jackie, his gray and black dog, skinny as sin, showed up from nowhere and sat by his side. "Come to see her off, have you?" he asked the dog. Jackie cocked his ears up and cranked his head at a tilt. "Me, too. Time someone laid her to rest, don't you think?" The dog stood and scratched his ribs with a back paw and sat down.

Old George kept the incinerator good and stocked up with chipped wood and split logs he stored to the side of the long brick chimney. He struck a wooden match from his pocket and nursed the small flames until they became big ones. He held the box in both his hands and closed his eyes.

"I know it's not much now, and it's coming from the wrong man, but I'm so sorry for what he did. All of it." He thought it sounded enough like a eulogy, at least as much as he could make up for a near stranger. He stood without saying much, and Jackie woofed at a cat prowling at a nearby pile. Old George came up with a little more he might say.

"And thank you for all you did for me. It wasn't a right road, I can tell you that. Not for you or for me. But I guess you can't always know the road, whether it's good or bad or nothing at all while you're on it. I suppose only when you got the chance to look back that you get to thinking on what's right and what's wrong. Sorry I wasn't there to stop him before it was too late. Guess that's all I've got to say," he said. "Except maybe goodbye."

He dropped the small coffin into the upper incinerator grate and closed the iron door with a rag. Black smoke poured out from the round brick chimney, and after a little while, no more. But he watched the black cloud wafting away for a minute, drifting somewhere east like an unhappy clump in the blue sky.

"You all done here, Georgie?" Sheila asked.

Old George turned and stroked the dog's forehead. "I think so. Nothing left for me here."

Twenty One

Los Angeles, 1947
Three Nights After It Happened

"I thought the Cloister at Dobbertiner See was far enough away. Nothing—no one could find me at the ends of God's earth. I changed my name. I changed my rank. All was silent for a time. There was foolishness on my part, I know. I was foolish to rest in the falsehood that a debt to pay would no longer be a debt to pay. And it demanded its wage, to be fed, that is. If not, the bargain would cease, and it would take me instead. I couldn't hide from what would be. No stronger force might exist, Father, than the craving to stay alive, especially if it means avoiding eternal doom."

"Try not to turn from Christ's mercy, Sister," the old man whispered.

His words, his sentiment alone, touched a deep wound and caused her to weep, for the first time she could remember across vast stretches of her life. "I am afraid, Father, that I am beyond the reach of such benevolence."

"Nonsense, child. The Lord's forgiveness eclipses all transgressions. For, he shed his blood so we may live."

"What do you know of the powers of Christ's mercy," she snapped, "when you've not sipped from the other cup? You've no idea of the advantages, far more bold and satisfying than the weak tea of mercy. And few of them have to do with Christ."

The priest held his tongue.

"As Christ shed his blood so he might save others, I, too, shed blood, though not my own. I did it so I might live… and be saved. I wasn't long at the abbey before the clergy made… discoveries. Gruesome discoveries, just as they had found at the cloisters in Budapest, and Copenhagen, and Nice. The thing had a voracious hunger for the sinful soul, father. And it found plenty of them then, as it does now."

♦

There were hissing noises and the sounds of air brushing in and out of a machine. It confused Ren. The sounds might have originated from above or below; it was hard to tell. He was dizzy and in pain—so much pain. But he sensed a hand holding his. It seemed warm and kind.

"He thinks I'm a priest," the officer said. He looked up at the nun standing over his shoulder. "I can't understand him too well, but it sounds like he's asking for—what do the priests call it?—oh, absolution."

"Are you Catholic, officer?" she asked. He nodded.

"He moaned yesterday. And the day before that, I heard some gurgling. But you say you heard the word absolution?" the nun asked. "What with the hoses and the bandages and the charred skin, we weren't expecting he'd communicate at all—so nobody has taken the time to listen."

Ren's vision failed him, but he recognized a woman talking. He knew he had one blind eye, and the other blurred for things that stood even a few paces away. A warm press of wrapped gauze covered his cheek and a wound over the left eye. Another bandage wrapped around his forehead.

He tried to say more, but realized he could not generate sounds. There is a certain panic reserved for the moment of realization when one becomes paralyzed and cannot speak. Ren was privy to that. He floated in a perilous world all his own, wrapped in a sterile cocoon, lying on a bed at the mercy of others. As soon as he tried to move a single muscle, pain shot with an intensity as bad as the searing from the fire itself. *Yes. A fire. There was a fire*, he remembered.

"Larson seems to think he's... *you*," the officer said to the nun. He shook his head and licked his lips. "Has he been conscious before this? Are you sure he hasn't said anything else?"

"Well, like I said, a few of the sisters have reported incoherent mumblings—an isolated moan here and there. But nothing intelligible," the nun said. "He's opened his eyes, too, but that's the nervous system operating, the doctors assured me. As I've mentioned before, it's likely a matter of time at this point. If he's communicated beyond his throat bubbling up, it would surprise me. Fire victims with this much body burned can't rouse much. And given the heat he inhaled, there'd be hardly any lining to his throat. To be honest with you, officer, if Mr. Larson survived this, what kind of life would he expect?"

"True. Poor bastard—oh, apologies for my language, sister," the officer said. "He did say something to me. Honest. He also said something like 'deal with a devil....'" He shook his head. "I'm sure he must think he's in Hell now. We still can't figure how he ended up burned like that in the rubble of the Downtown Hotel. The guys wrecking the joint heard his screams as soon as the dust settled from the first smash of the wrecking ball. Anyway, Larson's car was parked in his driveway, so he didn't drive there."

The nun crossed herself. "The Lord works mysteriously, sometimes, Officer. But to answer your other question, Mr. Larson's always had a fixation on that subject. Ever since he was a boy... when he lost both of his parents, he's perseverated on it... 'the devil this' and 'the devil that.' He was like that every day. We tried every procedure, both spiritual and scientific. Even discipline couldn't stop his rambling about Satan. And... we've come to this day..."

The officer nodded. "By the way," he said, "the district attorney is appreciative that you would admit him here again, after all that's happened. Understand, sister, you were all Larson really had. Besides, the next closest facility was out in Camarillo, and they wouldn't have the history with him like you. He wouldn't get the same care, you see? We figured he had the best chance of survival at Cyprian's. The D.A. keeps asking if there's even the slightest chance he'll make it, and if so, when he might be well enough to get up on that witness stand. All of Los Angeles needs him up there to say why he did what he did," the officer said. "That's why we want you to take extra good care of him."

"We will, Officer. But I'll tell you this—not even the doctors can tell us what motivates someone to commit such... acts. Please tell the District Attorney if Mr. Larson can survive, he's likely gone too far... mentally, just too far. Who knows if he'd make any sense to anyone involved? But I understand your need, and we'll do our best to preserve him and bring him back to health," she said.

With her words, Ren remembered it all, as if someone had switched on the radio. The memories flooded back with grief and emotional convulsion. His wife. His child. Sunnie. Were there others, too? Others whose names he did not know?

Ren's awareness burned his soul. The creature that followed and tormented him existed. Mr. Crooked. He was there at every turn. In every mirror, going to work, making love to Gloria, stroking his daughter's hair when she was asleep—always using Ren's hand. The lung pumps connected to him filled and compressed in rapid spasms. His eyes flooded with tears that overflowed to the bandages.

The officer hung the clipboard back on the bed and tipped his hat.

"Well, what should I do about him asking for forgiveness? I mean, will it help? Will he even understand?"

"You said you were a Catholic, Officer. Have you had the

sacraments of late?"

He nodded.

"Well, for the sake of mercy, hold your hand up and make the sign of the cross over him… like this… say whatever may soothe him. Everyone needs a small grace, Officer, even someone who's done as much destruction as Mr. Larson."

He followed her instructions, but all Ren did was stare out at the vague moving shadows with his unbandaged, blood-clotted eye.

"We'll all say a prayer for him in the meantime? Hmm?" the nun added.

"Of course, Sister," the officer said. He moved out of Ren's vision range. The other black shadow in the room grew taller, as though moving toward him. Ren struggled to focus.

"For your reference officer, it's Reverend Mother," she said.

"Of course, Reverend Mother," the officer said.

"We'll all say a prayer for Mr. Larson, that the Lord may forgive his sins," she said. She bent low, and Ren made out the face of Reverend Mother Margite gazing with the eyes he had thought were so cold before, so immune to others' suffering. Now they looked drooping and heavy-lidded like one who'd seen enough of the world's sadness. She grasped his hand. She smelled well-scrubbed with lye soap.

"Won't we, Mr. Larson?" she said. "We've fixed you up before. At least, we thought we did. And now, well, here we are." She paused. "Enough said." She wasn't sure he could listen with his ears singed off, or whether he followed anything at all. He had a complex and advanced mental case—more so than other patients she'd seen at St. Cyprian's. It had always been that way, ever since he was a boy living in the children's asylum.

Ren blinked and in that instant, his vision returned as clear as a July afternoon. In front of him the Reverend Mother Margite's face twisted into a fiendish grin. Her eyes, hot coals, burned in an eternal blaze. Her hand no longer seemed soft, but scaly and cold, like a snake or a lizard. Her clawing grip clamped down, crushing bones, and long nails sliced into the backs of his hands. "We'll all say a goddamn prayer so that your fucking blackened soul doesn't burn forever, lost in a forgotten fiery pit of hell, now won't we? No one will smother you in your sleep, now will they, Mr. Larson? Will they?"

Ren felt his heart spasm, and then there was the weight of a thousand bricks inside his chest, pressing, pressing.

Then there was no darkness, as he'd expected. There was no light, either. All that existed was fire, an endless expanse of fire.

Twenty Two

Cat Island, 1948
One Year After It Happened

Old Nany Root had lived in her small, pink, paint-scrubbed shop on Cat Island since the beginning of time. The old mothers whispered this story, at any rate. Nany's place took up a thin slice on a dusty side street. She came from Pigeon Cay Beach, and that's where she'd always be, some folk claimed. Though reports spread that she'd left for a time to fetch her sister from America. Plenty of folks figured it was only gossip, since Nany came back alone.

Islanders rumored that while she was abroad, she'd killed a man. They said she'd sent him to burn in all damnation for some terrible thing he'd done. Then again, they also believed in a half-shark, half-octopus *lusca* lurking around the underwater caves and rocky blow holes, waiting to drown unsuspecting souls. Such lore and partial-truths spoken in hushed voices and worried glances were part of island life. No one sifted out for certain the whole truth from custom, or from what folks repeated simply to scare children into obedience.

Nany sat on a folding chair, dented and rusted a bit in the back.

She placed herself near the floor fan which blew up her plain white dress, billowing it outward in the lower regions and puffing it up past her bosom. The room smelled like cedar and herbs burning in the incense bowl over the hot coals that nestled in the sand scooped up from the shoreline.

In the humidity, Nany's ritual attire stuck to her back like wax paper on jelly, but she maintained it as a custom and wore her tall white turban, too. She required them for special nights like tonight. Heat be damned, delaying the rite for another full moon was out of the question. Tonight, the dead might return more than at other times of the year. So sticky or not, she bore the turban and the ceremonial dress. Both were necessary to show respect, to be pure and clean in the presence of the ancestors and the *Loa*.

She closed the shop by sunset, but three girls remained. One mother had left her two daughters for Nany's instruction. Girls might take to the work of healing and hexing, and if a young one had a knack for the work, it was better than selling conch shells or cloth to tourists. Though most mothers understood what Nany taught—on general terms—they also thought not to inquire about the specifics. Too unnerving. Despite that, they trusted Nany would take care and never harm a young one. The last of the three girls had come to the shop on her own, despite her mother's inebriated objections.

The three of them lit candles and poured out salt from a canister around the circle in the middle of the floor. They wore white dresses like Nany, each differing from the other based on what their mothers could afford or whether there was a hand-me-down available.

Nany made her own clothes when she was a girl, learning the ways of the Loa from Tubah, her godmother. These modern girls had it easy, Nany thought, going to the local shop and buying what they needed right off the round racks as if they were living in Beverly Hills. Tubah didn't stand for such luxury. "You have to sew the dress by hand," Tubah would say. "That way, if you do things right, you sew the magic with your stitches." Nany had to make her garment of new cloth, too, set out overnight so that the moon might approve, and the warming sun would shine down to chase away the evil eye or any spells that may have set in along the way.

Some customs had to give way to change, Nany understood. But other things were enduring.

"Justice, come out here, child," Nany said.

Justice was now fifteen, and while Nany was gone those years ago, she worried about her. Rightfully so. Her mother drank too much, and her father, God rest his soul, came to an untimely end. Seems he drank from a bottle of rum and lost all his senses. He tore with his bare hands right into his stomach and pulled out whatever he might grab. Justice wasn't around to see what happened, but her mother was. Since that time, Justice's mother had taken to the bottle herself and become more pugnacious than a child should bear.

The girl started showing up around the shop more often than not with bruises and cuts on her face. Like today. Justice came around in the afternoon to set up for the ceremony with a puffed up and scraped eye. Looked to Nany like the work of yet another angry fist.

Justice took over things while Nany was away, buying and selling what the women of Cat Island might need from time to time to appease a quarrel or bind a stray husband to the wedding bed. Wasn't much to it, at least in Justice's mind. She always had a gift for things like this. It didn't hurt that if she caught the customer's eyes, she'd know right away what they came in to buy and for what purpose.

Sometimes women would ask for a love spell, when in their hearts they were looking to put a fix on a lousy husband. Once Justice saw what the truth was, she'd give proper advice. Sometimes she'd begin pouring herbs, bundling branches, roots, or leaves from their stinky old jars into a cone of paper, and telling folks what they had to do with them without stating what she secretly knew.

But she was smart enough to understand that other parts of the art took more time. They took more time and a learned hand to show her the way, so she waited those months until Nany came back. She waited on the dusty front porch, right outside the patched and sagging screen door, until her auntie, her godmother, Nany Root was for sure well and back.

Nany never fetched her sister—not alive anyway—and that saddened Justice. Nany missed Sunnie, and she never discussed the details of her disappearance. But Justice looked in Nany's eyes and just knew. One time when scanning Nany's eyes for answers, Justice saw fire and blood and three corpses standing in a blaze. It didn't bother her to see these things. One day she might have to be brave and face the fire herself. The knowledge that Nany shared came with responsibilities and a price, and she felt that coming.

The price wasn't like that warned of by the priests. In fact, Justice reckoned that Jesus had done nothing that made her feel so alive, so purposeful in the world as helping the women of Cat Island with her special talents. The priests and her sodden mother promised that Jesus might save her soul in the end, if she prayed and took communion. But she wasn't sure that souls needed saving, at least in the way they told her. There wasn't anything soiled or broken that the world and all its ways didn't make so in the first place. And there wasn't anything crooked that the world wouldn't straighten out, eventually.

Because waking the dead demanded solemnity and a certain formality, Justice set her mind just so. But she couldn't help smiling a bit, knowing that Nany would yet again have her beloved sister by her side, if only for a flicker. Every year, she seemed further away than the last. But Nany wanted to see her anyway.

"Had go, darlin. Can you fetch for Nany what she brought back on her travels?" Nany asked the girl. Justice nodded. She scurried toward the back, where the long workbench stretched out beneath the fluorescent lights.

"And bring Nany a cup of ice. It's hotter than the lakes of fire on a Saturday night," Nany said.

Justice brought back a small wooden box and a paper cup with some ice cubes.

"Just set that box down on the altar, dear," Nany told her. She nabbed the cup of ice from Justice's hands, took a rattling cube out, and rubbed it across her brow. Nany sighed, not from the heat or from weariness of the late night ceremony. She realized her time remaining was more momentary than she'd expected. It wouldn't be long now, so these girls needed to know and learn and do. She saw no point in easing the girls into the matters at hand tonight. Besides, words alone wouldn't make the visions they'd soon see more palatable.

No, they had to do the rite, plain and simple. The girls had to learn the time-honored procedures and stomach the results, or else they'd be left with nothing but a collection of hunches and small guesses. Or worse, they'd have to turn to someone like Taja, who would only use them to aggrandize herself and never teach them anything of use.

"Girls, it's time," Nany announced. The three students who were readying candles, filling the altar with fruits and cigars, candy and holy water giggled and held hands in a circle around the gathering of old wooden crates stacked up in tiers. The chicken in its cage at the lowest level of the altar clucked as though speaking in sentences, drawing attention to itself.

Nany heaved herself upward with a grunt and a click in her hip. She hobbled to the circle and joined hands with the young ones.

"Justice, the box," Nany said. "And turn off the lights."

Justice pried the lid up and extracted a severed human hand, a woman's, brown and dehydrated now. Nany had dipped the hand in melted beeswax and fitted the fingertips with string wicks. Justice noticed, buried beneath the coating of wax, a beautiful diamond wedding ring fitted on one finger. After Justice turned off the glowing fluorescents, Nany took a lit black candle and used that to light up the hand.

"Hold tight, girls," she said. "And don't be afraid. Whatever you do, don't let them know what makes you scared. They're here because I called them. They help me, and they'll help you one day."

Shadows danced with the hesitant flame-light. In the room's

corner, several shadows pooled and thickened until they moved from where they were on their own two feet. At the edge of the circle, Charlene stood holding around her shoulders a black Spanish shawl studded with red embroidered roses. The girls gawked.

Charlene moved her mouth, but no sound came from her. Instead, a black snake slithered out and dropped to the floor. When she closed her mouth, the most horrifying collection of screams filled the room. The two younger girls gave each other worried looks, but Justice followed Nany's rule and showed no visible reaction.

The snake wound sideways, back and forth across the floor until it reached the altar. The creature sprouted legs like a black crab, and a man's face mounted atop them. Nany recognized him, for she owned him now. The strange being climbed up to the candle and took bites from the fingers. A wet black ooze seeped from the creature's mouth while it munched on decayed flesh.

"Time for you to work," Nany said. She broke the circle of clasped hands long enough to approach the altar and uncork a rum bottle. "In you go." The creature hesitated, first exploring the rim of the bottle with one of its wet, glistening, tar-like claws, and withdrawing. "In you go or it's back from where you came," Nany warned. She lifted the ceremonial dagger she'd brought back with her and stabbed the creature down the middle. The abomination shrieked and puddled into a liquid shadow that bled into the bottle. She crammed the cork down and patted until she had the thingum secure.

"Charlene, you need to go back. I'm warning you not to touch one of these young ones. Now off with you," Nany said. She opened a powder bottle, sprinkled some in her hand, and blew at the apparition. The spirit screamed and shook the windows before collapsing into a thousand black spiders that fell like a splashing wave onto the floor and scattered about as a great scurrying mass.

"Well, that's it then," Nany said. She blew out the candles on the altar and puffed on her cigar one last time. Justice gazed at Nany, waiting to spot the look of disappointment for her sister never arriving. But Nany seemed content with peering through the green bottle glass at what was inside. The three girls began dismantling the altar.

"What is that?" one of the new girls asked. She watched with doubting eyes the bottle dangling in Nany's hands. The child was too sensitive, and Nany could see it. She'd have to break her of that before the girl could rightly claim power.

Nany held the container up and swirled it, listening to the insides. "This is my helper, child. Just like Charlene, who was quite old. Passed down to me from Tubah, she was. Might have been more than a hundred years by now. Old ones fight back and take on a life of their own. A new one was what we needed, didn't we? This one is a man. He come all the way from America. Do you know where that is? One day, you'll have helpers all your own. Maybe even this one."

"Why do we need helpers?" the smallest girl asked.

Nany spoke to the child like an elementary school teacher. "There are more things in life than you imagine, child. Takes time to understand them. You need the light, but sometimes the dark, too. There are thingums in the nether worlds, dark ones, nothing but pain in em. Powerful. Don't touch em, you hear?" Nany asked. She placed a finger on her nose, and she swirled the bottle again. "Like touching electric wires. No. That's what helpers are for. They fetch em to do what you sometimes need doing."

"How did you get this one?" the child asked. She looked down in deference, or maybe fear. The poor thing was possibly unnerved from what she'd seen. Spirits and helpers and spiders and all, Nany figured. Still, each of them had to learn to stand up, walk on their own two feet.

Nany regarded the bottle for a long time before saying anything. "Some things take a small sacrifice, child, like that hen over there. Some things take a bigger one. But knowing like that takes time, child. First comes the seed, then the root, and then the flower—all in that order. Can't even make flowers grow faster if we wished it."

She patted the smooth bottleneck and turned to Justice. "I worry for your mother, Justice. Drifting day by day, poisoning her mind. Is that a way to live? No way to raise a child proper, I say. A child needs love. Child needs attention. Why, she put you in harm's way once already, didn't she? Might do it again if she gets to washing her pain down more than she already has. Licking her wounds like a dog in a back corner. Only now, she licks em with a bottle… and a belt."

She stroked Justice's cheek with her free hand. "And no harm should come to my Justice. Sweet Justice. Knows more than she ought and seen more than she should. Nany would raise you proper." She placed her hands on Justice's with a squinted eye and a nod. "Give her this with my blessing, now won't you? Copp'r knows what to do. Been doing it for decades already." She kissed Justice's forehead and blinked with both eyes and a short smile.

Justice grasped the bottle and gazed down at it, nodding in understanding. "I suppose Mamma can always use one last sip," she said.

She blazed down the road from Nany's shop, barefoot, colliding with the dark, and even more, to be with what lies beyond that. She took the bottle understanding that there's good and there's evil, too. But there were lots of things in between all of that. And sometimes, just sometimes, helpers have got to help.

ABOUT THE AUTHOR

Timothy Roderick is a southern California native and he lives in Los Angeles. Many cultural influences meet at the crossroads of his writing. His works explore where magic meets myth, the supernatural meets mind-states, and where karma and redemption intersect. In addition to writing dark fiction, Timothy is also the author of five other nonfiction books including award winners and those that have appeared in the Time-Warner Book of The Month Club. For more information visit timothyroderickbooks.com.

Made in the USA
Monee, IL
08 February 2021